Michael Cannon lives in Glasgow and works at Strathclyde University. His first novel, *The Borough*, is also published by Serpent's Tail.

A Conspiracy
of Hope

Michael Cannon

Library of Congress Catalog Card Number: 96–67903

A complete catalogue record for this book can be
obtained from the British Library on request

The right of Michael Cannon to be identified as the author
of this work has been asserted by him in accordance
with the Copyright, Designs and Patents Act 1988

First published in 1996 by
Serpent's Tail, 4 Blackstock Mews, London N4
and 180 Varick Street, 10th floor, New York, NY 10014

Phototypeset in Bembo by Intype London Limited
Printed in Great Britain by Cox & Wyman Ltd., Reading, Berks.

A Conspiracy
of Hope

Part One

1

When I left school I thought I knew everything. Since then I've often thought of the same image which typifies me the day I left. I didn't like school very much. I had a kind of unspoken agreement with my teachers: they thrashed me for cheek and laziness and I ignored their instructions. It wasn't a very good school. If you weren't sniffing glue or setting fire to your desk then you were the least of their problems. Imparting knowledge seemed to be something incidental; absorbing it sheer accident. Sometimes they would beat it into us: Shylock's soliloquy and six of the belt if you weren't verbatim. To do them justice, they weren't social workers. It can't have been easy.

It must have been irritating for them with someone like me, someone vaguely intelligent who could have done something, someone who could have helped their abysmal hit-rate. I remember bits of phrases on the bottom of the report cards: 'squanders his opportunities', 'gifted but obstreperous'. It didn't help my marks but it did wonders for my vocabulary. So did the letters they sent home, which I intercepted. Early rising has never been in my line. I'm more the noon type. I'd rather read about the dew. I'd wait for the postman in the early hours with a steaming kettle ready in the kitchen. I dictated, and my friend, Thomas, would write my replies. Thomas could write like an adult. Thomas had pubic hair in nursery school. Thomas was sent home in primary six with a note about his four o'clock shadow. I dictated that reply also. We were eleven:

Dear Mrs Maguire its not Thomases fault that his
growth is so noticeable and I know some folk who
would give their right arm for a beard like his is. His
mother my wife took hormoans when Thomas was
no more than a feetus to help with the indescribeable
pain of gesticulation that only a woman can know
and I dont think its fair that our poor boy is held
responsible for the consequences of what the doctors
will say will happen when it doesnt like those babies
who are born stuck together or without heads.

No one was fooled. They weren't fooled either by the doctor's
line I had him hand in to say his suspected meningitis would
keep him away from learning the Canadian barn-dance. He
waited years to retaliate. He had the advantage of a precocious
puberty. When my testes finally succumbed to gravity he told
me I could swap my balls around without pain.

He was wrong.

He also wrote an excuse for me which I handed in to the
swimming coach.

'Your father didn't write this did he?'

Too late I realised why Thomas had handed me the envelope sealed.

'No, sir.'

'Follow me.'

Thomas and his cronies chortling as the sound of the belt
resounds up the corridor. The note thrust back into my
blazing hands, I painfully unfold it and read:

Please excuse Jamie from doing physical education as
he has pulled a muscle in his cock.

Signed

His dad

If it taught me nothing else, it taught me the value of being
able to think on my feet.

'This script bears a remarkable resemblance to that of the girl who sat beside you in the examination hall.'

'Indeed, sir?'

'And that of the boy who sat in front of you.'

'Really?'

'And the textbook you were asked to put in your bags before the exam began.'

'I exalt a healthy eclecticism, sir.'

'You mean you copied.'

'Semantics, sir.'

'A. J. P. Taylor gets full marks. You get a D minus and a letter sent home to your parents.'

Another early rise.

In those days unemployed school-leavers were still entitled to sign on for unemployment benefit. Before we could do so we needed a school leaving certificate. This had to be signed by your form teacher and every other teacher who allegedly taught you anything. The maths teacher signed when I handed in my maths books. The chemistry teacher signed when I handed in my chemistry books. There's no point in going through the whole doleful catalogue. I had all the signatures bar one: history. There was a snag: I'd lost my history books. When I say 'lost' I mean I'd left them somewhere around the school.

The teacher was a fat greasy man with epic dandruff. We didn't get on and he'd used me as a scapegoat when it suited. I hovered about till he left the room, then went in and burgled his store-cupboard. It took a while to find a set as tattered as I'd left mine. Also, each time we were issued books we had to sign a sticker on the inside cover with our name and class. These stickers were self-adhesive on one side and allowed space for about eight signatures. Eight years of abuse from careless adolescents was a reasonable life expectancy for any book. The only books which looked as if they could pass for mine had stickers which were filled up. I stole new stickers. They looked incongruous. I dirtied them on the storeroom floor. I scribbled pencil marks on them and smeared the graphite with spittle. Then I forged the previous seven names in block capitals: MARTIN BOREMAN, TULULLAH BANKHEAD, SAVONAROLA, ZORRO, CESARE BORGIA, B. L. Z. BUB, OTTO B. I. O'GRAPHY and eclipsed them with a flamboyant signature which arrested the eye and, hopefully, obscured the rest for as long as I needed.

He came back into the room. I couldn't leave the cupboard. When I saw him go out the door again I slipped out. He came back almost immediately. He must have forgotten something or been idling just outside the class. He stared at me, trying to work out how I'd got there.

'Leaving certificate, please,' I said.

'Sir.'

'What?'

'Leaving certificate please, *sir*. You've not left yet.'

I didn't say anything. I handed him the paper.

'Books?'

I handed those across too. He looked grudgingly at the pile and at the paper in his hand and then scribbled his close signature. I took the paper from him and started to walk towards the door. He had picked up the first of my books.

'Robertson!' he shouted. I turned. His face was very red.

'What?' I could have said 'What do you want you fat bastard?' but that would have degraded the exchange to the level of personal acrimony, which he could have dismissed as what he had come to expect. He seemed to be summoning himself.

'I haven't got all day,' I said. The realisation that he had no jurisdiction over me stopped him in his tracks. I walked out. I could see him shaking.

And the image I think typifies me? Butch and Sundance at the last stand, bloody but unbowed, rushing out of the cantina, guns blazing, into the unanticipated fusillade which shreds them to cheese. 'Dos Gringos!' from the incredulous Bolivian Captain, slapping his subordinate in fury at the pitiful odds pitched against his professionals. Freeze-frame the heroes in mid-stride as volley after volley is discharged to assuage the

Captain's anger. Fade to monochrome as they disintegrate in the salvo. Fade sound of repeated fusillade to cracked pianola splashing out a hesitant waltz. Cross fade to me standing at the open school gates facing the outside world with my arms raised above my head as if I'd actually won something. Me, Butch and Sundance, and the insuperable world.

I'm not one given to self-indulgent reminiscences, but when I think of me standing at those school gates, knowing so little I didn't even know how much I didn't know, I feel sorry for myself. I really do.

2

I remember I left school mid-week. I never had any plans. I've never had any plans. I was all prepared for an extended vacation which would mellow in time to premature retirement. For some reason I could never fathom, my parents have always lived by a curious Presbyterian work ethic. There's no excuse; they're not even that religious. Dad had a series of aphorisms, which extolled the cardinal virtues of thrift and hard work, printed in bold gothic script and framed in brushed metal. These were dotted around the house. He nailed several above my bed, including EVERYTHING IN MODER-ATION, EXCEPT MODERATION. This should have been above their bed. It might have accounted for the fact that I was an only child. Did they expect me to imbibe the good messages in my sleep? All these allusions to noses against grindstones and shoulders to wheels. Dad often talked about labour being its own reward. How? How many people do you know who get up at six and commute two hours each way for the love of it? I don't know any, but then most of my friends are like me.

If I have to go to the fishmonger's and the bank in the same day I usually want a lie-down afterwards. I don't mind reading about hard work, but that's about as far as it goes. I

read Tolstoy once, *Anna Karenin*, and there's this Levin character, who has any amount of couches to lie on and any amount
of vodka to drink, and yet he goes out and works with the
peasants, wielding a scythe and carrying stacks and stuff like
that. He thought that labour was its own reward too. It's
perverted. And for him too it was tied up in religion. Conse-
crating labour to you-know-who. What's so wrong with
apathy? I'd consecrate my inertia if I was religious, but I'm
not. I've always had leanings towards religion. I've always had
leanings towards anything I could lean on. And if you're good
you go to Heaven. And who have you ever heard of doing a
hard day's work in Heaven? Hell, maybe. Stands to reason
Hell must be work, since so many people are always telling
you work is hell. Maybe if you're one of those industrious
types Heaven for you is a golden plough and a limitless furrow.
I veer a bit more towards the Eastern orthodoxies, with copu-
lations six centuries long and a pile of toast with lashings of
hot tea when you come up for a breather.

Yes, I've always had leanings towards religion. But unless
you're naturally credulous it requires a certain rigour of
thought, and even the thought of the rigour of thought tires
me out. I got as far as the leap of faith. The very word 'leap'
put me off.

The second day of my new-found release I'm lying in bed
having a good time not thinking about much when dad
comes in.

'Up,' dad says peremptorily. 'You'll be late.'

'Late?' The concept of time is one I've never had much
truck with, especially when I'm in bed.

'You heard your father.' My mother squeezed in behind
him. There was now two too many people in here.

'You can't lie here all day.'

I looked at my alarm. Perhaps 'alarm' is a bit of a misnomer.
It's never alarming; it's never set. It was seven-fifteen.

'It's the middle of the night!'

'If you weren't up by the time we left we know you
wouldn't get up,' she said.

'You heard your mother,' he said. It's this ludicrous habit they have of always corroborating one another, no matter what the other says. It's as if it takes a consensus to constitute a truth. And it's a private club. And it can be anything: 'Buenos Aires is the capital of Poland,' followed by the inevitable 'You heard your father'; or 'Jonah swallowed a whale,' and its concomitant 'You heard what your mother said'. There's also another one dad tries on with me from time to time. It's usually 'so-and-so' followed by 'Or you're no son of mine!' It's usually said in anger. How can anyone make an ultimatum out of something that's been and gone?

You know what I think, I think I'm no son of theirs. I think there was a big mistake. I don't look like them, I don't talk like them, and we don't share the same ambitions. They have the same ambitions and I don't have any. I think I was swapped in the maternity unit and that I'm really the son of an English nobleman who did nothing professionally. I don't think I'm a horny-handed son of toil at all. Truth be known, I find them a bit common.

'You'll be late for your appointment.'

'What appointment?'

'At the Labour Exchange.'

'I only left school two days ago!'

'You don't want to squander your chances.'

'You heard your father.'

'Lots of school-leavers around soon. You want to get in early. You want to get in on the ground floor.'

How the fuck do they know what I want? No one but the self gets privileged access to their own psychology. I'm the only one qualified to look in and I don't know what I want. Or I do. What I want is for these two to leave me to go back to sleep while the school-leavers queue from the playground to the Labour Exchange and occupy all available vacancies.

I retaliated by monopolising the bathroom and standing under the shower till dad's colon nearly burst. An hour later, with only a grudging piece of toast inside, I found myself heading into the city.

3

'Have you any previous experience which you think may be of use?'

'Lots.'

'Such as?'

'Bit of this, bit of that. Y'know.'

'No.'

Rhino-grey carpet tiles. Rhino-grey filing cabinets. Rhino-grey everything. Salt and pepper expanded-polystyrene ceiling. Booths divided by partitions comprised of compressed wood-shavings then painted – grey. Behind those filing cabinets lurked the corporate threat of a grinding bureaucracy that might find me a job.

Did the people here arrive like this or did the surroundings do this to them? They're a caste, the lowest echelon civil servants. They work in a system as rigorous as the Indian social strata. Untouchables deal with corpses and excrement. Lowest echelon civil servants get the administrative shite.

They were all lack-lustre. All except the one I had in front of me. Early twenties, pretty, intelligent eyes (what was she doing in here?), quick manner, random strands of dark hair which fell across her wide forehead which I wanted to brush away. When she wrote, her pink tongue stuck out between white teeth.

'I was speaking hypothetically,' I explained.

'I've got a form to fill in Mr Robertson.' Pause for effect. 'Any useful work experience at all?'

'Jongleur.'

'Sorry?'

'I was an itinerant minstrel.' She didn't believe me. 'I went around rescuing imprisoned monarchs. Two bars on the lute and they were sprung. Girls threw their pigtails out of the window at my approach. I've broken hearts and hymens all over Europe. One pluck and it was all over.'

'I've got a job to do even if you haven't. There are other candidates Mr Robertson.'

'Who am I to stand in the way of a better person?'

'If we're not satisfied that you are genuinely looking for work, or willing to accept a job if one is offered, then you don't get any unemployment benefit.'

'My mind is always employed.'

'You wouldn't know it looking at your educational qualifications listed here.' She held up the sheet.

'I'm a student of the University of Life.'

'That's what they all say.'

'You don't know what it's like. The poetry I have torn from myself. My life is my work. Always to burn with this hard, gem-like flame. The modes of passion I have lived through in a single human existence.'

'After three months on the dole?'

'No one said it was easy.'

'There's a word for people like you Mr Robertson: "work-shy".'

'That's two words.' She licked her pencil. I could see her scan the vacancies. I began to panic. ' "Work shy", such an ugly expression don't you think? I prefer to think I'm suffering from a bout of occupational dismotivation.'

'Have you anything constructive I can include in this clause under past experience?'

'Aesthete.'

'You know, Mr Robertson, there's a technique which lots of people I interview use.'

'Interviewees?'

'They don't do it so glibly as you, but the intention is the same. They give unhelpful, or sometimes even hostile, replies to sabotage the interview.'

'Perish the thought.'

'The unemployed get sent in battalions to places like this by the benefit people. I see scores of them every day. And among a hundred hopefuls you get half a dozen drones like yourself.'

'That's sexist.'

'Perhaps it is. I only know I don't see so many female sluggards. And what really gets my goat is that ninety per cent of the poor people going for even dead-end jobs haven't a chance. But they don't give up trying and they deserve better than to be tarred with the same brush as the likes of you.'

'Steady on.'

'There are enough people who can't work through no fault of their own. It's up to the rest of us to do our best.'

'This is turning out like a temperance lecture. You haven't been talking to my dad have you?'

'I'm going to give you one last chance. So far, under work experience, you've given me pyrotechnician, exorcist, town-crier, jongleur and aesthete. Have you anything with practical application to add?'

'Metaphysical poet.'

'Some of the people who sabotage these interviews . . .'

'Sabotagees?'

'. . . only come for the statistical credit of having sat an interview. Their unemployment benefit depends on it. I, however, operate a policy: no co-operation, no credit. Occasionally I even go so far as to make it quite clear to the benefit people that the candidate arrived with no intention of accepting employment were it offered.'

'I'm living on my nerves . . .'

'But as you probably know, you're permitted more than one refusal before benefit is rescinded.'

'Three. You're permitted three.'

'My records inform me you've already used up two in twelve weeks.'

' "Rescinded", now there's a nice euphemism. I knew you weren't a civil-service pleb when I took one look at you. You know, you have a very elegant turn of expression. Very – '

'So basically this is your last chance and I've got you by the balls.'

'Forthright. Shoots from the hip. I like that in a woman. Must we continue this conversation here? I have a little *pied-*

à-terre not far away. It's not much: some wisteria, a creaking gate, a thatched roof, the faithful old retainer, as far as my dole money stretches. You know. I thought that perhaps we . . .?'

'You're young. You're unemployed. You have no job and no prospects. You have no work experience going in your favour. You should be glad of anything which comes your way. The only thing you have to recommend you is a vivid imagination and a fancy turn of expression, which some people might find amusing but which only irritates me when I have a job to do.'

'Are you sure you haven't been seconded here?'

'I think you better start taking me seriously, Mr Robertson. I think you had better consider your next answer very carefully.'

'I like the cut of your jib.'

'Have you ever had any amateur dramatic experience at school? Have you ever acted?'

'*Have* I ever acted? Have *I* ever acted? Have I ever *acted*? Have I ever *stopped*! "Is this a lager I see before me?" I – '

'Whoppers. High Street. Monday. Nine a.m.'

'What!'

'I'm offering you a job.'

'Oh for fuck's sake!'

'Shall I record that as a refusal?' The pen hovered. The lights were going out all over Europe.

'Whoppers!' A chain restaurant offering mechanically-recovered meat between thin rolls to the proletariat! I hear they have a twenty-four-hour drive-in branch in Stratford offering a Bard Burger.

'They issue you with a beefeater costume and a latex head, I believe. It should be ideally suited to one of your theatrical bent. The job involves raising the restaurant's profile and picking up litter.'

'Whoppers! Be reasonable.'

'Someone has to do it.'

I looked at her for a gap. There was none. She continued.

'Alternatively, the local engineering works are having their summer intake. I can give you details on how to apply. If I have it on file that you are in the process of actively looking for jobs there will be no need to rescind your benefits. You'll have to convince us that you have every intention of working if a job offer is forthcoming though.'

An application is at least one step removed from actual work. I thought of Whoppers and shuddered. The man in the latex mask.

'You're a hard woman Miss . . .?'

'Here are the addresses.'

'Whoever you are – I have always depended on the kindness of strangers.'

'Next.'

4

There's something I had better explain about my attitude at this time. It's embarrassing to repeat but it has to be said. When I saw that competent young woman in the labour exchange I started to sweat. I talked rubbish nineteen to the dozen, not just because of the awful prospect of work but because she was – a woman.

When I left school I'd been seeing Deborah for a while. We practised ten-play, that's foreplay for two-and-a-half years without a consummation in sight. For the first year we were the kind of couple who only ever saw one another during school hours. We'd stand in one corner of the playground, not holding hands, and I'd lean at improbable angles in a ridiculous attempt to look nonchalant. The end of that year saw us at the school dance, when I tried to put my hand up her duffle coat and was given lines by the teacher trying to chaperone a hundred kids bursting with new-found puberty.

On our anniversary I grappled with the catch of a brassiere flat as a ribbon and spent the following eighteen months sucking Deborah's incipient breasts into a semblance of their now pendulous proportions. I never got near the nether regions. It was a frustrating apprenticeship and I would walk home of an evening flexing my exhausted lips and wondering at the mystery of a woman who could make me feel so wonderful and so bad. She left me sufficiently unsatisfied to ensure I'd always come back in the hope of more. Perhaps it was a tactic. Perhaps she was cleverer than I gave her credit for. At any rate, I'd already made a big investment: eighteen months of pressing my throbbing courgette against her thigh while we queued for rhubarb crumble and custard. I wanted payment in full, with dividends.

I carried the vestige of those days into working life. I once explained my philosophy to Thomas: The great metaphysical answers to the great metaphysical questions, alpha and omega, all the beginnings and all the ends, all consolation and all truth worth having was to be found at a point somewhere roughly in the middle of a woman's body, at that trapdoor to ecstasy where her legs meet at the top.

'Who would have read so much into an arse-hole?'

'You're a philistine.'

'And you're a virgin.'

And so I was, the oldest in the Western hemisphere. Or so I thought as I walked in through the dark of the hangar doors and asked where the exam was.

5

It gives a false impression to call it an exam. Myself and perhaps forty other hopefuls, beetle browed, sitting in that classroom while a foreman holds up some contraption which looks like a solid cube with various levers sticking out of it. He moves one lever from side to side and the others move in various ways. One goes up and down, one retracts and moves out. On the paper in front of us we have a page on which are printed a series of alternative mechanisms which would allow this movement to occur. Each alternative is like the cube in cross-section, with pulleys and cogs and fulcrums and stuff like that. Four alternatives. The first two were unnecessarily, absurdly complicated. You don't need all that stuff for simple clockwork movement. The third was a minimalist proposition with two cogs and a sort of fan-belt linking them and nothing else. Unless it all went on by telekinesis this contraption wouldn't get off the ground. That left number four. I'm no mechanical genius, but it looked as if all the stuff was there to get the motion going I'd seen demonstrated. By default this was the only one anyone could go for.

Well it was the only one I could go for. I looked around and there was half the quota scratching their heads in the sunshine and looking perplexed. I realised I'd better be careful. I had every intention of failing with dignity and a sufficiently narrow margin to convince the unattainable woman at the employment exchange I'd put my best foot forward and it just wasn't good enough. But among candidates like these I felt like Pythagoras. I pointed at the only feasible alternative and passed the message around by winking and turning the book side-on to as many people as would look.

There were several more tests like that and I realised that the only qualifications really necessary were two arms, two legs and a head. I spread the good word on every occasion. I'm quite an accomplished cheat. The papers were called in and we were asked to come back in an hour.

So we loitered in the sunshine outside the factory, me and a clump of tense sixteen- and seventeen-year-olds. They stood together for comfort, smoking cigarettes and conducting an autopsy of the paper. I lay on my back in the grass with my hands behind my head, stuck a tuna sandwich in my mouth and ate it with the force of gravity. No one came to talk to me. They seemed to think I was possessed of great composure. Actually I was a bit worried. I had advertised all the correct answers to those around me and recorded as many wrong answers as I reasonably could without obviously sabotaging my paper. But if these fidgety teenagers were acceptable material I had better do something convincing or I could be out of being out of a job. The very thought made me sweat.

We were called back in again. A series of names were read out. Mine wasn't among them. I breathed a sigh of relief.

'Those of you who have just heard their names read out won't be further required. Could the remainder come back at two o'clock prompt.'

They'd winnowed out most of us already. I walked out the most bitterly disappointed person in the place.

6

I've been going out with Jamie now for almost two years. Mum says starting that young does more harm than good. I don't think it's too young. I think starting at our age makes it seem almost meant. I said as much. Dad says 'starting' better not mean what he thinks it does. I used to be able to talk to dad about anything. After he first met Jamie he kept telling me the way to Hell is paved with good intentions. Dad and I don't talk the way we used to. I miss it. So does he. Jamie never really talks to my dad, or his own. Jamie says parents have a jealousy gene that kicks in at thirty-five, and a special 'fuck you' gland that produces chemicals to make them want to mess it up for anyone who's having a good time. He's always saying things like that. I wish he wouldn't. I don't see why we can't all just get on. I like my parents. I don't see why it should be so hard.

I ask Jamie if he thinks things between us were meant. He says I was meant to do something with this unless I want him to die of a burst courgette, and then he does the canteen-queue things against me. Up till now I've always said no — after a while. The whiles are getting longer.

He's going for a job next week so we can be together. He says he wants to be an apprentice engineer and for me to live with him. He says that I'll have no money and he's racking his brains to think of a way I can possibly pay him back, and do I have any ideas. I said

*it will be special for us, living together: meant. He asked for something
in advance. He's always joking like that.*

7

I turned up ten minutes late and didn't even offer an excuse,
but it was no good, they were waiting for me. Perhaps, I
thought, to use one of Deborah's expressions, I was meant to
get a job. Perhaps employment and me were predestined for
one another. Fate isn't blind, it's rationally malignant.

I wanted to explain to them that my being here was an
administrative error, that I didn't see myself so much a potential employee, more as a complete leisure concept. They
thought I'd turned up late because I was nervous. I tried to
make them think otherwise. They took whatever I said as
bravado. They made allowances for me. I looked at the other
hopefuls, about fourteen of us. I had heard there were five
vacancies. Another besuited man came in. He caught sight of
the boy at my side and shot a quizzical glance at him.

'How many eighths are in an inch?' he asked of the boy,
over the heads of the rest of us. The boy looked uncomfortable
and gazed around at the rest of us for moral support. He was
suffering the ravages of adolescent acne. His gaze came to rest
on me. There was something desperate in his look, imploring.
In the best of all possible worlds a boy like this would get my
job.

'What,' I whispered, 'a whole inch?' I didn't intend the
joke to be repeated aloud.

'You mean a whole inch?'

The man snorted, turned his back on us and walked towards
the front of the room. There was something like a simple
examination booklet in front of us.

'You can open now and begin at once. Calculators are
permitted. You have one hour exactly.'

There was the turning over of sheets and the sound of

suppressed breathing. Questions occurred throughout the paper with space below for each answer. It wasn't one of those examination papers with the questions on a separate booklet which you get the chance to mull over before setting pen to paper. The first couple of questions required basic arithmetical skills, then they got progressively harder, with the same time limitation on each. It looked like an elementary IQ test. Most of the other candidates had the foresight to provide themselves with calculators. Thank God I hadn't. Perhaps I could fail the arithmetic miserably and give the impression I couldn't count. If I failed to show the working out they couldn't give me consolation marks for employing the right method.

The scrofulous boy at my side produced a slide rule. Honest to God, I thought, this kid is one of life's victims. He probably holds up the queue at the butcher's trying to work out the required weight of meat with his book of logarithms. I deliberately dallied over my arithmetic too long and wrote down vague guesses at the answers. The statistical chance of being correct was huge. As for the rest of the paper, most of the questions only required bringing some common sense to bear. I gave them the once over, signed my name with a flourish and closed the book in forty-five minutes flat. I collected some glances. The kid at my side was still wrestling with his slide rule and on page one. He gave me a look of true pathos.

The papers were collected in. We were shown into the works cafeteria. I lit a cigarette. Everyone looked tense, refusing to make eye contact with one another. No post-mortem of the paper was conducted this time.

The same besuited man came into the cafeteria. He read another list of names. Mine wasn't among them. They weren't required either. Fuck! That left six of us. We were shown into an office suite. Two moderately high-powered looking individuals came in and asked us questions as a group. Perhaps this was to measure our inter-personal skills. I gave a good impression of a surly lout. They adjourned. They came back. Myself and the spotty boy were asked to come into an adjacent office. Through the glass partition which separated us I could

see the looks of relief and pleasure on the faces of the other
four as the man who hadn't come with us talked to them.
All four were obviously in. One vacancy left between the two
of us. I could feel the bile of rising panic.

We were seated in yet another room, a big room, one with
a huge desk and an oval table ringed with chairs. The man
who had conducted us there left. Another entered. He was
hulking and crammed into an obviously expensive and ill-
fitting suit. He looked like top dog around here. This was his
office. He cut the other candidate, the spotty one, a friendly
glance. This was a hopeful sign. He sat down at his desk and
started flicking through one of the examination scripts. From
my distance I couldn't see which. Then he started talking. He
had a thick accent, had obviously pulled himself up by his
bootstraps and was obviously proud of the fact. He talked
while he flicked through the paper before him without looking up and I had no idea which of us he was talking to.

'There's something to be said for going by the book. I've
always done it myself. But you have to be careful to leave
room for the others too. We can't all be pedestrians. I've
always had a grudging admiration for the reckless innovator.
But this . . .' he said, throwing down the paper he had in his
hand onto the desk and staring fixedly at me.

I walked out ten minutes later via the now empty cafeteria
and ate a pensive yogurt. Then I walked through the hangar
doors of the main building out into the sunshine beyond. I
smoked a thoughtful cigarette. I could hear footsteps above
the noise of distant machinery and saw the other one, the
spotty one (I found out his name was Peter), emerge into
the sunshine too.

'I'm sorry,' I said.

'Sorry for what?'

'Sorry for being employed. Sorry for taking your job.'

'You didn't take my job. I'm in.'

'I thought there were only five vacancies.'

'Five advertised vacancies. I was always in. He's my dad.'

And not only that but, as subsequently came to light, the

other four were always in too. One was the son of the sarcastic man who asked Peter how many eighths were in an inch. He was marketing executive and there was a bit of family rivalry there. One was the nephew of the man in charge of quality control. One was the son of a man who owned a firm which supplied components at preferential rates (from now on), and one had a dad who was a master mason with a variety of contorted handshakes. So much for meritocracy.

'There was only ever one real vacancy. They're obliged by law to advertise the rest, but now you're here, keep it to yourself. You were always in, right from the first selection.'

Fate, kismet, the ineluctable course of history, call it what you will, it had it in for me from the start. I walked out of that place in a fit of depression that would have done credit to Dostoyevsky. There was one consolation: if I had got a job then I had kept my part of the bargain. Deborah's mum went to the bingo these nights. I was going to go round there and give her the seeing to of both our lives.

8

It didn't quite work out as I had always planned it would. There was me and there was Deborah. She's all but naked and sitting on the hearthrug. The mother is at the bingo. The father is, where? Who cares, as long as he's elsewhere for as long as it takes. The curtains are drawn, presumably attracting the attention of the neighbours in the balmy summer night. The windows are closed. The front and back doors are locked with the security locks on and the dead-bolts drawn across. There is about as much chance of coitus interruptus here as there would be in Fort Knox. History isn't going to shanghai me this time.

There's me and there's Deborah. I seem to have used the word 'love' quite a few times in the past few sentences. At

every impediment and coyly-guarded button, at every recalci-
trant zip, all it takes is the word 'love' and – open sesame.

'Jamie, don't you think . . .'

'It's all right, we're in love.'

And:

'Don't force the catch, you'll tear it.'

'God I love you. Take it off for me.'

And:

'Do you remember the first time we talked in the playground?'

'Not half as much as I'm going to remember this. We can
reminisce later. Take that off too. And that. And . . . I love
you.'

Now she's completely undressed and lying on the hearthrug.
She's not as developed for her age as I am for mine. Perhaps
that's why she needs the placebo of the word 'love'. I'm no
veteran but I look down at her and drink in her youth, the
full length of her pale, leggy body. This girl will go places,
she's got the full regalia. One of these slender girls who won't
lose a waspish waist but will end up with the contours which
make me want to cry. But looking down at her, two trembling
virgins, posterity is the last thing on my mind. Her tits are
burgeoning and she has the aureola with inset cherries that
drive me berserk. I can't remember what colour her eyes are.
Her nostrils are flared and she has a soft blonde down on her
upper lip. But the agonising smudge of her pubic hair is more
than I can bear. The Shulamite in the *Song of Solomon* is a
tawdry frump compared to this girl. I'm on the threshold of
ecstasy, the point of combustion. I kneel and bend over her . . .

Don't ask me how it got past the dead-bolts and the security
locks and the burglar alarm, but fate gate-crashed the tête-à-
tête. Destiny trampled all over me. Kismet shafted me up the
arse and the next thing I know some cosmic saboteur has
thrown half a pint of warm mayonnaise all over my belly and
I've given Deborah a cream rinse all over her face and hair.
She jumped up screaming in surprise and rushed to the toilet
to get the stains out before her mum came back with her

furry donkey or beach ball or whatever the fuck it is they win at the bingo these days. I sat pulling the stuff out of my navel and wondering at the volume produced by two-and-a-half years' foreplay and the malevolence of cosmic design.

Premature ejaculation? Tell me about it.

9

The first time we were together we were both really nervous. Things were a bit hasty at first. Jamie said maybe the hearthrug was meant to get a shampoo. We got better the next time.

'Jamie,' I said, 'if I was a cat I would purr.' But by that time he was asleep.

I got the quilt from my bedroom and covered us. I stroked his face while he was asleep. I kept thinking nothing could ever be the same again. I kept him there as long as I could, then I woke him up. He looked under the quilt and said 'fuck the rhubarb crumble', but he was ready for seconds. I told him dad was due and he put his clothes on quick enough. When I said goodbye to him in the hall I could hardly bear to let him go. I'm in love.

10

I had a month before my job started. I read lots. I've always read lots. I shagged Deborah as much as I could. I saw Thomas the day after the first night. He'd passed her house, shuttered against the sunlight and guessed the rest. He was sitting with his friends drinking while I was busy being thrown out of the pub for being under age. He's older than I am and even if he wasn't, he looks it. So do his friends. I received a round of applause when I walked in.

'We saw you coming,' Thomas shouted, 'and I said "that's the stride of a man who's done it". Didn't I?'

They all agreed and I got another round of applause.

'Deborah's gain is the Vatican's loss,' I said, trying to quieten them down.

'How many rounds were there?' He was still shouting.

'One' I said. 'She won by a knock-out.'

I looked young enough without being the cause of all this rowdiness. I tried to dissociate myself from the shouting, walked up, ordered myself a drink and was ordered to leave. It's like the black and white films when people are thrown into dungeons. They're always thrown, usually down a flight of stairs. They're never just put there. Similarly, I seem to have been thrown out of a lot of bars. I'm never just escorted.

Having left the pub I bought myself a couple of cans in an off-licence that serves children, went to the park and took stock. For a long time now I had been vaguely depressed. It wasn't just the impending employment, which was enough in itself, it was something besides. As I said, I've never had any plans, but strange as it seemed I had the feeling that somehow, somewhere, things had gone off the rails. Shagging Deborah was good fun as long as it lasted, but it was more than just my gonads that exploded that night. All this nonsense about alpha and omega, beginnings and ends, the metaphysical answers to metaphysical questions, all the cosmic mystery dispelled in a seismic shudder and a few pleasant emissions. I used to think women were little walking pockets of secrecy, and now? I'll have to find something to fill the void.

There's a pleasant candour in Deborah, but she's not going to teach me anything. What I need is an older woman, a gymnast with a fertile imagination and a filthy mind.

Deborah and I went at it hammer and tongs right till the night before I was due to start work. When I left her house that night my dick was stinging, I could hardly walk and the thought of an eight o'clock start next morning made me feel as if I was entering a gulag, not an apprenticeship. On the way out she handed me sandwiches wrapped in tinfoil for my lunch next day (prawn mayonnaise with coleslaw), kissed me and wished me good luck.

I used to wonder what that old mystic raver Blake was on about when he talked about his dark satanic mills. Not any more. I've seen one. In fact, I work there. I walked through the hangar doors the first day and I felt like I was entering the underworld. Those portakabins bolted together that had served as some of the offices during the interview turned out to be the garden spot of the place. Come eight o'clock a kind of steam whistle sounds and all these automata lounging around in overalls get up, walk to their places and all hell breaks loose. Machines start turning and grinding and forklifts drive about and crane booms pass overhead and blue flashes of electric are burst out of molten welds. It was like something Hieronymus Bosch might paint in one of his less frivolous moods.

There was a bit hived off where the six of us were supposed to start, a kind of training centre. They all looked as if they felt privileged, even Peter. 'Your dad owns this place,' I said. 'If you had any real talent for engineering you'd start at the bottom as a Vice-President.' The rest of them smilingly agreed. 'I don't know what the fuck all of you are grinning at,' I said. 'With the start all of you seem to have had in life I wouldn't call an engineering apprenticeship anything to write home about. If I had your kind of advantages in life I'd be in bed right now.'

That made them give pause. Six young men, at a nervous age, thrust into unfamiliar circumstances, establishing a pecking order, trying to impress. It's a recipe for tension. Evidently I'd done myself a favour, pre-empting the rest like that. And all because I was understandably hacked off. I found out later that they held me in some esteem for the outburst, were even a little frightened of me. And some of them looked pretty tough, in a boyish sort of way. I'll let you into a secret: I'm an abject coward. If I'm ever forced to be in the proximity of a fight, I hold the coats. I was only ever in one fight myself, in the playground. There were several opponents ranged against me and I had the option of choice. I chose the youngest. The smallest. She won.

So there were five vices in a row and a special one they had installed for the favourite son. Ours were all beat up with generations of abuse, like my old school books. His was new, refulgent. He offered it to me. I declined. 'You'll need it more than me, Peter.' Here we were supposed to stand for the best part of a year and learn the rudiments of engineering. And the first task? They give us a rough lump of metal and a draw file and tell us to make a perfect cube. The other five set about this with great gusto. They reminded me of Donald Duck's nephews. It's easy enough to get one face perfect. The next one is more difficult to get perfect and at right angles. The third face more difficult still. And so on. The last side is a killer. But they weren't daunted. 'What a fucking waste of time,' I said to them.

I considered the problem for a while, while the piles of shavings around their vices grew. At the end of some days I was obliged to steal some of their shavings and sprinkle them round my bit. Sometimes I think I expend more thought and energy in not doing a thing than I would have spent if I had simply done what was asked of me. Sometimes I'm tempted out of laziness just to do the work, but it goes against my principles.

I considered some more, then I took my lump of abused metal to one of the tradesmen out in the factory floor standing beside a milling machine. I asked him to make me a cube and there was a hundred fags in it for him. Twenty minutes later I've got a gleaming dice which I take and rough up a little with my file to give the impression of being hand-made. Out of those already handed in I get top marks. Peter's doing his best to be a chip off the old block but looks about as competent with a file in his hand as he had with a slide rule. The end of the week is the deadline. Thursday and he's nearly in tears.

'You want to impress your dad, don't you?'

'Yes.'

'Give me your metal, two hundred fags and twenty quid and no questions asked.'

'I couldn't.' I shrug and turn away. I know his dad doesn't stint in anything but affection and I'm gambling that the son's got more money than pride. 'I mean . . . all right.'

Next day I pay off the man with Peter's cigarettes and stand in the machine shop chatting with two crisp ten pound notes in my pocket watching another dice roll off the production line. We break open the carton and I smoke a few of his fags to pass the time.

By the end of the month I feel, like my first year at school, as if I've exhausted the possibilities of the place. Friday afternoon and a member of staff I've never seen before brings in the wage slips. She looks about twenty-five. She has a voluptuous chest, long legs, blonde hair that's come out of a bottle. She looks like the type who would wear too much lipstick and smoke in bed. The type you would hesitate to introduce to your mother.

Halleluiah.

11

A photograph: six of us in overalls, nonchalantly leaning on one another, class of . . .

Extreme left, Kevin, son of the marketing executive whose father had derived such an obvious pleasure from disparaging Peter at the interviews. The family rivalry hasn't been passed on. Kevin, lackadaisical, a man after my own heart, prematurely aged, in whose face I can already see the emerging skull of senility. Middle height, thickening, lounges a little, too open-minded to harbour a baseless grudge, or too apathetic, or both.

Second left, Scott, whose father is a master mason of the district and elicits many respectful whispers and curious handshakes. Scott, irreverent, standing with overalls peeled back, one breast bared, one trouser leg rolled up above the knee, holding a black ball in his outstretched hand. Scott, who apoplexed numerous relatives by the distribution of copies of this photograph. An elegant boy with a line in droll exchanges. Scott, my pal.

Third left, Bruce. He frightened me then. When I look at that picture he frightens me even now. Tall, spare, mercurial, possessor of homicidal strength with a temperament to match. He spent the first two weeks at the fabrication bench, manufacturing pointed stars from aluminium sheeting with a pair of snips, grinding them to razor edges and annealing the tips at the furnace. He then made a human effigy out of spare overalls stuffed with toilet paper, pigskin gauntlets and a welding helmet, and proceeded to perforate it with the stars he threw with daunting accuracy from forty feet back. Stars radiated from its face, its groin, its throat, the place above its heart – if it had one. When I think of my initial insult to them all it frightens me still. When not devising means of inflicting pain on non-existent opponents (no one in their right mind went near him) he was inventing tattoo motifs on scraps of paper. After every payday he would present himself to the tattoo 'artist' for more unflinching mutilation. We were regaled as a group with each new wound. Monday morning he'd stand on the fabrication bench and drop his trousers. From one cheek of his arse a skull with a Roman dagger thrust vertically through stared out at us. Beneath, in Gothic script, read the legend 'Pure Sex'.

'Exactly what kind of girl are you trying to attract?' I couldn't help myself.

'Fuck knows. One out for a laugh. Fancy a tattoo yourself?'

'About as much as I fancy conscription. If I was ever forced to get a tattoo it would be of a microbe or some sub-atomic particle – actual size.'

'I'm looking for ideas for my next one.'

'How about an eagle – '

'Fuckin' ace!'

' – swooping down on a herd of ravening wolves jumping over a waterfall in full torrent while an iceberg crashes into an arctic sea in the background with gigantic columns of spray and an approaching tidal wave.'

'Fuckin' ace! I was thinking of getting my prick done like a shark, with the teeth on the bishop, so that when some bint pulls back the foreskin, 'stead of being given the gladeye by the one-eyed milkman, like she's expecting, she gets a row of teeth.'

'That'll be nice for her.'

'Fuckin' ace!'

He just got progressively more scary. Bruce, a young man of great criminal pretensions destined to be fulfilled. His father was in charge of quality control.

Fourth left, Gregor, assiduous, serious, a young man with the kind of dynamism that makes me tired to look at. A young man who knew his limitations and persevered to push them to the limit. Son of the man who sold components to the firm at preferential rates, Gregor sought to use them to the best of his abilities. Aside from Peter he had the most to prove. I, needless to say, had nothing. Gregor, micrometer in hand, always ready. While the rest of us unashamedly pored over soft pornography, his lunch-time reading consisted of magazines full of satisfied civil engineers and happy tractor drivers. Gregor: prosaic, staid, dependable, predictable – not my favourite.

Fifth left, and, uncharacteristically, with Gregor's arm resting on his shoulder – me. You can vouch for my character. I'm the only one sitting, on the fabrication bench. Everyone else is standing in front of me. In my left hand I hold a lighted oxyacetylene torch, from whose vaporous tip I light a cigarette clamped between my lips. The act requires my full powers of concentration. My brows are knitted. The flame is unseen, marked only by its corona of heat distortion. My right arm, characteristically, rests on Peter.

Sixth left, or extreme right if you want to be pedantic about it, Peter. Peter, whose hysterical acne you know, at a glance, will endure into his fifties. Peter, with most to give, given most, with most to prove and, perhaps, most to lose. A hesit-

ator, an ingénu, generous to his bootstraps. Reticent with
men, excruciating with women, given to uncontrollable
blushing whose bloody fluorescence draws stares across a bus
terminus. Peter, with the most unfortunate level of intelligence
possible, that which is astute enough to look at itself dispassionately and doesn't like what it sees.

'We needs must worship the highest, Peter,' I said.

'What does that mean?'

'It means, watch me. Watch the way I can order a salad roll
without going red, the way I light a fag, the way I talk to
women. Got it?'

'Yes.'

My protégé? No. Nor his father's son. An epigone, not a
chip off the old block. He wouldn't found a firm manufacturing marine pumps and measure his success by the number of
women he could fuck while keeping it from his wife. If Peter
came out of an apprenticeship with a few botched metalwork
exercises and the wit to rebut the insults of common exchanges
then he had done more than could reasonably be asked.

Peter: flawed, limited, spontaneous at a month's notice, a
social cripple with the wit to know. My favourite.

All this might give the impression that it was nothing but
good fun and camaraderie (and there was a lot of that), but it
wasn't as good as it sounds. Months at a time we'd all be
together in the training centre, avoiding whatever Bruce's
latest projectiles were, arranging nights out (I was self-
appointed social convener) and doing little work. And then a
few months farmed out to work with some tradesmen or
other on the factory floor. These men I found universally
boring, purveyors and consumers of infinite pornography,
insatiable readers of the tabloids, football fans, the type of
people who can get excited by spot the ball.

A typical exchange:

'Sometimes you know, sonny, I take a pot of jam up to bed
and smear it all over the wife's tits and lick it off.'

He's saying this while looking at a picture of a Puerto Rican
porn star with a vagina like a gashed watermelon. This must

be what the psychologists mean by transference. I've seen his wife. She looks like him and he hasn't changed his cardigan since he started with the company.

'Really?'

'But sometimes I don't bother with the jam.'

As far as intelligence was concerned I came to think of him and his ilk as products of genetic espionage, informed on the need-to-know basis. They needed to know how to roll a fag, order a hamburger, shag their womenfolk and make more of themselves. In another ten generations they might evolve to making their own salad dressing. Perhaps not.

And then a few jubilant months back among my fellow apprentices. Bruce had taken to filling empty milk bottles with acetylene gas, sealing them with sellotape and throwing them in the furnace. They exploded in a thousand shards, like an anti-personnel device. He frightened me more and more every day. But the rest were all right. And I had decided to educate Peter to alleviate the boredom.

'You know what the best thing is about being an auto-didact?'

'What's an autodidact?'

'Someone who doesn't have to sit any exams.'

'So what's the best thing about it?'

'No one telling you you failed.'

'Can I be one?'

'Be my guest.'

When he told me he had a girlfriend I thought I hadn't heard correctly. Perhaps he meant a friend who happened to be a girl, someone you grow up with and play kiss cuddle or torture with till they take a fancy to someone more cultured, someone without stabilisers on his bike. But it turned out to be more, someone he had asked out. It must have required a burst of epic confidence on his part.

'So is she good looking or what?'

'*I* think so.'

The usual oblique answer. When someone asks you 'Is she good looking?' everyone knows what the question means and what the answer is. If they end up saying 'She's got a lovely personality' you usually wind up with a farmyard animal. He suggested a foursome. Out of vindictive curiosity I couldn't help but agree.

Deborah was beginning to blossom. I couldn't keep my hands off her tits. They attracted me like loadstones; like a magnet wheeling to magnetic north my hands would find her tits, and standing at bus-stops I'd find my hand ramming itself up her skirt. The summer was worst. My hormones and her summer dresses. And the thing was, the more times I said the word 'love' the dirtier she got. I was keeping 'I want to have your child' in reserve for a filthy climax when we finally decided to go our separate ways. All in all, I was ready for a fairly drab night with Peter and his dowdy girlfriend, where I'd concentrate on Deborah's contours and perhaps get the frisson of a grope under the table.

I was there and Deborah was there. Peter was there and Julia was there. Julia: guarded, unsure, hesitating and with a figure that would make the Pope chuck his job. 'There must be some mistake,' I almost said. Her colour was exquisite. I pride myself on noticing such things. Starting at the ankles, it took me three minutes to get to her face. It took her three minutes hesitantly to spit out that she had heard a great deal about me. The colour spread from her creamy cheek down the columnar neck and disappeared into her cleavage, dissipating, I imagined, over her swelling breasts. Well, I nearly exploded. Her and Peter. I know he was my friend and all but somehow I felt he didn't deserve her. I looked at him. Was he appraising Deborah the way I was Julia? I don't know how I know, but I know he wasn't. Was either of us wrong? I can't help it if I'm just a dirty bastard.

It was a restaurant of the cheap and cheerful variety, with a minute dance floor where people tried to cavort in two square feet and bumped into the tables. The staff were slow and struggled through the closely packed customers, retaining whatever good humour they could. I was obliged to rub against Julia and conduct a conversation through the noise. I left Peter and Deborah to it.

'Have you been going out with Peter long?'

'Three years.'

Fuck me!

'You didn't meet him in a pub then, not at that age.'

'We met at the Youth Fellowship.'

The Youth Fellowship is a pseudo-Christian Boys' Brigade and Girl Guides combined. They take you on outings and try and inculcate decent values while the boys and the girls try to shag each other behind the bushes. All except for the ones who take it seriously.

She took it seriously.

I could imagine in my mind's eye the prototype of two people fucking. I could substitute the image of Julia for the woman. That was easy. It was enjoyable. With no hesitation I could substitute the image of me for that of the man. But I somehow couldn't superimpose the image of Peter on top of the image of Julia. It just wouldn't go.

The meal wore on. Peter was glad I seemed to be getting on so well with his girlfriend but he and Deborah seemed to be making heavy weather of it. She went for extended leaks and repairs to her make-up. He soldiered on manfully, and between snatches of our conversation I'd hear prosaic descriptions of soldering irons and such stuff. While Deborah was away I asked him to go up to the bar for some drinks and turned my full attention to Julia. She was chewing – hesitantly. She did everything hesitantly. If the unimaginable ever happened and she and Peter ever got down to fucking, they'd probably approach one another across a bedroom like two stick insects, antennae quivering. That's not what she needed at all.

I watched her chew. I could imagine her teeth, lacerating the meat. Somehow the thought of all her physical functions gave me a thrill. I could get aroused thinking about her peristalsis.

'I want you to piss all over my face,' I said – almost. I knew at least several foremen and a few teachers who would have taken me up on the offer. I leaned across. She stopped chewing.

'I hope this doesn't sound . . . trite. Perhaps I shouldn't . . .' I managed a blush.

'No. Go on.'

'Have you ever met someone for the first time and you feel an affinity there, and you know it's because of something . . . something . . . spiritual?'

She stopped chewing, hesitated, swallowed, blushed, nodded. I touched her arm. There was no reproof. Deborah came back from the bathroom. Peter came back with the drinks.

Physical contact without the straight-out brush off: it was more than I ever achieved at school, something to be going on with.

When we'd gone our separate ways I was walking along with Deborah. She rolls her hips as she walks and sometimes I listen out for the sparks of static from the friction of her nylon thighs. Tonight was one of those nights.

'You and Julia seemed to be getting on like a house on fire.'

'Yes. Don't you think she and Peter are well matched.' It was a rhetorical question. I was being ridiculous.

'Do you think you and Julia would be well matched? If I wasn't here, I mean.'

'Don't say that. I don't ever want to think of your not being here. I can't imagine anything being worth anything if you were away.'

'Jamie, oh Jamie.' The feeling in her voice made me almost ashamed. We linked arms. We reached the bus-stop.

'Besides, with you it goes somehow further. Don't ask me how. I know it sounds ridiculous, but it's something . . . something . . . spiritual.' She drew me down towards her chest, her hands mobile in the thickness of my hair. When my voice came out it was muffled.

'Is your mum at the bingo?'

1 2

I've been here since seventeen, since I left school. I'm twenty-five now and feel like a veteran. Every year I've seen them and every year it's just the same – another intake. You can almost catalogue them: the wide-boys, the shy ones, the ones with acne, the brawlers, the ones who will end up drunks, the one with the dad who works for the firm. The would-be womanisers annoy me most. When I was seventeen, seventeen-year-old boys didn't entertain me. I went out with someone who was twenty-three, who had a car and could take me down the coast. And now, eight years on, I'm supposed to be amused by tipsy virgins who touch me up at the works' night out.

I don't know if it's me, if it's just that I'm getting older or they're getting worse. First week of the new intake and I take down the wages and I get the usual bunch of apprentices staring at my tits. Or not the usual bunch. There's at least two who have dads who work here. One looks almost retarded. This place is becoming incestuous. Pretty soon you won't get a job here as an apprentice if you've only got five fingers on each hand. There's the usual maniac and the usual array of skin complaints. And then there's this other one. When I go over to him he's reading the soft porn which always seems to litter the place. Most of them at that age try and close it over or hide it when they see me. He was sitting, not even making lip-service to work. He didn't even have the decency to look embarrassed. When I stuck out his wage he took it without even looking up. It annoyed me.

'You never been taught any manners?' He looked up at that and looked straight at me.

'What's bothering you, the pictures or the fact that you haven't succeeded in getting everyone in the place to look at you?' He was smoking. He was cheeky. He was quite good looking I suppose, and knew it.

'That's disgusting.'

'Don't mock talent. She can get them to cum at the same time. No mean feat considering there's six of them. And here she is sharing

a cucumber with her landlady. Now that's what I call friendly. I wouldn't mind being her greengrocer. Imagine all the vegetable antics you could get up to after hours with her.'

'Stick to the pictures, sonny. It's the closest you'll get.'

He had gone back to the pictures and was ignoring me by the time I spoke. I wanted to take his hair and crack his head off his vice. None of them ever talk like that to me.

'See you next Friday. You'll think about me,' he said, still without looking up as I walked out. The irritating thing is, I did think about him.

1 3

She waltzes in every Friday. She's tarted up to the nines. She's just put on more lipstick. Because of the reason for her being there, everyone is glad to see her. Everyone wants their pay packet and if she's obliging enough to bend down so we can look up her skirt, so much the better. She milks it. She needs the adulation of a bunch of spotty pubescent boys because if you take a look at her, a good look, you can see that time's running out. And she knows it. Common people age quicker. It's just a sad fact of life.

The roots of her hair show. She's thickening at the waist. If she had a job standing up she'd have varicose veins in two years. Her looks are fading and things are already beginning to go south. Her appearance owes everything to preparation and the time she takes to make herself up probably gets longer every morning. I imagine she's already reduced to salvaging with cosmetics what she once had without. Her looks appeal to sexist bastards who look at her as a weekend hump but she's nobody's long-term prospect. Bastards like me. She absorbs compliments – she needs them. She needs reassurance too. She jokingly mentioned her crows' feet and waited for someone to dismiss them as laughter lines.

'Nothing's that funny,' I said.

She's brought me my wages a few times now. I don't queue for them. You get the same amount of money whether you wait five minutes more or not. She manufactures lines now to meet me with. You can tell the time taken in rehearsal. But she can't ad lib. Last time I pre-empted her. She sat on a stool and called out names, handing out wages like corrected homework. She called my name. 'Shut your legs,' I said from where I was sitting, 'there's a draught.'

She's not like Deborah and she's not like Julia and she fascinates me by her possibilities and her tawdriness and her knowledge. I want to kiss her because I'm only young once and it will lose the potency if I don't do it soon because the discrepancy in knowledge between us will iron itself out. Somehow I think kissing her will be like rubbing my face round a full ashtray.

14

I crossed the Rubicon. Four nights on the trot I came in drunk and incapable. I've taken to getting horribly drunk of late. On the fourth, a Friday, I evidently brought a girl back with me. I don't remember. I was told by my parents the next day. There was no trace of the girl, no warm dent beside me on the mattress, no fortuitous stains on the hearthrug – I checked. I assumed it was Deborah and the next time we met I skated round the topic.

'Did you enjoy yourself last Friday?' My opening gambit.

'Yes, it was lovely. And you?'

'Mmmm . . .'

'I'd no idea it was so long.'

I gave a manly shrug. I thought perhaps I'd blacked out the night because it was so bad or embarrassing. Things were looking up.

'The climax was just . . . just . . .' She couldn't find the words. I must just be that kind of a guy. Deborah in paroxysms and me trying to hoist Mr Floppy. Even with a semi I'm hot stuff, bending it in with the best of them. You've either got it or you haven't.

'Soaking?' I said.

'Y . . . es.'

'And how was I?'

'You,' she said. 'You weren't there.'

The filthy cow. Three non-committal remarks later and I find out from her that she went to the opera with her dad to see *Così fan tutte*. Opera's just a lot of fat people shouting at one another in German or Italian. And I wasn't there. Who was I with? All it takes is for me to sleep with one more woman and I've increased my score by one hundred per cent.

Whoever I was with, she had a profound influence on my parents, although they didn't see her either. They heard me knock over the hat-stand, the drunken laughter, the noise of a woman's raised voice 'Rejecting your advances' as they put it, the noise of preliminary sexual strife, the sound of the front door slamming and me scraping my way up the hall staircase to my bed. I was woken up with a tap on the shoulder, the room lurched into focus and they were standing over me like two grim sentinels.

'What kind of time do you call that to be getting back last night – or should I say this morning?'

'You heard, your father's asking you a question.'

'And with a woman.'

'A woman? I had a woman?' I was instantly cheerful.

'You heard your father. Stop sniffing your fingers, it's dis-gusting.'

'Dis-gusting!' he echoed.

The long and short of it was an ultimatum. One more woman back under those circumstances and I was dispossessed, no son of theirs.

The way things turned out it seemed almost orchestrated. A week later, lying in bed, dad began to feel the preliminary rumblings of indigestion. Kidney beans are his idea of exotic cuisine, and they'd been taken out for a korma. He scoured the bathroom cabinet unsuccessfully for Epsom Salts and came downstairs. At the confused acoustics he opened the lounge door. I was stark naked standing with my back to him, facing her and the wall. Deborah had hitched up her dress and perched herself on me, arms round my neck, crook of her knees in the crook of my elbows, supported centrally by the moist socket. The trembling of my knees tapped out a sporadic morse on the fluted radiator – it was this that he had heard. She froze when she saw him silhouetted in the doorway over my shoulder. Some internal sphincter contracted and gripped me.

'Oh! That was nice. Can you do it again?'

There was nothing for it. She wouldn't continue. I lifted her off and searched for something to slip on in the gloom. I wondered: if I got pictures of my dad and flashed them to Deborah in the middle of a session, would she grip like that again. I hope so. Perhaps we could condition the reflex – Deborah and her contracting vagina.

I padded across the linoleum of the kitchen barefoot. He was standing looking morosely at a sparse medicine cabinet. There was no point in even trying to mollify him. I could only call his bluff.

'Dad, I'm no son of yours.'

He looked me in the eyes and looked down. I followed his gaze. In the gloom I had put on Deborah's panties, my still weeping dick stuck out one leg.

They gave me my bed to take with me. I think this was more a question of hygiene than generosity. They also gave me a kettle, some deck chairs, some mildewed carpet stored in the garden shed for years, and an old radio. And some money. Given their limited means I suppose they gave as much as they could. Given my limited means I got what I could. I was wrestling over the dilemma of a dingy flat in a nice area, or a nice flat in a dingy area. They would both cost about the same. I did my arithmetic and settled for a dingy flat in a dingy area. I moved in with what I had. Deborah's parents gave me an old cooker. The apprentices chipped in and bought me eight dozen cans and a beer dispenser.

I looked around on my first night. The evening light was slanting in and I could see the floating dust exhaled from my folded carpets. Everything was in boxes I had taken from the supermarket. The noise of occasional traffic came up from the street outside and I could hear the kids from across the way, playing in the swing-park with burdocks growing out the fractured tarmac. My windows were dusty with frames rotting in the granite. The floorboards were bare and erratic. Through the open door of the hallway and bathroom I could see the ancient toilet, surrounded by smelly carpet tiles I had not yet had the courage to lift.

'Bijou,' I said aloud to myself. 'Ascetic and compact with a certain . . .' My glance wandered and I caught sight of a single rose perched in a slender sterling vase on the mantelpiece, and beneath it a card with bold lettering – Deborah's unmistakable script – WELCOME HOME. There were beads of moisture on the green stalk and the folding petals. And suddenly the vibrant beauty of the thing, the perfection, simplicity, vernal freshness, threw it into grotesque incongruity. What right has something beautiful to be here? I thought, and looked around some more.

'It's a fucking dump!' I said, and burst into tears.

1 5

I've settled in. The place has a certain tawdry charm. I bought a saucepan. I'm beginning to cook. Deborah's cohabitation is still on the unspoken agenda. She cohabits with me two week nights, creeping home in the early hours and letting herself in with her own latchkey. She cohabits most Saturdays and leaves at the same time. I'm usually fast asleep, contentedly farting in post-coital stupor.

Living alone is good. I spend lots of time thinking about

Julia and the wages clerkess, whose name I have found out is Diane. Sometimes I think there must be more to life than avoiding work and lying about a flat planning strategies to fuck women, but I can't for the life of me think what that is.

I've started to act as go-between with Peter and Julia. We've even gone out as a threesome, minus Deborah. When I look at those two, I wonder how on earth they managed to stay together for so long. He's so fond of her it's painful. His acne flares at her glance. He hasn't got round to sex because he thinks she's far above him, from some empyrean realm he would only pollute. Personally I think she looks one of those quiet types who turns into a raver. I'm speaking with my wealth of sexual experience, you understand. They're about as communicative as two retarded protozoans. I've spoken to them separately. Every Monday Peter gives me an autopsy of the weekend, which includes lots of breast beating, swearing eternal fidelity and protestations of his unworthiness. No wonder they've never got very far. She must be bored to tears. If there's one piece of knowledge I wish I had possessed at eighteen it's that girls like sex as much as boys do. It's not a case of being let on sufferance. They actually want to. Julia said to me:

'I think coming home to someone . . . the television . . . a shared book, maybe . . . holding one another . . . And afterwards. The pleasant shared drowsiness.'

' "And afterwards".' It reminded me of one of those thirties black and white Hollywood numbers, or the pink-ink romances written for old blue-rinse virgins. He carries her over the threshold. She's lying on the bed, suggestively rubbing the counterpane, all pulsing acquiescence. He leans over her. Cut to waves crashing on a beach. Was it the Youth Fellowship made her go in for these circumlocutions? All she really wanted was a good shag. And who can blame her. So I said to Peter:

'I think it's something ephemeral Julia's looking for from you because that's what she's like herself. She's a creature of tissue . . .' I thought of some of her tissues. 'It's not the grossly physical that attracts a woman like that. Carnal things are more likely to dissuade her. There's something about her, something you wouldn't want to contaminate by mere contact . . .' I tailed off and looked upward: my pre-Raphaelite look.

'You think so?'

'Honest to God.'

Poor bastard. And I said to Julia:

'He's a cerebral person, Peter. If you want to remain with him you have to understand that. Don't expect to be swept off your feet. He's the type of person you grow into and enjoy, in your declining years, the fruits of speculative culture with . . .'

You should have seen her face. I think the 'speculative culture' really got her. She looked exactly the way I imagine I would if some red-hot date took me home, peeled off her coat, and suggested a game of all-night cribbage. She asked me round some more. My time as emissary began to employ more nights than their nights with each other, and since I could hear Peter's woes all day free of charge, most of my nights concerning them began to concern us – Julia and me. Deborah began to tire of the arrangement:

'If he can't make it work with her on his own after all this time, what chance do you have?'

'Perhaps they only need a little more push. Another little nudge to consummate things. You wouldn't deny them that? It could make all the difference. Remember ours.'

'I don't want to have to remember.'

Nor did I. I wanted to go in for frequent reconsummation whenever possible. There was something about Deborah. Perhaps because she was the first. Perhaps because she was the only. The crimson rinse of her complexion, the dimples above her buttocks, her vagina: deep, replete, orchidaceous. I could imagine her beautiful in pregnancy, her convex stomach, strawberry breasts, the honey of her sticky legs and children pushed out as easily as a breath from her wonderful insides. Kids I could teach to make sandcastles. The home-made bird table in the back garden. Christmas and a real tree, with the tang of pine and laughter through the house. A Sunday-supplement existence. Fidelity seemed so seductive. I had to fight it long and hard.

'So what's happening tomorrow night, Julia?' I said when next I got her alone.

'There's a Youth Fellowship meeting.'

'Aren't you a bit old for that?'

'I'm one of the organisers now. I thought it best to stay on and try and give something back. Give the other kids the opportunities I had.'

'What fucking opportunities?' I wanted to say. Peter goes back from time to time too and teaches kids to be as much of a social fuckwit as he is. Instead I said: 'Is Peter going to be there?'

'Yes.'

'And you're attending too?'

'I'm supposed to be.' You don't have to be too sharp to pick up on an opportunity like that.

'I haven't had a good talk in ages. Come out with me.'

'I don't know . . .' She dawdled with her voice. She dawdled with her foot, describing unintelligible patterns on the ground. I thought: she's unsure; she wants to come but I've allowed her too great a degree of freedom. She wants things taken in hand. She wants to be found in the grip of something bigger than herself, something abstract which she can foist the blame for her complicity on.

'You could come after the meeting, say nine o'clock?'

'I suppose . . .'

I felt suddenly tired of all this shy virgin stuff. I knew then that some day no aphrodisiac would drive me to these lengths, but while I still cared enough to walk ten miles for a random shag, I should make use of the facility. All the same, I wanted to push her off the parapet.

'I'll see you then.'

'Yes . . .'

'Come round to mine.' I moved away, deliberately, without looking at her. Until now we'd always met on neutral ground, in bars and once in the park, chaperoned by an unwitting Peter. The tone I'd used was almost peremptory, denying her the freedom we both knew she didn't want. And then I said, almost as an afterthought: 'Bring Peter, if you like.'

It was a good acid test. If she turned up at mine she hadn't been pushed, she'd jumped.

1 6

I'm beginning to remember who she was, the woman I brought home and with whose antics I scandalised my parents. The woman of my dreams, of my débâcle. The woman in my dreams. She's Cleopatra, sitting on peacock feathers and transported to my parents' lounge. The plaster ducks at her shoulder don't strike me as incongruous. A eunuch is swinging a censer. The queen gives me the gladeye, beckons me with obvious intent. The eunuch comes forward to unrobe the queen. A thick serving woman arrives with figs.

'Dad! Mum!'

Or she is the woman in the postcard from Greece, stuck on the wall above the fabrication bench at work with a piece of bluetack. She is frozen in mid-frolic, emerging from the swimming pool, while around her suspended droplets and fluted columns of spray hang like iridescent satellites brushing her body. She is a caricature of femininity wearing a leopard-skin G-string. She climbs from the card and stands full length on the fabrication bench, glistening. She nonplusses the apprentices as she stands there, Aphrodite in a G-string and high heels, among the broken scraps of metal and discarded welding rods. She steps down and beckons – to me. I drape my coat around her shoulders. I give a cavalier wave to my colleagues who stand there, open mouthed as we depart for the bus-stop, calling in only for two special fish suppers en route. Seconds later we are rolling among the brown wrappers on my parents' rug in front of the fire when the walls part and they stand there, the couple in American Gothic, he with the pitchfork. And superimposed on these figures are the faces of my disapproving parents.

She is the lawyer dressed in matching tweed skirt and jacket, her taste a little too precious, a little too conservative and at odds with the fullness of her lip. We climb the stairs to the flat she is buying on my behalf. The landing curves and transforms itself into my childhood bedroom, with hanging model aeroplanes suspended in an improbable dog fight above my bed. Pieces of the bike I dismantled as a boy still lie scattered around the floor and ledges. I point my collection of marbles out to her, my dead tortoise, the dried-out frog spawn I spilt on the bedside rug. She ignores me and tears the chignon from her head, peeling off her blouse as the hair cascades around her now bare shoulders. I grasp her. Mum enters with a mug of cocoa, dad brings up the rear with a plate of digestive biscuits.

A psychiatrist would have a field-day with this. Always I'm caught *in flagrante*. Nothing is ever consummated while they are around. And if this sexual object with whom I am tantalised is becoming less exotic, she's also becoming more real. Pretty soon she's going to become so real I'll find out who she is. Who is she? What did we do that was so bad I feel compelled to consign the act into the obscure backwater of memory? Who is that girl?

1 7

No one would ever guess. Julia writes *erotic poetry*. It's not very erotic and it's not very poetical, but it's a start. She turned up, alone, with a sheaf of papers she clung on to like it was her whole inheritance. She guarded them so tightly, a poker-player staking it all. She obviously wanted to be asked. I set about brewing tea and carried on as if there was nothing unusual. She followed me into the tiny kitchen with her clandestine bundle. She had to tear this from her chest to accept the cup I offered. She returned to the lounge before I did and shouted through – shouting was something she never did – that she was going to the toilet – something she only ever referred to at other times circumspectly. When I came through the papers were strewn strategically on the coffee table, or rather the upturned boxes I used as a coffee table. Out of sheer bloody-mindedness I decided not to read them. I did, however, go through the pockets of her discarded coat, hoping to find some condoms. I had a plentiful supply myself, of various flavours, but I wanted her to provide them as a sop to my vanity. She had none.

She came back and stood with her back to the electric fire, the red light shining on the back of her moulded calves. I drank my tea loudly and decided not to say anything. Eventually, without once having met my look, she stooped down, rummaged among the paperwork, and selecting a sheet began in a tremulous voice to read:

> All through the weft and weave of us,
> I spiral round your curling form,
> I cleave to me, I cleave to us,
> You grow in me, my fabric torn,
> Suffuse me yet with your sweet dye,
> Press me to death and softly gore,
> That I may sleep and I may lie,
> Decline to live and die once more.

And looking me straight in the eye she said: 'I take my analogy from tapestry.'

I suppose at such a time I should have felt ashamed. I didn't. Well, I thought, copulation and carpets, a dirty poem like that's got quite a lot going for it. There's 'a good shag', 'shuttlecock', 'well-laid' and any number of poetical double entendres someone of such a frame of mind might wring out of it. And the old play on die and orgasm might be a bit hackneyed but does the job after all. I always felt I would have had something in common with Donne when he gives us the low down on his bit of stuff, relishing her curves and grooves like a randy map maker. Me and Donne would have been pals.

'There was an old man from Nantucket . . .' I began. I cut it short when I saw she wouldn't see the humour in it.

She had some other poems, similar stuff. The curious thing was, when she read aloud, as if describing abstract love between two prototypes, she wasn't in the least embarrassed. We both knew the poetry was about us. But when she stopped she didn't know where to look. I sat her down and me opposite, either side of the electric fire. I suggested candlelight: 'Mediaeval,' I said. 'Older than love.' Although fuck knows what I meant by that.

'Nothing's older than love,' she said, and while she read I drew my chair closer to her, stanza by stanza. By the end of about the fifth poem we were practically knee to knee. I sat on the floor, leaning my head on her knees and staring right up her skirt. I wondered if she'd put anything on, or taken it off, for me. Unfortunately, she didn't appear to be wearing suspenders. I stroked her leg and momentarily she paused in her reading. When she started again I kissed her thigh. Her voice wavered. I persisted.

It's at times like this I feel like giving vent to my full powers of expression and laying it on the line, as it happened blow by blow, the perfume of her sex, the grain of her skin, the unpractised sticky fingers. And it's not that I scruple to do so. For the sake of perversity – cut to waves crashing on a deserted beach. I'm keeping all the best bits for my monograph, *Principia Erotica*. Cut back to a whispered parting, a shamefaced 'good night' in the darkness of the street outside my flat, unnecessarily furtive in the desolation of the early hours. Shamefaced and furtive on her part that is. Me, I was ready for a brass band. If I was a tribesman I'd have cut another notch in the fertility totem and shown everyone. This deserved a lie-in. This deserved a day on the sick. I lay on the couch, smoked cigarette after cigarette, and thought of an appropriately bogus excuse to phone in the following day.

1 8

I don't know if a day off the following day was such a good idea after all. I got time to think. A kind of moral rot temporarily set in soon afterwards. I woke up, not thinking of Julia but of Peter. And then I thought about Deborah. And I thought again what crap all this metaphysical stuff about the middle of a woman's body being the zenith and the nadir was. No wonder I felt a sense of moral dislocation. When you've had heaven, what's left?

I called in my miserable excuse which no one believed, lay back in bed, let out a happy sigh and all of a sudden I found myself getting all speculative.

I thought about last night, the smeared emulsion of her sex in the candlelight. I was right about that being mediaeval. And then I caught myself thinking about what those times would really have been like, with the superstition and the agency of God and the Devil to be seen in everything you do, in the sun that grows the crops and the blight which takes them away. And I began to wonder if I would have been different if I had lived then. Things might have been easier to grasp then; I might have been religious; I might have believed something. And then I caught myself thinking, no, that's easy, any time is equidistant from eternity. And then I thought, for fuck's sake! What's happening to me? Here I am, I've conned the taxpayer out of a day's labour, I'm lying in bed, I've cheated on my girlfriend, I've screwed my best friend's girl, I've gained some valuable experiences – why am I not happy? It's inexplicable!

If you believe all those old tragedies and that self-awareness comes through pain, then I'd rather be shallow and happy. But you have to be vigilant: profundity keeps creeping up. I need something to believe in. I believe Peter is my friend; I don't like him any less because of what happened last night. And Deborah and Julia, they don't bear comparison. I like them. They're both different and enjoyable in every way.

I thought of all the compensations I could, and still I wasn't happy. I needed a challenge. I needed a direction, a goal worth pursuing, something of substance in this superficial morass of all my petty wants and likes.

I mulled this over for a while. I came up with an answer. I was happy. I knew what I needed to do. I needed to fuck Diane.

1 9

It's a small firm: perhaps fifty tradesmen, a third as many again in administration, half of which are women, and a few apprentices. They hold an excruciating annual event which is supposed to promote a sense of camaraderie. It doesn't. It's destined to fail even if it wasn't for the one crucial factor which destroys any possibility of success from the outset: tickets are issued in pairs. You are supposed to bring your partner.

If it wasn't for the wives and husbands and boyfriends and girlfriends of the work-force the social night would be like any other. They'd all fall into their usual coteries and the M.D. would walk from group to group making futile attempts to integrate the company. He'd be treated to a reverential hush that lengthens into embarrassment all round. He'd make a few vulgar quips to show he hasn't lost the common touch, trump up a few reminiscences of his days of working with his hands, a nostalgic reference or two to the dignity of manual labour – the whole Gunga Din scenario compressed into eleven unanswered remarks – hand out a few cigars and return to the top table through the strata of middle management. Then he'd sit down and thank Christ he wasn't still vegetating with the type of people he served his apprenticeship with.

He's a fundamentally unhappy man, Peter's dad. You can tell. There are the subtle signs: the way he hates anyone with a bigger car than his, the way he shouts at everyone, the way he spreads rumours of management buy-outs to test the water, the way he hands out redundancy threats like confetti, the way he announces discriminatory Christmas bonuses over the tannoy and comes down to the shop floor to relish the effect. He's crossed one threshold and hasn't put his foot on another. He ensures the managers he employs are university graduates to a man, so he can disparage them for their lack of practical experience. He makes anyone who can spell 'marmalade' feel as if they had grown up in privileged circumstances. And he secretly derides those who didn't claw themselves up the way he did. His wife looks like one of those expensive Chinese dogs whose skin is too big for their bodies and hangs in folds about them. He grudgingly acknowledges Peter and lets everyone know without saying so that the boy's an obvious disappointment to him.

And as an example of the management of this work-force he's not alone. A lot of them seem to model themselves on him and affect his belligerence. So even if it wasn't for the boyfriends and girlfriends, the wives and husbands being there, the night would be a failure anyway.

But the partners are there, and the shop-floor boys who pore over tits in the tabloids and have pictures of steaming labia posted above their lathes, introduce their womenfolk to one another and mentally note how they do or don't fancy yours much. Since most of the work-force are men, there's usually a lot of bemused womenfolk walking about who introduce themselves to one another across the social boundaries. There's the laying on of hands and the clumsy introductions. There's one way of staying above it all, just get stinking drunk and enjoy the spectacle for what it is: a night founded on spurious bonhomie which is in its death throes by nine o'clock.

Deborah was there with me wearing an off-the-shoulder something that had stopped me dead when I went to collect her at her parents'. I enjoyed walking around with her and collecting all the stares. Kevin and Scott and Bruce and even Gregor came up and clapped me on the back in the spirit of randy camaraderie, as if complimenting me on my choice of horseflesh. The stares were blatant enough to make a scene with some of their girlfriends. I caught the old tradesman who had disclosed the stories of smearing jam on his wife's tits giving Deborah the gladeye across the room. No wonder some girls feel intimidated with dirty old bastards like that around. It's different with me, don't ask me how. I look at Deborah with unbridled lust and she just loves it. Last week I asked her to put toothpaste on my dick before we had sex because the tingle is supposed to be good fun and she just laughed all night. She's got this short skirt with a split up the side she wears only for me. When she crosses her legs you can practically see her fallopian tubes. It's bloody marvellous. It's at times like that I want to drink her bathwater, to floss my teeth with her G-string. It's times like that that almost make me want to be faithful.

I spotted one of the foremen I particularly dislike. We never hit it off from day one. He said I'm lazy. He was standing beside a woman of arresting ugliness. She could easily have been his pet iguana or his dad. I took Deborah by the hand and led her across.

'Deborah, my favourite foreman. Mr Twidell, my girlfriend, Deborah.'

He grudgingly took her hand.

'I don't believe I've met your lovely wife,' I said. By his look I already knew the kind of report I'd get in my continual assessment. Who cares? Who the fuck wants to be an apprentice anyway? I knew an introduction wasn't going to be forthcoming so I turned to her anyway. 'Evening, Mrs Twidell.'

'Aye.'

The single syllable was bitten off. It was a moot point which of them was least attractive. Perhaps they took succour from the other's ugliness.

'Your husband helps me manufacture things, Mrs Twidell.

We stand together at the forge, shoulder to shoulder, sweating manfully, doing manly things.'

He didn't know how to respond. His wife looked perplexedly from one to the other, trying to fathom this banter. Deborah had seen me do this before and was inching away, embarrassed. I stopped her drift with a question.

'Haven't I often mentioned to you, Deborah, how Mr Twidell and I do manly things together?'

'Yes . . .'

'Yes, Mrs Twidell. A manly man, your man. A man's man among men.' He was small and skinny and had a complex. 'Full of machismo and masculinity.'

'Robertson,' he breathed.

'And it's not easy to be a man's man among manly men exuding masculinity.'

'Jamie . . .' It was almost a plea. She smiled deprecatingly at the couple and drew me away. Mrs Twidell was still looking bewildered and after a whispered comment from her husband stared at me and said 'Fucking wanker!' loudly enough for most to hear. There was a local dampening of conversation and many looks. He looked livid, almost as angry at her now as at me. I waved them a fond farewell.

'What's the matter with you?' Deborah said. 'It's not even as if you're drunk.'

'He's a miserable old cunt.'

'Why do you do these things? They can only bring you harm. What gets into you?'

'And his wife's ugly. They deserve each other. Do you think they ever fuck?'

'Jamie . . .'

'I hope they live forever.'

The only good thing about these affairs is a free bar. It's not expected that anyone will abuse the privilege. Another time, another place it would be Sodom and Gomorrah and Pandemonium; but with so much to lose, the money saved on beer wasn't worth it to most people. It depends on you. I felt restless before I had even called in for Deborah. I felt shackled and provincial and angry at the world at large for being oblivious to my larger destiny, despite the fact that I didn't know what this larger destiny was myself. And against the backdrop of my discontent, Deborah's love and desire and the desire of Julia and the friendship of Peter seemed inconsequential. Even Deborah's slender neck, which I usually gloried in, annoyed me. In short: I was cramped and selfish. Froward. A cunt.

Peter arrived with Julia and I could see her look round to find my gaze to avoid as soon as she stepped through the door. This lack of eye contact seemed to be her idea of discretion. I took a hold of Deborah and walked across and breezily lifted a clutch of drinks from the passing bar staff. I half spilt one on Peter's leg as an introduction, took Julia by the waist and forced my face into hers. Her shoulders were bare, like Deborah's, and she wore antique black gloves which came up to her elbows, an attractive contrast to her pale skin. I wanted to see her wearing only the gloves and black stilettos: the five of spades. I held her at arm's length.

'Why don't you kiss Deborah like that, Peter,' I said. He started forward awkwardly. 'Kiss of the robot. No tongues.' And then to Julia, 'You're late. Down the Youth Fellowship?'

'Yes.'

'Pass round a few improving tracts? Give any . . . recitals?'

She stared fixedly at the ground.

'Save any souls?'

'No.'

'Get any converts?'

'I don't – we don't try and convert.'

'No?'

'No.'

'Well what's the point in all that then?' I didn't like myself even as I was saying these things. This was a novel experience for me. My tongue had a distaste even to make contact with the lining of its own mouth. 'I've always had reservations about the moral credentials of people who are prepared to tell me what to do.'

'I don't tell people what to do.' There was a crust of pain under the smile. I could see it clearly. Pain and confusion and the effort of trying to read something better into my motives that wasn't there.

'You just show by example?' I picked up another drink.

'No, I don't think I'm entitled.' She looked about to cry.

'Nor am I, and whoever is must be crippled in one way or another,' I said, and proffered a toast: 'The able-bodied.'

Julia found her make-up in need of repair and left to do the necessary. Peter looked in confusion from her retreating back to me, anticipating some telepathy which he was excluded from. Understanding nothing he followed her to take up watch outside the women's bathroom, waiting for her to emerge.

I drifted around and said hello to various people I immediately forgot. I had a feeling of unreality about the whole affair. It had nothing to do with the drink, although that didn't help. I was only half aware of Deborah beside me, and each time my eyes alighted on her I felt half-surprised afresh, and pleased with her appearance.

I made a point of going back and seeing Julia and Peter. Her eyes looked smudgy despite the efforts at repair. I did my level best to be charming, fighting my way through the glass air that seemed to be separating me from everyone else that night. I started a conversation involving the four of us and discreetly nodded towards the other two when Julia decided finally to look at me. It was an all-encompassing nod which could have said 'I only appear callous to deflect any suspicions,' or equally could have said 'Take off everything under the dress and meet me in the cloakroom.' And for some reason I can't even begin to explain, I didn't like myself for it. She looked at me clearly and drew back her shoulders and shyly smiled. I don't know what interpretation she put on my words but it obviously pleased her.

There was a buffet of sorts and a crowd of people shuffling round it. I excused myself and left the three of them in the

queue. Peter had lifted an extra plate and was beginning to
assemble an additional meal for me.

'Anything to make you happy,' I said, and left for the airy
foyer. The hallway was crowded with people I didn't particularly care to meet. I moved outside and stood in the night air
smoking. I threw the end away and watched its glowing
trajectory.

Diane came out. Whether or not she came out because I
was there I've no idea. I hadn't noticed her inside, perhaps
too preoccupied with the formlessness of the evening. I looked
at her closely, making no attempt to conceal the scrutiny. She
returned the look in kind. She was wearing no rings. I hadn't
noticed any before. If she had an escort she didn't appear
bothered at leaving him. She was tastefully dressed, which I
regretted. Deborah and Julia were both tasteful dressers.
There's no novelty for me in the subtle colour which sets off
the cheek or hair. I want something glaring, a rapacious
mouth, Circe with a henna rinse.

Neither of us spoke. There was a static in the silence and a
challenge to see which of us could endure longer. I lit another
cigarette, tired of the game and walked away. I could hear a
forced peal of what was intended as ironical laughter.

I walked round the circumference of the building twice. It
was ugly and municipal. Perhaps it was cheap. When I walked
back in a group had formed round Peter and the girls, or
rather, round the girls. Gregor was standing next to Deborah,
looking oafish beside her slim body. Strangely enough Diane
was there too, standing beside a nondescript man from middle
management in a cardboard suit, her beau for the event.
Bruce was making slow chopping motions with his hands,
demonstrating for a horrified young woman I had never seen
before some means of disembowelling a hypothetical attacker.
I saw him take out a handful of coins and place them between
her fingers, shaping this into a clenched fist radiating metal, a
make-shift knuckle duster. Peter handed me an enormous
plate of food I offered around. Diane accepted and seemed
piqued I hadn't taken the opportunity to speak.

'What's it like, being a lackey?'

'I like your dad's suit,' I said, inclining one eyebrow to her partner.

'You expect me to rise to that?'

'Why did you come over here? Just curious, or perhaps lonely? Searching for your lost youth? He must be a big boy by now.'

'Can I have the last one of those?'

'No.'

'Why?'

'Because it pleases me to deny it to you.' The boyfriend, or whoever he was, was staring by this time. I took the last of the canapés, asked Bruce to open his mouth and shoved them all down. More people were staring. I waved to Mrs Twidell and shouted. 'One left,' I lied. Then I went in search of more drinks.

A band came on, four men in rented tuxes battering out a strident ragtime, raggedly at that. By this time the groups were entrenched. Some women took the initiative and started dancing with one another, finally goading their partners on to the floor. I danced with Deborah and Julia and, to her surprise, Diane. Bruce danced and threw himself about spasmodically. I don't think he appreciated the distinction between rhythm and combat. I dragged Peter up. He stood in a state of nervous paralysis, twitching intermittently as a concession to the music. I dragged him up at the same time as I hauled Diane on the floor. She seemed fascinated by his social ineptitude and that kept the conversation going with a swing till she sat down. By that time you could almost say we were pals. I don't think she ever doubted my designs.

I went in search of more drinks. Some other people had also loosened up. Peter's dad was standing with the Twidells. He had undone his bowtie and was smoking a bigger cigar than he had offered Twidell. The foreman's face wore the most obsequious smirk and his wife looked as if she would pass out with the privilege. Since my interview I've only ever spoken to Peter's dad once, when I tried to embezzle a contribution out of him for a bogus charity walk. Peter says he thinks his dad found out. Peter thinks his dad has a secret liking for me because I'm on the make. I've seen the old man myself down on the shop floor asking around. I think he knows about the engineered cubes and me doing his son out of cash. If he hasn't done anything about it by now he never will. I walked up to him and slapped him on the back.

'El supremo,' I said, 'give us a cigar.' Twidell stopped in his tracks and then smirked further, obviously thinking I'd gone too far. The old man reached into his inside breast pocket and brought out a small box, took off the top and offered me one.

'Not one of those,' I said, pointing. 'One of those,' I said, pointing again. He reached into his other inside breast pocket and produced another, bigger box. I took a Corona. It took about six inhalations to get it lit. Twidell was chagrined. I looked at him.

'Size does matter. Don't you think?' He didn't say anything. I put one arm on Peter's dad's shoulder, one arm on Twidell's and exhaled a huge cloud. 'I didn't know you two were so matey.' Twidell looked petrified by this time. Peter's dad just looked bemused. 'That room of Mr Twidell's, you know . . .' I stopped to suck another lungfull, 'you'll have to break down a wall or something. Scarce room to swing a catamite. When he takes in some of the younger apprentices for his manly advice, it's such a squeeze. We could barely see the boy from the tool store for all the condensation.' Another lungfull and I watched the cloud hang between us. 'It's been such fun. Must dash.' I left without looking back.

I got Deborah and Julia up to dance at the same time. I was all for a ménage à trois where we rub into one another for a bit of musical frottage, but they were having none of it. I drank some more. Kevin, the son of the marketing executive, was making advances at some girl he had brought here to impress, and being as unsuccessful as I was. As compensation he was all ready for a fully-fledged debauch. The music had petered out in a stiff 'auld lang syne' and coats were already

being produced. Kevin, with a typical gesture, invited all the
table back to his parents'. 'They're away,' he said.

'Are they rich?' I asked. Deborah and Julia chided me at
the same time and looked embarrassed at the coincidence.

'Stinking,' he said.

'Drink?'

'Loads of the stuff.'

'I'm in.'

So were most of the rest, including Diane and her beau.
He took some quiet persuading in the corner. Perhaps she
was giving him a bit of frottage. Whatever she did worked.
He was ready to spend the rest of the night with a bunch of
tipsy adolescents who made him feel his age.

Someone drove me and Deborah. I don't know who. I
wasn't asked for any money so I assume it wasn't a taxi. The
drink had started to take effect by then. There were other
people in the car, Scott and a girl I didn't recognise. She
wasn't dressed for the occasion. She hadn't been at the dance,
she was striking enough not to have gone unnoticed. He must
have somehow struck up sufficient acquaintance between the
dance and the door of this car to persuade an unknown girl
to accompany him to a party full of people she had never
heard of. Lucky bastard. I wish I could do that.

I remember large gates and a gravel drive. A couple of other
cars followed us in. Two were taxis. Kevin and his crew
disgorged from one. He was being prodigal with a huge wad
of notes. I crunched across.

'So where's the heraldic animals then?'

'Fuck off.'

The house was as large as Peter's dad's, the car in the
driveway bigger, which accounted for the family rivalry which
hadn't been passed on to the sons. I'd seen the interior of
Peter's dad's house. It was like the interior of Peter's dad's
head: ostentatious and bursting with expensive gewgaws. But
this was tasteful. In fact, as I later found out, it was on the
grounds of taste that Kevin's parents boycotted the dance.
Every year they find a previous engagement so they don't have

to witness the cringing spectacle of Peter's dad holding forth on the dignity of labour and displaying the remnants of his calluses to the soft-handed men he threatens with the sack.

'Aye,' said Kevin, in a fair imitation of Peter's dad's tone, 'times were hard. We done our best or we done without.' He flung open the doors of the cocktail cabinet and waved us all forward. I found two types of cognac I'd never heard of. I claimed a cocktail shaker and started mixing concoctions and handing them round. The speakers crackled into life, Artie Shaw playing 'Begin the Beguine'. The pithy eruptions of opening beer cans could be heard all over the place.

Kevin and I sat on the floor seriously drinking and smoking cigarettes, with an arm around each other. I'd lost track of the girls. Bruce came along, produced a large knife and suggested we all become blood brothers. Kevin said that he loved us both: we could drink his booze, drive his car or shag his wife, but he wasn't risking contamination. I said likewise. Bruce said none of us were married or had a car and that the booze was Kevin's dad's. I vetoed the whole thing by admitting to cowardice. Peter passed, looking aimless and vaguely apprehensive.

'You want to lighten up,' I said, flourishing a drink.

'You haven't seen the girls, have you?' he asked.

'Girls . . .' said Kevin, tutting and shaking his head from side to side. And then, again, for effect, 'Girls . . . What do they do? They take your confidence an' take your money an' . . . an' . . . they break your heart.' He looked about to cry.

'What the fuck are you talking about?' I said. 'You're a sexist bastard like me and you've never wanted to give anything to any girl but the shaft of your dick. You've never been in love. You wouldn't know what love is.'

He nodded sagely and seemed to find even this sad.

' "What if", I often say to myself. "What if." ' He stuck his hands in front of my face. 'These hands. They could have helped other people. They could have been the hands of a great surgeon.'

'Well they'd be fucking wasted attached to a brain like yours then, wouldn't they? You know what blood's made up of? No? Neither do I. Could you memorise the function of the liver? I doubt it. There's only one organ in your body you've memorised the function of, and your hands have more to do with the maintenance of that than saving other people's lives.'

'True,' said Kevin. 'True . . .' And then he was sick. Peter ran to get a cloth.

As a matter of fact, we were so boring and drunk that the girls seemed to find more fun talking to one another. And who can blame them? If you look at most women as life-support-systems for a vagina, you can hardly expect them to find you interesting company. I can be boring at the best of times, and when I'm drunk it's yawn city. Deborah and Julia and Diane seemed to be getting on. Now there's a trio. I had an image of me in the slave market, some Patrician with a watered silk toga, buying those three as a job lot and taking them home for communal baths followed by some manual sunbathing. With my left arm round Kevin I could feel the receding spasms, as his mouth continued to pump a diminishing flow of slurry down his shirt front. As Peter remarked, lucky it was a parquet floor.

I was piqued by the sound of women's laughter. You can stand just so much macho puking. I wanted to be sitting among them, looking at their lips and cheeks and hair and breasts. Somehow the aggregate of their beauty seemed greater than the sum of its individual parts, just like Deborah. To appreciate her fully you have to see the whole customised package. Diane's man was sitting on the edge of the group of girls looking embarrassed. I handed Kevin to Bruce with instructions to keep him this end up and walked over. They fell silent at my approach. It didn't need all my powers of observation to tell I was being excluded.

'We were talking about abuses of human rights in these third world countries,' I said, waving in the direction of Kevin. They seemed to find it difficult to credit. Bruce had a hold of his jaw and Peter was ineffectually dabbing him here and there with a damp cloth. Slumped between them he looked like a smear of ectoplasm on the wallpaper. 'It upset him so much he vomited,' I explained.

'Your friend was sick over a discussion about abuses of human rights in third world countries?' asked one girl, incredulously. There was something quite aggressive in her tone. I don't know who she was with.

'That's right.'

'Which third world countries?'

'What?' It was a feeble reply. Though the gauze of drink I couldn't think of a single third world country.

'You heard.'

'Oh . . . Conuszuela.'

'Where's that?' She was inexorable.

'It's between . . . Parador and . . . and . . . Buruguay . . .'

'What language do they speak?'

'And the way they treat one another . . .' I said, trying to lead the conversation away from uncomfortable specifics. 'The men get circumcised in the undergrowth at puberty, using friction and a hollow bamboo cane . . .' I half closed my eyes and averted my glance, as if scrupulous over divulging the gory facts. 'And they treat their women like cattle. It was too much.' I waved again in the direction of the brown smudge that was Kevin.

'The difference here,' said the same girl, 'is only one of degree.' She then went on at some length about the patriarchy in general and gave some uncomfortable instances from the present company, how we were all macho bores and got drunk together and clubbed like some masonic order, leaving our partners, who didn't know one another from Adam, although she said Eve, to introduce themselves to each other. There was a murmur of consent from the other womenfolk at this point. She used this as a launching pad and went on at great length about other things. This was a two-can job. I fished a six pack from the fridge and deliberately distributed four among the women only. It didn't work. She'd got up a head of steam. All marriages were tyranny, all rings were shackles, all penetration was rape, all foetuses belonged exclusively to the owner of the placenta, all men were redundant, etc etc. It was an intergalactic conspiracy since time immemorial, bolstered by convention, the church, the press, the media and any other manifestation of human organisation. Personally, I've never been a member of anything in my life and I've never known anything that organised. At the penetration being rape bit I looked around and knew she'd lost the ground swell of support from the women.

'So who are you here with?' Kevin wailed from the corner.

'See!' she said. 'Typical. You can only identify with me as long as I am associated in your mind with a man. As an individual I am invisible to you.'

'What,' said Kevin, 'with an arse like that! I just want to make sure you're not a gate-crasher who's going to steal the cutlery.'

'I was invited by Sonia.'

'Who the fuck's Sonia?'

'A draughtsperson from the drawing office,' I interrupted.

'Oh Sonia.' He was reviving by the minute.

'Even as we speak she's upstairs in your parents' bedroom, probably being a discredit to her sex by letting Malcolm, the sexist, lumpenproletarian, electric-arc welder, violate her feminine integrity with his purple patriarchal totem.'

'Jamie!' The querulous reproach, again from Deborah and Julia simultaneously.

'You disgust me, you all disgust me,' said the girl, indicating the boys present.

'Let's have a straw poll,' I said. 'Hands up all the women who want to keep their feminine integrity intact for the rest of their lives, in other words no more shagging.' There was a lot of uneasy glances, but no hand movements. The girl gave a sign of complete exasperation and lurched towards the kitchen. It was only then I realised how drunk she was.

'Don't worry dear,' Kevin again, still lying against the wall. 'You're in no danger of penetration here.'

'Perhaps she's going to prove how redundant men are by pressing herself against the washing machine during the spin cycle,' I said. 'I think women should pay a surcharge for that at the launderette.'

'The strange thing is,' said Bruce, 'she's not half bad looking.'

'Probably a dyke.' Kevin's reply, not mine. I admit the provenance because you'd have thought it was me that said it by what happened next. I turned back from Kevin to the company and began rubbing my hands, as if relishing a good evening ahead. And would you believe it, the whole bunch of women had ganged up on me. They all started speaking at the same time but there were a few memorable remarks that stung more than most.

Deborah. *My* Deborah: 'So, you feel smug having scored points and hurt a nice girl like that in front of all her friends?'

'What friends?'

Julia, *quiet* Julia: 'Some of her views might have been quite extreme, but she made some good points. And you think you dismissed them all with the weight of insults from you and Kevin?'

Diane: 'And she's just split up with her boyfriend.'

So out of sheer bloody-mindedness I said: 'Oh is that all. Bruce, do me a favour. Go into the kitchen and stick your hand up her skirt, tell her she knows she wants it, give her one from me and tell her we don't hold any grudges in here if she wants to come back afterwards.'

There was a deluge. I raised my hands above my head as I walked away at the hoots of derision, as if protecting myself from a pelting. When I reached the front door I padded my pockets, looking for a cigarette. The whole night had been behind glass; if it didn't work I could write it off as some second-person fiasco. Curious how, like this, I always sought the air alone.

I came out and felt as if I was coming up through an ice floe, cracking my way into space. Almost immediately from the other direction I could see Diane approach. My first thought was the most pragmatic: she must have left the back door as soon as I left the front, and she's done it that way to disguise the rendezvous. She was walking towards me purposefully. Any other night and I would have been ready for the verbal cut and thrust. But right now, for the life of me, I simply couldn't be bothered with the banter. She didn't stop walking and spoke while on the move.

'Just who the fuck do you think you are!' It wasn't a question. There was a metallic note in her voice which belied the taste of her clothes. She looked hard, rapacious. Getting towards arms' length and still she wasn't slowing. I leaned towards her, took the straps of her dress in one hand, crushing her breasts together, and pulled her towards me, jerking her out of her stride. I kissed her very hard and in the same moment she put her hands on me and bit my lip. There was a moment of true illumination as we were framed in the headlights of an approaching car and I felt a sudden electrifying surge of déjà vu. The hand in my hair pulling me in, the blood on my lip. The synthetic woman of my fantasies in my parents' lounge took shape and I realised it had been her I had been with, mobile, vicious, pliant. And I had done nothing. The moment of illumination continued till the lights were turned off and I heard a discretionary cough from the figure emerging from the car. A woman. A man preceded her and was approaching across the drive.

'What the hell's going on here!' I recognised Kevin's father's voice. The woman was padding up behind him, unsteady on heels not designed for speed or the unevenness of the driveway. I slipped in through the front door, determined to retrieve my coat and what drink and women I could and vanish before the débâcle.

2 0

Fires blazing in collapsed superstructure. Smouldering gable ends. Bloated headlines in a greasy puddle. Tottering walls of graffiti sagging with old blasphemies. Peeling bill posters and blowing litter. Floating garbage. Broken panes of coated algae. Exuberant weeds.

My dreams are saturated with images of ruin and the vegetable forces which cannot be stopped. There are no people in this scheme of things.

2 1

At work, Peter and I live within a mobile boundary whose radius is no more than thirty feet. He is never much further away than that and seldom comes closer. He is a questioning presence, like a blur in the corner of my eye. For three days I pretended not to notice. With the others I filled the days with remarks about the inopportune timing of Kevin's parents. He enacted for us the consternation of his mother interrupting two strangers welded to one another on top of their marital bed. She has burnt the counterpane. We all laughed and Peter, not wishing to feel excluded, held his sides and rocked slowly. It is impossible to teach a sense of humour.

Several times I came close to talking, pretending not to notice the brittle air. He looks at me with a kind of deferential mistrust and answers in stammering one-liners, as if we had never really met. If I haven't gone half way to meet him, I haven't gone half way to meet anyone. If you don't know who your friends are, who do you know? I have never wanted anything from him except friendship and to fuck his girlfriend. It's the nearest I've ever got to philanthropy.

'How's the Youth Fellowship?'

'Fine.'

'Julia says these days you don't go so much.' He gave me a glance which was almost pained. 'That neither of you go.'

'Yes.'

'Lost interest?'

'Yes.'

'How are you getting on with your old man these days?'

'Fine.'

I tried about six more sallies and was met with the same monosyllabic replies.

'For fuck's sake,' I said, 'you were never the most exciting person around. If you've ever had any moments of real conversation I'll bet ninety-nine per cent of them have been with me, at my instigation. The rest you had in your sleep. A catechism isn't my idea of a good chat.' He didn't say anything.

'That cube you paid me to make, I didn't make it, I had it machined.'

'I know.'

'And I overcharged you. I had you pay for mine as well with a bonus into the bargain.'

'I know.'

'How do you know?'

'My dad told me. My dad knows everything that goes on round here.'

'How long have you known?'

'Since the following week.'

'Since before we were friends?' He didn't answer and just looked dismally at his metal toe-capped boots.

'For fuck's sake,' I said again, half under my breath, and turned away.

'I'm sorry,' he said.

'What are you sorry for?'

'I don't know. You're the first person who's been like this to me, who didn't care about my father.'

'Your father's a wanker.' He coloured. I modified it. 'Your father's a bully.' The fact supplanted the evaluation. We both pretended I hadn't said the insult.

'You're the first person who's been like this to me who didn't want something from me.'

This just about summed up my point of view also. Why did I feel such a shit? And besides, his emphasis on 'me' . . .

'You know, don't you?' I said.

'I don't want to know.' I half turned away. He touched my arm.

'Whoever said anything's exaggerating,' I said.

'No one has said anything.'

I shrugged him off and walked to the limit of our membrane. I knew he was watching as I lit a cigarette beside the furnace. Who the fuck needs friends anyway.

I spent the remainder of the afternoon in a glaze of concentration. I even worked to take my mind off things. Twidell seemed to think this some kind of a ploy. Come half past four I walked out without returning the goodnights bade me. Peter was still the same distance behind me and looked as if he would draw level by the time I reached the main gate. 'Don't,' I said to him. He stopped, a stone in the midst of the stream. His face looked like a kid. I kept on walking.

I went home and made a meal I didn't eat. I turned the radio and the television on at the same time, waiting. Let the technology of distraction fill the hiatus till we keep our appointments. The noise was still blaring when the bell rang. Another clandestine arrangement. Secrecy had lost its flavour for me. She was coming, she had told me to 'Get things sorted out.' I opened the door and hauled her into the hall.

'You told him, didn't you?'

'Told who?'

'Didn't you?'

'I didn't tell him anything. I didn't have to. He saw us. He sees us. He knows that it doesn't matter how many people there are there. He knows we're . . . together . . .'

'This isn't my idea of together,' I said. 'I don't know what "together" means.'

'You don't mean that!'

'I don't know what "we" means either. I've never been a member of "we". How do you join? How much does it cost?'

'Have you ever meant anything you said? This isn't you. I've seen you and this isn't it. There's something wrong and I don't know what it is. We can make it better.'

'There you go again. Who can make it better? Who's "we"? Can Peter get in on the act?'

'You bastard. Did you ever think of Peter when you touched

me? Did you ever think of me when you touched me?' She looked wonderful. I'd never seen her face so animated. 'And you bring him up now. Why? An easy means of disposal? For purposes of hygiene? For your convenience?'

'This,' I said, 'is the nearest I ever get to "together".' I took hold of her and started tearing at her coat. She let me do it and didn't put up any resistance, looking at me hollowly.

'Don't you dare let me, you fucking cow!' I shouted. 'No one ever let me!'

I threw her coat on the floor and tugged at the shoulder strap of her dress. I could hear the material give. One breast, surprisingly, popped out, rolling like a questioning eye. It somehow looked obscene. I grasped it. 'This breast is mine, not yours,' I said. In my haste, dragging her into the hall, I'd left the front door open. We were standing in the shabby lounge. Deborah walked in and looked at us expressionlessly. When I saw her I tugged down the other side of Julia's dress, exposing the other breast. I turned her round to face Deborah and pushed her in front of me, bared to the sight of the other woman. I reached my hands over her shoulders and gripped her.

'I know,' I said to Deborah, 'I'm a cunt.'

I walked past them both and out the front door and down the stairs and into the street. There's something wrong, I kept thinking, something far wrong. I don't have a plan, but somewhere it's gone off the rails. Things aren't working out. I want a life crowded with superficial incident. I don't want to draw breath. I want to be a hero in a picaresque novel. I want my existence to be one long romp.

I had plans at least for the next twenty minutes. I knew where I was going then. I'd been there before. She lived alone the way I did. I battered on her door and she answered abruptly, as if she was expecting me. When she opened the door she didn't look pleased.

'Let me in.'

'You're not expected.'

'I wasn't expected the last time either and that didn't stop either of us. Let me in.' She didn't move. She looked hard. I didn't really want her, but at that moment I wanted everything else in the world even less. There was a tone behind me I should have recognised, the low-pitched hum I'd heard often enough at the work gates. I went on ignoring it. She didn't. It was the slow movement of a perfectly tuned car, large and powerful, the noise of surveillance. It stopped. He got out and began walking up the path. Still he hadn't seen me. She was at a loss. He saw me. He stopped. He knew, the way Deborah knew. He had a bottle of wine in his huge hand. I wonder if he gave Peter many brothers or sisters this way. He said to me: 'You're out.'

I walked past him and past the car he had been careful to park away from the street lights. In twenty seconds I heard the car start up again. He was fastidious enough to drive in the opposite direction. I turned in time to see her walk back into her hallway alone, the light from the area that was not her body streaming past her into the night.

I walked back to the place where I lived. My front door was still open. Both of them had left. I packed some clothes and took what money I had. I crunched my way through half a dozen energy tablets and knocked them back with a pint of cold water. I doused my head in cold water, pocketed the rest of the tablets and left, closing the door behind me.

2 2

Everything was as frenetic as I could have wished, aside from the timeless speculations of bus-stops, night driving, the moments of interior logic I cannot legislate for which catch me when I'm not vigilant. I went to London. Where else. It's the catchment area for all the opportunist vagrants, and the vagrants. I failed in London. It's easy to do. You just start out without any plan and end up washing dishes in large restaurants in the West End, scrubbing away in the early hours to make ends meet, the way anyone without an option does. I washed enough dishes to make the break.

I went to the States on a wing and a prayer and a visitor's visa. No work permit. I had an image of an opportunist's paradise which took in the tired, the poor, the huddled masses, and fleeced the lot. I had an image of me as a fashionable barman rubbing elbows with the sophisticates of New York till I got things sorted out. What 'sorted out' meant I'd no idea. I'd spin bottles, make connections, concoct exotic drinks and seduce beautiful women.

'Do you like cocktails? Would you like me to tell you a few?'

I had the lines worked out. I had no skill but an aptitude to learn enough till I learned how to get by without working. I had everything going for me. I failed. It's even easier to fail in New York than it is in London. In my experience there have always been more people than jobs, and most of the candidates have a start over me in as much as they want to work. And if you don't have a work permit there's always a dozen poor Puerto Ricans, Hispanics or Blacks willing to do the job for half the wage I'd take. And they're willing to work even harder.

So when I wasn't washing dishes I walked up and down New York through the thoroughfares of money. I looked at the beautiful women and the handsome men and the shimmering cars and the unapproachable shops and at the exclusive sub-current of money. There was old money and ostentatious money and dirty money. There were strata within this club that some kinds of money wouldn't get you into. But if you didn't have the lustre of money you didn't get past the doorman. They're trained, these people, these lackeys. One glottal stop out of place and you find yourself showing your roots on the pavement outside. The whole thing was pathetic, superficial, ethically misconceived – everything I wanted. I didn't get as far as pressing my face against the dining room window.

I'd occupy some of the slack hours and get a heat by going to the cinema. The films were American schmaltz mostly.

These people have an insatiable appetite for sentimentality. Everyone lives happily ever fucking after, except in the sad films, and they're fucking worse.

I went to the bus station and bought myself a ticket to Dudesville, hick town America. I'd read enough road books. I was going out there to discover myself. I'd no more idea what 'discover myself' meant than 'sorted out' did, and anyway, there was a fair chance I wouldn't like what I found.

Getting on for dark. Small town with a single main street. Ten minute break. The bus stops. We all trundle sleepily out. Coke machine on the porch of the garage. Old man in dungarees sitting beside it in a rocking chair. I approach the machine parched and pump in the required coins. Nothing. I do the same again. Nothing. I tilt the machine and then deliver strategic blows. Nothing. The old man has watched the whole proceedings:

'It's broke.'

'Welcome to America,' I said.

I went to Arkansas. I went to Idaho. I went to Nebraska. I went to lots of places. I had no itinerary. I didn't discover myself. I saw a string of big cities and hick towns. I got poorer. I ran out of money in a small town in the mid-West whose only industry seemed to be bizarre clergymen. There was a proliferation of sects here which baffled me. They threw money at these people with Messianic fervour. Their television was full of them. The congregations struck me as conveniently gullible. If they could support this many peddling the good word they could sustain one more. It was either that or be reduced to shining shoes. I found myself an upturned orange crate and an appropriate junction. I nailed together a collection box.

'As ye reap so shall ye sow, and so shall it be shown that he whosoever sows upon stony ground, howsoever humble, shall not bring forth progeny, so it is written . . .'

It wasn't bad for a first go. I'd never read the Bible but I didn't think I'd have any difficulty sounding Biblical. Just throw in a few archaic expressions and mangle your syntax.

And if you get in trouble say anything vaguely philanthropic about your fellow men. A crowd had begun to gather already. I gave them another five minutes of this indiscriminate stuff.

'And if ye give ye are blessed. And most blessed are those who give with no thought of recompense. Give readily and be blessed. For who would confront their maker unshriven? Go to God knowing you have given and you will receive it a hundredfold.'

Someone at the front who looked like a college boy said, 'Doesn't that contradict what you just said? If you know you're getting it back a hundredfold then it wasn't done with no thought of recompense.'

'Oh ye of little faith,' I said, because I couldn't think of anything else. More people had started to gather. It's the accent, I thought.

'Come down from the mountain of pride! Leave the waste-land of debauchery! Wallow not in the morass of sloth! The way of the righteous is steep. The path of the pilgrim is stony. Swerve not from the true way!' I was getting into my stride now. A few coins had jingled into the box and I even saw a folded note or two. I'd noticed a bar up the street with an exquisite looking Filipina barmaid. I'd paid my last dollar on the price of a beer to sit on a stool and stare down her cleavage while she wiped the bar. Perhaps if I collected enough I could go over and strike up an acquaintanceship. She might live near the place. Perhaps I could shake hands with her tits and she could give me the kind of American hello my loins were desperately in need of. It was getting to the stage where I'd nail anything with a skirt and a pulse.

'For remember, when He, He, raised his hands thus and a hush fell upon the multitude.' And a hush really did fall upon them. I knew then this was the land of opportunity: there were dollars in demagoguery. 'And He turned to the multitude and He said thus: "Unto the strangers who come among you bringing the word, stint not in your offerings towards them. For what succour you bring them will be brought you. What dollars – alms, alms, you give them will be given you. Gold will rain among your ranks for the generosity you have shown the man who brings this word among ye." This He said when —'

'Where?' From someone. Not someone, a dark man with a strange dark hat. Lank hair hung in straggling rats' tails from under his homburg. He wasn't alone. There were several in the audience with the same manner of dress and the same fervid look in their eye. I didn't like it, I didn't like it at all.

'What?' I said.

'Where was He when He said this?'

'On the shores of the sea. He'd been out for a stroll on the waves to catch some fish.'

There was a low mutter from the others who were with him. He didn't say anything but just stood there looking at me unswervingly.

'And how do you know this?' he asked.

'It is written —' I began.

'Where is it written?'

'The afflatus is no longer with me,' I said, standing down from my crate. 'I cannot spread the word with so many who doubt about me. And besides, it's getting dark.'

I picked up my home-made collection box and began to weave my way through them. They didn't disperse as I hoped they would. They were all looking at me quite grudgingly now. They didn't move for me either. As soon as I was free of them I turned the corner and, once out of sight, ran as fast as I could. No one pursued me. I broke the box open. There was a ten dollar bill, a five dollar bill, several one dollar bills and quite a lot of change. I wasn't going to start a franchise with it so I doubled back some half hour later and found the bar with the Filipina barmaid.

She was a nice girl. In other words she wouldn't have anything to do with me. I squandered ten dollars in buying beers and craning to look at her breasts. She realised that quickly enough and went off to wipe elsewhere. I splashed my beer to no avail.

I left about eleven. I'd no idea where I was going. The

place was too small to house a YMCA. I'd an idea of finding a cheap hotel and doing a runner. When I'd left the light of the bar and was in the deep grove of darkness between two tall buildings, a hand touched my shoulder and spun me round. I hadn't heard anyone approach. I didn't see his fist either. I could hear my nose from the inside of my face, cracking inwards. Through the blur of pain I could hear shuffling feet and a whispered confab. Then there were several pains simultaneously. Either he was hitting me very quickly while running round me or I was surrounded. Someone planted a blunt boot in my balls, which expanded with more pain than I thought the cosmos could contain. I folded. The beating seemed to go on and on. It went on until I could look down and see, beneath the County's bedclothes under which I lay, a catheter rising from my groin dripping reddish fluid through a transparent tube into the bag suspended at the side of my bed. My arms were strapped in some way that left me almost incapable of movement. So was my neck. People came and looked at me from time to time. The policeman who walked round my bed appraised me from various angles with as much sympathy as he would have expended disparaging a car he had no intention of buying, kicking the tyres and pointing out spots of rust. For the first time in my life I made a plan: when this was all over I would walk outside into the pitiless sunshine and dissolve in the glare.

'One of the best, or worst, I've ever seen,' he said, with obvious relish. He cradled the bag the catheter fed into, feeling the weight of the fluid I'd leaked. 'The doctor tells me you'll piss blood for a while. They did a job on your kidneys. I figure baseball bats wrapped in newspaper. The print left some smears on you. If they can't cure you in here they can at least do the crossword. Nothing structural though. If there had been it might have kept you here. And none of us want that. Do we, sonny?'

But he only said that to me much, much later, after an abyss of pain when I lay in the dark, holding my balls, feeling the inside of my cracked teeth with my tongue. My back felt corrugated. I couldn't focus or make a noise. I felt warm blood from above my hairline dripping behind my ear. And even then, throughout the pain I felt something worse. It was knowing that the system might patch me up, that's what its dispassionate charity is geared for, but there was no one who really cared. I'd squandered the right to elicit care.

I'm lying here, I thought, and I'm not in a town. This isn't the mainland, or even a peninsula. It's an island. The man got it wrong. What did he know. He was only Dean of Saint Paul's and one of the most moving love poets in the language.

Poets.

Fuck 'em.

Part Two

2 3

When I left school I thought I knew nothing. Since then I've often thought of the same image that typifies me the day I left. I suppose it was a good school of kinds. It groomed me. A few generations ago it groomed us and people of our ilk to be the wives of diplomats or captains of industry. We were expected to be women who took on the vicarious status of our husbands' professions. There was a vestige of that left even when I attended. We hadn't produced any suffragettes. We were led to look on any excess as a kind of vulgarity. It strikes me now as the kind of place you send your girls to if you want them to gain admittance to a university, to use the right cutlery, and to feel thwarted when it matters most.

We were sent out of that place in droves to the older universities in St. Andrews and Glasgow and Edinburgh and Aberdeen. Some went south to Oxbridge. We inhabited the professions. We met ours and people like us who filled up the over-subscribed faculties of law and medicine and veterinary sciences. Or we studied history or literature or languages. We did not study the social sciences. There was something vaguely indecent in that, something 'leftist'. We became barristers or teachers or linguists or women of dependent means, who had husbands who could keep us in the style which we had been taught not to fall short of, even if we could not provide it for ourselves. We never became secretaries or supermarket check-out operators or cinema usherettes. There was an unspoken policy about such things. Although there was obligatory Religious Studies, conducted, like all our other classes, by a woman, the 'family of man' was something abstract which started and finished outside the school gates. It was a club for the less fortunate. We were a privileged sorority and were always made to remember the fact. To become a waitress or a window dresser or any of the thousand ordinary things needed to let human transaction occur, was to let the side down. No one ever said it aloud.

There were lots of us leaving the day I left. When I stripped the sheets from my bed the last morning I remember looking sadly down, realising I'd never sleep there again. Sadly, but only for a moment. I was glad to go. I met a girl one holiday in Ireland, two years ago. She was two years older than I was at the time. She told me about her boyfriends and the gamut of stains her mattress collected by the time she was my age. She concealed it from her parents. I felt sorry I had no stains to conceal and no one to conceal them from.

We were a single-sex antiseptic school. I never knew any lesbians. We weren't taught by these masculine women of hearsay. The swimming coach was frail. There were no Jean Brodies here either. There was nothing ardent about them at all. They looked as if they'd come here to escape. I'm not calling into question their abilities or their intelligence. I once overheard the milk boy say that 'all half of them need in there is a really good fuck'. It was a vulgar thing to say, a man's panacea. And yet, half way back to my room I burst out laughing. Perhaps he was right. I knew I formed none of the schoolgirl attachments to their teachers girls are supposed to. It was impossible with the desiccated spinsters I could see age by the day. It would have been nice to have been taught by a young vital woman we could have had something in common with.

Perhaps that's why I thought I knew nothing. I knew I'd been shut up for years with ageing women, outside the mainstream of people and things. And there had been no reprieve. It's not even as if I could have gone home in the evenings. There was a kind of perpetual moral surveillance. I knew I was a hot-house plant. I knew I knew little about the way things are, the way I would have to be if I was to get on. I'd done well enough at my studies. I'd the choice of universities and subjects. There were many who had not done as well as me and somehow still thought they had emerged from this place fully prepared. They didn't even know how little they knew. I almost felt sorry for them.

And there were even those reluctant to leave. There was a mousy girl who lived down the hall who took refuge in her books and didn't like taking her holidays. Perhaps this place instilled self-perpetuation by giving rise to such people. I could see some return here to teach. In my crueller moments, watching them file into assembly, I played a private game of spot the premature spinster.

We all got together after assembly and the headmistress gave a valedictory speech of kinds. It sounded hackneyed even to me at that age. It was full of moral injunctions and suppressed references to illicit sex. I felt like summarising it at the top of my voice: 'Don't screw around, and if you do, don't get caught. Don't conceive until you can afford the fees for this school. Don't become someone who washes hair for a living in a salon, and if you do, don't come back!' It lasted ten minutes and towards the end I had to stick my knuckles into my mouth to stop myself from laughing. It was contagious. Towards the end she noticed it and began speaking faster, unloading on us the moral baggage supposed to sustain us for the rest of our lives. I looked round at the girls I had befriended and I knew I would see increasingly less of. I felt sorry now, but I knew I wouldn't in six months' time.

She was really speaking rapidly now. She finished and received some desultory applause. We filed out. I was last to go. She stopped me at the door. 'It's not because of what you just instigated,' she said, 'but for motives I hope you recognise as good when you're old enough, that I feel obliged to say something to you.' It was the typical kind of preface of hers which made me wince. 'The trouble is, I don't know quite what.'

'Perhaps the die is cast.'

'No. I refuse to believe that. Not at your age. You're very

clever . . . ' And then, as an afterthought, 'You never really made an effort to fit in.'

'It's not something I ever wanted.'

'No, I realise that now.'

'It's awful, not believing in the team spirit and being sent to a place like this.' This place had been her life. My future, at least for the duration of my time at university, was mapped out. She thought I was being rude since, for the first time, I could do so with impunity.

'I'm sorry,' I said. 'I didn't intend that to come out the way it did.'

'You're a clever girl,' she repeated, 'and I think I understood you more than you appreciate. I did what I could. I tried to save you from some of the excesses. You don't know half of what goes on in the staff room. You won't come back to us, I know that. But don't speak unkindly of us, and don't discredit us. Perhaps we have done more for you than you know. After all, none of us know how you would have turned out had you gone elsewhere . . .'

Her head quivered very slightly, not with anger but with the infinitesimal motions of age. There were liver spots on her hands. Her skin was grainy and gathering round her old neck. I felt ashamed.

'I'm sorry. I'll do my best, for both of us.'

'I know you will.'

I went to shake her hand and, for the first time, she leaned forward and kissed me on the cheek. It was not the first time we had been alone. Perhaps, knowing we were going our separate ways, she also felt she could act with impunity. I felt stunned. I left before I said anything else hurtful.

I had one more call to make before I left and I was looking forward to this even less. I had to go and see my housemistress. She also taught me English Literature. I dreaded the meeting, not because I thought she didn't like me but because I knew she did. I was her favourite; I shone in her class, but that wasn't the reason: she thought she saw something similar in us. I've no idea what. I liked her and felt horrified that she might be right. She had censored her life the same way she took care to expurgate our texts.

'Come away in, Rachel.' The colloquial edge she had fought hard to maintain in this place. And again, 'Come in . . . we'll have to make much of you since we won't be seeing you for some time.' The 'we' was a way of distancing herself, absolving herself from the crime of blatant affection. 'I wanted a last talk with you. And . . . and . . . to give you something.'

The last thing I wanted was a few more homilies to carry away with me. She busied herself about making tea, as much for the distraction. I realised she was more nervous than I was.

'I suppose you must get used to it,' I said, trying to sound matter of fact. 'Losing people each year.'

'We do, we do. Although there's many it's no great loss to do without.'

'They don't all get this treatment at their departure?'

'Some get the tea. None but you have received the Dundee cake. It's a rare accolade.' She said it to introduce a note of levity. Now there were no more distractions she was obliged to sit opposite me. The tea was set to infuse. She had the same infinitesimal motions and liver spots as the headmistress. The bones of her face were fine, the taut skin over the cheeks almost translucent. When I sat there I could almost feel the bird-like pulse. What makes them like this, these aged sensitive women? Nothing had rounded the corners on her, she had none of the calluses where she needed them most. I could imagine a man's hand, encompassing her face and breaking it to fragments without effort. Had she come here like this as a young woman? Was she ardent and had become friable with age and neglect of the attentions that really mattered?

'Do you know the syllabus?' she asked. Her voice had a beautiful sing-song cadence to it. She was from the Islands.

'No, not really.'

'Do you have a book list?'

'No.'

'You're very neglectful.'

'Don't chide, please. Not on my last day.'

'I'm sorry.' No teacher had ever apologised to me before. This was the nearest to official sanction of independence I'd get. After this I'd hardly be surprised if they stamped on my forehead 'grown up' at the school gates. Now we were both embarrassed. A silence grew.

'I'm going to study Donne,' I said. This was news to me also. I said it to fill the gap.

'You like the metaphysical poets?'

'I don't know. My reading has been . . . desultory. I know I like Donne.'

'I also liked Donne at your age.'

John Donne, 1572–1631. We were taught the dates as if it meant something. I thought: He died hundreds of years ago and he's younger than you are now. I thought: He would never have become your age. I thought: He plotted the contours of his woman's body with the intricacy of a loving cartographer and an ecstasy that I feel when I read it even now. And there you sit. And look at you. I thought: How could you like such a writer as more than an intellectual exercise and let your juices run dry alone? I thought: You are an old stick inside a Macintosh raincoat. I thought: I will never allow myself to become like you. Perhaps this was a day for caustic introspection. Perhaps she knew what I was thinking. Another silence fell between us. She poured the tea and offered slices of Dundee cake.

'I have a present for you,' she said, leaving her tea untouched and getting up. I think the present was intended as the culmination of what she imagined would be a pleasant farewell. With things not going according to plan she was obliged to produce the props now. I was expecting a volume of Tennyson, more poems of action, spirit and adventure. She produced a slim volume of Sylvia Plath, a first edition of her later poems. Inside she had written an inscription: 'To Rachel with fond regards from Anne. Literature is all very well, but don't put the cart before the horse.'

I don't know what I had ever done to deserve such trust. She was blatantly warning me against her mistakes. No one had ever made themselves that vulnerable to me before. I couldn't eat. I stammered a thanks and stood. She stood also. I thrust the book into my pocket gracelessly, shook her hand and almost ran out of the room.

And the image which typifies me? Becky Sharp hurling Samuel Johnson's Dictionary out of the window as the carriage departs from Miss Pinkerton's establishment for young ladies. I'm not that rebellious or that ungrateful, and I don't think I came out prepared as one of nature's opportunists as she was, but nevertheless it is the image which remains. Perhaps I am there in the carriage, handing across the book to be jettisoned, lobbing out one bore to remain with the rest. Fade to me standing at the school gates, standing unsure on the threshold of something new. Fade up the tingling clarinet glissando that opens 'Rhapsody in Blue,' as I put my best foot forward.

2 4

There was a train to the local station. My parents live in an affluent suburb of Edinburgh, close enough for my father to commute to the city for work and for my mother to shop. Neither were in when I arrived. I stood in what used to be my bedroom and hesitated unpacking. This would be a summer of unreprieved domesticity till the start of university term; I half contemplated taking my bags and leaving before they knew I had come back. I had some wild fantasy of lounging around Lake Como for months but, having no money to get there or to live on once I'd arrived, and no one to go with, I soon gave the idea up as lost. When I was a schoolgirl, all those hours before, I used to act rebellious by handing in my essays late.

I left my bags symbolically still packed for three hours and walked around the rooms. My parents have a huge bed, not for the reason of erotic manoeuvres, but privacy. They sleep more like two single people in a double bed with the hinterland between. I think for years mother has imposed a ten o'clock curfew over this area. I had a sister who died before I remember her. I was two and she was four-and-a-half. I don't think my mother even considered having another. She had decided she would bring two children into this world. The fact that one died before she was five years old didn't appear to affect mother's decision. Two children were had and if they didn't reach adulthood she sadly chalked the loss up to the law of statistics. I've no idea how stricken she was. I came out through Caesarean section. Mother wasn't going to have more scars to provide me with a replacement sister. I don't know everything that went on, what say my father had in the size of our family. My mother seems to think large families indecent, third world. I don't really know my parents.

They live discrete lives, mother and father. They have separate dressing tables at either end of the room they inhabit. Father has a sombre mahogany dressing table covered in dark-wood hairbrushes, redolent of antique masculinity. No mirror. Mother's bureau has a frontal mirror and two angled panes in which she can catch herself in double profile. There is also a hand mirror to enable her to scrutinise her coiffure from all sides. Her dressing table is light pine. They have an ensuite bathroom with 'his' and 'her' washbasins. The only things their loins now share is the toilet, and I think father uses the main one in the top hall. Yeats said that love has pitched its mansions in the place of excrement. He didn't see my parents' bathroom arrangement.

Beside father's washbasin is a badger-hair shaving brush and an antique shaving mug. The other necessities are kept in his small cabinet. Mother's basin is surrounded by all the paraphernalia of a woman who has made a cult of her own femininity. She has nothing else to do with her time. Perhaps this is the way she repays my father, being all the flighty things it suits them both to pretend a woman should be. My father is a senior partner in a prestigious firm of solicitors. I hear they were contemplating a merger but that, had the merger gone ahead, one of his colleagues at his level would have been a woman. There were tentative discussions and the inevitable expense account dinners. The merger failed. Having never met her, mother spent two days afterwards impugning the other woman's 'femininity', implying the lack of it. In my mother's scheme of things, being a well-kept woman precluded the possibility of being anything else.

I could hear a car in the drive. This early in the afternoon it couldn't have been anyone else. Mother doesn't work, she does the kind of things rich women do. She'll get involved in charity as long as it doesn't entail meeting destitutes. She went to the same school I just left. She came in and presented me with her cheek. I did likewise. We collided in a soft puff of her powder and she made a puckering noise with her lips in the air next to my right ear.

'I'm sorry I wasn't here to meet you. Have you been here long?'

'An hour. Perhaps two.'

'Was it sad? I imagine it was sad.'

'Yes,' I said.

'It was sad for me too. It seems so long ago, but I remember it was sad.'

We stood about three feet apart and thought about how sad it was. For a moment I got the grotesque feeling that shrugging off that place had given her more grief than the death of my sister.

'And now the summer,' she said.

'Yes, the summer.'

'There's a collation for you in the fridge.'

'Collation' is a code word in our family. It's a misnomer, a bit like the word 'family'. 'Collation' means a meal mother has had the domestic rustle up and doesn't know what it is herself.

'I have to go out again soon,' she said. And then, as if this sudden absence struck her as somehow mercenary, 'It will only be for a short time. I'll sit with you, shall I?'

'Yes,' I said. This sounded similar to the interviews I had just left. Perhaps it's too easy to be dismissive, but somehow this conscientious 'sitting with' does not strike me as the normal transaction that mothers and daughters enjoy. If you love someone shouldn't it just consist of the joy of the other's unaffected company? I'm sure I don't know what it is, but I know that this *isn't* it.

Mother made us some tea. I saw her unconsciously choose the china service normally reserved for visitors, replace it on the shelf and deliberately pull down two mugs. She served me sitting through in the front room. She gave me tea and handed me a tea-plate with an eclair which she had put there with a pair of tongs. I looked at the tongs, embarrassed for us both. She was sitting propped on the edge of her seat, leaning forward, as if trying to establish telepathic communion. She caught my glance at the tongs and hesitated. She appeared to be trying to suppress the idea that I was a visitor.

'Your father will be home soon.'

'Is he reconciled?' He had wanted me to study law. When my sister was first conceived he began forging nepotistic links across the Edinburgh legal fraternity in readiness for the son he never had. They were still there for me to inherit, to compensate in enthusiasm for what I lacked not being a man.

'He says we'll see what you make of yourself.'

'I'll try not to be a disappointment.'

'I know you won't let us down.'

How? I thought. How do you know I won't let you down when *I* don't even know that? Your idea of success isn't mine, so in all probability I will. So far my whole life has consisted of not letting people down: not letting them down with my behaviour, my marks, my pronunciation, my dress. And now I'm not to let them down with my ambitions or the way I go about fulfilling them. 'Mother,' I wanted to say, 'don't hold your breath. The way I feel just now, if the mood takes me I'll go and live in some polygamous squat and practise free love behind a hessian curtain with eight tinkers.'

'More tea?'

'Don't let me keep you if you have an appointment,' I said, a shade too enthusiastically. An appointment could mean getting the dog shampooed. To give herself the illusion that she is not inert, mother ties her life down to a series of spurious imperatives: 'I must pick up the canapés!'. It's motion of a kind and I won't deny it to her if it helps, as long as she doesn't lie about it to herself or to me and tell me that chronicling small beer is a vocation.

'If your father comes back soon don't spoil your appetite. We'll eat early.'

'All right. Goodbye.'

'Goodbye. I won't be long.'

I heard the engine start up again. I went through to the kitchen and picked at the 'collation', some coleslaw and prawns beneath cling film. I went into father's study and looked at his books. He has all the Waverley novels bound in morocco. They stand in formidable panoply beside his encyclopedias.

John Donne, I thought, where are you when I need you?

2 5

They arrived home at the same time, in their different cars. They parked in the garage. I saw my mother wait for my father before she came into the house. Perhaps she was glad of the reinforcements. He came in carrying a bottle of wine. There are gallons of stuff in the house, but for the return of the prodigal he had bought this specially. He made much of decanting it in front of a candle flame. When we sat down to dinner he sniffed with the preamble of a connoisseur.

'Red, is it?' I asked. He smiled obligingly.

'Was it sad?' he asked.

'I don't think it was as sad for me as it was for mother.' My mother's parents, God alone knows why, made sacrifices to send her there. I get the impression the fees didn't make a substantial dent in my parents' income.

'And now the summer,' he said.

'Yes,' I said. I downed a large draught at one gulp. A flicker of disapproval appeared on his face. Expression is rare. My mother has acquired a habit of my father's of rendering her face immobile. They also seem to try to talk without moving their mouths. It's a curiously phlegmatic trait the Anglophile strata of Edinburgh adopt, a ludicrous attempt to mimic the habits of the English aristocracy. There was silence of sorts. There was also the question of money. I have an allowance which father pays monthly by standing order. Many of the past summers consisted of trips of one kind or another with the school, outings of an improving kind. Last year they took us to Luxor. Nicole looked like losing her virginity to a Dragoman. 'It fell through, or rather it didn't,' she announced to us later in the room. She lay back and fell asleep watching the slow rotation of the ceiling fan. I suggested we break her hymen and write to her parents. It was a natural presupposition at a school like that that you went on holiday and no one bridled at the cost. Father didn't anyway. Reduced to a monthly allowance it looked like a tame summer. If I showed any of the wayward symptoms they'd read so much of I think they hoped to curtail me by withholding money. Half the girls I'd known at school were drugged by the stuff.

'Do you have any plans?'

'I'm thinking of taking a job.' They exchanged looks.

'What kind of a job?' It was mother who spoke while pretending to be engrossed in the gooseberry fool.

'Bar work perhaps, or perhaps selling copies of the *Socialist Worker*.'

They were quietly apoplexed.

'Why this compunction to work?' father said.

'Money.'

'You have your allowance. Do you have plans for the summer which mean you'll need more?'

'No, no plans. But I don't think I ought to accept an allowance any more. Not at least over the summer when I'm capable of earning for myself. When term starts, and if the workload means I don't have time to keep down a part-time

job as well, then, if you don't mind, I'll probably be glad to
come back and talk about an allowance.'

As soon as I said I was thinking of giving up my allowance they exchanged another look. This time it wasn't
guarded. They smiled an indulgent smile at one another and
then at me.

'I've set my alarm for early tomorrow,' I said. I hadn't.
'Perhaps, if there isn't a coffee-morning or anything crucial
on, one of you could run me to the employment exchange?'

2 6

It was all bravado. I admit that. If either of them had openly
taken me up on the offer my enthusiasm might have evapor-
ated over night. But neither of them gave me a lift. I think
they thought my flimsy plans would be overcome by inertia.
I ate breakfast looking round, loathing the place. I made
plans. I caught the ten-fifteen into town. In those days that
was my idea of an early rise.

Till then, for me, Edinburgh was a place dotted with points
of cultural interest which teachers dragged us round, crocodiles of bored schoolgirls arranged in appreciative formations
before gloomy paintings in the Scottish National Gallery. Or
it was the site of my mother's recreation and forays of pre-
Christmas shopping with me on an epic and indiscriminate
scale. Even then, as a child, I remember my feelings of almost
morbid sensitivity, sitting in our commandeered taxi with a
mother happily surfeited with purchasing, laden with parcels
as people outside bent into the driven rain and a ragged man
stared vacuously. Where do they go? I often wondered. When
I went to the employment exchange I found where lots of
them go.

The first thing that struck me was the place itself, the drab
uniformity. Even if finances necessitate that everything be
painted one colour, why that colour? It looks calculated to

depress. It succeeds. Perhaps it's the decor that does what it does to the people. Once I'd had a look at the walls I took a look at the people. They blended in, queues of grey people looking quietly despondent. A few, admittedly, looked cheerful. Perhaps unemployment agreed with them. But the atmosphere overall was one of resignation. There were men in their late forties looking as if they had reconciled themselves to this shuffling attendance for the rest of their working lives. Nothing at school had prepared me for this.

I wasn't prepared either for the rudeness of some of the people who worked there. I joined the wrong queue. When I'd waited twenty minutes I arrived at the wrong desk and the woman simply pointed to the back of the right queue. 'I'm not obliged to do this,' I felt like saying. 'My father would pay enough for me not to have to come here.' I hadn't opened my mouth yet and I knew I stood out like a sore thumb. I had had a bath to come here. All the clothes I had casually put on cost more than a week's wage of most of the vacancies I'd seen advertised. For the first time I saw myself as they must have seen me. My hair is in good condition. My complexion is thankfully clear. My shoes have the sheen of leather that someone has carefully worked. I have the lustre of money and I'm sitting here with less than five pounds in my pockets.

'Next.'

I am addressed across a booth, partitioned from the other booths by panels which appear to be made of compressed pencil shavings. It is a concession to privacy and does not affect the acoustics at all. I can hear the conversations quite clearly going on to right and left. The woman opposite is middle-aged. She has a kind face. She looks tired. Perhaps she did not slice a lemon into her bathwater at half-past-nine this morning.

'I'd like a job please.' She does not seem surprised at the sound of my voice, but then she can see me. The conversations going on at both adjacent booths suddenly cease. I hear a snigger. I can feel my face redden.

'Have you had a look at any of the vacancies advertised on the cards?'

'Yes, yes of course. I'm sorry that must have sounded vague. The point is that I'm going to university in October, so basically I'm willing to do . . . anything.' She looked as if she was trying to conceal a smile. Someone in the booth next to me, a man's voice, had started a ridiculous parody of mine.

'Have you any previous work experience?' I must have looked vacant. She tried to help me. 'Perhaps a summer job.'

'No. I'm sorry. This is my first summer job.'

'Don't worry. Perhaps something you studied at school may have been of use, like secretarial studies?'

'It wasn't that kind of a school.' There was another laugh from somewhere. Her lips compressed in a line and she shook her head slightly while looking at me, as if confiding that the best tactic would be to ignore the laughter. I couldn't hear any other voices now. I felt as if everyone was listening to us.

'You must appreciate that most of the employers we advertise for aren't looking for temporary workers. Not unless they specifically say so.'

'Yes.'

'Have you thought of bar work? If you got a job in a bar you wouldn't have to give it up at the start of term. The flexible hours can be quite good and the money helps you with your grant.'

'Yes,' I lied. I hadn't even thought about a grant. With my father's income I didn't think I'd be entitled to money from the state. I just assumed I'd be paid for from some source. And if I stopped to think about it, which I didn't, that meant my father.

'There are some specific cards for vacancies in retail and catering. You'll get bar work listed over there.' She pointed.

'Yes, but if I'm able to do bar work during term-time I might as well do something else while I have full-time leisure. Perhaps you could help me find the kind of job where I might . . . learn something.'

She tried to dissuade me. There were various posts for

office juniors she tried to veer me towards, tacitly instructing me to lie as to my availability. She might almost have been in league with my parents. I thought that if this experience was to be worth anything I had to do something incompatible with something father would have arranged for me.

'I've brought this card here.' I handed it across. She accepted it wordlessly and studied the details for a moment. She picked up the phone. There was a brief discussion in which I was referred to in the third person. She even mentioned, without looking at me, that I was only available for the duration of the summer. After another exchange she put down the receiver.

'Monday morning,' she said, 'eight o'clock.'

'Eight! Couldn't they make it later; flexible hours or something?'

She shook her head. She told me what bus routes the place was on, presupposing I would be travelling from the centre of town. She asked me where I lived. I told her. There was another adjacent snigger.

'Good luck,' she said, and smiled, as if I needed encouragement.

'Thanks.' I stood and instinctively leant forward to shake her hand. She looked bemused and wished me well. Perhaps it's not a reaction they normally elicit.

2 7

'I've got a job,' I said. It was over the inevitable meal. With a house this size we can all contrive to avoid one another till meal times.

'What kind of a job?'

'Manufacturing.'

'Manufacturing what?'

'Carpet sweepers.'

'Where?'

I told them. They didn't say anything. Mother put down her fork and raised the serviette to her mouth in a slow gesture of precise gentility. Their stifled reaction was not one of perplexity or anger or worry, but of embarrassment. It was contagious. I began to feel it myself. I felt obliged to enthuse.

'I'm not actually making carpet sweepers, I'm providing components to the women on the production line who assemble them.'

'We should be grateful for small mercies,' father said.

28

Mother was 'indisposed' the night before my first Monday morning. 'Indisposed' is one of her words. 'Soupçon' is another. I called up various of my school friends, feeling the need for some kind of approval from some quarter. Most of them were away somewhere doing money kind of things. From the rest I got a mixed reception, from, 'What on earth for?' to, 'Find out if they need anyone else.' I held tightly on to Bo-bo, the bear I'd refused to throw out, and fell asleep as the first light was showing.

I got up to the house in silence. Mother's first appointment was a bring-and-buy sale in aid of something worthwhile and started at a civilised hour. I moved around the half-lit kitchen making my breakfast. Father arrived downstairs as I was finishing up. We said little. I noticed the deft movements I had not seen before. It must be a manner he has perfected, moving with trepidation round the expensive rest he has purchased for his wife. I shouted goodbye from the bottom of the stairwell as loudly as I could. Father came out annoyed and handed me the 'collation' on a paper plate wrapped in cling film.

The factory was an old brick affair with a replacement zinc roof. It looked like a vestige from the industrial revolution. When I walked into the gloom no one offered me any help or

direction. They were women mostly, of various ages, quietly
smoking while they waited for their shift to begin. I stood
feeling redundant and thinking how well my worst clothes
looked. One woman stood up, inhaled while she walked
across, and standing in front of me said, 'Clocked in have
you?'

'No,' I said.

'We'll have to see about that then. Can't have you standing
around without getting paid for it.'

'It's a closed shop,' another woman said. They all laughed.
I didn't know what a 'closed shop' was and I didn't see the
humour.

'Can't have you not getting paid for not doing anything.
Put us in a bad light,' said yet another woman. They all
laughed again. By this time I knew they weren't using me as
the butt. I laughed with them. I took the snack from my bag.

'Is there a fridge where I can put my lunch?'

They all stopped laughing. The woman who was near me
took the paper plate and handed it round. There were some
prawns and some fish pâté on a bed of iceberg lettuce and
sliced capsicums. They all looked at it through the cling film
like some religious totem, passing it from hand to hand. It did
the rounds and came back to me. The woman who had
taken the lunch from me reached into her locker and produced
a brick-shaped object wrapped in kitchen roll. She unwrapped
it to reveal some outsides of bread with cheese and what
looked like a stain of chutney between.

'You can put your lunch with mine and hope for fuck's
sake we don't get them mixed up.'

They all burst into hoots of laughter. It wasn't malicious. I
was astonished: it was the first time I'd heard a grown woman
swear. She put the sandwiches back and laughingly offered to
find me a vacant locker. She put out her hand. 'Agnes,' she
said. I shook. Her hands were coarse. A bell sounded. They
stood up, threw their cigarettes on the stone floor and trod
on them.

'You were here on time,' a girl my age said passing. 'We

seen you. If they give you a card today and you don't clock in for another hour don't let them dock your wages.'

I didn't know what 'dock' meant but I could work it out. I assured her I wouldn't and thanked her for the concern. When I spoke several heads already passed turned and looked over their shoulder. I thought: My God, what a terrible mistake I've made.

A supervisor found me. I was allocated a locker and given an overall. It was called an overall but it was really just a nylon slip which buttoned over your dress or trousers or whatever you happened to be wearing. I had noticed that most of the workers were wearing trousers. They gave me a card. The supervisor showed me where my card would be placed alphabetically in the list. Perhaps with my clothes and my voice she didn't trust me to know the alphabet. She looked about the same age as Agnes, in her fifties, but I later found out she was only in her mid-thirties. She showed me how to put my card in the slot and punch in. She suggested I go ahead.

'What about the dock?' I said. I could feel myself blush.

'What dock?'

'Sorry not dock, docked. I don't want my pay docked. If I punch the card now the salaries office will assume I came in late and pay me accordingly.' I was being forward. I was in breach of one of my mother's cardinal rules. The woman looked at me in surprise. So far we'd traipsed round things and she'd pointed and commented in a bored monotone.

'Punch the card and I'll initial it with the correct time written in.'

I punched the card. She wrote something and initialled it and put the card away without letting me see. Then she took me to a place on the shop floor where there was a vacant table with what looked like a plastic chute leading off. Surrounding the table were a number of tea-chests with their contents spilling out. The floor was also littered with the debris. Gesturing me to watch she took from one of the chests two wheels of moulded plastic about two-and-a-half inches in diameter and one inch in thickness. A central hole was exposed, only on one side. From another box she took a metal rod of the same diameter as the holes and about fourteen inches long. The rod was fitted into two of the holes as an axle and the assembled part slid down the chute. Then she did another. Then another. Then she started a fourth.

'I think I've got it,' I said.

'You sure?'

'Obviously I'll not be as proficient at it as you, but I can learn.'

The irony was wasted. She stood beside me and watched me do five. Since the holes were only one side of the wheel and there wasn't any other permutation of axle and wheels, it was impossible to do it wrong.

'When you run out of parts have the boys bring you more from stores. When you get the hang of it we'll put you on bonus.'

'Thanks awfully.'

Dotted at various distances there were other tables with solitary women doing similar things. At a further distance still was a row of women working on parallel ranks which must have been production lines. From the noise of the thing there must have been electrical and pneumatic tools of some kind. Despite the noise I wished I had been over there with the other women. The place was the size of an aircraft hangar and I imagined it possible to be lonely there, which was strange because I'm never lonely when I spend my time in the house strategically flitting from room to room to avoid other people.

It wasn't at all like I had imagined a factory. There was nothing in the way of heavy machinery. It's difficult now to remember how I had imagined a factory would be. I think I imagined it to be like something from a Dickens novel with inexorable engines, grime and a cacophony of noise. Lots of these people seemed nice. The room was dotted with opaque skylights and the impression inside, despite the exposed brick-work, was of a large airy space. The offices occupied the mezzanine which ran the width of the wall at the short end of the rectangle which made up our factory. There was a row of perspex cubicles. I could see male faces staring from these windows. The canteen and executive offices, I later found out, were housed elsewhere.

Within half-an-hour I was bored to tears and the bin at the bottom of the chute was filled to overflowing. I didn't know what to do and just kept on assembling. One of the wheel assemblies rolled over the pile and kept going down the gangway between crates. Men were watching me from the windows and seemed to be laughing. I noticed also that some of the women from the assembly lines were looking at me expectantly. I pretended not to see them and began to work faster. Eventually one of the younger women, the one who had warned me not to have my salary docked, came across.

'What's the score? Where's the stuff? We're on bonus.'

'I'm sorry?'

'Bonus. We're on bonus. You on bonus?'

'I've no idea. No, I don't think so. The supervisor said something about putting me on it.'

'If you're not on bonus you're on basic. Basic's shite. Management. Christ! Fuck 'em. If we'd a union in here everyone would be on bonus. How much have you done?'

I pointed.

'Christ. That all? Since when?'

'Perhaps forty minutes ago.'

'Christ!' I began to think she hadn't a very pliable vocabulary. 'Look,' she said, pointing to the production lines, 'see all those women hanging about?'

'Yes.'

'Well they're waiting on these. And they're on bonus. Understand?'

'Good Lord!' I picked up a handful and began walking. She stopped me.

'Sit on your arse. That's what the boys are for.' And then, without moving, she shouted at the top of her lungs 'DREW!'

A boy materialised from among the packing cases. I say 'boy', perhaps he was nineteen and certainly older than I was, skinny and above middle-height. He had an Elvis haircut,

greased back and combed with precision. The maintenance
of this obviously monopolised all his pride in his appearance.
The rest of him had been left entirely to chance. He still had
a trace of acne. He had D.E.A.T. tattooed across the knuckles
of one hand. I later found out he had intended this to read
'death' but had miscounted either the letters or his fingers.
The back of his other hand read ECSTASY. Both tattoos had
been done with a compass and a bottle of ink. He had a
cigarette balanced on his bottom lip. I came to recognise this
as a permanent feature. I thought: My God! what a specimen.

'You new here?' he said, looking at me.

'She's new and she's going to university so piss off.' I hadn't
said a word about university to anyone.

'My looks, your brains,' he said, still looking at me, 'we
could do somethin'.'

'We didn't ask you over to socialise,' said the girl at my side.
'We need those wheel assemblies over there right now.' There
was a finality in the way she said 'now'. It frightened me.

'Keep your pants on, doll,' he said, obeying nonetheless.
He fetched a barrow with an empty bin, replaced it with my
full one and made to move in the direction of the production
line. The whole thing was adroitly done, the most impressive
fact being the way he effortlessly balanced the ash of the
cigarette to prevent it from falling. He had been intimidated
into action and tried to make his movements look as slow as
possible whilst keeping up enough speed to mollify the women
who were by now all watching. He took the cigarette from
his mouth at last, threw it on the floor and ground it out
with his heel. He nodded at me in a deliberate manner, as if
there was some unspoken agreement between us. I saw the
spare cigarette from behind his ear slide down his collar. He
immediately started chewing and I realised there must have
been gum in his mouth all the time as well. He summoned
what he seemed to think a 'knowing' look. His eyes flicked
above my head and I followed his gaze to the men in the
offices.

'The bastards!' said the girl beside me who had watched

the whole exchange. She took a step towards the boy who lost his languid manner and rushed off with the barrow in alarm. Then she turned towards the offices and, opening her overall, lifted her sweat-shirt, exposing her huge breasts to the office staff. A burst of hysterical cheering broke out at the production line. I was paralysed.

'Fucking men,' she said. And then, extending her hand: 'Morag.'

'Rachel,' I said, taking it automatically.

'Well, Rachel. Best piece of advice, and don't take it wrong – '

I waited.

'Don't arse around when other women's bonuses are at stake.'

'Of course not.' I smiled at her. She smiled back. Then nothing happened till I realised they were all still watching from the production lines. I put my hands in my pockets. Still nothing. Then I realised she had been elected to come across to get me going and ensure I provided them with enough to maintain their bonuses. I was galvanised into action and began to assemble wheels and axles at a furious rate.

'Thanks,' she said, and began to walk back. 'Don't take any snash from Drew.'

'I'll keep that in mind.' What on earth was 'snash'?

'If he doesn't get the bin across on time, kick his arse. If he touches you up and you're too shy to do anything about it yourself, tell me. Or even better, tell Agnes.'

'I will. And thank you.'

I worked incessantly without looking up. When the bin was full there was no sign of the slovenly boy. Curiously enough I was embarrassed to shout here, where shouting was the order of the day, whereas I have no hesitation about shouting at home when I know it flouts every rule. I was embarrassed to shout for him but I was still more in awe of the consequences of not providing the women with enough work. I went looking and found him sitting on an up-turned packing case, playing solitaire. When he saw me coming he took a deep inhalation of his cigarette and ran his fingers through the precise hair. It was a habit I got to witness many times. I imagined oil collecting under his fingernails at each of these affected gestures.

'I need a bin.'

'We're both men of the world here, doll, except you that is, and we both know what you need. Look no further. I'm your man.'

'Fuck off.' It was more a shibboleth than an obscenity. I'd passed the test.

'You just failed the test. I thought you were different. That's just what any of them would have said.' He looked genuinely put out and I thought I'd caught a glimpse of vulnerability that made me warm to him.

'I'm sorry,' I said.

'That's more like it. The Trocadero. Eight-thirty. Be there.' He turned to go.

'Don't ever presuppose anything about me again, especially that I'd go out with a spotty oik like you. If you don't empty my bin now and provide me with another I'll go and tell Agnes that you're responsible for them not making up their bonuses.'

He looked hurt again but this time I was firm and stared at him till he'd done as I asked. I caught an approving nod from Morag and waved back with a gesture of solidarity I'd never felt at school. It took me till the afternoon break to work out why: at school there had been no men.

I returned to my bench and chute and began assembling again. By moving the tea-chests closer together and next to where I stood, and by arranging the axles in a pile at my right hand, I found I could work more efficiently. I tried several more permutations in a small time-and-motion study, all the time ensuring a plentiful supply to the production line. By eleven-thirty I'd arranged the desk and components in three different ways. Perhaps, I thought, I have a flair for ergonomic management. Then I realised why I was doing it: I was bored. In just over two hours I'd ceased wringing any further enjoyment out of it. By the looks of the rest of them, and the accustomed speed with which they worked, it seemed as if they'd been doing this for years.

By the end of the day, with the incessant noise and standing, my temples hurt and I felt as if all the blood in my body was washing sluggishly round my ankles. When we clocked out I received a few words of encouragement from some of the ladies and the offer of cigarettes from more. It was something I began to notice: as soon as a bell rang they all automatically produced cigarettes and lit up.

I walked out the main door feeling dowdy and exhausted and happy. We dispersed at the road and I shouted goodbye to one or two who had gone out of their way for me. A hand touched my shoulder and I turned to find Drew who had run to catch up.

'Where are you going?'

'Home.'

'Where's home?' I told him. He looked momentarily crestfallen. Again, caught unawares, I saw something unaffected. I could have liked him if such incidents weren't covered up by his stupid veneer of macho composure. As soon as he was away from the rest and not worried about making an impression, everything about him improved.

'That's funny, I live near there.'

'No you don't. The only people who live near there are people like my parents.'

'And you,' he corrected. I don't know if he intended to sting me but he did. I hate comparisons with my parents.

'I'll live elsewhere, given time. The only thing that concerns you now is that I'm going to a place where you don't live.'

'Who the fuck wants to live in a place like that? I bet you don't get any ice-cream vans.'

'What's that got to do with anything?' I imagined my mother cringing at the sound of Mr Cappochi tinkling his way round the mews lanes with his carbon monoxide and his double nuggets.

'Well how do you get your fags?'

'None of us smoke.'

'See!' he said triumphantly, as if having proven a point.

'We don't have ice-cream vans because if we did the residents would form a vigilante committee in minutes to keep away anything that would affect property values – including you.'

He looked at me without saying anything and walked away. Up till then I'd still been happy. I caught my bus annoyed at him for having disrupted my peace of mind and for causing me to vent the kind of snobbery I'm most ashamed of. But I was more annoyed at myself, because I thought my veneer was thinner than his and who knew if what was underneath was any better.

29

'I didn't get docked,' I told my parents.

'That's nice,' mother said.

'They tried to dock me, but I was up to them,' I lied.

' "Dock",' father said. 'Isn't that what they do with dogs' tails?'

He knew what 'dock' meant even though mother was mystified. I went into an elaborate explanation of how they tried to do me out of money by subterfuge but that, despite my accent, I proved to be more worldly-wise than any of them had anticipated. I didn't mention that any of them had been nice, or the co-operation they had shown. I presented an image of me, composed, alert, outwitting a factory of plebeian opportunists. Mother and father, in their genteel solidarity, chose not to say anything further. They chose to show no curiosity whatsoever, perhaps hoping this tacit disapproval would dissuade me from going back.

I thought of something one of my teachers had said to me. She said that you should always talk about other people as if they were there or you knew would hear what you had said.

She hadn't grown up in a Stalinist commune. She wasn't trying to teach us caution but kindness. I never knew anyone who lived up to the rule. At school, half the joy of knowing other people was the opportunity of doing a hatchet-job on them when they weren't there.

I thought about what she had said, and the way I'd just distorted the story of my day, at the expense of people I half knew, in order to get some kind of response from my parents. I'd failed. It was an unworthy lie that hadn't even worked. I felt angrier now than I had on the bus after my encounter with Drew. I focused it all on my parents. I continued to talk for a while about work and then I said:

'And that's when Morag flashed her tits and got a round of applause from the rest of us.'

Mother stopped chewing. She didn't look at me but quietly put down her knife and fork and rose from the table, excusing herself. Father stood up and threw his napkin on the table. He left after her and I could hear them talking in the lounge across the hall – the cadence of subdued reproach.

'Does no one in this house apart from me have breasts or what?' I said to the cornice-work, hoping my parents would hear. 'I'd rather die an old maid than have kids who grow up in an atmosphere where the mention of bosoms halts a meal. Bosoms,' I said, and then louder, 'Bosoms. Big bosoms. Breasts. Tits. Mazoombas. Bristols. Mammaries. Knockers. Huge, huge, HUGE, knockers.'

It's just as well Morag hadn't shown us her arse too.

3 0

Three weeks. I'm a veteran. I'm on bonus. After two days they wouldn't allow me to sit over tea being quietly exploited. They goaded me. I was more afraid of their reproach than I was of a rebuff from the supervisor. 'Put it this way,' Sandra said to me, 'you don't have to do it for yourself. You'll leave.

No one really expects you to stay. You're not losing that much out of it. Maybe your parents'll make it up. But whoever replaces you might not have an old man who's rolling in it. She's almost certain not to. And if they've got away with not paying bonus to you, why should they pay her?'

The logic was flawless. Half of Drew's friends on the shop floor were semi-literate, but they could count the odds and winnings on a betting slip instantly. They knew how much I lost by the hour by not being on bonus. With the ladies all egging me on I walked up to the offices, past the perspex cubicles on the mezzanine, and along to the supervisor's office. By the time I arrived it was obvious something was happening and the whole factory was watching. I felt like Oliver with his bowl. I knocked timidly. No answer. I knew she was inside. The psychology was obvious. I summoned myself and walked boldly in. It was her break too, she was listening to something on tape. At the sight of me she took off her earphones and seemed to consider for a moment.

'You're on,' she said.

'What?'

'Bonus. That's what you came about, isn't it?'

'. . . No. I . . . I was thinking about the work rota.'

'There isn't a rota.'

'Yes. Exactly. It seems to me the jobs are uniformly monotonous. Three weeks would drive anyone to distraction. If – if we alternated it might up production.'

'It might.'

'It would seem like obvious psychology to me.'

'Studied psychology have you?'

'No.'

'I'll bear it in mind.'

'And I'm still on bonus?'

'You're still on bonus.'

I tried to draw the conversation out further to spend more time in the office so I could pretend to the ladies I had had to fight for the concession. But then the supervisor wasn't bad, and why do her a disservice when she hadn't done me one?

I broke the news to them when I got back.

'I'm on bonus and we discussed the question of a rota.'

'What rota?'

'Didn't it ever strike you that the jobs on the production line are terribly boring?'

'Yes.'

'Well then, if you take weekly turns at doing something else it might not become so monotonous.'

'It might not. Didn't it ever strike you that the longer you do something the quicker you get at it?'

'Y . . . es.'

'And if you're on bonus it means you get more money for the more you do?'

'Y . . . es.'

'And don't you think with families to feed we'd rather be bored during working hours and earn more money?'

'That never occurred to me.'

'So, basically, fuck the rota.'

'Yes,' I said, 'fuck the rota.'

The bell sounded. We all returned to our places. It had been more of a disappointment than they thought. For the brief span of time it had taken me to walk from the supervisor's office to the ladies I had thought it within my grasp to do something for somebody. I had supposed that I had had a flash of insight which, with the daily grind year in, year out, they had never experienced. Also, if a rota had come into effect, I wouldn't be at a table out on my own and I really wanted to be with them on the production line, to hear what they talked about and what their families were like.

Patterns began to emerge that third week and I began to notice things. I noticed the age discrepancy between them and people like my mother. Without the time which money affords, the rejuvenating lotions, the long baths, the uninterrupted sleeps, and, most noticeably, the carelessness of a replenished cheque book to dispel money worries, they looked older. Sometimes much older. And harder. Morag, scarcely older than I was, had a face like a map. Sandra, in her mid-thirties, had had jobs like this since she was sixteen and had been standing day in and day out for the past fifteen years. The sluggish uphill trudge of blood had left her with ripe varicose veins. The mottled 'corned beef' complexion of the legs was something common to all of them and something they didn't hesitate to talk about.

They also talked about lots of things in an unashamed way I hadn't heard before. They were totally unaffected in their discussions of sex and didn't scruple to go into the kind of detail which left me shocked and curious and horny. Nicole Lingard split her hymen with a fountain pen one day in third-year trigonometry when the teacher had temporarily left the class. That obsessed us for months and was the sum of our pooled sexual experience until the same girl was caught on one of our school trips giving a knee trembler to the off-duty concierge in the linen press of a small Paris hotel. She was escorted home early the next morning before we had a chance to talk to her. Her parents were instructed not to send her back next term. She bequeathed us intrusive surveillance for the rest of the holiday, and her gorgeous reputation. Her removal had been so total, so efficient and so clandestine, that she became the stuff of legend; we invented her cutting an erotic swathe down South America, leaving her wake littered with dark Lotharios. We abstracted her out of existence, and with her went our only real connection with sex.

Sex. It had been on my mind for years and was getting more insistent all the time. The women at the factory talked about it with a hearty relish that made me wonder if my parents were the same species. They went into it with the kind of anatomical detail people ascribe to macho rhetoric. (I don't know if men talk like this.) And they were self-disparaging in their humour. Agnes said that breast-feeding three children had left her with tits like spaniels' ears. They got as much mileage out of descriptions of their Caesarean scars and stretch-marks as they did out of their husbands and boyfriends.

'Touch his toes? Touch his toes? He can't even see his fucking toes. He only ever gets to see his dick when he takes a stiffy, and these days that's usually only once a week, after football on the telly on a Saturday night, with a lot of help from me. A lot. I've whipped a dozen meringues a lot easier.'

'How do you . . .?' I asked. She was fat herself.

'It isn't easy, dear. Imagine two jellies on a washing machine during the spin cycle and it gives you some idea. That's why it's only Saturdays these days. Twenty years ago he was built like a whippet and we went at it like a couple of stoats in a sack every time we had the chance.'

Twenty years ago, I wondered, did my parents go at it like a couple of stoats in a sack every time they had the chance, or did mother slide in beside father with the light out and suffer his caresses? Is there a protocol for a bourgeois orgasm?

Sex in the head and becoming worse. Morag recognised the fact, or perhaps just the symptoms. She told me once, as a casual aside, that she lost her virginity in the rank vegetable patch of a convenient allotment on the way home from a talk given by some Catholic luminary of the Legion of Mary. Her memories are sketchy. I was appalled she remembered so little about it.

'I thought it would be fraught with significance, every detail committed to memory. What was his name?'

'Don't know. Can't remember.'

'Can't remember?' I couldn't disguise the surprise. She looked at me, a look of close appraisal.

'It's high time you had a shag. Drew likes you. He's a nice boy, underneath it all. Get him away from his friends and he'll drop the act. When he's on his own you can manage him. If all you both want out of it is a shag then take precautions and where's the harm? I think he's softer than he looks though. Don't hurt him.'

Perhaps for the understanding and the blatant compassion, for me, for Drew, for the situation, perhaps because I could never have imagined such a conversation with my mother, and here was a woman scarcely older than I was showing the concern I should have had from another quarter, I thought there was something inevitable in her words. Perhaps I just wanted sex and have retrospectively invented all kinds of reasons to justify myself to myself. At any rate, I did what I had been taught to do to get the ball rolling, the only thing I could think of doing, I invited him home for dinner.

3 1

'What are we having tonight?' She was standing by the kitchen sink when I came in.

'Rainbow trout.'

'How many did you get in?'

'Enough.' There was already a perplexed note in her voice. The ritual meals of my first return had been abandoned in the light of my haphazard schedule. Many times recently, with money in my purse, I had called in late afternoon and left garbled messages with Dora, 'the help', as to my whereabouts and deliberately vague alternative arrangements. I had gone for drinks after work with the friends I had made there. In all the time I can remember, my father, with the crushing schedule of work he feels obliged to meet, has usually failed to make dinner on week nights. A solitary evening meal is something my mother is accustomed to. I attend by default and was surprised she did not read something into my motives when I called to state, categorically, that I would be there.

'Will father be here?'

'Perhaps. Perhaps later. I'll make enough.'

'If there isn't enough it's all right.'

'Enough for what?'

'We can easily go elsewhere.' He wasn't even here and already I began to think everything was going terribly wrong.

'How many?' she asked, without looking up.

'Just one. A boy. A man. A man I met at work and assumed

you wouldn't mind if I invited. You've always encouraged me to bring people round.'

'Of course I've encouraged it. I've always encouraged prudence and foresight and common good manners too.' She reached into the drawer and produced the enamelled napkin rings we had only used half a dozen times in my life. I walked through to the lounge with a feeling of mounting dread. For the past three late afternoons, after work, I'd had heavy snogging sessions with Drew in the locker room, sitting with my knees clenched under the onslaught of his baboon gropes. I'd allowed my knees to slacken the width of a hope. I was just waiting for the venue of my choice, nothing too tacky. With a house our size I'd been silly enough to imagine the two of us free for a sexual romp in one of the rooms, when the time came, with mother and father conveniently somewhere else, doing whatever they do. From the hallway I could hear her, quietly insistent, as she spoke on the phone, summoning him back.

Father arrived. He and mother had a quick confab in the hall and then he came into the lounge, deliberately seeking me out. I was sitting on the settee. He came and stood in front of me.

'All right?' he said. For a moment I thought he was going to shake my hand. Without pausing for a reply he walked to the cocktail cabinet. 'Gin and tonic all right?'

'For God's sake, I'm not one of your clients.'

'No. Of course. You have a young man coming I believe.' The last part spilled out hurriedly, as if, for want of a common denominator, he'd prematurely blurted something he had intended working up to.

'Yes.'

'And what does he do?'

'He provides components to women on the production line who assemble carpet sweepers.'

'Quite. A sort of . . . facilitator.'

'Yes . . . It's not an issue.'

'Of course not,' he said with exaggerated warmth. Mother

was hovering at the door. He looked at her and he looked at me and he looked at his shoes. 'I think I'll just change.'

Mother followed him out of the room. I've noticed how she does that now, dogs his footsteps rather than be left alone with me. Five minutes later they reappeared. In as long as I can remember father has worn a shirt and tie to dinner, my mother what she deems to be the feminine equivalent.

'Oh my God!'

Father was wearing a cashmere v-neck sweater with a polo neck of the same material below and a pair of worsted trousers. It was the type of outfit exclusive golf clubs permit as mufti on the nineteenth hole. Mother wore a matching his 'n' her sweater with a silk neck scarf and Italian vicuna wool slacks. The whole ensemble was the self-conscious 'at home' wear of a couple of extras from a James Bond film. It was my turn to remonstrate.

'There's the doorbell.' Mother disappeared into the hall. I ran to overtake.

There is an elaborate inside door of stained glass, and the outside double doors. In the area between is a spacious conservatory, brightly lit from all the glass, and tinged green with the number of plants. It's a room in itself. When I tugged open the doors Drew stood on the threshold looking hesitant. He walked in and took my hand with a kind of tepid reverence, as if re-evaluating my worth in the light of these unaccustomed surroundings.

'Where's the TV?' he joked. I laughed, too loudly, and at his vulnerability felt a sudden surge of affection for him. I slipped my hand in his and led him through to the lounge, consciously trying to cover the tattoo across his knuckles with the bar of my thumb, disliking myself for doing so.

My parents stood like sentinels in the centre of the lounge.

'Mrs C,' he said to mother, extending his hand. She took it, looking at him askance, unsure if the form of address was some whimsical joke she couldn't fathom. He took father's hand in turn. He was wearing a cream suit that looked as if it was made of anaglypta, a yellow tie with a gold tie-pin,

white socks and burgundy shoes. In that lounge of muted
sepia he seemed more three-dimensional than the rest of us.
From inside the voluminous suit he produced a half pound
box of milk chocolates he handed to mother and some cheap
Lambrusco he handed to father.

'You want to try some of that,' he said.

'Yes,' father said. And then again, 'Yes.'

'We're having fish,' mother explained. 'I've had the wine
chilled.'

'Sound,' Drew said.

We went through to the dining room. Even with the leaves
removed the table is a long oblong. Without waiting to be
seated, Drew placed himself at the head of the table. I was
placed at the opposite end. I didn't feel like abandoning him
to scrutiny all the way out there. There was no help for it.
Mother produced the avocado.

'So, Drew,' father started, 'I understand you're involved in
the production side of things.'

'Yeah, I shunt the stuff up and they assemble it.'

'Assemble. You hear that Marjory, a facilitator.'

'Yes,' mother said.

'Good stuff this, Mrs C. Bit slimy, but good.'

'Yes. I suppose it is slimy. Curious consistency. I'm not sure
I would have used the word "slimy". Certain textures in
vegetables I never took to. Personally, I never saw all the fuss
over asparagus.'

'Candour,' father said tendentiously, 'is a dying art. Don't
you think?'

'Don't know,' Drew said, his mouth half full. 'Whether you
mean it or not it sounds like the kind of thing people say on
late Saturday-night talk shows to sound different.'

I wanted to snog him then and there. Father poured some
wine. Drew coloured at the unexpected discovery of having
committed some gaffe. I felt for him, thrashing around to
make an impression when he didn't know any of the house
rules he was violating. The movement of his adam's apple as
he drained the glass fascinated us in the brief silence. Putting

the glass down he saw my parents watching him and felt obliged to speak.

'Keeping the Lambrusco till later, are you?'

'Yes,' father said. 'The best till last, like the wedding feast at Cana.'

'Where?'

'It's in the Middle East,' I said. Father looked at Drew and me and smiled widely.

'Middle East,' father repeated, shaking his head from side to side and tutting amusedly. Drew looked at him blankly and then glanced towards me for explanation. I could only shrug. Mother, feeling excluded from the arcane joke, fussed uneasily over the arrangements. Unless everything conceivable is easily to hand she feels negligent as a hostess. She takes her responsibility seriously. It is the nearest thing she has known to a vocation.

'So Drew . . .' she began loudly, perhaps hoping to propel herself into some meaningful exchange by the momentum of her opening. 'You . . . you like the wine?'

'Bloody good. Any more?'

Wine drinking in our house is done frugally and with an elaborate preamble. Father lifted the bottle from its terracotta cooler and took his leave almost gleefully. He didn't go straight to the fridge, where there's always an indifferent bottle of white cooling, but went through to the back and returned with an ice bucket and a bottle wrapped in wire that looked very expensive. Whenever he's away it's always wine he brings back.

'It's not many times we entertain,' he lied, by way of explanation.

'Nice house,' Drew said, accepting a huge glass without demur. The glasses were long-stemmed. Drew held his by the bowl. My mother can drink from a glass and leave it looking unused. She holds the stem lightly sipping like a dragon-fly exploiting surface tension, leaving mark of neither finger nor lip. There is a rumour that she once vomited at a dinner party with such decorum that no one knew, averting her head slightly and puking with a suppressed spasm into her glass with no overflow. One minute she was drinking Chardonnay and the next holding a glass of what looked like frothed oatmeal, which she took to the toilet and quietly disposed of. She was so discreet the story has no corroborators, but it is the type of thing she is mortified by and would never make up.

Bearing the brunt of her horrified expression father told the whole story.

'Not to worry, Mrs C. I once leaned over the deep-freeze of Safeway to get something and gagged last night's dogburger over the free range chicken.' Dad shook in uncharacteristic mirth. Drew was undaunted. 'Why is it that it's all right to eat fish with the heads on but if you served chicken that way everyone would lob their tonsils all over your tablecloth?'

'I . . . I really have no idea,' mother said.

'Excellent,' father said.

We finished the fish. Mother brought in the Cranachan, one of her specialities, a dessert made of oatmeal, cream, Drambuie and raspberries, served, inopportunely, in long-stemmed glasses.

'Thank God, I thought this might be the kind of place where they bring you in the pudding and then set fire to it. And Mrs C, you haven't . . .,' he made gagging motions over the glass. Colour drained from my mother's face. Father clapped his hands together and said, 'Precious . . . Precious.' I wanted to say, 'Drew, shut the fuck up.' It occurred to me that father might be egging Drew on to new heights in order to satisfy his own curiosity, or conduct some kind of social experiment, or goading him to new depths in order to demonstrate to me what a fool I was making of myself.

Mother left her dessert untasted. She seemed unable to look at the glass or at any other food. I cleared the dishes away and fetched the cheeses from the kitchen. She followed me in and stood beside me for a moment, taking and wringing my hand without looking at me in an instant of unprecedented warmth, as if expressing solidarity in the face of universal male ghastliness. 'Mother,' I wanted to say, 'I don't find men so ghastly. Although he's no genius and not much to look at, I want Drew to roger me rigid so I know what all the fuss is about.'

When I got back Drew was halfway through the second bottle and firing on all cylinders.

'. . . all the dreadful things you think can happen. It's all happened before. Earthquakes and the like. Don't dismiss mythology so lightly. They knew what they were talking about. Take the five horsemen of the Acropolis. There was rape an' famine an' war an' . . . an' . . . unemployment, an' . . .'

'Prohibition,' father said.

'Exactly.' Drew spontaneously laughed. So did I, although I had no idea what I was laughing at. So did father. It occurred to me we were having a good time. Mother looked in, smiled wanly and immediately retired.

'Or Dante's seven circles of Hell,' father said, getting into the spirit of the thing, 'each one worse than the last. The first is a never-ending bus journey on public transport with a child behind who cries non-stop and kicks the back of your seat.'

'And hacks up on your head,' Drew said.

'And the second is a permanent visit from the VAT men where you are given three minutes to justify a bogus return while they wait in the outer office.'

I felt like contributing to the hilarity.

'Or you're destitute on a desert island and the only thing that washes up is the ménage à trois sex manual.'

Father stopped laughing immediately. Perhaps profanity is a male preserve, or perhaps the mention of sex stopped him in his tracks. Drew poured father a stiff one. Father paused for a moment and seemed mollified.

'I must say,' he said, addressing Drew, 'you've got the appearance off to a T.'

We looked at one another.

'Down to the tattoos. How did you do them, with a biro?'

'Well . . . ink.'

'I half think Marjory thinks you're bona fide.' There was an uncomprehending pause and then he went on. 'How long are you staying?'

Drew looked at his watch. 'I've no idea. The buses don't run up here. No point. There'd be no customers since everyone's got a car. I took a taxi here and I'm going to have to get one back so I didn't think there was any rush.'

'I don't mean to dinner, I mean at work. When does term start? The same time as Rachel's?'

Everything exploded. The whole night had been conducted by father on the presupposition that I'd found a soul mate at work who was also idling time till university started. I don't think he could conceive of me finding anyone attractive who wasn't on their way to becoming something else.

'You know, father, a degree isn't the *sine qua non.*'

'The what?' from Drew.

Father stopped smiling.

'What exactly do you do?'

'Like you said, I'm a facilitator.'

'Whom do you facilitate?'

'Anyone who wants to be . . . facilitated. Morag mostly, and the other girls.'

'You provide people with components?'

'. . . yes.'

'And they manufacture carpet sweepers?'

'. . . yes.' The pauses between each answer were lengthening as the recognition dawned upon him that he was being appraised.

'And you've done this, I suppose, since you left school?'

'Since I first got a job.'

I had to interrupt.

'Work's scarcer than you think when you don't graduate from a good university with a vocational degree. Drew was lucky to get it and he's held the job down responsibly.' I sounded like a probation officer called as a character witness by the defence, and I didn't even know if this was true. I doubt if he'd ever held anything down responsibly. When I recall the situation, what angers me most is that I felt obliged to justify to my father someone I had chosen to invite. It was just a dinner, not a contract of marriage. And in as much as I felt the need to justify his job, his dress sense and his conversation, I failed to realise how much of my father's baggage I carried around with me. To tell the truth, outside of work I was secretly ashamed of him myself, and I think at that moment he understood.

There was a long silence. Father looked at the remains of the bottle and said, 'Do you want any more wine?'

'No thanks. I've had just about as much as I can swallow.' He rose from the table and the serviette in his lap fell on to the floor. 'It's earlier than I thought.' He was looking at me now. 'There's no need to call a taxi. If I walk to the main road I'll pick one up. I might even be able to get a train. At any rate, there's plenty of time.'

He gave a final nod to my father and walked out of the room. I caught him in the hall. He kept walking and didn't say anything. I held open the inner door and he walked through. I held open the outer door and he walked out. I knew that unless I did something he wasn't going to speak. If he left in silence, tomorrow would be impossible. And the days would get progressively worse.

'I'm sorry. I suppose if I went home with you they'd be nicer to me at yours.' He didn't say anything and just walked away. I watched him till he turned the corner. It was a balmy night. I wanted to cry. I went to my room without any detours. I have an ensuite bathroom. With food I can exile myself for days, as I did when I was a kid, reproaching my parents with my absence and thinking up melodramatic scenarios of the aftermath of my suicide. But I didn't feel indulgent just then. I just felt sad for Drew and angry at myself for not realising beforehand what a bad idea the invitation had been for him.

There was a knock on the door, I don't know how long later. It opened slightly and mother stood on the threshold. She appeared nervous to come in. I didn't say anything.

'I heard what you said at the door to him. People don't

necessarily get nicer the less money they have. The poor don't have a monopoly on decency.'

'That's no excuse.'

'No. I know.'

'Why has it taken you seventeen years to say something like this to me?'

'I don't know. I'm sorry.'

'Yes.'

'Goodnight.'

'Goodnight.'

3 2

There was one sure way to make up. Even if it doesn't heal the breach you can always depend on a man to go through the mechanics. He avoided me most of the next day. When I needed components he contrived to have someone else deliver them. When we were clocking out I deliberately hung back. I found him in the cloakroom standing around for no apparent reason. Perhaps he knew and he was giving me an opportunity to rectify things. I walked up to him when he was facing the wall. He knew it was me. It could only have been me, at that time and that place, our trysting place. I took him by the shoulder and turned him round. He looked at the ground, like a surly child and refused to look at me although we both knew why he had waited behind. I grasped his oiled hair and cranked his head erect. When he looked at me I kissed him and slid my tongue between his parted lips. His whole body grew immediately stiff. I sat down slowly, still kissing him. He was easy to bring down. He sat beside me on the bench. I took one of his hands and placed it on my breast. And then I parted my legs wider than his wildest hope.

Once I'd let him touch me for a few minutes I stood up. So did he. The nearest toilet was the men's, but I'd passed that before when the door opened and the odour of stale urine wafted out. I was prepared for a lot but I wasn't prepared for that. Love isn't pitching its mansions in that place of excrement. I led him towards the ladies'. By some absurd taboo, with one hand up my blouse and the other down my tights, he was reluctant to come in. I took his hands out of my clothes and pulled him inside. I chose an end booth and closed the door behind us.

I opened my blouse. I wasn't wearing anything underneath. I put down the lid of the toilet seat and stood on it. My plan was to perch myself naked on the cistern while he sat on the lid of the toilet, then lower myself on to him. I took off my skirt and my tights. I looked at him wondering if he had the initiative to take off my knickers. He hadn't. I stood out of them and turned to face him feeling vulnerable on the raised pan, my navel level with his face.

I don't think he'd ever seen a vagina before, despite the fact that he'd just attempted to force eight fingers into mine. He looked at me unblinkingly, mesmerised by the triangle. He leaned forward, touching both my ankles, running his hands up both legs. It felt wonderful. He curved his hands round my buttocks and towards the front, converging on the thatch of hair. He seemed apprehensive now to touch me there and brought round his fingers with the kind of delicacy I'd never seen in him, as if being permitted to touch the last member of an endangered species. I leaned forward to kiss him. My breasts are fuller now, heavier, but I remember I felt the weight of them for the first time that late afternoon when he cupped me in his hands and squeezed me so tight I gasped. He was trembling through his lips and hands. He still hadn't taken off any clothes. I pushed his face backwards and raised my eyebrows. Realising, he began tugging at his dustcoat. His movements looked almost manic. If there was any thinking to be done I decided I'd better do it. Women are better equipped for it at times like this – at any time. We have to be. We suffer the consequences.

'I think there's a machine,' I said deliberately. 'In the men's. A machine.'

He had pulled down his trousers and was trying to take them off without first removing his shoes. He looked bemused for a moment, pulled up his trousers and ran out, leaving the door of the booth open. I reached forward and pushed it closed without pushing home the bolt and then resumed my position. I heard him yell to me from the empty cloakroom beyond: 'I'll have to get some change.' The voice was as manic as the actions. I looked down at myself from the vantage of the cistern, blouse open, breasts loose, legs parted and thought: Is this really me? It was. I was beginning to moisten at the prospect of the next few minutes. All that money, all those Latin verbs, all that decorum culminating in a sleazy fuck in a cloaca.

He wrenched open the door and stood there with one arm rigid, triumphantly brandishing a packet of three, three feet in front of his face.

'Well go on, put it on.'

Another blank look.

'You know how to.'

'Of course I know how to.'

But he didn't. I wanted him to take off his shirt before his trousers so I stood down and began to unbutton it. His skin was creamy and pleasant, with no hair besides a soft down. He seemed little more than a large boy. His body was taut and marvellously pliant. When I had taken off his shoes he managed his trousers and pants but insisted on turning to the wall to put on the condom.

'It always embarrasses me when a girl watches me do this.' I knew then he had never done this before. At that revelation my nerves vanished.

I was sitting on the lid of the pan watching his trembling buttocks as he wrenched and swore. I stood up and looked over his shoulder.

'It won't work,' he said. 'The fuckin' johnny won't peel back.'

His dick was erect and blue, looking bruised with the attempt of putting the condom on backwards. I'd only ever seen pencil illustrations of an erect penis in sexual manuals and biology textbooks before. It looked angry purplish. I wasn't to know then this was its natural colour with the surge of blood. The branching veins were pulsing. I was fascinated. I wanted it inside me.

'You're trying to put it on backwards.' I knew about condoms. Nicole Lingard carried them always. We'd peeled them on to bananas, our toes, the spikes of railings, anything that caught our childish fancy. Standing with my breasts pressed against his back I reached round. He let his hands fall by his sides. I took the condom from him and turned the opening round. I took hold of the shaft of his dick. The reaction was stunning. I peeled the condom on. He turned to face me. I could feel the rubber baton graze my pubic hair.

I sat on the toilet and opened my legs. He sat between them. I half stood and was half lifted on to him. When he penetrated me he immediately stood up cradling my bottom and turned me with my back to the door. He didn't look strong enough to sustain this. My arms encircled his neck. He pushed further in. It felt fantastic.

'Fuck me till your boots fill up,' I shouted.

He battered me against the door. My head jarred against the coat peg. I thought: Latin verbs – you can keep them, except for the verb to fuck, whatever it may be. I didn't think that. I thought that afterwards. At the time I didn't think anything. I just thought how wonderful it felt to have a vagina that could make you feel like this. Do all women have it? I felt sorry for women who don't have my vagina.

He stopped dead in a paroxysm that left me feeling that I hadn't had the better part of the deal after all. He didn't say anything. His eyes rolled and with me still astride him he sat suddenly on the lid of the pan. His head lolled back on to the cistern where I'd been waiting moments before. He looked beautiful. I grasped his oily hair for the second time, tilted his head towards me and took his bottom lip in my mouth.

'Thank you,' he said, with utter sincerity.

I sat across him and felt him shrinking inside me, two virgins with the bravado gone.

3 3

There's this bint in the work. Nice girl. Good family, y'know. Nice house, and they eat cheese after a meal instead of as one. She sort of took a shine to me. 'These things happen,' I said to her. Didn't make much difference. Never does. Not that there have been that many, but, y'know. When all you work with is women all day every day – things happen. With the best will in the world you couldn't stop it, and anyway, who'd want to.

This bint though, this girl. Rachel. Type you know you could hurt. Type to lose her heart. 'Rachel,' I've said, 'these things are biological. It's nature, that's all. Procreation. A sperm meets an eggule and makes a zeitgeist. Don't make it something it isn't. Don't get yourself hurt.' But you know how it is. I've said it lots of times before with the best of intentions, but if a girl sets her heart on you. Well . . . We're all men of the world.

I thought we could keep it to just a passing friendship on the way out from work. But she kept stopping me, for one reason or another. I knew what it meant, but I didn't tell anyone.

Except Kevin and Scott and Daniel and Jack. And I told them separately and I told them not to tell anyone else.

For one reason or another she'd want me to walk her back to her house, to carry things or give her directions because she'd forgot where she lived. I usually stopped short of going in. It seemed the decent thing to do. Don't ask me why. It's foolish I know, but I suppose I'm kind of old-fashioned that way.

Then she invited me for a meal. I couldn't not go. It's a nice house. A big house. I could see they'd lots of money and that it embarrassed them. I'm atune to those kind of things. 'Listen,' I said to her parents, 'don't let it bother you. It doesn't mean anything to me. "Consider the chillies, they reap not neither do they sow." ' That seemed to make things go a bit easier. Up till then I think they thought they'd someone on their hands who wouldn't know what cutlery to use. I think they were pleasantly surprised. More. I think they thought I was good for their daughter.

I suppose in a way I am good for her. Someone had to be the first and it's better it's someone nice. Someone who knows what they're doing. It was good the way it worked out. I met her the day after dinner at hers. She caught me up in the cloakroom just as I was leaving. She was upset and I put my arm around her. One thing led to another. You know how it is. And you know how special it is for a girl the first time. I tried to make it as nice as I could for her. It was. She told me so afterwards. I didn't say much. I don't tend to talk much about these things. I didn't tell anyone.

Except Kevin and Scott and Daniel and Jack and I told them separately and I told them not to tell anyone else.

3 4

'You bastard! How could you?'

'What?'

'It's all over the men's toilet walls.'

'How do you know?'

'Robert told me.'

'Cunt. How does he know?'

'Because he watched Kevin and Scott and Daniel and Jack write it. And what I want to know is, how the fuck do they know?'

'How should I know?'

'Don't plead ignorance with me. You know why makeshift macho bastards like you cum so quickly?'

'Why?'

'So they can run out and tell their friends.'

I froze him out for a week, even though I kept wanting to do it all again. When I went to the toilet I never used the end booth, out of a sense of nostalgia. I didn't stop talking to him completely, I just confined myself to business. He came near me on every pretext. Even through my anger I found something endearing in him, penitent, inarticulate, hoping to penetrate my good graces, or me, just by the act of being ubiquitous. I kept up the act for spite and made sure it never affected the supply of components to the ladies on bonus. I was chastened by Morag:

'Give the boy a break. You went out for a fuck and you got one. You used him as a mobile prick. What do you expect?'

'He told all his friends.'

'You told me.'

'That's different. I didn't tell everyone else.'

'I did.'

'Oh . . .!'

'You can lose your temper with me if you want. You can lose your temper with everyone who knows, or who's talked about it. That wouldn't leave you with much company around here. In a place this size did you really expect everyone else not to know?'

'I don't know what I expected. Becoming common currency like that sort of debases it.'

'And where did this celestial act take place?'

I didn't answer.

'In a bog, that's where. You go for a fuck in a toilet out of curiosity. What of it? Do you think you're royalty? How much do you think everyone else cares? You were a three second exchange over a Jaffa cake. "Drew and Rachel. Did you hear? No? In the toilet after work." And then we got on to the bingo. Do you want us to turn the cubicle into a fucking shrine?'

I didn't know what I wanted. I just knew I wanted it somehow to be different. Underneath it all I thought I was different. Better. I forgave him of course. I forgave him on every imaginable occasion, at every convenient opportunity, in any convenient locality and in lots of inconvenient positions. He'd done his reading since that first encounter. I began to sense his moods and read the nuances. His parents never went away, and if they had, there were any number of brothers and sisters around the house all the time.

I was invited round to his house only once. It was like living in a corridor. His family were fractious and seemed to be coming and going all the time, lots of them. There seemed to be a number of on-going arguments that they took up whenever enough of them were present to make it worth their while. The night involved eating a makeshift meal in flux as people came and went. Halfway through the night his parents went out. We were left sitting on the settee with the plates on our laps in front of a blaring television. An elder brother and two sisters sat with us also. He looked at me apologetically and I could sense his embarrassment as he went through comparisons, or imagined I did. He suggested we go for a walk. If he had had Morag for company he wouldn't have extended the same invitation. For the first time it occurred to me I might be doing him more harm than good.

My parents went away to the Algarve for their time-honoured ritual. We spent a glorious fortnight in their house. We had baths together a lot and drank lots of father's wine. We used their bed and their bathroom and fucked frenziedly on the stairs, the kitchen table, among the ferns in the conservatory, sweating into one another as the plants flourished. We desecrated every room and every surface. We smeared each other with everything edible we could find in the kitchen. Sometimes I thought of my parents and their clinical pairing as I took him inside me and rocked on his cock, the tail wagging the dog.

Everyone's bonus suffered. I spent my days in a wide-eyed torpor waiting for the night. I could see him feeling the same way. The reprimands didn't matter to either of us. We had the same sense of lightness, of unreality. We became more frantic as the fortnight came to a close. We retreated, fucking room by room as I tidied up in the wake of our desecration. The bathroom was last. I only realised how far things had gone when he came in while I sat on the bowl, knelt in front of me and kissed me while I pissed. I hadn't ever envisaged anything like that; it wasn't in the least embarrassing and didn't seem strange.

When I'd finished he handed me a square of toilet paper, and when I'd cleaned myself he pulled the handle for me. I could feel the cold water flush an inch from my bum. I reached for my tights, the elasticated band drawing my ankles together. He stopped my hand and said:

'Rachel. I love you.'

I was glad there was nowhere left to fuck and that they were coming back tomorrow. I looked down at my ankles clamped together and tried to concentrate on my actions as I could feel him desperately read my face for some sign of reciprocity.

3 5

I didn't save very much money. I don't know if I even learned that much. I matriculated among a bunch of virgins which gave me a temporary sense of being pleasantly world-weary. The ladies in the factory gave me a beautiful send-off, gave me more than I deserved and took me out to places I'd never been before and got me gloriously drunk.

The conversations with Drew became painful, and petered out with a sense of desperate futility on his side. Besides sex we didn't have much going for us as a couple. I had taken that as being read all along. He hadn't. He made some heroic attempts at being interesting and began to manufacture conversations as a pretext for throwing in the esoteric facts he had memorised the night before in the public library. I think he thought that that comprised intelligence. He once told me that George Sand was really a woman who published under a pseudoplume. I can't begin to describe how much this depressed me. He became hoarse with desperation and I couldn't look at him when he began to talk about South American lung fish or the Copernican revolution. And he was always brought back with a note of jarring authenticity as he lapsed into the kind of thing he'd been talking about most of his life.

I left without the financial independence I naively thought

a summer could afford. Agnes gave me my valedictory speech
when, in front of the other ladies, she said: 'You're all right.'

Drew made himself scarce on my last day. I was glad for
both of us. Even though I knew it was coming to an end I
couldn't have stood continuing to work there if he had left,
and now he was going to have to stay while I went on to
bigger and better things. Morag told me he never said anything
about the fortnight we had spent in my parents' house. To
smother talk of antics like those in a situation like his was the
greatest compliment he could have paid.

He wasn't loitering in the cloakroom as I picked up my
coat for the last time. Out of nostalgia I took one last look at
our cubicle and found a single rose waiting for me on the
cistern.

I heard he left shortly after I did and became some kind of
itinerant. I took the precautions. I'd known enough to ensure
I wasn't impregnated. He hadn't.

The day I left my parents to go to the university accommodation I butchered my hair with a pair of kitchen scissors
and put on a pair of working-men's boots, and with a sense
of militant self-desecration, marched into the future.

3 6

Continually arriving late, I sat up back of the lecture theatre.
Within a fortnight I'd already begun to view a nine o'clock
start as onerous. So much for the fresh air Presbyterianism of
schooldays. The lecturer spoke so quietly I had to strain to
listen. I was also keeping late nights. I was drunk on the
freedom and the bonhomie. I'd met some boys. They didn't
appear at all like Drew. My flatmate, Gorjeit, invited them
round. We burned joss sticks and talked to the early hours
about Art. At least the boys did. Martin did. The fact that he
didn't know anything about the subject he was expatiating
on didn't deter him. It took me years to realise this.

I don't know where Gorjeit's predecessors came from. She spoke with a Glaswegian accent. She was small, very small, fragile and dark and exquisite. Her eyes were large and dark and receptive. She looked like the last of a species which only came out at night. She was nervous and exceptionally sensitive.

'I think Martin likes you.' It took her three drinks to say to me.

'I think Martin's young. I think Martin likes Martin.'

But Martin was in my English class and after two weeks of hearing distinctions of hamartia and hubris and talk of the democratisation of tragedy versus the classical canon drift up through my reverie from the podium below, it was Martin who offered to lend me his lecture notes in preparation for the first class exam.

'I think I've got the gist of it,' I said. I was confident in my abilities.

'Yes. Of course. I sometimes think they say everything they have to in lectures in the first ten minutes. The rest is crap to fill up the hour. There's more lecture time available than there are worthwhile lectures to occupy it.'

'It's not only true of lectures,' I said.

'You're always late in the mornings.'

'Is this a lecture?'

'A cautionary tale. I was just thinking that if you missed the first ten minutes you missed the best part. It might be helpful if you looked over the notes I've made.'

'Thanks all the same. No, really. I can't depend on the lecture notes to get me through an exam. I've always done the background myself.'

'Fair enough.'

It was like that at first with Martin. We were both nervous of one another and liked one another and jockeyed for position. One good thing about being in his company was picking up his rigour of thought. That wasn't all that rubbed off. So, for as long as he was there, did his manner of speech. He spoke in perfect prose. And he was funny. All of his sentences had a beginning, a middle and an end. He could have been punctuated. When he was with us there were none of the painful tailings-off we lapsed into when he left. Some of us were funny and some of us were articulate, but only he could keep all the balls in the air at the same time.

When I went to examination halls for the first exam I came away with the vague feeling something had gone wrong. The results were posted outside the department a week later in order of performance. After that day I learned a consolatory technique: start from the bottom and work your way up, not the other way around. The longer you don't encounter your name the more optimistic things become. I was stupid enough to place my finger at the top of the list and begin to run down. That way my ranking could be seen at a hundred feet and so could the consternation on my face. My first thought was that this must be a clerical mistake. Was there anyone else called Rachel Carey? When I'd convinced myself there wasn't, I began to look for names of people I knew. It's petty that happiness is dependent on comparison. I didn't mind so much being bettered by people I didn't know. I looked for Martin. I found him. I realised I'd been a big fish in a very small pond. I asked Gorjeit not to ask him round for a while.

He turned up allegedly to give Gorjeit back a book. His hair was as dark as Gorjeit's and his skin as white as mine. He was small and handsome. On paper they'd make a nice couple. And she was keen on him.

'She's not in,' I said. He was on the doorstep brandishing her book.

'I know.'

This threw me. 'You'd better come in.' Once he was in I realised there was no reason for him to be there at all. I could have taken the book off him on the doorstep. At a loss, I headed to the kitchen to make the obligatory coffee. He looked inquisitively around. I searched for him with the two steaming mugs. He was standing in the spare room.

'When does the third girl arrive?'

'Next week, supposedly. She's from Malawi.'

'Which room is yours?'

I nodded my head. He walked in uninvited. I followed him with the mugs. He stood on my rug, next to my bed, looking around, taking inventory. He said to himself, or to me: 'Unframed Pre-Raphaelite prints, Warhol's Marilyn Monroe, some fashionable teen-angst rocker, old joss sticks, potpourri, amphora pot, dirty tights, books, notes, unmade bed.'

'Here's your coffee.'

'Self-consciously a student bedroom.'

'Gorjeit's not in.'

'You already said that.'

'Gorjeit likes you.'

'I know.'

'Did you come here to gloat?'

'I came here to have sex with you.'

'You've got a nerve.' He had more to recommend him than the flow of his balanced sentences. He had a nice physique, with the musculature of his torso hanging easily from the cross-spar of his shoulders. The coffee went cold.

It was beautiful, as long as it lasted, and different from Drew. But as soon as the pleasure was over I began to feel stabs of remorse I couldn't explain to myself. I sat up and wrapped the duvet half round me. That left him exposed, lying torpid on his front. The cleft of his spine was so deep it cast a shadow that ran from his shoulder blades to the base of his spine, resuming again with the notch of his buttocks. He was tousled, with his head half turned, half his face buried in the pillow. He hadn't shaved for a couple of days and I ran my fingers lightly over the stubble. He also looked beautiful. I felt worse. If I had smoked cigarettes I'd have smoked one then. It seemed the kind of decadent gesture a girl with poise would have carried out. I wanted to feel blasé, as if having sex in the afternoon with a passing acquaintance was the kind of thing I did without thinking about.

He looked up. He reached over and began stroking the inside of my thigh.

'What, again?' I said. He rolled over.

'Not just yet.'

'No. I can see that.'

'Your skin is wonderful,' he said.

'I was just thinking the same thing about you.'

'Well,' he said, rolling again on to his front and kissing my thighs, 'two blemishless people in a bedroom of Eden. We can kid on they never ate the apple.'

'I don't think it would be so much fun if it wasn't naughty.'

' "Naughty". Are you a public school girl?'

'You wouldn't think it, looking at us now.'

'Why? Don't public school girls fuck? Where do all the public school descendants come from? Osmosis?' He parted my legs with his hands.

'Gorjeit likes you,' I said.

'You said that already. We haven't plighted our troth you know. She won't commit suttee and throw herself on my funeral pyre. I only met her a week before I met you. The sum of our acquaintance probably amounts to three coffees and two joss sticks. You've spent a lot more time in her company than I have.' He had reached my vulva with his fingers. 'I like you.'

'Obviously.' I drew the duvet tighter round my chest. Above the waistline I was all remorse. Down there I was all his.

'Anyway, you can't legislate for who comes to like whom.'

'It's just like you to use a word like "legislate" when you've got your fingers in my vagina.'

'I know. Aren't I "naughty".'

'Bastard.' I thought: I'm becoming a woman of the world.

'I didn't go to public school, but then, at a time like this, does it really matter? "When Adam delved and Eve span, where was then the gentleman?" Here's to the apple. Talking about eating forbidden fruit . . .'

He slid his thumb to the base of my anus and parted the lips of my vagina with two fingers of the same hand. It was very practised. I saw his head bend till it submerged beneath the duvet and felt his tongue slide the length of the cleft.

'Oh fuck,' I said. The tongue momentarily retracted. His voice came out muffled from between my legs.

'You can still borrow my notes if you like.'

3 7

I borrowed his notes. I didn't sit with him because we saw one another often enough at other times. Gorjeit talked about him intermittently and I didn't have the courage to tell her that we were an item. After a fortnight, and three more frenzied afternoons, I began to doubt whether or not we were an item. When it suited us, we slept together. We agreed not to sleep with anyone else or, if we did, to tell the other. I liked his conversation. I began to notice his looks less than the animation of his face. It was lit from behind with intelligence. He was never publicly demonstrative or put his hands on me in company. We argued, we debated, we locked horns in and out of bed, and within the easy constraints of this sexual fondness which would have appalled my mother, I found, for the first time in my life, a kind of happiness.

My concession to study was a place near the front of the lecture hall. Even when late, I was adamant I would sit there. I'd turn up late and tousled and clatter down my books. When Gorjeit was away for a week Martin stayed over and I turned up consistently late five days running. Martin stayed in bed: it was my turn to take the notes. It's an old lecture hall panelled in fumed oak and with hard benches. The steps are steep and old, the acoustics unforgiving. My entrances began to have a marked effect on Dr Foster. Once I'd been there three minutes his delivery began to falter. After class I'd buy croissants and hurry back to the flat to meet Martin. I'd heat them with coffee and get melted butter smears and coffee stains on my sheet. Martin was quite blasé about this too.

'It's all organic,' he said, brushing the crumbs to my side of the bed. I told him about Dr Foster.

'Perhaps he's just got a good sense of smell.'

'What's that got to do with anything?'

'You go in there first thing after a night here still radiating pheromones. You stink of sex. So do I and I can smell you from here.'

He was exaggerating. I had my clothes on.

'At least I'm dressed.'

'That's another thing I wanted to talk to you about.'

'But I'm dressed.'

'I'll bet you wind up one of those middle-class housewives who won't have a fuck in case it smudges their mascara.'

'I'm going to the library.' He made a lunge. 'It's your turn for the dishes,' I said, closing the door.

I'd never worked less in my life, but I did enough at least to appease the markers. I've always had an instinctive gift with exams, of giving the impression I know more than I do. It's not something I should be proud of, but it's always got me by. I received good marks and comments that I should learn to marshal my ideas better, ideas that I didn't have. Gorjeit came to know about Martin and me, it was impossible not to. We all ate at the same cafés and had the same friends. Both of us knew the other knew and both of us skated round the subject. We'd suppressed the topic so long it adopted a weight of silence. Gorjeit broke the taboo unexpectedly.

'This is silly. Have him round to dinner and I'll cook for you both.' She was standing in the kitchen, the sink looking disproportionately high against her small body. I leaned down and kissed her.

I read widely. Most of it had nothing to do with the curriculum. There was such a frequent flux of people through the flat that I learned to concentrate anywhere. I read while living in a corridor. I picked up bits and bobs anywhere and, for the first time in my life, began to think I was clever. Martin told me I was 'squandering my time in eclecticism', a very Martin-type phrase. Our flatmate from Malawi failed to materialise, and through some administrative error we managed to get the flat to the two of us for the remainder of the academic year. The spare room was seldom vacant with the number of people we had coming and going. Gorjeit, an aspirant physicist, took up with a sombre mathematician. They would sit at all hours in silent telepathy, barely touching, a curious bookend to the daemonic romps of Martin and me. I think I was their idea of a bohemian because I went to see plays by Tom Stoppard and argued about existentialism till the early hours with Martin between fucking. Gorjeit introduced me to her beloved. He was so boring I gave him the credit for existence on a mathematical plane beyond my ken till I found out he was just dull, in every sense of the word. I told Martin.

'That's what education is,' he said. 'A continuous process of debunking. You learn to see through the veneer. I'm just dreading you finding me out. I've only got three ideas and I told you them all the first day.'

Life became a series of pleasant tangents. I joined a film society and watched incomprehensible foreign films with opaque subtitles and drank cheap dry wine in the cinema out of polystyrene cups. I emerged in the daylight with my friends drunk in the early afternoon. Martin told me I was being self-consciously 'naughty'.

'Best have a bit of a "lark",' he said, using raised forefingers to denote the inverted commas as he had an annoying habit of doing while pretending to be pompous, 'before you start prowling the Young Conservative Club for a prospective spouse.'

'Fuck off!'

'I hope you don't use that kind of language in front of Tarquin and Philippa at the mixed doubles.'

The first term ended in a series of premature Christmas celebrations. Then everyone went their separate ways. I saw Gorjeit off from Princes Street on the train. We were only a month and fifty miles apart but I felt like bursting into tears for some obscure reason. I had never felt this way when parting from my school friends. Martin would have some trenchant and cruel psychological observation at my expense ready if I told him so. I didn't. I went back to the flat and called up lots of people, all of whom had already left for the break. I hung around for two days, bought frugal presents for my parents, nothing for myself, and window shopped for the things I couldn't afford. I hoped mother would keep the receipts of her presents for me so I could change the things I didn't want for those I did. I read more books, missed Gorjeit and Martin, both for different reasons (I don't know who most), and felt the weight of a phone that refused to ring.

On the third day I was walking in Rose Street and I'm sure for an instant I saw Drew. I was aware someone was watching me in the throng and by the time I'd located the eyes they had withdrawn into the dark recess of the pub they'd emerged from. He must have seen me coming, watched me pass and slid back rather than acknowledge me. I didn't blame him and felt ashamed my actions had given rise to such pained behaviour in another person. The time on my hands gave me too much opportunity for self-assessment. At the risk of cross-examination for all my months of neglect, I fled home.

3 8

Martin visited in the dog days between Christmas and Hogmanay. His family wasn't rich. He said the amount of food we had in our house was obscene. He brought the kind of critical scrutiny I didn't mind levelling at my parents but resented having directed at them by others. Father showed him his collection of decanters ranked in their tantalus. Martin accepted a drink and toasted Greek gods and the bourgeoisie. He obliquely ridiculed mother for her affluent domesticity. When she happened to mention the kind of books she liked he said, 'Well, having as much time as you have, you would like them, wouldn't you.' It wasn't a question. He told me father was a part-time dilettante and mother a step away from *Readers' Digest*. 'Does she improve her word power for the Presbyterian coffee mornings?' And later, after he questioned her about her 'charitable' activities: 'There seems to be a crippling lack of free will on the part of all these unfortunates who have your mother's charity inflicted on them.'

It was a discordant week. They were sensitive enough to notice and felt somehow impotent in the face of someone who disparaged them for the bric-à-brac they had surrounded themselves with.

Consciously or not, I think they had collected the trappings of wealth to give themselves some social altitude and now felt displaced at being sneered at by someone they thought themselves entitled to look down upon and who had somehow upstaged them by applying rules they had never heard of. And it wasn't as if they could attribute Martin's attitude solely to envy. He didn't covet anything. And he was cleverer than they were. And we all knew it. I think father thought longingly of Drew's malapropisms.

We left the day before Hogmanay. He shook father's hand and asked my mother not to feel reticent if she felt like passing on any crochet tips. My parents stood together on the doorstep, arms linked, looking perplexedly at their daughter with the shorn hair methodically throwing off everything they had striven for. They looked suddenly older. I was glad to go.

Martin's parents lived in a small house, inhabited for New Year by themselves, Martin, his two brothers and three sisters and their partners if they had any. His brothers and sisters were of various ages. Two still stayed at home. Martin was third oldest. There was a pervading aura of Irish Catholicism. Despite the crush and the abundance of drink, unmarried couples slept separately. I'd expected something different of this iconoclast. At university, in my parents' house, wherever, he hadn't scrupled to ridicule anything and bring his caustic cynicism to bear. Here, confronted by the gentle reprimands of his parents, he would inexplicably blush. He kept his irreverence to himself.

'You're a fraud,' I said.

'I know. I'm actually a Jesuit priest in disguise, a fifth-columnist among all the nihilists at university. The Vatican pay me by the convert.'

'You're being glib, but you're a fraud all the same.'

'I know. Do you hate it?'

'No. When I see you talk to your mother I like it very much. Especially when you blush.'

'I don't blush. I suffer from localised and very sudden rashes.'

We left two days later. Sitting by his side on the upper deck of the bus crossing the South Bridge, I watched him exhaling in relief. I realised then how much of him was bravado and that he spent more effort than anyone else I had known in disguising effort itself. The defences were temporarily down and I didn't like him any less as he had feared.

'Thank God that's over,' he said, taking great gulps of air. 'Let's go back to being us.'

'What's "us"?'

'You've developed a very disconcerting habit of quoting people.'

'I got it from you.'

'I know.'

'What's "us"?' I repeated.

'Well, I don't know about you but I'm a dirty bastard. There's no one in my flat yet. Let's go back to mine and shag till term starts.'

'Is that all we've got going for us?'

'Depends if you're talking about us or "us".'

'Bastard.'

'You know you really ought to do something about that vocabulary of yours. What did they teach you at that school? What did your parents pay all that money for? I grew up on a council estate and you're the one who finishes conversations with "fuck you" and "bastard" and all those eloquent disclaimers.'

'You were nice for about three days there.'

'And now I'm me again.'

'Yes.'

'And we can get back to where we left off. I think I was holding your tits.'

'*Is* this all we've got going for us?'

'No. Not all. I'm really clever and you're not bad. We've got lots of the same interests that require intelligence. But right now I'm not really interested in your brain.'

'Most of me that doesn't meet at the top of my legs is pretty redundant to you, isn't it?'

'Depends what you mean by "pretty".'

I nearly said 'Fuck you!' Neither of us spoke for some time.

'Your stop?' he said. If I wasn't going with him this was my stop. 'You don't have to come with me if you don't want to. I can always find someone else who needs a loan of notes.'

I stood. I hadn't intended a gesture but once I was on my feet there was no going back. To concede was ignominious and not to was to allow the situation to continue of its own momentum. I walked deliberately forward and down the metal stairs. I listened for the noise of his feet behind me. After all, my flat was empty too. The doors closed and the bus moved off. I could see him sitting on the top deck, the back of his head to me as he stared resolutely away. A caprice had gone further than both of us intended.

The snow was falling, turning into a wet diagonal sleet. Umbrellas bent in unison at the cutting gusts from the Forth.

3 9

There were the initial two weeks of melodrama that broken romances go through at that age, where we deliberately went to the places we knew the other would be. I took succour in pointedly ignoring him. I don't know if he did me. Despite the fact that she wasn't in any of the classes Martin and I both attended, I gave Gorjeit his notes to return to him. I only found out later how unfair my action was: her mathematician had begun to bore her and she still looked for Martin in any company. But that kind of immature grief is selfish and I wallowed in the wreckage of our romance, confident we could pick up where we left off whenever we had each satisfied our self-respect.

After another month I began to grow less sure. I missed him. I missed him in my bed but mostly I missed him for other things. I missed his reproaches for my sloppy way of thinking and speaking. I missed his humour. There were so many of us in the group that the lack of a partner wasn't the social inconvenience it would become in later life. If my mother didn't have my father for a partner her evening social life would die. It wasn't like that. But we knew many of the same people and went to lots of the same places. We were constrained by how much we could afford, Martin more than me, and it was inevitable we would meet.

He came up to me in the bar of the film society after a double feature. We'd gone separately with separate friends and now stood hovering around the bar in one nebulous group, buying drinks in ones and twos since no one could afford a round. I was standing with Gorjeit and her mathematician, witnessing another romance in its death throes and being silently miserable. When Martin approached, Gorjeit tactfully guided her boyfriend to a discreet distance. I had been mulling over tactics for this moment for a week and had decided upon a certain initial hauteur which would diminish by instalments in the face of his contrition. He had been brought up as a Catholic: he told me no matter how hard you try to renege you can never escape the vestige of a Catholic education; contrition informed his values. I had imagined our reconciliation in graphic detail. My big empty bed was within walking distance. I thought of him and me in it, talking in whispers in the aftermath the way we used to. It would be difficult to maintain my composure for any length of time.

He stood in front of me and blushed the way he had in front of his mother. My heart grew hot. He hesitated before he spoke.

'I missed you!' I blurted out. 'I really missed you . . .'

'I know. That sounded blasé, the way I hadn't intended. I think we missed each other. Look, this contriving to avoid one another — it embarrasses me. This isn't a big place and we know lots of the same people. Even if we don't arrange to we're going to meet unless one of us goes into hibernation.'

'I know.'

'I've been rude before and I don't want to be rude now.'

'That's nice. I don't want to swear either.'

'Just because it didn't work doesn't mean we can't be sociable to one another.'

'Of course not.' I tried hard to immobilise my face. He nodded, still blushing. As with my father I thought for a moment he was going to shake my hand. He nodded again and half turned. I stopped him with a stupid remark: 'Do you have someone else?'

'No.'

I was hoping he would ask me the same question, as if our mutual availability somehow predestined our reconciliation. He didn't. He returned to his friends. Gorjeit came back. With one look at my frozen face she unloaded her mathematician, disappeared for a moment and returned holding both our coats.

'I don't think it's a good idea for you to drink any more.'

'No,' I said.

'I'm finished, are you?'

'Oh yes.'

'Come on then.'

She helped me on with my coat and said my goodbyes. When we were in the street she linked her arm in mine. We must have looked incongruous: me, tall, slender, Aryan; she small and dark. I was not only glad of her company, I felt as if I couldn't have walked home without her. It's a journey I had made dozens of times previously and would make dozens of times again, but that evening is the one evening I remember with startling clarity. It was a crisp February night. The stars were clear. When we left the thoroughfares our footfalls sounded heavy in the wide streets. One of the roads was cobbled and I imagined sparks rising up in the cold air from horseshoes before the car had invaded. I stopped.

'You can imagine, can't you, the sound of the heavy Clydesdales clopping up these streets. More comforting than the way things are now. Fewer and fewer things are organic.'

'I never really gave it much thought.'

'And the plume of their breath in the night air from their nostrils, hanging for a moment in front of their faces before it disperses.'

'I'll make us some coffee.'

'The aggregate of suffering presses down on this planet. It accumulates, like strata. Tiny griefs like amoeba petrified in amber.'

'Please, Rachel. Please . . .' She began to guide us forward.

We got there, through the amber air, our footsteps ringing like Clydesdales in the tenement close. She took off my coat and made us coffee. She sat beside me, sipping, and took my hand, tolerating the silence.

4 0

There's a blurred period for a while, a time of indistinct moroseness. I hadn't realised till then how much I cared for him. I seemed to stumble for a long time, not just figuratively. I became clumsy where previously I had been deft. Gorjeit watched me crash around the flat, chipping her precious things she couldn't afford to replace. She didn't once complain. Her patience was exemplary, greater than mine. I've gone through and witnessed histrionics in others since and I know this wasn't them. I honestly think at the time I would rather he were dead than suffer the indignity of seeing him and knowing he wasn't mine. I felt a sense of loss I had nothing to compare with. I realise now, with the advantage of retrospect, that I'd stumbled with ease across the kind of match most people don't achieve most of their life, no matter how hard they look. The conscious search is counter-productive. That's another thing it took me a while to learn.

I did what most people do: I took refuge in other people.

I went through several boys, slept with a couple of them too. They were astute enough to recognise in me the limit of what I wanted, or was prepared to give, and tailored their attentions to suit. Perhaps I even got myself a reputation. One of them was quite wonderful to fuck with, which I did at every available opportunity and venue. He had no conversation. I became addicted to the climactic moments because they became my few times of complete forgetfulness. I don't think it was the same for any of them. I think they just unburdened themselves in me as a convenient vehicle. I stopped when Gorjeit came in one morning. Whoever I had been with the previous evening had left. The bedclothes were strewn. She handed me some tea she had made and looked obliquely at the bed, not wishing to appear too obvious.

'I saw you last night,' she said. She was facing away from me. 'You left your door open. Did you do it on purpose?'

'No. Does it upset you?'

'Yes.'

'I'll make sure it's closed next time.'

'That doesn't matter. It only matters that you don't care. You don't care, do you?'

'No.'

'They're not even nice, some of the boys you go with now.'

'I know.'

'They only want to use you.'

'I know.'

'I saw you. Only for a moment. I couldn't help it.'

'It's all right.'

'No. It isn't. He was penetrating you. Your eyes were glazed. It was almost as if you didn't know what was happening to you. And I thought – she's just a penis.'

She started to cry.

I don't remember much of the remainder of the year. I spent lots of time with Gorjeit and some of her friends. I kept up with the girls of my acquaintance. I couldn't help keeping tabs on Martin despite myself and took no pleasure whatsoever in learning that he hadn't found anyone else. If he had I might have been more wretched, if that were possible. I knew he knew about the other boys I'd been out with and fucked. I thought that might assuage something but it didn't. I scraped an entry into my second year and went fruit-picking in Kent for the summer.

I came back thinking that there is something more mellow about the English. And it's not just their climate. The scenery is less grand. It undulates. Or perhaps it was just a therapeutic break, having spent too long walking the same paths and meeting the same people. It was a relief to my frayed nerves to know no one and be sure the next corner didn't conceal Martin, and that he wouldn't crop up in the next conversation, or mention of him be conspicuously excluded for my benefit. We were paid a pittance plus accommodation, but the food was good and we had a sense of camaraderie. I wanted to fancy some of the boys but just didn't. I drank most of my wages, spent two months of pleasant thoughtlessness and stopped a month before term with almost nothing. I wasn't above asking my parents for more and spent four weeks inter-railing with Gorjeit.

We returned together and got the flat again, which we had angled for. By coincidence we were allocated the same flat-mate. This time we were told the girl from Malawi was sure to materialise. She did.

Her name was Stephen and he came from County Cork.

'I'm your new flat-mate.'

'The new flat-mate's a girl.'

'Nobody's perfect.'

'And she's from Malawi.'

'Her name's unpronounceable. It won't fit on the nameplate.'

'We don't have a nameplate.'

'That's all right. I brought my own.' And he had. 'I'll let both of you put your names on it, if you want. You can even go first. Sort it out among yourselves. I'm not fussy.'

He had met her on the steps of the university accommodation office on her way gracefully to decline the offer of our room since she had found an alternative with another girl from her country. He steered her in the direction of a café, reduced her almost to tears with tales of his destitution, stuck her with the bill and had her gratefully conspire in the fraud. She collected the keys, handed them to him and saw us once a month afterwards with her flashing smile when she turned up to collect the rent she owed on his behalf. She put up with his dilatory payments (despite being badgered for the money herself), his excuses, his drunkenness and his petty larcenies, because she was captivated by the bursting personality of a penniless alcoholic who masqueraded as a writer. So was I. Even Gorjeit wasn't impervious.

He was always working on some dog-eared script he said was 'cooking'. That was his metaphor for sloth. He was a mature student, a misnomer in his case. He was forty. He had got in by the skin of his teeth and intended continuing in the same way. In the first three hours Gorjeit saw him for the charming parasite he was. I didn't. I bought him the things I could afford and fell into a routine of leaving him in the lounge most mornings poring over the morning papers with the can I had already fetched him from the fridge. Perhaps it's inevitable that talent will out. I don't know if he had any. The things he read me were, I think, deliberately fragmentary and too dislocated to pass an opinion on. I know I never got a foothold; I don't know yet if he ever did. If he had I presume I would have heard. He had many saving graces, but the most important, and it was important, was that he cared for people. He cared for them more, I think, than he cared for himself, and he was as unstinting in extending hospitality as he was ready to accept it. He would give you whatever he had, though he never had much.

I attended lectures regularly. I turned up on time and handed in my essays promptly. I gained respectable marks. I ensured I wasn't included in the same tutorial group as Martin who, I heard, had turned quite gloomy.

Initially I sat at the back. The tutor's voice was so soft I was obliged to come nearer the front. His baldness became more apparent the nearer the front I got. The obvious attempts at camouflage emphasised his lack of hair. He grew one side long, combing the parallel lines across the exposed crown. No one was fooled. He looked like a young old man. I later found out he was an old young man. At our initial meetings I treated him with the kind of deference which assumes a huge age discrepancy and which he must have found insulting. After a while I ceased to notice how old he was. Perhaps I orientated myself towards him because he was so unlike Martin. I'm not capable of the kind of dispassionate self-assessment that might answer my questions.

His name was Dr Hawking. Julien. An androgynous name, Dr Julien Hawking. He had led the kind of sequestered academic life I thought true only of Oxbridge dons of the Edwardian era. He had lived with his mother till he had gone to university, University College London I think, and paid diligent weekend visits home while he lived a quiet undergraduate routine from Monday to Friday. And then he had come up here to lecture, and stayed. His routine had altered little. He compensated for his absence from home by assiduously wrapping parcels of Arran mustard, Kirriemuir gingerbread and any Scottish provisions not easily obtainable down south and sending them to his mother with whimsical little notes to cover the vacuousness of his existence. He had a sister, older than he was, a younger version of the mother herself. They kept one another intermittent company. I imagined them in their genteel lounge in the Home Counties, passing time in the lengthy afternoons. I have no grounds for these speculations.

I gleaned most of this over a period of time. When he first stood up, an uninspiring figure in his old man's clothes, and told us he was lecturing on Byron, I giggled. I couldn't help it. The incongruity of a hero and sexual renegade, a man of hemispherical infamy and this frowsty bachelor in Donegal tweeds made me laugh. Would Byron have thought Dr Julien Hawking could do him justice? The sound trickled round the

room, eliciting little humorous bursts as it faded. He coloured.
I tried to atone by asking questions at the end, something
seldom done. He answered by addressing a point several feet
above my head. I thought he was angry. I was wrong.

I was assigned him as a tutor. I handed in a reasonable
tutorial paper. We were obliged to read our efforts aloud to
the other few people in the tutorial group. He seemed to be
particularly censorious on mine. I thought he was being vindictive. I was wrong again. The first time I had an individual
tutorial we drank tea and ate biscuits and overran by almost
an hour. I had been there allegedly to discuss the piece I had
submitted and the quality of my work generally. When I was
putting on my coat he handed me the corrected work.

'What mark did you give me?'

'Does it matter?'

'Yes. I need a benchmark of some kind. How did I do?'

'You did well enough. I find marks so hard to give.'

'You're scathing?'

'No. Not at all. I just find it difficult to evaluate someone
else's thoughts, never mind pass judgement on them.'

'Is anyone ever *wrong*?'

'I don't know. I like to think of them as less right.'

'What if they disagree fundamentally with something you
say?'

'Why shouldn't they?'

'I'm not sure I envy you your uncertainty. Somehow I think
if I were in your position I would want to be more sure. Am
I "less right"?'

'No. You are not critical but you are sensitive enough to
feel.'

'And that's enough?'

'I think so.'

'You seem sure enough of that.'

'Yes.'

I thought of Stephen and any sensitivity he might have
beneath the drink. I began to wonder what in his life was so
bad that he sought to elude it by the temporary suicides of

his repeated blind stupors. Gorjeit still told me things Martin
said. I even missed his merciless pontificating. He had talked
to her about Stephen. He had said that he liked Stephen but
that Bohemia shelters lots of charlatans. He said the 'isms'
opened the floodgates for anyone without talent to claim a
vocation. He said 'don't mistake obscurity for credentials,
or sensitivity for creativity.' The sudden thought of Stephen
saddened me. He couldn't create and I don't think he possessed
the powers of discrimination to tell what was good from what
wasn't in others' work. On my way out I stopped.

'Dr Hawking?'

'Julien,' he corrected.

'Do you ever try and create anything? To write?'

'I know enough not to try.' And as I turned to go he said,
half to himself: 'To bring anything into compass is to bring it
to a personal level, to your own scale, whatever that is. Whatever I touch, I belittle.'

I saw quite a lot of him. I had tea with him in his frugal
little flat. 'You can't be hard up,' I said. 'What you want to do
is spend a little. Don't stint yourself. You're a long time dead.'

There was a wistfulness about him that made any of my
troubles shrink in comparison because, with him, it seemed
almost congenital. He seemed always to be looking for something that didn't exist in any sufficient quantity at all. I felt
obliged, in his company, to act with uncharacteristic flamboy-
ance and to colour at least as much of his life that I touched
as I passed through.

'Julien, Martin, Stephen,' I said to Gorjeit. 'Fucking men.'

'Fucking men,' she echoed. I'd never heard her swear, or at
least use 'fucking' as an adjective. I gave her a standing ovation.

'Let's throw a party,' I said.

'Yes. Let's.'

41

When I recounted some of the incident to a colleague of mine he said: 'They say that when Mussolini ran the show the railway timetables were kept to the letter.' After a contrived pause, during which I sat bemused and silent, he went on to add, 'Mind you, Fascism seems an exorbitant price to pay for punctual trains . . .' No further explanation was forthcoming. Perhaps he takes a pride in being whimsical, or imagines himself to be humorously so. I have it from a reliable source, which I'm not prepared to name, that he has a gift of making what is already obscure seem even more opaque. At any rate, I think I was supposed to take from this that there was more to it than a disembodied reference to Italian trains.

He couldn't be expected fully to understand. He wasn't in possession of all the facts. No one is, except me – and Rachel of course. We've never mentioned our reciprocal feelings, so it's hardly surprising that an outsider, denied the privileged access we both enjoy, fails to understand.

Rachel and I have a tacit understanding. The age difference is one reason we don't advertise ourselves and, of course, that kind of gap inevitably means that our social circles are very different. We cannot curtail our respective social lives because of some common prejudice. It's right that she should have her separate social life and I mine. There's no reason why she should be denied the company of people her own age.

She makes full use of this carte-blanche to be with whomsoever she pleases. I've always been rather a home bird and my duties inevitably kept me in anyway. Marking papers occupies more time than you might imagine. In the past I may have been stupidly jealous on one occasion, or two, but such moments were fleeting and, thankfully, uncharacteristic. I no longer listen to ill-informed gossip. The attempts I made to incorporate her into my own small coterie had nothing to do with keeping 'tabs' on Rachel. Her refusal was her prerogative. I found it complimentary to be invited to her party.

I'll admit I was a bit anxious at the prospect of being with all her friends for the evening. I envisaged a 'them and us' situation that might degenerate into a 'them' and me. This wasn't the case. It was a more heterogeneous group than I had imagined. I think they had brought back several people at random from the local pub. There was a drunken Irishman there who seemed nearer my age than theirs.

Perhaps it's not really surprising that the mental image I had had when anticipating the party was so inaccurate. Student days, when I experienced them, were less liberated. That's probably more to do with me than my times. The angry young man was still in vogue when I studied. I was more bookish than most of my contemporaries. I'm not saying that I didn't have a good time — my work bore some fruit — but in view of what I saw that evening, looking back I now regard my undergraduate days as abstemious. Postgraduate life was just an extension of that. I'd fallen into habits: women seemed to remain in purdah and I've never been able to drink.

I mixed easily that evening. If anything I felt slightly bizarre because of my very ordinariness. Not that anyone else would have noticed. It's a modest ambition to remain anonymous and I'm sure I succeeded. I'm sure no one noticed me besides those I introduced myself to, and those Rachel brought across.

She was a marvellous hostess. She seemed to be everywhere at the same time, solicitous to everyone. There didn't seem to be anyone she didn't try to spend some time with. Naturally, I'd have preferred to have been with her more, the atmosphere being as relaxed as it was I'd have liked to have been more publicly demonstrative of my feelings than normal, but it's unreasonable to monopolise the time of a hostess. And she's so vivacious. I assumed she was more that way when she was with me but it appears to be her natural state. Always laughing, always touching. She's not guilty of that stupid Anglo-Saxon reticence that I'm prey to, of maintaining some silly inviolable body space that impels me to shunt away on a park bench, or in the tube, despite the fact that the other person's two feet away. Rachel has, thankfully, dispensed with such absurd taboos.

The most curious of those I talked to seemed to say the least. Rachel introduced him to me with a generous sweep of the arm that seemed to indicate the whole room and drew the attention of practically everyone in it. She stood there at the head of the coffee table with us on either side, facing one another, for all the world like some silly set piece. I never noticed her leave, only the awkward silence that everyone seemed simultaneously to observe. I seem to remember he broke it, but not what he said. For want of something better to say I gestured to some of the political posters and asked him if he had any. He said no.

The conversation was desultory and made more difficult by the pop music, which sprang to life from time to time and was played at needless volume. In something he said he threw in a reference to Jane Austen which seemed scurrilous and out of context. I subsequently found out he is on the course and doing well, despite his lack of effort. He left early and, as far as I know, for no particular reason. On his way out he asked me if I'd enjoyed the circus. Rachel, ever solicitous, saw him to the door. I wandered over to talk with some other people.

After a while I noticed people partnering off and couples beginning to drift away. Compared to my accommodation the flat was old and huge. I confined myself to the three doors I already knew: lounge, kitchen and bathroom. Eventually I found myself in the kitchen. A couple sitting tête-à-tête on the pine bench whispered to one another as I entered. After a few minutes they got up and left. I thought of finding Rachel. I stared for a few minutes into the punch bowl, which contained a little blood-coloured liquid and the residue of some sliced and pulped fruit. I syphoned off what little I could extract and went to distribute it – to provide a helping hand and look for Rachel at the same time. The lights had been turned low in the lounge and I stumbled over two people lying entwined on the floor. What punch I salvaged went untasted. Several people waved me away and I didn't like to interrupt the couples. The unknown doors I left alone. I couldn't find Rachel, so after a while I went back to the kitchen.

As I say, it's unreasonable to monopolise a hostess and I couldn't expect her to spend every minute with me. I had one last look in order to say goodbye, but still couldn't find her. No doubt a girl like Rachel has a thousand and one things to do. In the hall I found my coat on the floor, supplanted from its peg by a jacket I didn't recognise. I looked round once more, just on the off-chance, before closing the *front door behind me. I'm glad for Rachel's sake that it all went well and that the party was such a success.*

4 2

I caught the tread of dancing feet, I loitered down the moonlit street, and stopped beneath the Harlot's house. I say 'I' because, curiously enough, I had actually received a written invitation. In this sense I think I was unique among the guests. It was the first communication I had received from Rachel in months and it had been scrawled, whether with contrived carelessness or not, on a piece of scrap paper. There was no 'RSVP', no 'And partner', just 'You . . .' I thought I was the one with the cruel streak. I think it was necessary for her little strategy that I turn up alone. I used to think better of her.

I'd been there lots of times before, but even if I hadn't, the place wouldn't have been difficult to find. The stereo was playing so loudly it practically flaked the stucco off the outside of the building. Someone I didn't know answered the intercom when I buzzed from the entrance. It was one of those buildings that look like a Greek wedding cake — but impressive nevertheless. When all's said and done, Rachel has a little money and doesn't know what poor is. She lives in places like this and considers poverty an arithmetical calculation. There is no squalor she wouldn't dabble in and allow her father to bale her out of once the experience has ceased to be novel.

I was buzzed into the lobby and climbed to the first floor of their flat. The main door was unlocked and I walked straight into the hallway. I could feel the bass line of the stereo through the soles of my shoes. I shed my coat and followed the noise. It got hotter and more smoky as I walked into the blare of sound and in the half-dark it took my eyes a moment to adjust. I put down my bag full of cans and a bottle and staked my claim. Then I looked around.

Half of the people I already knew. They were huddled in little groups shouting at one another through the noise. Every time the music temporarily stopped they would continue to shout, then look sheepish, and the noise would resume. I had been half of a mind not to come. Things between Rachel and me had been strained and were only beginning to plane out on an even keel where we could be reconciled to being friends again. I don't know if she had expected more or not, but any chance of being anything other than friends had been ruined when I was forced to witness her silly retributive phase where she slept with as many of my 'friends' as she knew would allow the news to get back to me. But she had taken the trouble to write and it seemed rude not to at least put in an appearance.

There were two effeminate looking young man staring round at everyone in a sneering sort of way, shouting their effeminate nasty little observations in one another's ears. Then there was Rachel, flinging herself with gusto into the role of party animal. She was giving the gladeye to some young man with a blonde on his lap. Whether or not this was expected to elicit some reaction from me, I don't know. When we first started she used to look at me the way she was pretending to look at him. He kept pulling the blonde girl's face up to his, tilting her head sideways when he stuck his lips on hers, glancing past her temple in Rachel's direction. Two can play at that game. Rachel looked at me, feigned surprise, excitement, rapture, the lot, and stood up. Next thing I know the lights are on, the stereo's off and I stand blinking in that fucking awful silence, led by the wrist to one side of the coffee table, facing her other victim on the other. Rachel stands at the head of the table bawling an introduction.

I spotted the other victim on entering the lounge. An Eskimo, beamed from his igloo to the Sistine chapel, couldn't have looked more out of place than that poor bastard. At my first recce I saw him fidgeting feverishly with a stupid bowtie. My second glance caught him patting his bald spot nervously and staring at the carpet as if its weave held the secret of life. He was the most alone person there, as alone as I felt and more alone than the drunken Irish tenant lying prone in a stupor behind the sofa. One girl I had not seen before, good looking enough to daunt any but the most drunken propositioner, stood apart as if asserting the solitude her beauty entitled her to. She even succeeded in making this splendid isolation look fashionable. Him, he just looked sad. He looked like an apology. Poor sad old virgin I thought.

If the outcome had been her intention, then Rachel stage-managed *things beautifully, right down to the positional arrangements: the eternal triangle with her at the apex. She had pulled the sofa and chairs around beforehand in a kind of amphitheatre. She introduced us to one another with a wide sweep of her arm, standing long enough to make her point. I was stupid enough not to understand. I watched her smile at the young man with the blonde, a triumphal little flick of the corners of her mouth that was gone before I'd registered I'd seen it. Then she flounced off somewhere and it was pitch dark for a minute and the thud of the stereo began again.*

My first impulse was to follow her into the kitchen, punch her in the tits and tell her what a middle-class cow she really was and how daddy couldn't foot the bill for the dilapidations this time. Then I looked at him and realised he hadn't even realised. The flare of hatred passed and I immediately felt more sympathy for him than I did anger towards her. And then, seeing how sad and alone she'd made him, more sad for him not knowing while everyone else did, and more alone for that reason too, I felt another burst of anger. This wasn't the episodic irritation I'd felt at her past acts of thoughtlessness but something more enduring, because his being alone and looking stupid seemed to have been part of her contrived arrangement. I wanted to leave right then but felt I couldn't leave him to face it out alone. Not that he knew. I'm not given to sudden acts of philanthropy and it's ironic that he didn't understand that I stayed for his sake. There must have been a complaint, because the stereo went down to a reasonable level, although the half-dark remained.

He remarked on the posters. He even believed them. How sheltered do you have to have been to be that stupid at his age? The people here were Civil Servants, angry young men after five and at weekends. Rebels! They wouldn't recognise a fucking rebel if they met him in the street. The rest? Students! They take a stance — they hand in their essays late! I'd seen enough of them to know and I didn't exempt myself from the general denunciation, although I'd noticed that only the more wealthy students, like Rachel, can afford foibles. The rest are too busy stacking supermarket shelves to buy their textbooks and make ends meet.

He asked me about her. That shows how much he knew. He asked me if I'd met her parents. I explained I'd stayed briefly over

Christmas. Perhaps it occurred to him then that I was one up on the familiarity stakes. Perhaps he saw me as a possible rival. Probably not. He asked me if I liked them. No one who asks a question like that of a stranger really expects a truthful reply. I said I hadn't sufficient in common with either her father or mother to form an opinion. He questioned me. He had the tact of a dinosaur. Perhaps he had lived too long alone. He wanted an exhaustive explanation. He didn't get one. I said I'd been home with her and it was all too much honey for tea at the old Vicarage. 'Jane Austen's got no balls,' I said.

I stood there till we were no longer a point of immediate interest. We stood long enough to prove Rachel's point: the scope of her charms, the catholic nature of her tastes. Then I left.

That poor man looked as if he would be free every night from now till senility. I once told Rachel she wasted her time in eclecticism. Now she's wasting his. She won't waste mine again.

4 3

When I think about the party I realise I'd based the whole thing on the absurd proposition that, brought face to face, my various problems would evaporate. Even so, given the naive hope the idea was founded on, it's still a wonder things went so very wrong.

People weren't scheduled to arrive till around nine. For most of them it would mean a preliminary drink in the pub. Not wanting to be the first, they didn't begin trickling in till tenish. After eleven there was a deluge and the flat lurched into motion. Gorjeit and I had had the buffet prepared by the late afternoon and sat amid the various trays of uncooked vol-au-vents and bowls covered in cling film. We made premature gin and tonics and drank more than half a bottle. I drank more than she did. She can't weigh even seven stone and two glasses produce the kind of blurred admissions it usually takes me a night to work up to. I needed the drink. I found myself in a state of agitation I hadn't experienced before at any of our other frequent parties. I think Gorjeit participated out of sympathy. By eight o'clock we were both fairly drunk. She wanted to go to bed then and there and would have if I hadn't prevented her. I intended getting much drunker.

We comforted one another by becoming in turn maudlin, ecstatic and obscene. I'd never heard her really lewd. It was that evening, sitting alone with her, I realised how close to finishing with her mathematician she was. She told me about their prosaic sex life, the standard grey underwear his mother bought for him and his father, underpants he could pull up to his nipples. I had an image of him in home-spun drawers that convulsed me with laughter until I realised I had mentally superimposed on Gorjeit's mathematician the face and body of Julien, looking equally sexless.

By ten I was hysterically happy, nothing could go wrong: Martin, Julien and Stephen would meet and gel, a happy symbiosis of nurtured academe, penetrating intelligence and Celtic charm. Julien would make some social connections with other students besides me and might even find a bookish young woman quite to his tastes. The fact that none of my invited friends matched the prototype didn't deflate me. Stephen would find the company sufficiently stimulating to be conscious at midnight for the first time in months and take from this a lesson that there's more to be found in life than the bottom of a bottle. If I could juggle so many types with such success Martin would realise what there was in me, we'd grope our way to a hesitant reconciliation and at least establish a date to meet alone.

I don't even know if in my heart of hearts I believed all this at the time, but I desperately needed some good news and if it wasn't going to come from outside I'd have to provide it myself. I'm not given to lying to myself, snorting coke, leading a conga or dancing round my handbag wearing white 'shag-me' shoes, but I'd have done practically anything then if it would have helped the evening to go well. I needed so badly for the party to work.

The first indication of how accurately I had prophesied came at around ten when someone I didn't know delivered Stephen. It transpired that Stephen didn't know him either, he was just some passing Samaritan who had picked up the bundle of clothes on the pavement outside which turned into a drunken Irishman. He shyly accepted an invitation to come in as recompense for his troubles. Even through the gin the sight of Stephen distressed me. He was incapable of walking. I left him on his bed and returned to talk to Gorjeit and the stranger. Later, he resurrected himself and made it back as far as the back of the sofa.

Julien turned up wearing a hound's tooth jacket and a bowtie as his concession to Bohemia. There were only a few people there and they had formed themselves into defensive little groups. More people and drink were needed before the talk would flow easily. I introduced Julien to everyone and spent as long with him as I could. I was still pretending to be a crowd, running from group to group trying to galvanise the party. When I swanned in carrying a tray of vegetarian sausage rolls I noticed with relief that he'd started a conversation with someone else. I can't be the only student in the world he was capable of striking up a rapport with.

Gorjeit got herself corralled in a corner with her mathematician. I think he anticipated being given the push and was remonstrating with her, in his telepathic way, sitting glumly holding her hand.

'Enjoying yourself?' I asked. He looked at me with a face of deepest tragedy. Someone brought in someone from the pub who didn't look half bad. Not too bright, but not half bad. I decided to look coyly alluring whilst at the same time quoting Kierkergaard and getting the dancing started. I led by example. I could hear fragments of Gorjeit's conversation till I turned the music up.

'But we just don't do anything.'

'We do the crossword.'

'Perhaps we're just too much the same. Perhaps to work it takes one of us to be outgoing.'

Taking his cue he sprang up from the couch and started dancing with me. I don't think he'd ever danced before. He stood rigidly and sawed the air with his arms like a windmill. His face was fixed in concentration. This was obvious purgatory to him. He would do it for the duration of the song to establish his flamboyant credentials and sit down for the rest of his life. Anyone who had been inclined to join in the dancing immediately resisted. Gorjeit blushed vividly under her dark skin. I endured for three awful minutes and lurched off in search of more drink.

I kept waiting for Martin to turn up. Every time the doorbell rang I ran to answer. Each time it wasn't him I took another drink. At each new arrival my disappointment grew and my ability to conceal it dwindled. I was reduced to thinking: Oh fuck, it's only you. I could see them any time. Where was Martin?

When I was convinced he wouldn't come I necked about another quarter bottle. Gorjeit joined me while her mathematician pleaded his case above the music, saying he would throw away his sensible shoes and lose the kagoul.

Gorjeit looked at me and said: 'You're so fucking drunk.'

'Since when did you start fucking swearing?'

'Since I learned it from you.'

Martin arrived. My heart dilated. I stood up, snapped the lights on and the stereo off. We all stood paralysed in the sudden silent glare. People looked at me expectantly. I introduced Julien to Martin bawling at the top of my voice. I can't remember what I said. People continued to look, obviously expecting more. I couldn't think of anything to say. I turned the lights off. Someone turned the music on. I left the room.

The good-looking boy was standing in the hall with a medic called Pamela, resting his hand casually on the curve of her pelvis which she was flinging out to accommodate him. I knew her vaguely. I walked into the kitchen and thought how simple it had all been in my mind. Why was it all going wrong?

There was a while when everyone was in the lounge before the party dispersed to the other rooms. The good-looking boy sat on the floor with Pamela across him. He kept tilting her face towards his to kiss her while looking past her eyebrow directly at me. I think in my numbness I even gave him some looks of encouragement. I don't know why. The person who had brought him came across at one point and said his friend had called me 'Two dark glances wrapped in tulle'. My eyes weren't dark and I wasn't wearing tulle. I later found out they got it from Proust and would trump it up at student parties to help one another with introductions to girls they wanted to fuck.

I managed to get Martin on my own for a few minutes. He said little and looked absolutely hostile. Although he wasn't capricious I think I could have accepted his reaction more easily if he had thrown a temper. I had two minutes of desperation when I raised topics and he disposed of them. He wasn't once rude. He left after another half hour. I followed him into the hall. When he opened the front door he looked round. I had a premonition then as I faced him, silhouetted in the light from the hall, that there was something inevitable in his leaving, that whatever meeting we might have from now on would be accidental and that, young as I was, one of the very few chances I would get in life at real happiness was going out the door with him.

I went to find Gorjeit and found Stephen instead. Someone, tired of tripping over him in the lounge, had organised his removal to the nearest bed – Gorjeit's. I lay down beside him. I couldn't face the lounge. The party was throbbing on sufficiently without a hostess. It's my party, I thought, and I'll cry if I want to.

44

When I look back now at the remaining two years of university, they seem fairly uneventful in comparison with the first two. Perhaps as many things happened, but not of the same moment. The novelty wore off. So did my histrionics. I ceased to see myself as symbolic.

Seeing Martin became very difficult. We no longer deliberately went to the same place at the same time. If we met it was indeed accidental. We struck up an unspoken bargain that whoever could most easily leave with the minimum of social upheaval, did so whenever we found ourselves in the same company. His studies took him an alternative route to mine, whether by design or not I don't know. He also made new friends and allowed the acquaintanceships we had in common to lapse. I felt things afresh at each stage of this systematic exclusion.

I drifted, in more ways than one. I drifted into several relationships but didn't throw myself at those boys with the same retributory zeal as I had when trying to reproach Martin for his neglect. Some of them I slept with, some I didn't. I was circumspect enough to mollify Gorjeit. Curiously enough, I felt no closer or more distant from them for sharing their beds. Sometimes it was enough to have someone there to hold hands with in the cinema or a shoulder to lay my head on. I felt empty. Perhaps they knew. They didn't demand anything of me I was incapable of or unwilling to give. Whether or not I chose kindred spirits or was just fortunate in my friendships I've no idea, but I know intuition wasn't a female prerogative among the people I knew at that time. I ended all of the relationships. They all went their way without rancour and some remained friends. I ached for what was missing but knew I had no grounds for complaint: I determined the terms on which the thing had been conducted and I had set the agenda.

Stephen took a year out in our third year. It's doubtful if he would have shared with us anyway. We had a fire inspection and his room, instead of being festooned with feminine paraphernalia and pictures of relatives from Malawi, was littered with empty beer cans, botched manuscripts and condom packets. His various little frauds had come home to roost. He hadn't done any academic work either. He made a special appeal to the university authorities and was given an appointment with his advisor of studies followed by another with the university psychologist. He fabricated for both of them a story of crumbling family-ties back in County Cork and a host of other mitigating circumstances. No one believed him. They gave him a year's grace to get himself sorted out. He celebrated that night by a binge that lasted a weekend. He had no shortage of people to drink with, who would pay the price of a pint for half an hour of his charm. Even so, I began to wonder how a man with no visible sign of support could sustain such a habit. He told me he subsidised it by not smoking. I had long since ceased to wonder at his capacity for drink. He said he would make use of the year to flesh out the bare bones of a novel which would explode everyone's preconceptions of the limits of the form. He didn't elaborate how. Martin, I heard, called Stephen's writing the 'stream of unconsciousness'. Gorjeit and I saw him off. He was going for the boat train. He was drinking in the early morning at the station. I held one of his hands while the other was busy with the can.

'When I die,' he said, 'open the window. It's the Celtic presentiment. I've got the third eye.'

'You've got double vision,' I said. 'We're all going to die, you'll just do it a lot faster than the rest of us at this rate.'

They didn't replace him with another tenant and we enjoyed the remainder of the year in one another's company. The following year I was late to arrive, coming down at the start of term with a bout of flu. We were no longer entitled to university accommodation and Gorjeit had managed to get rooms for us in a labyrinthine flat in Bruntsfield, which we shared with three other girls. One worked at something financial in the city, one was a nurse who spent much of her time doing shift work, and the third kept a room ostensibly as a token of her independence while living most of the time with her boyfriend in Stockbridge. We kept a sense of camaraderie going by arranging fortnightly meals which we cooked in turns. Everyone made the effort to attend. They were good company. The nurse was a vegetarian, as was Gorjeit. It was a communal flat but to all intents and purposes Gorjeit and I had the run of it to ourselves and kept company more with one another than with the rest of the tenants.

I kept up with Julien, more out of a sense of obligation than anything else. He hadn't made the connection with other students I was hoping for; the bookish girl never materialised, or if she had she would have been equally shy and socially inept and they would have passed one another like ships in the night, agonising over an introduction both were too embarrassed to venture. When he gleaned my motives for continuing to see him the invitations to toast and sardines in his sparse little flat stopped. When we met in the department he would come across and spend five conscientious minutes talking while we both fidgeted to be apart. I seemed to be spending the second half of my time at university throwing off ties I had made in the first.

Gorjeit became ill in the summer before the final honours year. I went to see her at her parents' house in a small village outside Glasgow. She had come down with shingles and the whole thing had been compounded by the state of her nerves. I knew when I saw her that she wouldn't be back that October. The illness had run its course before I saw her but she was obviously unwell. I surprised her parents by asking them if I could stay the night. They were only too glad to have me. I surprised them further by saying there was no need to make up a bed as I'd share with Gorjeit. We had a family dinner around seven o'clock with the parents and two of Gorjeit's younger sisters. Gorjeit picked at her food and went to bed looking exhausted around nine. I spoke to her parents for the sake of courtesy for another hour and then went to join her. She was in her pyjamas reading a book and waiting for me. I had to borrow one of her father's T-shirts to sleep in, having brought nothing with me. Nothing any of the women of the house wore would have fitted.

'You can borrow my toothbrush,' Gorjeit said.

She read aloud to me from the *Rubaiyat* of Omar Khayyam which I had given her as a present our first Christmas as friends. Then she put the light out and we lay down. I put my arms around her while we talked. I could feel the vibration of her voice through her bones. She wasn't robust at all and I had leaned on her for three years with my petty griefs and the assumption of the importance of my own destiny. And she had given all the help unstintingly. It had taken me this long to realise that I didn't have the only bruised heart in the world.

'I'm sorry,' I said, without explanation.

'I know,' she said. And then she kissed me goodnight.

I wrote to her religiously, monologues full of the inconsequential trivia we would have exchanged over a coffee. I missed her terribly. I didn't want to share with anyone else. I took a bedsit as near the university library as I could for my final year. There was no sense of camaraderie with the other people who lived in other bedsits. The rent was collected every Friday by a grubby man. I exchanged pleasantries every morning with an old woman carrying a sponge-bag as I left the communal bathroom.

As I said, I drifted in more ways than one. In the past year I'd read whatever took my fancy and had attended lectures in subjects that had nothing to do with the curriculum. In those days I was fiercely curious but, as Martin would have said, paid the price for my eclecticism. I knew when I returned for the final year I would have to put in a considerable amount of directed work if I wanted to come away with a respectable degree.

Life began to follow a predictable course. Lectures were

few and far between; we were expected to teach ourselves. It suited me. I moved between my bedsit, the library, the small shops where I would buy things for tea, the houses of my few friends and the pubs where we habitually met. Occasionally we would make a foray to the dowdy dance-halls in Lothian Road. Occasionally I would entertain or eat at a friend's. I no longer had the freedom of a whole flat to move around in and kept the noise down at late hours. My paths became circumscribed by the routine I deliberately set myself. I got a lot of work done. A curious sense of finality set in and I would catch myself thinking: that's the last time I'll read that, or do that, or see them, or come here.

Just when I'd reconciled myself to this imposed solitude Stephen came back. He arrived unannounced one Wednesday evening around seven o'clock when I was drying the tea dishes I'd just washed. I answered the front door to be confronted with a huge and various bunch of flowers he'd stolen from every garden en route from wherever he'd come from. He stood there, swamped in an army greatcoat far too large for him and which looked as if it had been slept in. A year had aged him visibly. He looked crumpled but refreshed.

'Honest to God, I've a thirst you could photograph.'

I burst out laughing and pulled him into the hall.

'Which way?'

'In there.'

He stood in the centre of my room and looked round with unaffected curiosity, the way Martin had a hundred years ago.

'I haven't got a camera,' I said.

'It's not a picture that would slake my epic thirst. Do you have a beer?'

'I don't think so.'

'Dear God! What kind of a house is this?'

'The house of a hard-working girl who's trying to hack it. Not a drunk.'

'Who taught you to be so cruel?' He feigned umbrage.

'If I don't have a beer I think I might have some gin or some other things. What else will you drink?'

'Everything.'

I found a glass and some supermarket blend whisky some-one had left. He looked at me and said: 'You haven't changed. You look exactly the same.'

I didn't say anything.

'All right, don't reciprocate. Cow. It's not as if I don't know what I look like. I'd like to take my liver out and wash it under a tap.'

It was too close to the bone. I changed the topic.

'Where are you staying?'

'Here and there. What are you doing tonight?'

'I had intended to go to the library and study.'

'Come out to the pub.'

'You haven't changed either.'

'God bless you for that. "I've crossed anters vast and desarts idle to get to you." You're not such an arid bitch as to deny me your company?'

I couldn't deny him anything. He endorsed the invitation by standing up and shaking the pocket of his coat, which jangled quite merrily with change.

'My credentials,' he said.

He was as generous as anyone I ever met. The change materialised into some loose coppers and keys. Once I'd bought him his third pint I said:

'Do they have paper money in Ireland too?'

'I've never been one to acquire much of the world's gear. You always knew that. Take me as you find me.'

There wasn't any other way he could be taken. I'd aban-doned any intention of studying that night and also wrote off the meagre contents of my purse as a calculated loss.

'Have you come back here to work or just to haunt the pubs?'

'I've come back here to fulfil my vocation.'

'Is three pints a good start?'

'What's the matter with you, woman? God knows what a year has done to my insides, but it's made you a cynical old harridan. Perhaps you just need a good shag. Bleak times are they?'

'If you're expecting more drink maybe you ought to trot out some of that famous charm I've heard about.'

'Charm doesn't work on people who know it's consciously being brought to bear. Besides, with you I don't want to have to behave any other way than me.'

'So what's "me" doing back here? Didn't things work out back home?'

'I get more mileage out of being a reprobate Irishman here than I do back home. Back home is full of them. And here I am,' he threw open his arms and raised his voice in one of those flamboyant gestures which incorporated the whole pub, and usually prefaced walking from group to group with the presupposition that he would be well received, 'in the city of the Enlightenment. I can work here, I can write great things. The afflatus is upon me.'

He opened his coat and took out the ubiquitous dog-eared script. I could never understand whether or not he really thought he had a vocation or if writing was a refuge and a conversational gambit. The script was hand-written in a sprawling style, with pencilled insertions. What I assumed was a colour-coded means of correction proved to be more haphazard. He wrote with whatever came to hand: stubs of pencils found in his pockets, biros stolen from banks, felt markers. Out of the pile of sheets only two dozen or so proved to have writing on them, the rest were there to lend substance. Most of the hand-written sheets were marked with careless circles where he had left his drinks whilst conducting work, such as it was.

I said: 'You can't matriculate till next academic year. Till I've left.'

'University's not the be all and end all. I've learned more from my peregrinations round pubs.'

'There's a lot of the old crowd who aren't here any more.' I told him about Gorjeit and gave a roll call of those who had dropped out or simply taken the option of a shorter three-year ordinary degree. Curiously enough, for someone who had such an abundance of natural affection, he didn't express the disappointment I'd expected.

'You get used to losing people,' he said. 'You have to learn to let go. It's the price you pay for being an itinerant wastrel.'

'Are there people you meet you know you can't do without?'

'There are people you find it harder to do without, and if you know you're losing them it's like losing another bit of skin.'

'Such as?'

'You.'

'Gallant, if predictable.'

'God, Rachel. What's happened to you? Perhaps romance hasn't come your way but you're young yet. You're not happy, but then, who the fuck is? How dare you be disillusioned at your age. You're infringing on my prerogative.'

'I've never noticed you being that disillusioned.'

'It's one of the tactics in my arsenal I deploy with girls I try and seduce: Celtic wistfulness.'

'I've never seen it.'

'I've never tried to seduce you.'

'Don't bother. It won't work.'

'I know. I realised that within ten minutes of meeting you. It won't work with Gorjeit either.'

'Realised that too, did you?'

'No. I tried to seduce her and she wouldn't wear it.'

'She never told me that.'

'I know. I asked her not to.'

'Even so. The little bitch. I'll have a few words to say to her.'

For an instant I was half annoyed at him for so easily putting an obstacle between Gorjeit and me. But only for an instant. If he'd made a futile pass at me and asked me to keep it quiet I'd have probably done so for his sake too. He looked dreadfully skinny. I wasn't hungry myself but I suggested we have something to eat. He made a show of reluctance, then agreed. I took him to a place I knew and forced him to eat more vegetables than he would have eaten in a year if left to his own devices. I paid the bill. Afterwards he wanted to go for more drinks. I refused.

'Look, Stephen. It's perfectly obvious to me that when we see one another I'll probably have to foot the bill. In as much as I can afford it I will, but I can't do it all the time. And I'm going to have to put in a lot of work between now and finals. It would be nice if we could agree to do some things together that don't involve drink.'

'I'm working on it. God bless you for your generosity and calling a spade a spade. I wasn't kidding or being gallant when I said what I said about you. I didn't find my way here because I had nothing better to do.'

He said goodbye at the next junction. When I asked him for an address or a phone number he said he'd be in touch with the details shortly. I offered him a bed for the night, emphasising 'the'. He'd more pride than I thought and graciously refused. We parted. I'd walked fifty yards when I heard him call me.

'Rachel.'

'What?'

'That Martin.'

'What about him?'

'He wasn't good enough for you.' He turned the corner and was out of sight.

I returned home one evening the following week to find an embossed card wedged in my letter box. On it was printed: STEPHEN KERR: NOVELIST. followed by an address in a seedy part of town and a telephone number. When I called the operator informed me the phone was disconnected and had been for a number of weeks. He came to see me before I had a chance to visit him. He had won the opportunity to have one hundred cards printed from a drunken post office employee who ran them off clandestinely after forgetting the capital of France in a pub quiz whose banality beggared belief. The telephone had been disconnected before the cards were printed and Stephen had had the number included in the vain hope that someday he would find the funds to be re-connected. Since then, for reasons he chose to be obscure about, he had been evicted, and had gone round those to whom cards had been distributed laboriously changing the address with a smudged biro. He walked past me into the flat and looked round till he located the card pinned to the felt notice-board above the desk where I worked. I watched over his shoulder as he cancelled out the address and added a second in his untidy scrawl. The second address was even less salubrious than the first.

'Spoils the effect,' he said, holding the card up to the anglepoise.

'Yes.'

'I don't suppose you want to go for a drink?'

'Correct. I don't. I wouldn't mind doing something else with you. We could go to the pictures.'

'I can't. My public awaits.' No matter where he went he seemed to surround himself with drunken acolytes.

'What were you inviting me out to?'

'To Bohemia. Whenever I can I try and extend to you the courtesy of seeing you alone. Tonight I can't and I thought you might find it entertaining to meet some kindred spirits.'

'I don't mean to be offensive, but if they're a bunch of clones of you, who pays?'

'Whoever. Tonight *I* have money.'

'How?'

'Yours is not to reason why. Why not come out and take advantage of it?'

'Another time,' I said, knowing another time he would have no money. He looked even skinnier than last time. 'If you really have money, and I know it's a big "if", why don't you buy some ingredients and make yourself a meal? You look awful.'

'A meal. I knew I'd come here for another reason.' He took down the card again and wrote a date and time on the reverse.

'What's this?'

'A dinner invitation.'

'*You're* going to cook a meal?'

'Yes. For us. I'm insulted by your incredulity. You will come?' He looked anxious, like a small boy.

'I wouldn't miss it. Shall I bring wine?' He reproached me with a glance for the superfluousness of the question. 'What colour?'

'Who cares?'

The meal was the following week. He'd left no phone number I could call to get directions. I provided myself with a bottle of Pinot Noir, some cheeses, which I knew he wouldn't think of, and some German lager. I had to use a map of Edinburgh to find the place. I took a bus to the nearest place I knew, then took a taxi. It didn't look the kind of district I'd feel at ease walking around after dark.

The close smelt of stale cooking and, faintly, urine. He had a one-bedroom flat on the first floor with his card sellotaped across the previous occupant's nameplate. The flat was larger than my bedsit. The hermetic mess that mirrored Stephen's mind was strewn everywhere. And he had two dogs.

In the kitchen I picked my way over a guitar, old Sunday supplements, the dogs' dirty eating tray, discarded shoes and other rubbish to get to the table. By some herculean effort of organisation he'd managed to clear a space and put out two settings, complete with tea plates. The rest of the table was occupied by half-written scripts, an open dictionary and a thesaurus. Other written sheets, whether intended as part of the same work or as separate pieces I don't know, were scattered in the hall and on the lounge floor. Empty bottles and cans occupied every available surface. A large black bin bag, stuffed to capacity, held more. Other brown paper bags clinked as he kicked them aside to get to the sink.

I found a bread-board and scraped it clean, arranging the cheeses on it. I opened the Pinot Noir. He had already opened a party-sized bottle of cheap Merlot and was swigging this from a tumbler. He poured me a measure in his only available wine glass and opened one of the beers for himself.

He gave me some soup he'd made by pouring the powdered

contents into an electric kettle and bringing it to the boil. He'd purposely done this in haste since he was alarmed at the speed with which everything else was getting ready. My help was vigorously refused and he vetoed any approach I might make to the cooker.

'This is the easy bit,' he said, pouring us both half a bowlful of tasteless green froth. 'If I can't do this on my own then I'm really fucked.'

I ate enough of the soup not to seem rude. When he realised I had had all I was going to eat he took the plate from me and threw both his and mine into the sink from three feet. Then he burned himself on one of the handles of the pans. It was an ancient cooker with a collapsed and sunken range. The lop-sided pots continually spilled their boiled contents, extinguishing the gas. There was a blast of warm air as he delved into the oven, returning with two plates which immediately burned smoking holes through the veneer of the kitchen table. I tried to shove old newspapers underneath. He came back juggling two silver-paper sachets which he'd cooked chicken fillets in. He slit both open on a plate and, before I could stop him, threw the paper containing the juices in the direction of the bin. The dogs fought for the spillage. He then produced some hard potatoes and some carrots and broccoli boiled completely anaemic.

'Fuck!' he said, looking at the assembled meal on the plates. Obviously this didn't live up to the prototype picture he'd seen in the book.

'It's fine,' I said, leaning across to kiss him, feeling immensely complimented by this botched attempt which represented so much effort in the confusion of his life.

We ate in silence, he initially glum. He could never remain in low spirits for long. I conscientiously ate everything, drinking frequent sips of wine. He drank wine with the same gusto as he did beer. I looked forward to the cheeses to replace the taste.

'There's coffee,' he said, 'with no sugar or milk. Or there's milk with no coffee or sugar. Or there's sugar without the rest. I know I've got one of the ingredients somewhere but I can't remember which or where.'

'Cheese will be fine.'

I excused myself to go to the toilet. When Stephen had shared with Gorjeit and me we had to badger him into taking his turn of cleaning anything. He'd even cleaned the toilet for my arrival and placed a vase of stolen flowers on the window-ledge. I think he'd used the towels for drying the dogs: they were covered in coarse, short black hairs. All in all the evening was turning out to be a triumph of achievement.

We talked about nothing in particular while I drank more than my normal quota. He drank consistently and interrupted me to say: 'I've asked some people about you. When we shared I spent a year drunk and it probably looked as if I didn't know what was happening. I watched you when Martin was around. And now he's not?'

'Yes.'

'Yes he is or yes he isn't?'

'Yes he isn't. You're not turning serious on me are you?'

'No. Just to say this. You seem to have worked your way through a fair number of men since then, if what people say is true. (It wasn't said maliciously),' he added, in parentheses. 'There's something sad about you just now that's very alluring. But don't become world-weary at your age. You might wind up the way I would be if I didn't have a vocation. Don't spread yourself thin on the ground, don't sell yourself short and for fuck's sake don't get infected. I'm sorry you don't have Gorjeit, but you've got me.'

He took a large swig out of the bottle. His cheeks were burning. It was the most effusive I'd ever heard him. I took stock: a penniless drunken fornicating wastrel of, at best, dubious talent who had never worked a day in his life, never held down any responsibility, never had more than transient relationships, never earned a penny, never supported himself and never had the consistency to complete anything, had orchestrated the whole night for the transmission of those few 'nes, because he was worried about me.

'Bless you for that,' I said, thinking how uniquely unqualified he was to pass on advice. Perhaps he even knew.

He walked me with the two dogs to the stop where I could catch a bus back and waited with me till the bus turned into the road.

'Do you ever think,' I said, 'of what will become of us all?'

'It smacks of long-term aims and permanence. A vista of more than three days appals. No, I never think.'

'If you never make any investments you can't expect anyone to make any in you.'

He looked nonplussed by that. I kissed him and got on the bus. Throughout the night he'd remained, for him, relatively sober and sadder. It was a lacking on my part that although I could diagnose the real cost of his fecklessness to him, I failed completely to see the symptoms of something other, or to plot the prognosis of his love for me.

4 5

I worked harder. I tried to contact Stephen but the phone number never materialised. I even went to the extent of spending one Saturday afternoon travelling to his flat. There was no response at the door, not even the manic barking of dogs which had greeted me on my first visit. I thought he'd turn up in time, but he didn't. I knew a sure way of finding him: I trawled the bars where he lived. They all knew him and had all seen him recently. By an unfortunate coincidence I always happened to be one bar behind, till I ran him to earth on Wednesday night of the following week. It was an old men's pub.

He was sitting in an alcove. There were two other people there but with the huge mound in the ashtray and the number of empty glasses, it looked as if lots of others had come and gone and these were the survivors. The dogs greeted me with enthusiastic recognition. He looked at me through a mist of lethargy and alcohol and seemed immediately to sober. He also became feverishly happy.

'It's taken me some time to find you. You haven't come round, you haven't phoned . . .' I tailed off, waiting for a reply.

'No.'

'I was worried.'

'Yes.'

As I sat beside him he angled his body towards me, excluding the other two from our talk. The gesture was superfluous, they seemed content to sit back and contemplate the table in a reverie of beer. I could see the point in being a happy drunk, but this?

'How have you been keeping?' I asked, aware of the bizarre formality creeping in which had never before interposed itself between us.

'How do you think?'

His face was the colour of whey. He looked awful.

'Why haven't you come round?'

'You really don't know?'

'No.' No explanation was forthcoming. I had recourse to the one topic which always loosened him: 'How's the writing coming along?'

'It's putrefying. I've an organ in me, just like all my others, but this one is responsible for writing. It's not a heart organ, or a liver organ, but a writing organ. A bit like the organ of generation, because it makes other things. But just like my liver organ, it's gone necrotic.'

'You're drunk.'

'Yes. But I've always had faith in my star before.'

I had to leave because I couldn't bear to see him like this: self-corrosive, dilapidated. He turned up two nights later with another bunch of stolen flowers, the inevitable beer and some hot-cross buns. He apologised for his behaviour and almost convinced me with his forced geniality. I heated the buns in the oven and offered him one with butter running. He accepted this and picked at it. His tea went cold and finally he confined himself exclusively to the beer till it was all gone.

Then he left and made an indefinite appointment for our next meeting.

I didn't see him for a month. I went looking for him. His name on the door had been supplanted by another hand-written card. I knocked and was told by the new occupant that Stephen had been evicted because of the dogs, and a host of other reasons, some time before his arrival. He didn't know how long ago. He had been there for five weeks.

I couldn't find him in the pubs either. He hadn't used up his credit, because he had none to use. Those I asked questions of asked after him with the same fondness as had set me on my search. I began to imagine plausible hazards: a drunken tumble into Leith Water, a haemorrhage in some quiet garret.

I found him by chance one evening on my way home, sitting on a bench overlooking the Meadows. He was pale and sober.

'Where are you staying?'

'Wherever.'

I took him by the sleeve of his coat and he stood up. I began to walk in the direction of my bedsit and took him in tow. He put a forefinger and thumb to his mouth and whistled. I'd forgotten about the dogs. I only paused for a second. With or without dogs, he was worth the effort.

I made him take a bath and recover his clothes the next day from the various caches around the city. We smuggled in the dogs also. My small room became indescribably sordid. He recovered some of his self-respect, but not the same ebullience. I had another set of keys cut and palmed off the old lady with the sponge-bag every morning with increasingly unconvincing excuses. I stayed out late to get the opportunity to study and we cooked together when I came home. He did his level best to keep his drinking down. Sometimes I thought he took my generosity for granted. He stuck in my throat and he stuck in my heart. One night, when I was tired, he took the dogs out as he habitually did, and when he returned, rather than occupy the camp bed I had made up for him on the floor, he came in beside me.

'No,' I said.

'Let me at least stay here then.'

When I woke up he was asleep, nuzzled into my armpit.

Looking back I think he realised then, with hopeless resignation, that if he could obtain this proximity without sex then
it wasn't ever going to happen. He never complained, but a
long time later he whimsically said to me: 'What's worse,
a loveless fuck or a fuckless love?'

I finished my finals. I did well. The night I finished I
gathered with other relieved individuals and drank myself
insensible. Stephen came along. We toasted his novel. For the
first time he helped me home.

'It sounds ungrateful,' he said, 'but in a way I'm sorry it was
you who found me. My life has been made up of temporary
reprieves, and when one presents itself it's almost impossible
to resist the offer. You don't know what it's like. You're hungry.
You're cold. You need a drink. If it could have been anyone
else except you. If it could have been a stranger. Indignity
doesn't hurt so much in front of people you don't know. And
you, what will you do now?'

'Why me as opposed to other of your friends?'

'I'm not in love with other of my friends. I told you, it
wasn't an accident I found you.'

'I expect I'll go away. That's what people usually do when
they're finished,' I said, in reply to his question, pretending I
had never asked or received a reply to mine. I still feel slightly
ashamed when I think of that. With other people he only
ever talked about things that didn't matter and he was that
way with me most of the time too. That declaration of love
cost him, and my only acknowledgement was to pretend it
didn't happen, a cowardly response. He colluded in the lie for
my sake. I knew then I'd have to go away.

I graduated and had pictures taken with mother and father
in the university precincts while I wore my hired gown. They
took me to a restaurant of my choice, the Café Royal, to eat
one of the most sumptuous meals I remember. I was grateful
to them both. Things were easier now I wasn't trying con-

scientiously to jettison everything I'd inherited. Two years previously mother's outfit would have embarrassed me, I'd have seen it as a pretext for display. Now I saw only a middle-aged woman who dressed carefully to celebrate with some pride the success of her daughter. I think we had all mellowed. Although I wasn't the son and law graduate he had hoped for, father accepted my success with the same show of reserved pride. I had invited Stephen to the meal on the condition he discipline his drinking for the evening. He gallantly refused: 'Thank you, no. It's a generous offer but no one on the outside understands the democracy of families.'

When I came back, he'd gone. There wasn't a letter or a flower or anything to mark his passing except the scratch marks the dogs had left on the skirting and the bed legs. To leave without trace was unlike his Gallic romanticism, but I'd seen him surreptitiously watching me as I dressed in my best for the meal with my parents and I knew, with impotent certainty, that everything I did, everything, every gesture and expression, only hurt him in his love. What could he have written? I think for the first time he felt something too sacrosanct for any of the public gestures which had come to be his vocabulary. He was larger than life because its mere ordinariness defeated him. I knew that, like Martin, any future meeting with him could only be accidental and that it would never be the same again. In my mind's dialogues I began to discuss him in the past tense.

I sat in my party dress and cried till I fell asleep. The next day I packed and wrote a long and effusive letter to Gorjeit. My desk had come flat-packed and I stored it at a friend's that way – a girl who was repeating honours. Everything else fitted into two small cases – the cargo of four years. I was prepared to forfeit my deposit to make allowance for the dilapidations caused by the dogs. I had some addresses in London, addresses of friends and places I could stay. I booked a ticket on the overnight bus.

Stephen had left his keys. I would post both sets when I left. I sat on the bed with my bags on the floor and watched it grow dark. I stood up and took a last look round before going. At the beginning of the whole enterprise this wasn't the way I'd imagined it to be, a leavetaking in silence. This was worse than just tame. What happened to everything, to the prospect of joy, the promise of love, the equilibrium of chance, the conspiracy of hope?

Part Three

45

Herr Metz has two Christian names: Frederick, his real name, which he uses in the restaurant, and Otto, which he uses in town, a deception he considers worthy of an Oscar Wilde farce. The spurious name is only adopted by him in order that he can perpetuate his little Anglophile pun. The front of his obscure car showroom is advertised by a flamboyant sign proclaiming: OTTO'S AUTOS, the humour being lost in the main to the good citizens of Athens on whom he plies his trade.

The showroom lies off a main thoroughfare in a nondescript dusty cul-de-sac. Most of the clients arrive by accident and are obliged to scrutinise the wares as they describe a slow U-turn around the battered relics which Herr Metz trundles out on to the road every morning and back every night. Many of the cars have papers of dubious authenticity and are capable of motion only through the circumspection of fate, which has not yet administered the *coup de grâce*. Some are from Eastern Europe, with basic parts rarer than a Fabergé egg. The more dilapidated remain in the dusty showroom, decaying in the kinder shadows. Some are even bought by customers with a sense of obligation to perpetuate the memory of their trysting days in such vehicles, or simply by people with more money than sense. Despite the state of the merchandise, and the appearance of the showroom, there is nothing underhand in Herr Metz besides his bogus first name. This is apparent on first sight. He is a huge, bearded man, unashamedly Teutonic, with expansive gestures and a ribald sense of humour. His colour is high, rubicund, from too much drink and much laughing, a jolly Mephistopheles. His fatness suits him. Inside him, he jokes, is a fatter man waiting to get out. He parts with the cars regretfully, having become fond of each one because of its foibles, which he is careful to point out to potential customers. He feels an affinity with old things which endure; there is a wellspring of optimism to be found in the contemplation of a car which refuses to disintegrate in the face of corroding destiny. He takes them in and appoints himself custodian of their remaining years, mentally promising himself a good home for each or no other home at all. He impresses this upon his customers.

His love of life is such that he can embrace inorganic things with room to spare. His lust for other things is unbounded. He has a diminutive wife, Inez, who has followed him through all the entrepreneurial disasters of his life because she knows there is scarce another such love in this world in which to bask. He has three adult children, scattered to the four winds by the same pioneering spirit which drove him to open a dowdy car showroom in Athens, who love him to distraction. Dogs follow him in droves, as do children. He will never have any money and he knows it.

Each spring he calls all his past customers to enquire after the health of the car. These are lengthy conversations during which he will give unfaltering diagnoses with instructions of what to do should some mishap occur in the next eight months, plus details of where cannibalised parts can be bought. This is in preparation for his short migration. In the summer months he spends his time with his wife running his restaurant on the island of Kyros.

His restaurant is as well, or badly, run as his showroom. It comprises a kitchen in full view of the customers, two dozen long, rough tables and a litter of various unmatching stools. The whole affair is under a bleached hessian awning which flaps cheerfully in the summer winds. Except for the stone floor, the whole construction looks temporary. Here the smell of frying shallots mingles with charcoaled sardines, broiled meat and the untutored bass notes of Herr Metz, to float out

over the clientele. The island has many casual cafés which play
the same indefatigable pop music. There are several reputable
hotels also with impressive à la carte menus and restrictive
dress codes. People go to Frederick for the food, which is
cheap and more than reasonable, and the ambience which is a
feast in itself.

He cooks with the same gusto with which he sings. He
sings requests. Left to his own devices he sings anything from
Negro spirituals through *Tannhäuser* to Tennessee blue grass
music of the most appalling sentimentality. The reverberation
in his raw voice rattles empty bottles on the tables. The cicadas
stop to listen when he starts. People wait patiently for their
orders, for the truth is that although many of the notes he
hits are wrong, his emotional marksmanship is unerring:
he can make the trees weep.

Most of his waking hours are spent in the restaurant, cooking for the clientele or drinking with them. When he is not
in the kitchen he is usually at the bar, monopolising the corner
stool with the ambiguous status of owner-barfly. Each year his
wife gives explicit instructions to the staff, limiting the number
of free drinks her husband can dispense with his indiscriminate
generosity. Unaware that some of his promissory notes go
unhonoured, he walks between tables shouting to the staff to
provide drinks here and there.

His wife is in no way mean, she is merely astute enough to
realise that generosity such as her husband's, for which she
loves him, must be quietly curtailed, or it will exhaust its
resources in two days. He would continue to distribute when
there was nothing left to give away. In his reflective moments,
which are few, he realises the need for discreet thrift to keep
their finances in some kind of equilibrium.

He knows also that Inez is as generous as he, she is just
more selective on whom to bestow such impulses. A partner-
ship such as theirs could not accommodate two feckless entre-
preneurs, or two accountants. Each morning she shops
assiduously, selecting only the best. Each morning she provides
him with raw ingredients. He spends his day among the

flaming charcoal grills belching out stertorous songs like some comic-opera demon. When he was twenty-three and fat Inez met him and said: 'You look like a character from Wagner.' Each evening, as he sits drinking among the stragglers, she collects the day's takings which she counts and notes in her little book of meticulous columns. She is making provision for when they can no longer do this. She has looked after him from the first day of their meeting, when she extricated a kernel of corn from his beard. She will look after him for the rest of his life. He is more than willing to defer to her in anything, trusting her judgement more than his own.

It was for this reason, the reserved but instinctive liking which Frau Metz took to the younger man, that Frederick developed such an affinity for Jamie Robertson. The German couple live in a plain house behind the restaurant. The walls are whitewashed outside and in. The floor is tiled and covered in scatter rugs. The furniture is worn and comfortable. They have a radio and no television. There are many books. On the wall above their bed is fastened a crucifix; Frau Metz keeps tenuous links with the Catholic spirit of her upbringing. She worships in no formalised way, but stares frequently at the image of a man hanging in pain till the sight penetrates her heart and she wonders if things wouldn't have been just a little better if we had all been slightly more predisposed to good. For this she would relinquish some cosmic free will. When her speculations make her sad she goes and looks at her husband who makes her happy. She vows to herself she will try and leave things a little better than she inherited them. She can do no more. She thinks if everyone did likewise the world might be a nicer place. We might all be more like her husband who, she knows, never concerns himself with such speculations. She thinks this is no bad thing.

She has had her husband outfit one of the spare rooms as an office. In this room there is a desk, on which sits a water decanter which is hourly replenished, a swivel seat, two occasional chairs for visitors who never arrive, and two walls of bookcases containing the ledgers and what books Herr

Metz has not scattered over the rest of the house. On warm days she has her husband erect a folding table on the flat roof and here she sits with what paperwork there is, happily studying the figures in the sunshine.

It was here that Jamie first met her, having walked into the restaurant in search of work advertised in a small shop beside the jetty. Herr Metz was eating a plate of anchovies with lemon. Licking his fingers he jerked a thumb in the direction of the house and said: 'Ask my wife.' No one answered Jamie's repeated knocks, and when a disembodied voice asked him to come up he had to step back and shade his eyes from the sun to see the small head above the parapet.

She shouted instructions. He had to enter the cool recesses of the house to find the stairs. When he emerged on to the roof his eyes had again to accommodate the adobe glare. When they had shut down what he saw was a tanned and delicate little woman in her late fifties sitting at a desk among fronds of laundry wafting in the warm wind. What she saw was a weather-beaten young man in his mid-thirties with clothes more worn than fashionable and intelligent eyes from which all expectation appeared to have receded. She knew why he had come and had made up her mind almost immediately, as she always did on such things. She was seldom wrong. But out of motives of sheer curiosity she asked him to sit and gently catechised him under guise of an interview. Neither were deluded and both knew this also.

She indicated the decanter and asked him if he would like a glass of water. He said he would prefer coffee. She told him where the kitchen was and gave explicit instructions where he could find things. She also asked him to bring to her a ledger in the bottom drawer of her desk beside the cash box. She handed him the ring containing keys to both the desk and the box. She returned to her papers while he went downstairs. He reappeared five minutes later holding two glasses of viscous coffee and the book under his arm. She asked him to sit opposite and went on with the interview. Her questions were deliberately vague, allowing the kind of non-committal answers she knew she would get. While he talked she scrutinised him closely. His skin was burned a deep umber, with a depth of colouring that could not be obtained in a summer of cosmetic exposure. He was spare and looked strong and extremely durable. Beside the vaccination mark on his left shoulder was a small starburst of some gouged wound. One of his eyebrows was misaligned, dragged off at a tangent near the temple by a faint cicatrix. The nose retained an oblique alignment from a previous break. Somewhere along the way she knew he had been beaten, but it had not defeated him and she liked him for this. More to the purpose, she associated him in her mind with her own deracinated children, regarding whom she often felt qualms of guilt at not having been a more orthodox mother. She would make redress by being good to this waif. She did not believe in the validity of this plan but she knew she would allow herself this sentimental lapse.

That night in bed she said to her husband: 'I'm glad our daughter is not going out with him. Work him hard and be nice to him. He needs it.'

When the interview finished she did not tell him he had the job, she simply said: 'Go and see my husband. He will tell you where to put your things.'

Jamie went back to the restaurant. Herr Metz, by long-standing clairvoyance of his wife's actions, immediately stood up from the bar when Jamie reappeared. He led the younger man out and even offered to carry the tattered rucksack as a gesture of goodwill.

The compound in which the owners' house stood was large, consisting of an irregular acre of compacted mud which, in the summer months, dried out to khaki dust. The whole area was surrounded by a chicken-wire fence whose rotting posts had been allowed to fall into dilapidation. Inez cultivated a small garden behind her house. The lush rectangle appeared in stark contrast to the surrounding clay. The staff quarters comprised several outhouses, each with rudimentary furniture and three or four beds. Jamie was later to find out that the segregation of the sexes was a rule more honoured in the breach than the observance, but that any lapse was dependent on obliging room-mates and a propitious work rota. There were two communal toilets, one of them chemical which most of the women refused to use, and two separate shower units, each with three shower heads.

His arrival was early in the season. They were easily managing on a skeleton staff. The itinerant workers would blow in and be hired as necessary when business inevitably picked up. But now he was one of the first and had the privacy of his own room, which he did not relish because he knew this state of affairs could not last. Besides which, his wanderings had taught him the kind of self-sufficiency which enabled him to enjoy privacy in a crowd.

He had not asked Inez the terms of his employment or his wage. Both knew he had no other immediate options. He knew she would not abuse her position of privilege. As soon as he saw her he liked her, and recognising the reason for her superfluous questions, knew that she liked him. He knew they had nothing in common and that she would approve neither nor be scandalised by anything he had done. Despite her husband's good nature, which he was glad to share in, Jamie knew Inez understood him best.

He started work the following day. He served drinks, washed dishes, cooked food, laid tables, cleaned the public toilets, swept floors, picked litter from the stretch of beach adjacent to the restaurant, chased lizards from the premises, disinfected the kitchen, unloaded supplies from the pick-up and did anything else demanded of him, without demur. He even, in his spare time, helped Inez cultivate the herb garden she had nurtured as a secret project for so long. Neither husband nor wife realised the metamorphosis which had occurred in the scapegrace who, without effort, insinuated himself into their life.

He worked longer hours than he would eventually have to when business picked up and the full complement of staff was reached. There was no door to lock, the restaurant being exposed to the four winds, and nothing to lock away anyway. If he was left sweeping after midnight Herr Metz would call him across and pour two drinks which he placed on the bar with patriarchal solemnity. They would drink slowly, sometimes in silence, sometimes with the older man relating anecdotes from his chequered history or about the obscure places he had been and the idiosyncratic people he had attracted like a loadstone. If Jamie took anything away from this it was a silent respect for Inez, who had endured the vicissitudes of fate as the consequence of placing her love and trust in a guileless buccaneer with the business acumen of a dog. If Frederick expected his revelations to be reciprocated, then he was disappointed. But he was not disappointed: he never asked any questions or demanded any explanations. Inez's tacit recommendation was enough.

Jamie enjoyed the unheard-of privilege of being asked to accompany Inez on her shopping trips. She shopped systematically and with great flair. He was not asked along for advice or even to carry out supplies to the pick-up, which he did gladly, usurping the delivery boy's position. He was asked along for company by a woman who was not lonely. He had never made friends with a woman before and was silently proud of himself for liking Inez without an ulterior motive. When he was handed his wages in cash from her every week he would count out a set amount and hand it back for her to put aside for him. Sometimes he would redeem the whole sum within days; nevertheless, this was the first provision he had ever made for the future.

On his day off he would explore the interior of the small island. He visited villages in the hillside with whitewashed houses clustered round a market place and church. The three main centres of population were on the coast and had been overrun by tourists. He went to the interior for peace, where he would buy goats'-milk cheese, coarse bread and coarser wine and eat and drink against the backdrop of the impartial sky which never clouded. He went to the coastal towns for women.

He felt now as if he had been travelling all his life. In his wake he had left more sad itinerant affairs than he could conveniently remember; hurried bivouac fucks which scarcely gratified the appetite of his loins and exacerbated another in his heart. An accumulated debt of longing now refused to be ignored. It frightened him, this wanting, and he would anaesthetise the desire by the flashpoints of loveless orgasms whenever, and with whatever women, he could. Each recrudescence found him hunting voraciously, looking for women he could dissolve into, instruments for the momentary negation of himself which absolved all pains for as long as it lasted. These were women who, in the main, only wanted the same thing from him, women he viewed as conduits, and to whom he would give his semen and nothing else, knowing that such an attitude would preclude him from realising what he knew he really wanted.

So he hunted among the tourists who came to the restaurant and even among the staff themselves when more arrived. He always kept matters discreet, not because he feared for his employment but because he did not want to incur the disapproval of Inez whose friendship, if not good opinion, had become necessary to him for reasons he did not understand. He fucked with women on beaches, in their rooms when they had one, in his room when the rota and their inclinations and menstrual cycles permitted – an unsatisfactory arrangement which required almost astrological confluence. Herr Metz came up to him one evening and handed him a key. This was to an unused guest room adjacent to his own house and with a separate entrance and toilet.

'You can use it one night a week on the night of your day off. No more. My wife sleeps lightly. I know it's not possible for you to make no noise, but bear this in mind.'

He patted the younger man's back in a gesture of masculine solidarity. He had never philandered in his life and never would. Jamie never knew whether Inez had been complicit or not in the matter of the key, but even if she was not he knew she would know because she knew everything that went on. She knew about Vanessa and Lesley and Dolores and another girl who had left in his memory only the image of a starfish birth mark on her buttock. These were young women and girls he trawled on the evenings of his days off. She knew about Estel and Nikki, waitresses who worked in the restaurant and had drifted on, Nikki because she was as restless as he and Estel because she was astute enough to realise how fond she was becoming of a man who only appeared at bedtime like the ghost of Hamlet's father, and even then only when it suited him. They would have left anyway, and there was no shortage of people to be found who would work a summer in the sun, but he decided to be more cautious in his relations with the bargirls and waitresses. He did not leave them alone altogether.

Only once did Inez interpose, when a young Scandinavian girl arrived during a heart-breaking sunset. Jamie had been the one to direct her to the house and had watched her proud shoulders and the svelte motion of her waxed buttocks with prehistoric hunger. After the interview with Inez she was shown her quarters and he again stopped to watch her walk. He was the last to leave, stacking chairs upon the tables to enable him to sweep the floor. When he heard the motion behind him he assumed it would be Frederick come for the customary drink he had come to look forward to. Turning, he was surprised to find Inez.

She opened one bottle of beer, poured herself a small measure and gave him the rest. Curious, he sat on the barstool and waited for a pronouncement.

'I know you know who I am talking about. Leave her alone. The last thing she needs just now is you.' She finished her drink in a single draught and left. He respected her prohibition because he knew Inez would have said as much to other people in *his* interest, not knowing that she already had.

He found it a curious exercise in self-control, watching Ingrid lay tables, peel vegetables and do even the most mundane jobs with animal grace. She was open and friendly and ready to talk. He had met many women whom he found alluring and who were in no way attracted to him, and he had learned in such instances to leave well alone. But he could sense Ingrid's vulnerability, and when she came to solicit his opinions and his company he knew there was an exclusive chink for him there which he could have driven a juggernaut through. But he didn't. She had a torrid affair with a Greek barman from one of the seedier establishments, like everyone else seeking refuge in other people from the memory of the love she had come to the island to elude. One evening, on the way home with her Lothario, they were ambushed by policemen who pinioned her lover with swift brutality and dragged him off in handcuffs. Jamie, having monopolised his own room, was nearly caught *in flagrante* with a pock-marked Spanish girl as Ingrid tearfully beat a tattoo on his door.

He took her back to her room and the following morning accompanied her to the police station. Hardened men from the mainland, deaf to her importunities, produced unimpeachable evidence that her lover was an accomplished polygamist with a string of wives to each of whom he swore undying love and whom he financed by a string of armed robberies. He also had a history of aggravated assault. He was escorted on to the ferry the following morning, handcuffed to two officers. She saw him off with Jamie at her side. They heard the lamentations of the barman who declared his innocence and love for Ingrid at the top of his voice till one of his escorts fetched him a cuff round the ear. Amused by the melodrama, Jamie draped his arm round Ingrid and was surprised by the spasms of grief he felt welling from the centre of her body. How inopportune, he thought, is the human heart. She momentarily buried her face in his neck and he felt the automatic tingle in his loins that contact with a pretty woman elicited.

A week later, the ceremony of departure was repeated as he saw Ingrid off. She would go to another island to eradicate the memory of her beloved criminal who had served his purpose and helped eradicate the memory of the man she had come to Kyros to forget. Is this, he wondered, what love for most people comprises? A patina on top of a veneer and strata of memories of things which might have been otherwise?

In time-honoured fashion, as he had agreed, he stood on the jetty and watched her waving arm till the distance separated them. As he padded back towards the restaurant he felt a certain pride in the knowledge that if she hadn't departed as intact as she had arrived, this had nothing to do with him. And then, for a reason he could not fathom, he felt a sudden lack. Inez was waiting for him on his return. Her face wore a look of subdued gratitude and she handed him a slice of watermelon with a glance that was worth a week's wages.

All the rest of the week he felt the same unaccountable dejection. Even in his brief celibate periods he now felt the weight of his organs: the sad ballast of his full testes, the disconsolate gravity of his heart. And without knowing it he was carrying the additional burden of his disenfranchised soul. He searched for the best palliative he knew: the cosmic fuck.

He found it in the most unlikely quarter, an Australian girl called Sandy who came to work in the restaurant. There were no proscriptions this time from Inez who felt she did not need to enforce them. Sandy was unprepossessing. She was small, with shoulder-length straw-coloured hair. She was fair-skinned and avoided the sun, which a lifetime in the antipodes had not inured her to. She was slender and breastless and looked as if her bones would crack on contact. He paid little attention to her beyond occasional conversations in the slack periods. She deliberately asked that their day off coincide in order that they could have a meal together. When he found out he did not object. He had no one lined up and she might prove to be an entertaining detour.

She knew about the key and asked him before they went out if she could share the room with him that night. He agreed. Then she asked for the key in order that she could 'Put the room to rights.' None of the girls he had been with before had ever scrupled at sharing a bed with him, redolent of all their predecessors; he was not meticulous in changing the bedclothes, a fact that only occurred to him when Sandy asked. Nevertheless, he gave her the key and that evening showered and even went to the extent of putting on some cologne lent him by Frederick to satisfy the hygienic scruples of a girl he doubted was worth the effort. Most of the time he simply smelled of the sea, where he swam several times a day.

He ate fried squid with squeezed lemon, and swordfish fried in garlic butter, with no regard for the heavy scent of his breath. He would eat anything that came from the sea. She ate the same as he did. They drank from pitchers of bitter lager, glass for glass. He was astonished that such a frame as hers could contain so much food and liquid. They stayed till late and afterwards walked on the beach. He now disliked the smell of cologne which hung round him, incongruous with his breath. He asked her to wait while he briefly swam, unless she wanted to join him. She sat on the sand holding his clothes, and when he came out took hold of his sodden hair to smell.

They returned to the room which she unlocked. The bed was unchanged and even unmade. He turned on a small table light and for a moment he could not see why she had wanted access earlier. Two smouldering joss sticks set vertically in a holder dispelled the mosquitoes. A decanter of fresh water and a bottle of wine had been placed on the bedside table. And then he saw: on top of the plywood chest of drawers were the papers, roaches and cannabis resin.

He undressed and lay down on the bed to watch her. She undressed with equal unconcern and when she was naked he could smell the sheer vitality of her across the room. Her small, flat body reflected its planes in the subdued light. He watched her sit on top of the plywood drawers and adroitly glue together with her saliva the biggest joint he had ever seen. Then, without speaking, she came across to him with the joint and an ashtray and a box of matches, laid all three on the bedside table, lifted one leg over his face with the other foot still on the ground, grasped him by the hair and pulled him to her, exposing the fragrant morass of her vagina to the startled solicitations of his mouth.

After a few moments she pushed his head again back to the pillow and lit the joint. Then she straddled him, taking him inside her with a long inhalation on the joint. He watched with curiosity the burning ember and hoped, lethargically, it would not fall on his chest. But she was too dexterous for that. She began to rock and inhale, rock and inhale, stimulating her brain and her vagina, rocking herself to a climax he found mesmeric in its self-absorption. He thought she had forgotten him, that he was relegated to the status of an adjunct to his dick when she shuddered to a slow climax, the first of many, becoming progressively more frenetic. Looking down at him she bestowed a grateful smile, the first real attention he felt he had been paid, and in gratitude inhaled deeply, bent forward, and blew two columns of green smoke up his nostrils while contracting her vagina and giving her pelvis a dozen spasmodic jerks.

Three things happened to him simultaneously: a field of sunflowers bloomed behind his eyes, the top of his dick exploded in a blissful Vesuvius, and he passed out. He knew, just before he lost consciousness, that this would be the apogee of their time together. He awoke to find her disengaging herself.

'How long was I out?'

'About five seconds. Don't worry, this often happens to them.' And then she said: 'I'm on the rag this time next week, so if you're game it'll have to be one up the shitter.'

He had been correct in his swooning intuition. Despite his attempts to replicate down to the minutiae the circumstances of their first fuck, he never again retrieved the chemistry of the instant or again achieved the same pleasure from her municipal loins. Nevertheless, she gave him more stimulation than he could ever remember. He began to count the days till his weekly freehold would come round again. Those were times of leisure. Other times he would sit with her in the sand and slide his fingers between her legs while her thick tongue probed his mouth. He caught himself almost obsessively plotting the constellations of freckles on her arched back as he took her from behind. He liked the smell of sticky cinnamon her skin gave off when aroused, a process he unconsciously reciprocated. On one occasion, in the kitchen, he was surprised by the heavy scent of cloves and fish which did not come from the ingredients he had to hand. It took him a moment to realise it came from himself, a tacky resin flooding from his pores in response to the girl who had stood watching him without his knowledge. He pressed against her hard and pressed her to the wall, feeling the throbbing of her tight body beneath the clothes. All he wanted to do these days was lie between her legs and howl like a dog. Just thinking about her now exhausted him. She was the most enervating obsession he had had.

He knew he had invested too much when in one week he saw her take home, or be taken home by, three separate men, and felt hypocritically put out by the presence of a libido more voracious and less discriminating than his own. He recoiled and began immediately to look elsewhere. When they stopped fucking they became better acquainted, friends even, and when she left to fornicate her way across Europe it was he who saw her off. Neither made any pledges to write, honest enough to recognise the separation as final. If they met again it would be by accident. She never used the deodorant of self-deception and she was not lonely. He was jealous and wanted to know how she carried it off.

'You just don't think about it,' she said.

'But what if you do?'

'Then you're not one of the elect.'

There were no histrionics of waving on the quayside. She gave him a final passionate kiss, said 'Bye, lover,' and strode on to the ferry without looking back. Previously, he had always been the one to leave; he wondered how many more of these departures he could absorb with resilience and why it was he was only honest with the people who were transient in his life.

Sandy left in mid-season having given only a week's notice. She never stayed long anywhere, feeling stultified after two months in any one place. When she left he found the few encounters he manufactured pallid by comparison. For a while he kept strictly to himself. Besides his late night drinks with Frederick and the occasional drinking friends he had made over the course of time on the island, most of his time was spent alone. He preferred Inez's company most, precisely because they could spend long periods of mutual silence without awkwardness. She never used superfluous words. Her sentences were brief and dryly humorous. She took him shopping with her whenever his absence did not inconvenience the rest of the staff, and was careful to conceal her favouritism.

His other crucial lack was books. His travels over the past years could have been plotted by the discarded paperbacks in his wake. Books were one of the few things he disliked leaving, but the weight of such a library could not have followed him around. He could recall, in order, the names of Madame Bovary's various lovers read ten years previously while forgetting the itinerary in the bus timetable referred to fifteen minutes ago. The best of his library he had subsumed. None of this was deliberate and he had never tried to interfere with the arcane process of his selective recall. The landscapes he had travelled through were tinged with the authors he had been reading at the time. He loved the gradual suffusion of the good writers' intelligence. He had the powers of discretion to choose what was better, but given a lack of alternatives he would read anything in English, absolutely anything. What might have served him as a profession, had he been more consistent, became a means of escape.

Inez had one book in English, *The Complete Home Doctor*, written in the twenties. It was more a textbook on how to avoid the medical pitfalls of colonialism, with detailed descriptions of tropical parasites and their consequences, a Baedeker for hypochondriacs, with lithographs of distended organs, swollen limbs and human colons infested by parasites. A small portion of the text was devoted to small domestic crises with appropriate remedies. He read the book from cover to cover and came away with the impression that he suffered from every symptom described, from housemaid's-knee to sheep-liver fluke. He confessed his worries to Frederick, who correctly pointed out that if his body was one big larval battlefield, how was it that he had not simply decomposed before now. Frederick had a cheerfully simple philosophy in this matter as in all things: everything we ingest is a drug of one kind or another, so why not go for those we enjoy best. Besides, he went on to say, the nearest you can get to asepsis of the gut or the bloodstream is achieved by strong drink: whisky, vodka, schnapps. 'You ever hear of a drunk with malaria?' Jamie could not think of one offhand and Frederick took this as sufficient corroboration and poured them both another.

Frederick had no books in English, or in German for that matter. All the books belonged to Inez. Jamie was reduced to loitering round the cafés, listening for conversations in English and wondering whether these people were worth approaching for any reading matter they might care to sell. He seriously contemplated holding up an appropriately worded placard at the jetty as passengers disembarked. A middle-aged woman from Yorkshire took pity on him and on her departure gave him two bodice-rippers which he read in a week. He would sit on the stone floor, in his kneeless bottomless trousers, and read articles from glossy magazines on the haute couture of Paris. Women with improbable figures pouted at him from the shiny pages. He would have forfeited them all for a decent read.

He was attracted first by the accent. A voice behind him asked for a beer and a salad with feta cheese and bread. By the standards of his upbringing it was almost accentless, worthy of a BBC presenter. It was his lunch time. He had gone to one of the adjacent cafés. Business at work was slack and Frederick told him there was no need to hurry back unless he saw things pick up. He had gone swimming and come here for a beer to take the taste of salt from his mouth. He swivelled in his chair to see the owner of the voice.

Prior to his collision with Sandy he had formed private theories of women's sensuality in relation to their looks or physical type. She had exploded that. The young woman before him was tallish and slender and Aryan. The incongruity of her ragged hair, which looked as if she had cut it herself, did not detract from the symmetry. Her eyes were intelligent. All this he noticed on second glance, since the first thing his eyes lit upon was the book she was reading and the promising silhouettes of several others bursting through her rucksack.

Without further ceremony he sat opposite her and said hello. She smiled her reply, refused the offer of a drink, and seemed quietly unimpressed. She found the restless motion of his eyes as he talked to her disturbing. From gazing intently into her face his eyes would continually flick downwards. She adjusted the open-necked shirt she was wearing, thinking how offensively obvious his attempts were to stare down her cleavage, till she realised he was trying to read the upside down title of the book before him. In relief she raised the cover to satisfy his curiosity. It was Turgenev's *Sketches from a Hunter's Album*.

He talked to her for an hour solely about books, without noticing that both their glasses were empty. It was the only selfless conversation he had ever made in his life, the only talk with a good-looking, unaccompanied woman which was not intended to culminate in an attempted seduction or to lay the groundwork for future sex. Frederick sent one of the staff to retrieve him. When he stood up and saw for the first time her empty glass, Jamie apologised for monopolising her time and paid the waiter to bring her another beer. Then he left in a hurry.

Rachel, left alone, turned over the conversation several times in her mind and felt pleased with what had occurred. Perhaps she had been wrong and his voracious looks belied him. She had only been travelling for two months and already had grown very tired of the harassments and masculine presuppositions which a solitary woman is prey to. He had offered her a beer without thought of recompense, the proof being that he had not tried to arrange another rendezvous. He had not talked about himself with the mistaken assurance of many of the men she had met: that they are the most interesting topic of conversation to others as well as themselves. Nor had he talked about her in an obvious way to find out if she was available, or to insinuate himself into her good graces.

The Turgenev was easy reading. When she was finished, and if the circumstances permitted, she would make a pretence of lending him the book. To give it as a present outright would look forward and with the itinerant population of these islands she did not seriously expect the book to be returned. Everything was in flux here, that was part of its charm and why she had come.

Back in the restaurant Jamie worked feverishly till closing. When he had time to reflect he thought over their encounter and wondered what the fuck he had been playing at, why he had squandered such an opportunity, how he could possibly have come away without having arranged another meeting. Even if he didn't get access to her library he might get access to her loins, or even better, both, one through the other. He was a great believer though in first opportunities, almost to the point of superstition. Having acted as he had done he felt the die was cast, and he would not approach her a second time uninvited.

Kyros is not large and in a land dotted with ruins of emblematic importance the island is historically insignificant. On one of the headlands, overlooking the bay and within walking distance of the restaurant, is a small ancient pile. Littered with discarded fruit rinds and desiccated condoms, it has become a trysting place for vagrant two-week tourist loves. Rachel saw this and saw almost everything else within a fortnight, deviating as far from the beaten tracks as the scope of the island would allow. At the end of that time she thought there was little of consequence left to see and had no real reason to stay.

Jamie provided her with the reason. She had watched him walk back to the restaurant from which he had been summoned. Although she knew he worked there she did not know he lived on the premises also. Having never heard of Kyros she had hoped it would be more inaccessible than it proved to be and she was still prey to the solicitations of the type she had come to avoid. She knew Stephen would have hated this place and took that as her yardstick for its vacuousness. The evening of the second day after their meeting she walked into Jamie's restaurant. He wasn't behind the bar or floating round like some casual maître d'hôtel as she had imagined, and the whole enterprise now seemed foolish as she clutched the book like an invitation. When she asked for the Scots boy she felt more foolish still: for calling him a boy when he was not and for not knowing his name. Perhaps, to these people watching, calling on a man whose name she did not even know was tantamount to solicitation. She soon learned his name, which was bellowed by Frederick into the kitchen, and taken up by the other staff till he was summoned by echoes, like a mediaeval monarch. He sauntered out, smelling of lemon juice, garlic and cooked fish. Everyone was watching. She could feel her colour heighten as she handed him the book, and for the first time in his life he could feel the stirrings of a subterranean blush. He scotched it by breaking into a wonderful smile of complicity which she, grateful to him for diffusing the embarrassment, returned. He asked for, and was given, ten minutes' grace, threw the apron he was wearing behind the bar, collected two beers and sat with her in the furthest recess.

He had read the book before but had the good grace to lie. He thought her reappearance a windfall, almost miraculous after the feeble initial impression he thought he had made. Now that she had taken an initiative he did not feel embarrassed to ask her to go swimming with him the following day during his lunchtime, which could be any time from noon till five o'clock, depending on the customers. These were still her first few days of an indefinite stay on the island; she was

not about to forfeit her explorations to spend all day on the
sand waiting to watch him swim for an hour. She politely
declined. He did not understand: why should a young woman
with no intention of succumbing present him with so public
an opportunity? It was a misconception shared by Frederick,
who had watched his kitchen protégé home in on any likely
woman with no more encouragement than the complaint of
a dirty fork. Unintentionally, he rubbed salt into the wound
by roaring 'Your Tiny Hand is Frozen' out from behind the
resonating copper pans and presenting them with what he
called his 'tête à tête' salad, a lettuce base with everything else
the island could provide in the way of vegetables, garnished
with anchovies and any fish with aphrodisiac reputations. She
was bemused and unsettled by the singing and the food and
left soon afterwards.

He looked for her on his day off with the pretext of
returning the book. She'd moved from the dilapidated place
she'd taken on arrival and he found her negotiating the price
of her new accommodation with a wizened Greek woman.
Inez occasionally took in stragglers who were prepared to
pay their way, but he thought an attempt to arrange her
accommodation next to his might be misinterpreted at this
stage.

'Take it,' he advised. 'It's a good price and as cheap as you
get here.'

He needlessly carried her rucksack to the room and further
proved his credentials by leaving shortly afterwards with a
vague invitation to meet him on the beach if she wanted, but
only if she wanted. She arrived an hour afterwards. Why was
it, he wondered, that she would accept an invitation now
when she would not previously? Both were offered with the
same fervour and the same sincerity, in as much as he was
capable of sincerity. She swam with him, splashing like a child.
He felt that she could not say no to his invitation to eat.
She agreed, unaware of the interpretation he put upon her
acceptance.

She chooses the place, another open air café. He has brought a top which he drapes round her shoulders, feeling a pleasant chivalry in his exposure to the sudden chill. It is his night of the room, but he will not play his trump card. They eat spiced meatballs and drink cheap retsina. At her smile he sees the discoloration of her teeth and wonders if his are similarly reddened. It does not matter. She drinks more than he does. He will not talk about anything that matters, recognising her state. It is the nearest he has come to integrity. As the place finally closes around them, he takes his leave and takes her with him. She is garrulous now, feeling for the first time in two months a sense of false security at being with someone she has chosen. He puts himself in her place and knows tomorrow morning she will regret many of the things she says, and perhaps even be angry at him for being an audience, unwilling or not. He is sensible enough to know such an anger is irrational and that her realisation of this will not abate it. When she has sobered up she may even shy from him, but just now he feels the night is his.

'Take me home,' she says.

'Home. What's home?'

'You feel that way too?'

'Yes.'

'Then take me back.'

He takes her back. It is a ground-level room she has to herself. She flops on the bed, limbs yawning, slumberous. He takes in all of her with his long look: the slender length of her legs, her flat stomach, the lolling curve of her breasts, her exquisite neck. He removes her shoes and after another tortuous contemplation leaves with the anguished satisfaction of a Dickensian hero knowing that it is a far far better thing he does now than he has ever done.

'Was I too awful?' she asks the following day. It is the time of his habitual swim and he cannot avoid the sense of satisfaction from thinking she had come here, at this time, for him.

'You were fine.'

'What did I talk about?'

'Your craving to have sex with me,' he catches himself from almost saying, and amends it to, 'Books.'

'You're lying.'

'Yes.'

'Will you see me again?'

'I don't know. I'm not used to being asked out by forward young women like you.'

'Liar. Tonight?'

'I work you know. I can see you tonight after midnight.' It was a gambit, what else is left open after midnight?

'Midnight! What else is open after midnight?'

'You public school girls play hard to get.'

'Bastard. When's your next day off?'

'Next week. I squandered my last night off carrying you home.'

'I'm worth it.'

'That remains to be seen.'

He loiters after midnight, needlessly tidying up the things he has already tidied. It is the first night he hopes Frederick will not materialise to share a nightcap. Frederick shows and she does not. The older man notices Jamie's thoughtfulness; he drinks quickly and leaves him to his ruminations.

She meets him on the beach again the following day. Her guarded independence baffles him; Sandy was a loner and did not compromise anything by sharing her body with whoever she felt like. He cannot help but feel as if he is being manipulated. Nothing is further from her mind. She has another novel for him.

'When's your next day off?'

'Two days after tomorrow. I doubt if I'll be finished reading the book by then.'

'Why does that matter?'

'I wondered when you might want it back.'

'That's not important.' She feels secure enough now to make the gift. 'You can keep the novel. Books are too heavy to carry around. I probably won't be here when you finish it anyway.'

He feels a sudden deadening at the thought of her departure. She has no set date to leave and no fixed destination. Her course is as truant as his has been for the past ten years. In a sense almost of panic, he exceeds his authority and offers her a job.

'It's a nice way to spend a summer in the sun and you might get some money behind you for whatever you want to do afterwards.'

With disarming credulity she agrees on the spot. He asks her to come round after six and goes looking for Inez with a feeling of trepidation, attempting to disguise his blunder by making out he has found a young woman for the vacancy who is an investment.

'There is no vacancy.' She is on her usual eyrie on the roof, with the laundry blowing around her like bunting.

'No one has replaced Vanessa yet.'

'No one has needed to.'

'It's not high season yet.'

Inez puts down her pen, folds her arms and looks at him directly. 'I've watched you chase half the young women who worked in here and most of the women outside. My heart goes out to you because, like pornography, that kind of behaviour never made anyone any happier. If you become happy it will be by accident when you've stopped looking so desperately. And now you want me to employ another young woman to make things easier for you?'

'It's worse than that. I've offered her a job.'

Her eyes narrowed. It was the first time he had seen her angry.

'Then you were foolish.'

'Yes. I was foolish. It's not the first time. I've never asked you for anything and I was no more to Ingrid than a friend because you wanted it that way. That must be worth something.'

'It's worth something. Tell her to come round at six.'

'I already have. She already thinks she's got the job. Please don't disabuse her of the idea, Inez.'

'I hope she is worth it. If she doesn't pull her weight you are going to have to work hard enough for two.'

When Rachel climbed up to the sun-drenched roof at six, Inez, with her customary prescience, saw in the young woman many likeable qualities and the foreshadowing of Jamie's grief.

Rachel pulled her weight and even occasionally usurped Jamie's place, accompanying Inez on her shopping trips. Inez liked her but was more curious to discover precisely what combination of qualities had attracted the young man of whom she had grown so fond. If asked directly, Jamie could not have told her himself. With her careless good looks and pleasing manner she became popular with the customers, many of whom asked her out. Practice had already perfected her inoffensive refusal. He came to value her for the attention she attracted and even more for the way in which she tried to deflect it. His colossal vanity magnified whatever scant virtues he could find in himself, whereas she was not vain in any way, either of her obvious intelligence, her natural grace or her looks. He thought this insouciance calculated till he knew better.

He asked Frederick that Rachel's day off be scheduled to coincide with his own. Frederick conferred with his wife, having realised from her obstinate silences on the subject that there was more to Jamie and Rachel than simply the usual routine of predator and willing victim.

'He will find a way to burn himself with or without our help,' she said. 'If it will not inconvenience you, do as he asks.'

They worked side by side. They were good as a team. He unconsciously memorised her gestures: the irritated flick of her head as the fringe, which had grown too long, fell into her eyes; the folding of her arms across her breast in resignation; the vexation of the chewed lower lip when confronted with something she was unsure of; the weary smile she would retaliate with when handed an additional job at the end of the day. He wondered what her manners in bed were like, having studied many. He imagined the curves of her pelvis and the gentle motions she would make in sleep. The pucker of her lips. The time he would previously have spent in realising these activities with whatever women would have him was now spent wondering what her underwear was like, and whether or not she would be a noisy lover. Would she moan or simply breathe in erotic sibilance? He was in over his head and still sinking in a morass of his own making. His propensity for self-delusion kept the fact from him.

They spent their days off together for three consecutive weeks from morning till night. She now lived on the premises and he kissed her goodnight at each of their partings. He would organise a whole day round that brief proximity. During an inauspicious evening, as they were stacking chairs after the departure of the last customer, Frederick came in from the kitchen and poured a drink for all three. She finished sweeping the floor and thanked Jamie with her weary smile when he handed across her drink. Frederick talked enough for all of them. She seemed preoccupied and raised her hand to stroke her temples. It was a gesture he had often observed, one she habitually performed when tired. She did it again. He felt an intense longing in the centre of his body at witnessing so trivial a motion, a longing that could not be reconciled to cause and effect. He tried to displace the sensation, push it down, attribute it to his lugubrious testes, thinking how easily pains of this sad ballast are remedied. But it would not move. A yawning cavity of growing proportions had appeared in his body. She did it again. The architecture of indifference he had built up over so long collapsed: a breeze blew across his heart and left him transfixed.

Until then Jamie thought of love, if he thought of it at all, as some kind of illness, a contagion that affected those not astute enough to fathom its purpose. Jamie had fathomed its purpose and knowledge was immunity. He knew that love was a genetic safety-net, a mechanism temporarily deployed to perpetuate the species when lust alone was not enough. Lust alone had always been enough. Jamie knew he would never be contaminated.

He excused himself, claiming a headache. He wanted to

return to his room to quell the riot of his blood. He did not trust himself to speak. By the irony which only love can elicit she thought he was in some way displeased with her to forfeit their goodnight.

He was reticent with her for days, doing what he could do control the aberration. Inez, omniscient as ever, had her husband reschedule the rota in order that they were not together all day, every day. At their next day off Rachel came looking for him, determined to have the argument out or in some way dispel the brooding atmosphere which had inexplicably fallen between them. She found him in his room, lying on his back looking at nothing.

'Whatever you do,' he said, 'don't become one of those women who put paid to any introspection by saying "what are you thinking about?" '

'I imagined you'd be thinking about whatever it is that has made you such bad company the past week. If you've kept it to yourself this long I imagine you'll keep it longer without any prompting from me. I'm going to the beach to read. You can come with me or you can lie and stare at the ceiling. If you stay, don't expect me to come back and try to cajole you out of your mood like a little boy. Coming?'

'Bless you, Rachel!'

'Jamie, pick up thy book and walk.'

He sat with her on the beach the way he had previously on many of their days off. The pages before him appeared bleached in the sunshine and he found difficulty following the lines. His concentration span was shattered. He was acutely aware of the rhythm of her breathing and thought of all the physical processes that were going on in her long body solely to allow her to sit there and read. He thought about her blood and her sleeping spleen and the subtle activity of a mind behind the young eyes.

'Rachel?'

'I'm reading.'

'What will you do after all this is over?'

'What's "all this"?'

'This summer.'

'I don't know,' she said absently, pushing aside a stray hair. 'Something else I expect.'

He looked at her, sidelong, watching her eyes flick absorbedly from side to side across the page before her. He had had no right to expect any other answer and if two months ago she had said she planned a future which incorporated him he would have been alarmed. And yet he suddenly felt he had been made accidental by the ease with which she imagined a life bereft of him.

'Where will you go?' he insisted.

'I don't know. Somewhere different. Questions, questions.'

He realised then what a crucial difference their ages had made in them. He had been travelling for over ten years, and for the past two nowhere for him had been any different from anywhere else. He was utterly rootless. He felt his migration was coming to an end. She was impressed by the places he had been. Both realised he was on his way back, whereas she was on her way out.

That night, over a dinner with copious wine, he screwed his courage to the sticking place and withheld the disclosure of his love for her, which in the brooding week he had come to admit to himself. He knew she was travelling as light as he had and would not be encumbered by the baggage of his love. Through a sustained act of courage he held back the revelation for the remainder of the summer. Sometimes he would have to leave her and go alone to his room or take long solitary swims. He cried, clandestinely, at least every day, wrenching sobs which ambushed him when he was not vigilant, which would not be denied, which necessitated burlesque exits to hide his shame, which exhausted and surprised him by their violence. He did not know where he found the reserves of strength from.

He planned to leave before she did, knowing he had not the resilience to watch her depart the way he had the others. The days remained clear and bright, if not so warm, till gradually the overcast days became more frequent. The sea contained the latent heat of the summer and he spent as much of his spare time in the water as out. The customers began to dwindle. Confronted with the situation of last in, first out, Inez would have been forced to let Rachel go first, but the natural staff attrition in a place where staff drifted in and out like fish among coral, enabled them to survive on a skeleton staff without any forced redundancies. The last two weeks consisted of only the four of them: Inez, Frederick, Rachel and Jamie.

Rachel found nothing sad in the situation in which she found herself, besides the annual regret which she had experienced for as long as she could remember at the end of each summer, and with more potency in the dying autumns. Jamie, whose premature departure was thwarted by a request from Frederick to help him close up, had to endure the continuous presence of Rachel against a backdrop of saffron afternoons and heart-wrenching twilights.

The last week there were no customers at all and their work consisted of preparing the place for an abandoned winter. The bedding from all the staff quarters was removed, washed and stored. The slender mattresses were hung up to blow through before being replaced. The walls were washed down, the floors swept and disinfected in a torrent of diluted bleach and dead insects. Jamie insisted to Frederick that he carry out all these offices for the room which he had been lent. On the floor he found burnt joss sticks and the roaches to commemorate Sandy's brief participation. The sheets had been changed, irregularly, but the mattress bore the brunt of all the juices exchanged, secreted or simply spilled. Ten years previously he would have looked on this as a calendar of successes. He took the evidence of these vagrant fucks outside and burned it. Inez, passing, looked at him askance.

'It was infested,' he said.

With the clearing of the staff quarters both he and Rachel were given separate rooms in their employers' household. All four worked hand-in-glove under the supervision of Inez. They ate together, like two old couples accustomed to one another, and with the closing of the restaurant cooked their meals in the small house kitchen. Inez often arranged that she and Jamie cook together while the other two laid the table. He realised how well she knew him when, as they stooped together to taste the contents of the pot with their fingers, she said to him: 'If things were only different this would be paradise for you.' That night Frederick produced a ferry timetable. He and his wife and Rachel pored over the schedule, planning their itinerary. Jamie planned to make his arrangements alone.

It was decided that they would all leave on the same day, three days hence. On their second to last evening Frederick, with theatrical elaboration, handed both Rachel and Jamie a card. It read:

Rachel and Jamie

You are invited to dinner on the roof chez Metz.
Eight o'clock sharp. Evening dress de rigueur.
We will provide the food and drink.

Inez and Frederick.

Frederick lent him a khaki shirt which hung like a kaftan and would have wrapped round him twice. He was also given a salmon-pink tie which, if nothing else, provided a splash of colour. When he approached the kitchen with the offer of help he was routed by the vehemence of Frederick.

'I am an artist! Do you think the domestic offered to help Leonardo with his Last Supper?'

The women were nowhere to be found. Inez appeared, coming down from the roof, wearing a simple white cotton dress. Her skin radiated.

'You look wonderful,' Jamie said.

'Save your compliments. You haven't seen Rachel. Here's cinzano. Take two and I'll send Rachel out to you on the terrace.'

Rachel joined him two minutes later. She had brought no

formal clothes with her besides a dark trouser suit with short matador jacket, the one gratuitous piece of luggage she had allowed herself for occasions such as this. She wore pendulous earrings like elongated drops of amber. He looked at her and said nothing.

'Am I all right?' She raised her hand to one ear, nervously. 'You beggar description.'

Inez asks them to come up to the roof. She has set out the table with four chairs and immaculate linen, the breathing wine, and the best of what matching cutlery she can find. The centrepiece is composed of flowers, jars of which are strewn everywhere. And against the gathering dusk she has lit candles, on the table, on upturned boxes brought up as temporary stands, on the edges of the parapet, on every available ledge and space, dozens of candles of all sizes, some floating on bowls of water, cupped in little vessels. Against the mosquitoes she has lit tapers which lend their fragrance to the flowers. Walking into the luminous space Jamie feels the same sense of unreality and reverence he has had when standing before the icons in the Greek churches he has visited. Rachel is enchanted.

They sit, finishing their aperitifs. The women talk and he is content to sit back and watch, listening to the clinking of ice in his glass. Frederick comes up with a tray of crudités and various dips. He is wearing his customary clothes in which he roasts himself daily in front of the gridiron. 'Chef's privilege,' he explains with a shrug. He warns them not to eat too much, the crudités are intended to pique the appetite. He has prepared them a German meal, which he produces in instalments to appreciative, if muted, applause, becoming louder as they drink. He clears the crudités, taking the tray with him, reappearing with beer soup with floating islands. 'The German brown beer,' he explains, 'is not available here. I have had to use what alternatives Inez finds for me.' They have cutlets and aspic with sauté potatoes and remoulade sauce. He has also made a chicory salad. They drink chilled Rhine wine. For dessert he provides them with Bentheim honey cakes, small, sweet and spicy. He reminisces over Christmas long ago with his mother, when this dessert was traditionally served to him as a child. He moves on to the topic of their children, their whereabouts and aspirations, slaking his thirst all the time with huge gulps of cold wine. Inez watches him with pleasure, her small face cupped in her hands. He is not given to maudlin introspection and is enjoying this aura of wistfulness he is conjuring with the wine and the light. He produces an exorbitant cigar which he lights from a candle, sitting back in his chair contentedly blowing out aromatic clouds. And then he begins to sing.

They are pleased to listen. There is nothing awkward in their silence. Darkness has almost fallen. His voice rises with the fragrance and the light to dissipate into the ether. He sings both parts in Bizet's *Pearl Fishers* duet, he sings songs from the Auvergne, he sings 'With A Song In My Heart', 'Our Love is Here to Stay', snatches from *Porgy and Bess*, 'Bewitched Bothered and Bewildered', 'We Kiss in the Springtime' – anything that comes to mind or is requested from his repertoire, finishing with 'On the Street Where You Live'.

Jamie watches Rachel as the sound wafts by, catching the glance of light on her amber earrings or the gloss of her moistened lip. He knows in advance that, without effort, every detail of the night will be committed irrevocably to memory. She continues to talk to Inez, quietly, as Frederick sings. The lack of an audience has never bothered him because he sings for himself. Occasionally Rachel glances across at Jamie, smiling shyly at him to ensure he does not feel ostracised in his uncharacteristic silence. The sun disappears in a final effort of colour. Against the harrowing canopy of the sky he watches her for the sixth time brush the stray hair from her eyes and consciously thinks to himself: If she does that one more time my heart will surely break.

He packs, as do they all, the following morning. Everything he has in the world would fit into half a supermarket trolley. He takes silent inventory, looking round, before joining the others with their pile of luggage in the hall. Frederick solemnly locks the front door behind them, handing the key to Inez for custody. The jetty is within walking distance. They shoulder the bags and walk in silence.

His plan to be the first to leave is to no avail. Rachel will take the same ferry as Inez and Frederick to Athens, using the capital as a springboard to whatever destination takes her whim. He does not need to launch from such a centre of communication. His leap is not so ambitious. He will snake his way slowly north up the coastline in easy instalments of islands and promontories. He is in no hurry, having nowhere to arrive at.

Their ferry is scheduled to arrive and depart two hours before his. He would have given a month's wages for the arrangement to be reversed. Somehow, if he had left first, he feels he could leave some of his colossal isolation with them rather than be marooned with it alone on the shore. To sail away when they are there would at least provide him with the comforting illusion of motion, of finally making headway through the series of half-acquaintances and unrealised tasks that have become his life.

Their boat arrives. He helps carry the luggage on board. They stand in a line to say goodbye to him. Frederick hugs him with the embrace of a bear. He has given Jamie their address in Athens. The younger man accepts the slip with embarrassment.

'Will we see you in the restaurant next year?' Frederick asks.

'No,' Inez replies for him. She kisses him and cups his face in her hands, speaking softly for them both. 'I am so very sorry.'

Rachel, at a loss, has written out her parents' address for him. 'If you're ever in Edinburgh . . . There's no guarantee that I'll be there, but if you're stuck you'll always get a bed for the night.'

He has no permanent address to barter, and would not do so anyway. He will not allow his feelings for her to dwindle to the travesty of a tenuous Christmas card. He looks at her with a momentary intensity which embarrasses them both.

'Go now,' Inez says.

He nods his head, and after a muttered thanks to Rachel goes ashore. His throat is blazing. He walks into the small town out of sight of the jetty. He feels the ineluctable weight of their difference. Any notion he may have had of a romantic leitmotif underpinning his destiny has long since gone, knocked out by baseball bats wrapped in newspapers. She is still young enough to hear echoes of the clarinet glissando as each opportunity presents itself.

Part Four

4 6

She wakes these days almost instinctively, at the preliminary movements of her baby in the next room. She is attuned to the small noises which precede Suzy waking. If not too tired she will have prepared everything the night before. She is deft and quiet walking around the early flat.

Suzy is not always immediately hungry when she wakes. Sometimes she is fractious. Sometimes she presents her mother with a serene smile of motiveless joy.

She dresses and feeds the baby before starting on her own regimen. Usually this is a hurried shower followed by wheaten toast and weak tea which travels with her from room to room as she rushes to get ready. Each morning, as she assembles her notes for work and Suzy's clothes for the day, she resolves to be more organised in future. She will get these things ready the night before. Even as she tells this to herself she knows it is a resolution she will not keep and that tonight will find her like every other week night, tired from work and from lulling a baby to sleep.

She is looking at herself in the bathroom mirror as she brushes her teeth, mentally running through the checklist of things she has to have with her on leaving the house. The sound of the radio echoes through from the kitchen. Some flecks of yesterday's toothpaste have sprayed on to the mirror and hardened. She picks idly at the granular spots with her fingernail while running through her inventory. She takes a swig of mouthwash from the bottle, rinses round and spits spiritedly. She collects Suzy, the buggy, her papers, money, her bag, sets the alarm and manhandles the baggage out the door in a hurry. As an afterthought she flits back into the small hallway and snatches up an umbrella from the coat-stand, rushing out before the alarm is triggered.

She takes Suzy in one arm and under the other tucks the folded buggy and the rest of her baggage. She edges down the flight of stairs cautiously to the ground floor. Her flat is a portion of a large house of the type built for Edwardian families. The central hall is flooded with light from the stained-glass door. On the floor is a jumble of paperwork that is the resident's mail. She places the envelopes on the dresser and scans quickly through. There is nothing for her besides a manila envelope that looks like a government communication or a bill. It can wait till tonight. Personal mail always piques her curiosity and cannot wait. Suzy is dipping her hand into soil from one of the potted plants. She gathers everything together again and goes out.

There are trees lining either side of the street. It is autumn, early. Her already buoyed spirits lift. Tiredness does not dishearten her these days. She sings to Suzy as she wheels the buggy, a collage of songs she knows and those she makes up as she goes along to amuse them both. The baby beats erratic time with her foot.

She lives on the outskirts of Islington, among rows of well-proportioned brick houses set in tree-lined streets. Her earlier years have given her a preference for this architectural symmetry. She has worked hard to be in a position to afford her small flat and family. She is pleased with herself.

She would not describe the place she leaves Suzy as a crèche. 'Crèche' suggests something organised, formal. When she first found a job in Highgate she also found a crèche which would take Suzy. Besides the fees, which were exorbitant, she found herself the object of undisguised curiosity, which she found insulting. The other mothers drove up in waxed metallic cars or even had their children delivered. Some were career women, the type she imagined she would have something in common with. It was precisely these women she never met, or only exchanged scant pleasantries with in the hallway as both hurried to keep separate appointments. Those who talked to her had the time to loiter. They were professional suburban housewives with more time than diversions. They drank espresso coffee together while paying to have their children amused. They looked askance at a mother who arrived on foot. They invited her to functions she could not afford. They had enough to make casual disregard of money their shibboleth.

She accepted one invitation to coffee, prepared for a ten-minute diversion for the sake of sociability. She expected a cup of instant in the lounge of the crèche, another sprawling Edwardian mansion. It involved a fifteen-minute drive outwith the proximity of familiar bus routes to an Italian café. She recognised the other cars parked outside. She drank slowly, answered their questions and prepared to take her leave. She had earned a morning off and had hoped to do many of the small things she had delayed since moving in. She was not prepared to squander the time discussing a husband's opportunities or to live by proxy. She refused the offer of a lift home on the suspicion that it was made not so much from motives of charity but curiosity, to see where she lived.

She found Mave Doyle, a sixty-year-old Irish woman who looked after the children of her friends, and friends of friends, partly as a favour but mainly because she had never reconciled herself to a house without children. She had had seven herself and spent most of her adult life with one in her stomach, one in her arms and the rest receiving instructions which they blithely ignored. She had succeeded in scolding them into some kind of harmony while her husband, a diffident Englishman uneasy with his wife's excesses, kept out of the way. All the children grew up like her, exuberant beyond their means, while the husband brought home a wage and grew progressively more transparent till eventually he could scarcely be seen around the house. 'He was a good man,' she said. 'He was never a nuisance, he left me well provided and when he died we were quiet all day.' She threw one or other of the children out of the house every week and told them never to darken her door again. They were always accepted back hours later, like prodigals, among slaps and tearful recriminations. She keeps meticulous tabs on each of the seven now that they have eventually left. Like all mothers, she imagines her off-spring have formed alliances with partners unworthy of them. She will divulge anything to anyone she has met twice and she assumes her audience is immediately familiar with her convoluted family history and blood-ties.

'Michael's an architect and keeps time with some girl in the office he's never had the nerve to bring back to meet his mother. "You'd think," I've said to him, "you were ashamed. You with more degrees than a thermometer and with your mother without an examination pass to her name. Well just remember this, Michael," I told him, "you didn't pick your brains off the ground." What I want to know is, who is he ashamed of, us or her? His brother, Jonathan, calls his bit of stuff a common-law wife. I call her common too. God save any of my girls from the lure of cohabitation. Mind you, our Theresa leaves that answerphone on days on end. "Your mother might not see everything," I tell them, "but there's those that does." "You mean dad," says James. "Don't mock the dead," I says, "you make your apologies and shut your mouth." "Which?" he says. Always had a quick turn of phrase that James, not like our Angela, and her with a face of a saint and a head full of broken glass an' fag ash . . .'

The list of names of her children reads like a hagiology. She has the centripetal pull of a mother none of her children will ever learn to do without until they have to. Every Mother's Day the phone rings incessantly and grown men and women wait their turn to be scolded and told how to live their lives. Every Christmas her whole brood descends for a tumultuous two-day beano that leaves the cupboards empty and the neighbours exhausted.

She heard about Mave through a friend of a friend. She tried on the off chance, afraid that the link might be too tenuous a recommendation. As she approached the terraced house for the first time she wondered what the vetting procedure might be. She found a frail old Irish woman smoking a cigarette, surrounded by children of various ages, crawling or playing. Toys and books littered the huge lounge where she was shown and seated.

'So what's your girl's name?'

'Suzy.'

'Suzy, is it? And where does Suzy go now when you go to work?'

She told her.

'I know the place, or if not the place the type of place. It's all fur coat and no knickers with that crowd. I'll bet they bring their children in dressed up. Is that right?'

'Yes.'

'Whoever heard of such a thing, dressing a child so they can go and play. Mine were never dressed. Still aren't. A shabbier crowd you never saw than my boys. The girls now, they're different.'

They were interrupted by a small boy tearing strips from the wallpaper. She stopped to scold him and seemed to think it worth the effort of reprimanding the rest while she was at it. The boy stopped tearing but besides that the torrent seemed to have little effect.

'Can yous not keep your noise down? Can't you see I'm in conference! Sorry about that. Where were we?'

'The crèche.'

'Oh them. Bet they take you for an arm and a leg.'

'Yes. Speaking of which, what are your rates?'

'They give me what it costs to feed them and some help with the electric. Some give more, but I don't ask for the extra, mind.'

She would have looked for concealed surcharges in such a vague arrangement had it been suggested by anyone else. But there were none and she was not disappointed. The truth was that Mave banked the cheques without counting and as long as she had sufficient to hold together her large house from falling down she didn't care.

Rachel was pleased and wanted her girl to come here. She

did not know who was conducting the interview. What should they do next, shake hands, sign paperwork?

'Tell me, does your Suzy believe in God?'

'N . . . no.'

'Well she will when I'm finished with her.'

'She's barely three!'

'Never too young. Last Christmas our Michael says to me, "I don't know what I'd do if I had a child and it asked me if there was a God." "Just because you turned out a heathen," I says, and he did, and it would break your heart, "there's no reason to deny your children the benefit of God." "Benefit," he says, "that's the point. On the other hand, it's a bit much to foist the rigours of existentialism on a child." "Existentialism. Existantialism is it," I says. "Is that what small boys smokin' behind the church is called these days? Michael," I says, "you're full of big words for a loveless gap and for all your qualifications you've no more sense than a boiled shite. You're a good boy and God hasn't forgotten your name even if you've forgotten his." '

There was no exchange of paperwork. She left Suzy with her the following Monday. After a week there was no fuss from the girl as there had been each day when leaving her at the crèche.

She arrives at the door. Mave answers with the ubiquitous cigarette stuck in the corner of her mouth. The house already seems full of children. There are also two adolescents who Mave conscripts. Rachel refuses the offer of coffee, she is already behind time. She leaves Suzy and makes the bus-stop with seconds to spare, browsing through her papers on the way to Highgate.

She has made use of her years spent in Spain and teaches conversational Spanish to whoever can afford to learn during working hours. Many of these comprise bored housewives who see Spanish as a pretext to get out of the house, and easier than German. Many remind her of the mothers she has met at the crèche. She also teaches English to Spaniards, a job she prefers. Sometimes she will spend part of her day travelling

to the homes of the language school's clients who are prepared to pay for individual tuition – diplomats and their wives.
She refuses to go to the homes of single men. When Suzy is
old enough she intends taking a further course in technical
translation in the evenings. She enjoys the company of work
but is bored by the halting conversations of a scarcely learned
vocabulary.

She has an ambiguous status in the office. The flexible
hours she has negotiated to accommodate Suzy have made
her motherhood public knowledge. Several have noticed she
wears no rings. She is naturally gregarious and yet never
mentions a husband or partner. She has brought Suzy to the
office before, unaware of the speculation this has invited.

Two men are in love with Rachel, or think they are. Arthur
Puxty, a ceramically bald man, as prosaic as his name suggests,
speaks fluent French and has lived in Paris without absorbing
a soupçon of its romance. He has walked countless times
round a city fermenting in love and not noticed. The only
effect France has left on him is a penchant for strong cheeses.
He wears striped sleeveless V-neck jumpers with acrylic
trousers. He collects bricks as a hobby and has his own pewter
tankard in the local pub from which he quaffs real ale in the
company of other veteran bores. He is in his late forties and
has fallen into the routine of rust. He has convinced himself
that his inactivity is by choice, that he is saving himself, and
that Rachel is the fortunate beneficiary of his abstentions.

Nick Burgess is not a linguist. He has a vague job in general
administration which entails anything from keeping ledgers to
unblocking the sink. As a result of his undefined remit and
obliging manner he is given all the detritus which others
consider themselves unwilling or over-qualified to carry out.
He accepts these without complaint. He is Rachel's age but
immeasurably younger. His dress, like his manner, is subdued
and careful. He nurtures his feelings for Rachel like a secret
flower. He thinks Arthur nice but vulgar. Always willing to
defer, he is patiently waiting till Arthur's blundering seductions
flounder and the coast will be clear for him to reveal his love.

He thinks Rachel cannot but be moved by the fragile beauty of the bloom.

It is a quick day. She has one class this morning and one early afternoon. Attendance is small, a full complement of only eight people. She can spend time over individual tuition. Between times she works in the open-plan office, preparing course-work for distance learning, compiling a shopping list, making vague plans for the future. She lunches on the grass with Alison, a colleague. The weather is still clement enough to eat out-of-doors. Arthur, senior enough to merit his own office, spends part of his afternoon shuffling papers near her desk and talking loudly about inconsequential things.

She leaves shortly after four. Mave would keep Suzy forever, there is no rush to get back. Mave's house is a thirty-minute walk. She can alter her route to pass whatever shops she needs to buy their evening meal. She enjoys the walk. When not involved she even enjoys watching the early evening rush, London in transition, its movement and distraction. She has never learned the protocol of the tube. She cannot gouge or push. She is not sufficiently cosmopolitan.

She walks and shops and looks, taking pleasure in a sedate pace in the midst of the flux. Her mood changes when she approaches the library near Mave's house. The book has been overdue for some time. She has deferred taking it back till the sight of it has become an open reproach. She can feel its guilty weight beneath the groceries.

The steps lead up a flight to the entrance, a Victorian vestibule. Inside, the atmosphere is removed from that of the street. The people here are browsers with a correct sense of time. She wanders purposelessly, picking out books, sampling at random. She can do this happily for hours, reproaching herself for all the intended books she has not yet read, revisiting others like old friends. Since moving into the district she has only been here half a dozen times. Thinking of all the unread stuff at home she replaces the book she has in her hand and turns towards the counter.

Two other people are ahead of her in the queue. She looks

absently at the man behind the counter while reaching into her shopping bag. A spark of recognition flashes in her mind as she pushes aside the vegetables for the book. She is not mistaken. His colouring is lighter than she remembers. She recalls him as cupreous. He still has the tone of someone who was once burnt umber. His hair is all there, the hairline slightly retreated but still intact. His temples are flecked with grey. There are lines of perplexity on his forehead and others from the corners of his eyes. Shadowed diagonals stretch from the flare of his nostrils to the corners of his mouth. His face looks more lined and less tense than previously. He has a becomingly vague air to him which has nothing to do with immediate incompetence but rather bewilderment at a deeper level. He is not as she imagined him (frozen in time which does not destroy but enshrines), but having looked at him twice she thinks the way he is is correct and cannot now imagine him otherwise. He is more handsome than he was, his face more creased, relaxed. Time has been good to him. He has not yet seen her. She realises, with a sudden sense of dread, that whatever changes time has wrought in her will be reflected in his expression when he looks up.

She slides the open book across the counter with the over-due date displayed. His eyes fall on this before flicking up to her. Her remark hits him as he sees and silently implodes.

'Hello, Jamie.'

He does not speak but looks from her to the book and back again, as if attempting to grasp the connection. He is having trouble coming to terms with a rendezvous of mortal significance being caused by something as trivial as an overdue book. He looks at her again, hard, still without speaking. She is shocked by his consternation, wondering if she is so changed. She wishes she had not come.

4 7

Jamie's peregrinations, which took him almost everywhere
except the polar extremities, deposited him in tawdry accommodation on the periphery of Lambeth. He lives in a multi-
racial enclave with shop signs in Urdu and Cantonese. He
does not have much money and it would be kind to describe
his apartments as modest. Neither of these factors disturb him
unduly. Although he appreciates the beauty of artefacts or the
utility of their design, he has never cared to acquire much of
the world's gear. Nor has he ever cared much for money. He
is looking for something more fundamental to help him with
his transactions. He is confused.

He has chosen to work in a library for reasons of seclusion.
He thought such an environment would give him the opportunity to think things through. That was three years ago. He
has only found more questions.

He is convinced that the surrounding rows of books slow
time down, like a lead shield protecting him from the
irradiations of the outside which he is exposed to between his
flat and his work. He is not trying to cheat posterity from its
inheritance and the inevitability of death holds no fear for
him. On the contrary, sometimes he feels a sense of comfort
at the thought of ultimate annihilation. But infinity makes his
head spin and he experiences awful vertigo looking into the
double chasm of time. As a result he has no plans besides what
he will eat for his tea tonight. He anchors himself with the
thought of sardines, the number of the red London bus he
will take home this evening, his chair before the banal television and the bric-à-brac of the world which everyone
inhabits.

Libraries are quiet, impartial. People who come here do so
for pleasure, without urgency. Besides the occasional vagrant
he has to escort out at closing time, the library is removed
from the exigencies of the street. The books exhale the cogi-

tations of better minds than his and he inhales their calming vapours.

Mrs Moncrieff, Jamie's landlady, has an unmarried, and perhaps unmarriageable, daughter. When Mrs Moncrieff first saw her new tenant she knew that a man such as him, with virtually no luggage besides the weight of ten years' disappointment, was not an ideal candidate for her Laura. He had seen too many things and by the look of him he had not been content to remain on the sidelines. But in one way he looked tired and if she knew how to go about it, Laura might snare him by his fatigue. Mrs Moncrieff saw that Jamie did not care how old he was whereas Miss Moncrieff, younger than Jamie by years, sat two floors down like the Lady of Shalott chalking up a calendar of regrets at the wasted days. Her mother was prepared even to compromise her own principles and allow Laura to cohabit with anyone of whom she now vaguely approved, in order to save her daughter from what she saw as the spectre of spinsterhood. His availability had been his passport, and once every month or so he would accept an invitation to eat sponge cake with the two ladies, mother and daughter, who daily became more alike. He would make a few ribald jokes and spice his conversation with mild innuendo to leave the ladies feeling pleasantly scandalised. He did this to earn his preferential rates. Then he would politely take his leave and trudge up the stairs. They would stand at their open door on the landing listening to his footfalls.

'That Jamie,' Mrs Moncrieff would say.

'That Jamie,' Miss Moncrieff would echo.

He found Laura quite the most dowdy thing he had ever seen. She often knitted. He found it easy to go into a room and not notice the bundle of clothes in the chair, or to confuse the knitting and the knitter. If he could have done so without repercussions he might even have seduced her out of gratitude to her mother, lain between her legs and given a few cosmetic thrusts to allow her to take something to senility besides a hymen left intact for lack of interest. He knew he would never do so. When he thought of her, which was not often, he occasionally wondered, with complete impartiality, what she would look like without clothes on.

His mind is elsewhere, exactly where he finds it hard to say. This huge opportunity he has given himself for introspection has turned out to be a double-edged sword. Often he wonders what he has done for things to go so badly wrong and what would be needed to fix them. Not a Mercedes, or a magazine-lifestyle walking golden labradors in the Home Counties. He has pored over his past thinking about the roads not taken and the possible consequences of decisions if he had chosen otherwise. He has not yet progressed to self-reproach. Nor does he blame anyone else.

Sometimes, emerging from a late shift behind his barricade of books into the metropolitan evening, he will look around at the phenomenal world and be appalled by the staggering banality of life, its inevitability, pointlessness, its trundling ineptitude. And then he catches a bus, buys an orange, exchanges hellos and weights himself with whatever trinkets he can to sink back into the flux.

He knows he has spent too long in the solipsism of a nurtured grief but he does not know what to do about it. He has practised not thinking about her and congratulates himself on a two-week absence of her in his thoughts. But then, he thinks, how is it I know exactly how long it is since I last thought about her unless I was thinking about her all the time? How can I focus on purging her from my mind when the very act of thinking of what I am trying to forget enshrines her in my memory?

He tried to cope with it as best he could by endowing her with so many remarkable characteristics that she became mythical. Given time, he thought, I will miss her no more than the Minotaur. In the unlikely chance of their ever meeting she would appear so insipid beside the Rachel of his dreams that she would just have to crawl away.

'Hello, Jamie.'

4 8

He is walking, hesitantly, through Lambeth to the tube station. She is pounding the chicken breasts with vexed concentration. He is plummeting under London with a growing sense of dread. She is pressing in the spices with vigorous apprehension. Both think this has been a terrible mistake. He looks at the swaying floor of the train and recapitulates: 'Hello, Jamie.'

Like Rembrandt, he has expected his taste in women to mature. He has waited to caress with his eye the sagging contours of a baggy woman with the same relish with which he would once have dwelt on the curves of her younger self. Unlike Rembrandt, his taste has remained almost static, juvenile. Perhaps, he thinks, the missing ingredient is love, or the continuity of the same woman in his bed over the years. For whatever reason he now finds the number of women who can undress in front of him with impunity is dwindling. It is not just him who is getting older, it is them, and he calibrates his years not by the growing number of lines on his face, the twinges in his joints or the incipient demands of his prostate gland, but by the striated buttocks, the dimpled cellulite and the sagging breasts of the women he occasionally receives in his tawdry rooms. He has been so in love with nubility for so long he has lost the ability ever to see beyond it.

'Hello, Jamie.'

He looked up. The mythical Rachel had been the same age as the girl who worked with him in a beach taverna, only amplified. Her lips were redder, her brain larger, her unfelt breasts more pneumatic, her conversation more precise, witty, cruel. That Aphrodite lacked substance and sank without a trace at the woman in front of him. He never saw Her again. What he saw was the girl of ten years' distance looking at him with eyes of a gentle woman. She had not changed much. She was unmistakably older but the years had filled her becomingly. She was still a young woman and, if not beautiful, more

alluring than he remembered before he began to embellish
her memory.

'Hello . . .'

'Rachel. My name's Rachel.'

'I remembered.'

He is still moving in slow motion. He can see himself from
without and he looks ludicrous. She thinks: I have changed
so much he does not even remember me. He thinks: I was so
little to her she thinks I can forget her name carelessly, like
something I threw away by mistake.

'I take it you never took me up on the offer and visited my
parents then?'

It is a foolish remark. If he had visited her parents she
would have heard. It is just something to say. His hand is
hovering over the book awkwardly. She wants it to be
afterwards.

'No. I never did.'

'Do you live near here then?' Another question. She does
not need an answer. These are gap-fillers till protocol will
allow her to go.

'Near Lambeth.'

'That's a bit of a trek.'

'You get used to it.' He thinks: Listen to me. This is the
kind of phatic drivel I despise. 'And you?' Riposte with a
question, recourse of the insipid and unimaginative.

'Not far. Twenty minutes' walk. If you're ever working late
you must come round some time.'

'Yes. We must make a date.'

'Yes.'

Neither says anything. He has never been at such a loss in
his life. Finally she says: 'How much?'

'Sorry?'

'The fine on the book.'

He waves, grandly: 'It's on the house.'

She smiles a shy goodbye and begins to move towards the
door. He knows if he lets her go like this, in awkwardness,
she will never come back or will avoid him when he is there.

He is frightened by the size of the stakes. He has never taken his happiness in his hands before.

'Please . . .'

'Sorry?'

'Don't go . . . Not yet. I liked our time in Kyros. I'd hate to think it all dwindled to . . . to awkwardness. Wouldn't you?'

She looks at him blankly, stunned by his unprovoked sincerity.

'No – I mean yes. I wouldn't like it either . . .'

'Did you ever hear from Inez or Frederick?'

'No. I would have thought they'd have contacted you first.'

'Yes.'

'So did you – hear from them?'

'No.'

'Pity.'

'Mmmm . . .' He thinks: what am I saying? It was the kindest thing they could do, not to write.

'Well . . .' She begins to collect her things again. He panics.

'I think I'm free next week.' He is free every night till Christmas, and the next. He would walk to China to have a drink with her. 'We could have a meal . . . for old times' . . .?'

She smiles, bewildered. Is it possible in such circumstances to refuse? 'All right. As long as it's not Greek. Wednesday?'

'Wednesday's fine. Where?'

'Eight o'clock on the steps outside.' They both know she is carefully choosing neutral ground. She smiles her goodbye.

The following Monday her plans for a babysitter fall through. She phones the library, hesitant.

'I don't think I can make Wednesday.'

'Never mind.' The concealed resignation and anger come through the line. She thinks: he does not believe me. He remains obstinately silent, refusing to offer some palliative like 'Another time perhaps.' The reproach prompts her.

'If you like I can make you something here.'

Another pause but of a different texture.

'I think that would be fine.'

'If you get a pencil I can give you my address.'

'It's on your library record.'

'Wednesday, eight o'clock?'

'Wednesday eight o'clock.'

She puts down the phone, half angry at herself and at him for having coerced her into cooking.

The doorbell goes. It can only be Mave whom she invited to come early. She speaks over the intercom:

'Mave?'

'What is this, a house or a penal colony?'

'Come up.'

Her hands are stained with saffron and paprika as she opens her door, trying to leave as few prints as possible. She can hear the older woman labouring up the stairs. Mave arrives taking draughts of air through her cigarette.

'God love us. Got an ashtray?'

'Come in.'

'How you manage those stairs God alone knows. And you with a baby and all. Where's Suzy?'

'In the lounge, watching television. Say hello and then come through to the kitchen and keep me company.'

She is busy with the salad when Mave comes in and lights a cigarette.

'I hope it's not going to be one of those healthy meals. Our Michael went out with one of those women who used to serve meals like what you would get at the bottom of a budgie cage. They had me round twice. I was invited again but my bowels couldn't stand it. He told me she once made him a lentil curry. God help the boy. They went their separate ways. I can't say I'm sorry. He broke her heart and she reamed his sphincter. What's this?'

'Garam Masala. Put it down and behave. And I hope you're not going to be crude when he arrives.'

'Me! I'm never crude. We all have the same functions, so where's the shame in that? So what's so bad about this man you've got coming round that you need other company? Is he a Tory?'

'I don't know what you're talking about.'

'Sure you do. I've been here for dinner before but then I was asked to come on time for the meal, not early as reinforcements. When I got that invitation the other day I thought I'd never known a grown-up woman in need of a chaperone before. It's just the kind of thing a chaperone is there to stop you from doing that you should be up to, a healthy woman of your age. Is he that ugly then?'

'No. He's quite handsome.'

'A Freemason?'

'No. At least, I don't think so. In fact, no. Definitely not.'

'He's not got one of them funny religions has he, one of those bald people with gowns and tambourines you see in Oxford Street?'

'No, Mave. He's not.'

'Has he been banged up in jail for two years and you're worried about his hormones?'

'No. It's nothing like that.'

Having exhausted the possibilities of disqualification, Mave settles herself resignedly to wait. She listens to the music playing in the kitchen and watches Rachel cook. The door goes again. With a few words over the intercom Rachel buzzes him up. She rushes back to the kitchen to slurp some white wine and wipe her hands before rushing back. Mave joins her in the hall.

The door of the flat opens on him standing on the doormat. He has brought two bottles of wine, one red one white, and a box of after-dinner chocolates. He smiles ruefully at her and colours on seeing Mave.

'Bring the boy in. His credentials are impeccable.'

He enters the hall, looks at Mave and says: 'I haven't been called a boy in years.'

'Are you married with children?'

'Neither.'

'Give him a chance, Mave. He's only got in the hall.'

'He's a boy. And what's your name?'

'Jamie.'

'A boy's name. And a fine name it is too. Let me take your things. I'm Mave.'

Mave takes the chocolates and wine and goes into the kitchen. Left alone they stand staring awkwardly at one another. She shows him hurriedly into the lounge and runs back to the kitchen. Everything is getting ready at the same time.

'He looks all right to me. Attractive I'd say.' She is holding the bottle of red up to the light. 'And the wine's not cheap stuff. You sure you want me to stay? Just say the word.'

In her haste, Rachel has not mentioned Suzy in the lounge. Jamie walks in to meet the inquisitive stare of a three year old. His last contact with children was when he was one himself. He immediately assumes Suzy is with Mave, a niece or grandchild.

'Hello.'

She doesn't say anything.

'What's your name?' He runs the gamut of superficial questions without receiving an answer. He gives up and sinks in his chair to watch the television. There is a cockney soap opera on. To him the characters look scrofulous or stupid or pathetic or all three. Within two minutes he thinks he has grasped the essence of the show: a series of contrived misunderstandings which conclude in tableaux of consternation. The little girl seems engrossed.

In the kitchen Mave says to Rachel: 'Have you any beer?'

'I don't know. Why, do you want one?'

'No. But he will.'

'How do you know?'

'Men always want beer. At least the ones I knew always did. Like sex. It's all that beer makes them fart so much.'

'Mave! You promised. There might be one in the fridge that Arthur left.' Mave begins to root at the back of the shelves.

'I can be crude talking to you. He won't hear next door. Didn't Suzy's father drink beer and fart in bed?'

'No he didn't.'

'No wonder you got rid of him then.' Before she can reply, Mave has produced a can of German lager and taken it through to the lounge. It opens with a pithy hiss and a plume of foam which delights Suzy. Mave hands the half empty can to Jamie.

'That'll quench your thirst.' The silence broken, Suzy speaks to him for the first time.

'You've got hair growing out your nose.'

'Old age doesn't come alone,' Mave says. 'My father used to sit in front of the radio and pull the hairs out of his nose with a pair of pliers. You're not at that stage yet are you, Jamie?' Before he can reply the child speaks again.

'And he's got dog's shite on his shoe.'

'He's got *doings* on his shoe, he's got dog's *doings* on his shoe.'

'A dog did a shite and the man stood on it.'

'Look, madam . . .' She turns to Jamie. 'Honest to God, I don't know where she gets it. Or rather I do. It's that Graham Ingles she plays with in the sandpit. Graham's another one I know. The nursery, you know. Nice boy but the busiest bowel you've ever seen. His parents think it's a form of self-expression. I'll soon learn him. I've got him nearly trained. He's like one of them psychological dogs, ring a bell and out pops a shite. Clap your hands, out pops another.' She stops and smells the air. 'But here now, I think she's right.'

His trousers have a knife-like crease that he is sitting in an uncomfortable position to maintain, at least till Rachel recognises the effort gone to for her benefit. Craning, he examines the sole of his shoe and finds the offending wedge, a viscous lump stuck between sole and heel. He looks around pointlessly. Taking off the shoe he hops to the hall door and down the stairs to the small garden outside. Standing on one leg he wipes his shoe against the kerb, tears up a handful of grass from the brief strip of adjacent lawn, and wipes the sole with a look of disgust on his face. Mave and Suzy watch him from the lounge window, as do the downstairs neighbours and the irate owner of the lawn.

He walks back up to the flat but leaves his shoes outside.

He goes into the bathroom to wash his hands. When he returns, Mave is on her hands and knees with a bottle of bleach and some kitchen roll. Fortunately, the floor is polished boards with scattered rugs which he succeeded in missing.

'Can I help?'

'It's done,' she says, and, turning to Suzy, 'It's time for your bed. You've got away with murder tonight just because we've got company.'

'Can I stay up and watch the man?'

'No. Believe me, dear, the novelty wears off in ten minutes. Bed.'

It is said in so peremptory a tone and so readily obeyed that he is surprised. He thinks: they must be good friends if Rachel allows the child to sleep here. He wonders if the two women are somehow distantly related. Not by blood. He finds it impossible to suppose two such women from the same stock.

Rachel comes in to announce dinner. She has changed her clothes since their brief encounter at the door. With heels she is taller than he is in his socks. He follows her through to the dining kitchen, treading on his trousers. She has set a table with glasses and candles and artfully folded napkins. She goes to the fridge to bring out the starter. Looking around he is reminded of Inez, their dinner, the light and the shade, Frederick's voice. She is as graceful as he remembered and he takes pleasure in the movement of her body.

She pours some wine while they wait for Mave, and straightens the already parallel cutlery. He is determined not to say anything inane. So is she. Neither speak.

'I think we should start,' she finally says, avid to occupy her hands and mouth. He proffers a toast: 'Good times.' The glasses clink in mock levity. He thinks: ten years and no change. I did not think myself capable of feeling like this again.

Mave enters. 'She's an angel when she's asleep, like most of them.'

'Did you brush her teeth?' Rachel asks.

'You're not trying to tell your Granny how to suck eggs, are you?'

Jamie says: 'I never understood that expression.' This goes unremarked upon as they eat. He feels it incumbent on him to say something, be witty, earn his keep. These halting starts are a new experience for him. He thinks of how, with ease, he can manipulate the conversation with Miss and Mrs Moncrieff, have them laugh despite themselves, provide them with the guest persona he knows they are looking for. He tries again: 'I didn't know what kind of wine you would prefer. There's some Bordeaux there.'

Rachel says: 'That's lovely.'

'I also brought some white Rioja. I didn't know what we were having.'

'Chicken. In spices. Either would be fine, I don't follow etiquette. I think there's so much snobbery over wine, don't you?'

'Yes.'

'Me too,' says Mave. 'Bordeaux. Where's that from?'

He answers. 'Bordeaux.'

'Well that's handy. Even I can remember that. Pretty convenient to name a place after a wine. Anywhere else like that?'

'Champagne, Cognac, Armagnac . . .' He runs out of ideas.

'They don't do that around here. I've never heard of any place called "Lager", have you?'

'No.' She lets them exchange a quiet grin of complicity.

'There you are, see. It worked. You didn't really think I was that ignorant, did you? But you smiled at each other and the ball's rolling. Aren't they, Jamie?'

He bursts out laughing and smiles at her in gratitude. He thinks: there is much to miss in this little skinny Irish woman. She pours herself a generous measure of Rachel's wine. She sits back, one arm folded across her chest, prepared to pontificate between sips.

Later, preparing to take his leave, he thinks Mave will never know how much he owes her. The meal and afterwards have gone well. Her humour and consistent refilling of their glasses

provided the lubrication for a night which otherwise would
have been his last with Rachel. A chance encounter spun out
to a failed evening would have made their separation permanent. He knows he could not have contrived another chance
meeting, loitered where he knew she would be. He has done
as much before. It is not his dignity at issue, but her credulity.
She is too intelligent for any of the techniques he has in his
arsenal to avoid loneliness.

He says goodnight to them both. Rachel sees him to the
door. He hopes he has a foothold, a place on the cusp of her
affections. He looks at the ten feet which separate him from
her door and thinks: if I can restrain myself from doing anything dreadful between here and the landing I might be invited
back under other circumstances.

'Goodnight,' she says, looking askance at him for the first
time in the night.

'Goodnight. And thank you.' He turns away before he blurts
out an invitation or gives rein to his feelings. He picks up his
shoes from the landing and walks downstairs carrying them.
The main door closes behind him, sending up a draught of
night air. If he had invited her somewhere or insinuated
himself she would have felt uncomfortable. She can only
glimpse a corner of his feelings. She likes him all the more
for not attempting to trespass. She returns to the lounge.

'Do you want to stay here tonight, Mave?'

'Why not. I'll sleep with Suzy. He likes you.'

'I know.'

'No. I don't think you do.'

He is walking through the strewn leaves to the last tube.
He has waited so long and loved so well he is arrogant enough
to believe he deserves some recompense, that there is something inevitable in himself and Rachel. But he knows that
first there is something he must do.

4 9

Almost two years ago, when he was working in a library nearer his accommodation, a woman came in. She drew his attention firstly because of the incongruity of her style of dress. There was nothing garish about her, quite the reverse. The district was poor, the signs in the library multi-lingual, as were the residents. As one of the free warm and dry spots in the district they were inundated with vagrants during the cold snaps or the long wet days. One of his daily duties, which he hadn't the heart to perform, was to retrieve the newspapers which the tramps stole to line their clothes as insulation against the cold of the winter nights outdoors. He found himself surreptitiously handing out old pink copies of the *Financial Times* so that they could quilt themselves with exchange rates against the rigours of the night.

She was tastefully dressed in muted autumnal colours. Each item of her clothes looked as if it had been bought to complement the other, not vaguely, like his, to match his parsimonious rag-bag wardrobe. There was an expensive resinous shine to her leather boots. Her hair and orthodonture had the lustre of money. She was not here for heat or a bodice-ripper or cliterature or one of the dog-eared detective novels which changed hands so frequently. She did not want to use the photocopying facilities. Their reference section was almost non-existent. She interested him, spending as much time in front of the books in Urdu, or the large print editions for the short-sighted, as she did in front of their paltry selection of classics. She was in her late thirties. She had corn-coloured hair. She was pretty, almost beautiful. He could not see the contours of her body beneath the comfortable folds of her clothes. She interested him.

Business was slack. He watched her and conjectured. She had already looked at her watch twice. He thought: she is waiting for a man, not her husband, although she wears a ring. If he does not turn up she will be angry or worried or both. If he arrives at the point of her departure she will forget the fact that he has kept her standing for half-an-hour. Her exasperation will evaporate at no longer having to be alone.

She was lonely. He could even feel it from where he stood, a breath of desolation which her wealthy smell could not mask. He wondered if he gave off the same forsaken odour. He was half tempted to look away but thought: why should I? I work here. If I stare to the point of being rude we'll never see one another again after she leaves this place.

She saw him looking at her and flashed a nervous smile. She saw him looking at her still and picked up a book to pretend not to notice his rudeness.

'That's in Urdu,' he said. She replaced the book and looked round for another. 'The periodicals are over there.' He pointed. She walked across to the table with a quick ironic smile of gratitude. Some ten minutes later a man, younger than her, came in wearing a midnight-blue cashmere coat. He was still carrying his car keys.

'She's over there,' Jamie said, pointing. The younger man looked at him with glacial contempt and walked across to the woman. Both were obliged to pass Jamie on the way out.

'Have a nice day.' He could not help himself. The younger man remained as before. Despite herself, the woman smiled.

When the door closed on them he dismissed them from his thoughts. It was a difficult time for him. For two weeks he had experienced a state of unreality he used intermittently to feel in his teens and early twenties. He ate out of necessity. The only regulating factor in his life was working hours. Sometimes he would read or walk all night, or wake ravenous and realise he had not eaten for two days. He did not feel cold, or warm, unless in the extreme. He felt careless of his actions and divorced from their consequences.

Two weeks later she returned. He was still in a state of unwanted limbo.

'Waiting for your Lothario?'

'I don't know what you mean.'

'At least you picked up a book in English this time. I was talking about the young man, well, not that young, who left in what the novelists would call a state of high dudgeon.'

'No. I'm not waiting for him.'

'Another one then?'

'Is this all part of the service?' Her lips were a tight line.

'How do you do it, that's what I want to know? Give me a reading list. After all, I work here.'

'If you'll excuse me.' She brushed past.

'Please yourself.'

Another man arrived. An older man, in his sixties. He had a kind face. Jamie looked at him and decided there was something Dickensian in him, a benevolent old philanthropist. But she didn't need cash. Unless otherwise unsatisfied she didn't look as if she would want sex from the older man either. Companionship then? Jamie knew then that she needed people. Almost instantly, at the realisation, he wanted her to need him, to lean on him, to fix something in the whole swirling constellation by being depended upon. He thought: I will get her.

She did not come near the place for over a month. When she came in, wearing yet a third entire outfit he had never seen before, he was waiting for her.

'I haven't seen you here for a while. Have you been when I haven't been working?'

'I don't keep a tally of your work rota.'

'Have you been here in the last month?'

'No.'

'Are you here to meet someone again?'

'I don't think that's any of your business.'

'I think it is. I'll tell you what I want to happen. I don't want you to go out with whoever he is or they are. I want you to wipe the sheet clean and go out with me.'

'You arrogant bastard.'

'Yes. Desire's like that. I suppose love is too. Arrogant and selfish. I don't want you to be enjoying yourself with someone else, I want you to be enjoying yourself with me. Even if that means making another person unhappy. Stop seeing your young man or your old man or whoever. I'm going to make an excuse of feeling ill and leave early, because I don't want to see whoever it is you're meeting. Jealousy is belittling. I don't want to spend the rest of the night thinking of another man putting his hands on your body. After this don't ever come back here unless you come back for me.'

'You fucking . . .' She petered out, appalled at herself. The word had been fully pronounced. She was as unpractised in swearing as she was unprepared for the ultimatum. 'This is a library. This is a public place. How dare you – '

'This is a dingy little library. The earth's covered in dingy little assignations. There's a whole world out there to rendez-vous in. This is all I have. Leave me alone or don't. Come for me or not at all.'

He walked away without giving her the opportunity to reply. She watched, still paralysed with anger, as he murmured an excuse to a colleague. She saw him emerge from the back a few moments later and leave with his coat on. He did not look back at her. Ten minutes later a middle-aged man entered, again looking incongruously well dressed, and found her standing in the same spot. Any careless observer would have seen her refuse his arm and the two leave together, he undoubtedly galled, she with her colouring still high and an air of repressed rage.

For the next few days Jamie wondered if he had been correct in the way he played his hand but knew he could not have played it otherwise. Sheet lightning intimacy had been a technique he had used in his younger days. Its cruder form had been the sudden physical contact of a hand laid on. He had refined this to a statement of intent, an ultimatum of sex which, when accepted, dispensed with the preliminary negotiations or the feigned reticence for the sake of form. This approach, of late, had become more of a necessity than an option. In his infrequent assignations he had lost the technique of conventional seduction, mainly because he did not care.

It was a month before she reappeared. She did not come into the library, she was waiting for him outside. It was winter, after dark. The ground sparkled with a hoar frost. She was waiting for him just outside the vestibule, in the light from the library. When she saw him coming she walked a little away from the others who were also emerging and stood beneath the lamppost. He watched this as he bade goodnight to his colleagues. As he walked across he could see she was summoning herself for her opening remark. He imagined she had rehearsed this many times in front of a suburban mirror for tonight's performance. He spoke first, while he was still moving, his remark preceding his arrival: 'Don't pretend you've come here to remonstrate. If you'd wanted to do that you would have done it two days later, in there where it would have damaged me most.'

'Do you imagine for a minute this arrogance does you credit?'

'No. I'm not looking for your approval.'

'You're a bastard.'

'And you're here. Besides, you told me that already. You didn't come here to tell me the same thing again.' His attention was drawn up. 'Look at the plume of our breaths.'

'What is this, the poetic technique? I knew boys who gave that up in their late teens.'

'Perhaps you did come here to remonstrate. I've been wrong before. If I'd wanted to hurt you I would have gone about it methodically. I only told you what I honestly thought. If you want to say bitter things say them now.'

'No, I don't want to say bitter things.'

Her neck was concealed by a silk scarf. He pushed this aside to look at its long columnar length. In the lamplight the flesh looked nacreous. He ran his finger lightly across. She did not move. He opened her coat to look at the clothes underneath.

'Tell me, do you choose your underwear with the same care?'

She did not immediately answer but stood still and let him

touch her neck. Then she said: 'Would you like to go for a drink?'

'No.'

She looked nonplussed and for an instant almost haggard. Then he said: 'I don't want to go anywhere public with you. I want to be with you on my own. If you don't mind things being too basic for our first time together you can come back to mine. We can't make too much noise because of my land-lady. If you prefer home comforts I'll gladly come home with you if you lend me a toothbrush.'

She smiled. There was something painful in her face, the anticipation of another happiness hazarded and perhaps lost. 'Mine,' she said.

'How do we get there?'

'I have a car.'

'Are you rich?'

'Yes.'

'What's your name?'

'Sarah.'

'Mine's Jamie. Jamie Robertson.'

'You're Scottish, aren't you?'

'Is the Pope a Catholic?'

She had a terraced house in Bloomsbury. The curtains were already closed on their arrival. The room he sat in while she made supper was panelled in dark wood. There was antima-cassar over the seats they sat on. A tall clock in the hallway stood like a sentinel and boomed the hour. Victorian pictures and seascapes lined the wall. She served tea in florid china cups.

'If you're rich why do you live in a museum like this?'

'I've only recently really had it to myself. Really, irrevocably. Do you follow?'

'No.'

'It was decorated to my husband's directions. It was a good decision to retain the original features but not to buy all that gloomy furniture. He equates gloomy things with good taste you see.'

'Why, was he once poor?'

'Yes.'

'And now he's rich?'

'Very. Have you . . . It's a strange question I know. Have you ever been rich?'

'My father was Governor of the Bank of England, my mother the only child of the Duke of Argyll and sole inheritor of the estate. I just dress like this and work in a library as an aristocratic foible because I don't know what to do with all my money.'

'I'm sorry. It was silly to ask.'

'Yes, it was. I'm not offended. Money's not something I ever considered much. I've only ever wanted what it could buy. I take it your husband's gone?'

'Yes.'

'Really and irrevocably?'

'The papers arrived a few months ago. But he wasn't here for a long time before that.'

'Other women?'

'You do ask a lot of questions.'

'You're going to take your clothes off for me later.'

She laughed. 'Yes, other women. Lots of them. Evidently he'd been doing it for years. I only found out latterly when I picked up the phone and hit the redial button by mistake and got a woman on the other end of the line. Then I went to the laundry basket and smelled his clothes to see if I could smell them, the other women.'

'And could you?'

'No.'

'Is that why you've been running about with all those pathetic specimens I saw at the library, to get your own back?'

'God no. He didn't know. He was too preoccupied with his other women. And even if he had known he wouldn't have cared.'

'Did you ever love him?'

'I thought I did. But now I wonder, and I suppose if I

don't know then I certainly didn't. I imagine love's somehow monumental, don't you?'

'So you got the inside of the house and he got the outside?'

'Put that way. Yes.'

'But you were rich anyway?'

'Yes.'

'That's handy.'

'And what about you?'

'Mind your own business you nosy cow.' He burst out laughing at the obvious look of shock on her face. It took her a minute to laugh also, which she did more out of politeness than understanding.

They drank some more tea. Making up his mind, he put down his cup and took hers from her. She turned towards him, her eyes dark and fluid. He grasped her hair hard and pulled her on to the carpet. She was light and malleable. He helped her undress with one hand while the other still held her hair. He stood above her and undressed. By the firelight her skin had lost its nacreous glow and looked almost dark honey. Her breasts were tight and responsive, their dark tips the colour of roasted coffee. He knelt behind her and took her from behind, pushing her head down to the carpet by the handful of hair, pushing into the melted wax of her sex. Leaning forward with his chest along her back he looped his arms under hers and locked his hands behind the nape of her neck. Above the beating of his own heart and the rhythm of his lungs and loins he could hear her quick gasping into the pile of the carpet. He pushed and pushed against her buttocks and at the imminent moment pushed a searing orgasm into her body like a hot wound.

When he slumped, his hands loosened but he was pleased still to imprison her by the weight of his body. When he rolled off she retreated some feet to the settee and looked at him, half frightened.

'Did you enjoy that at all?' he asked.

'What do you care? You don't want my money. It's what I'll use to pay you.'

He thought: She's trying to assume callousness. The rest of her is even more easily penetrated than that. I will have to be careful.

'You could always leave a note in the complaints box at the library.'

'Bastard,' she said, amiably.

The bath was a huge cast iron affair on legs fashioned like lions' paws. She scented the water. They lay at opposite ends while he prodded and tickled her with his toes.

'If I stick my toe right . . . there,' she squealed and splashed, 'I wonder if you could get athlete's quim.'

'You're utterly revolting.'

'Have you any champagne?'

'Yes.'

'And cigars?'

'And cigars.'

'Do me a favour and get some. Just once in my life I want to be fucking urbane.'

5 0

The German lager which Jamie drank when he was at Rachel's for dinner had been left there by Arthur Puxty, a remnant of the night he had attempted to gain a foothold. A man of menopausal tastes, if juvenile urges, Arthur lacked not only the subtlety but the patience to prosecute his designs gradually. Blithely ignorant of his own shortcomings he decided, upon his fifth meeting with Rachel, that she passed all his tests. It never occurred to him that he might not pass any of hers and that a young woman could fail to want a prematurely aged man who collected bricks. As far as he was concerned the only fly in the ointment was the child. Upon reflection he decided that this might even be a blessing in disguise. He was currently reading an American book on positive thinking whose author was capable of construing a holocaust benignly.

Arthur reasoned that, being young, Rachel would want
children, or at least a child. One was already provided. There
was no need to make more, the arrival and care of which could
only interrupt the life of conjugal happiness he envisaged. His
bricks were fairly robust things, it wasn't as if he collected
porcelain or fine china, so that was all right even if the child
was clumsy.

The more he thought about it the happier the arrangement
in his own mind became. He was even prepared to move, to
have a herb garden, to cut down on his nights out with the
real-ale society and his own pewter tankard. Sex was something abstract that never really entered the calculation. The
few sexual encounters he had had in his life were entered into
in the same spirit of determination with which, as a schoolboy,
he had donned his plimsolls and baggy shorts and splashed his
way doggedly round the cross-country with other muddy
schoolboys. As a student, in Paris, he had watched the kissing
of insatiable lovers with the impassive curiosity of a palaeontol-
ogist examining shales. Such scenes excited his interest, not
his hormones. He had known a French girl there, sharing
accommodation in the same block, who was aroused by his
receding hairline, his brown cardigan, his chequered slippers,
his incipient interest in bricks – or at least claimed to be.
When they were alone together she told him she wanted him
to suck her toes and do all manner of unsavoury things to
her. She rubbed his crotch with her stockinged foot. He was
petrified with astonishment. She took his dick out with her
hand and with a few expert motions brought it to veinous
and strident attention.

'You have the dick of an old man,' she said.

He continued to look in astonishment at this angry member
as if it was more an adjunct to her rhythmic hand than to his
rigid body. Half a dozen more fluid motions of her wrist
brought the inevitable conclusion. He was horrified.

'I'll never get this stuff off my cardigan!' he said.

Such incidents were the zenith of his passion. His loins had
since fallen into disuse. Occasionally, even in his late forties,

they would protest against years of neglect and present him with viscous offerings in his pyjamas to wake up to, or truncheons in his trousers if he unwittingly sat above the back axle of a vibrating bus. He thought the whole arrangement perverse and untidy and would have preferred the species to be wind-pollinated.

The more he thought about the child, whose name he could never remember, the more pleased he became. If Rachel wanted sex he was prepared to make an effort on Saturdays, but it was less likely that procreation was on the cards with one child already there. So reasoned Arthur. He also reasoned he could appeal to Rachel by appealing to the child.

So he planned continuously, whether he saw Rachel at work or not. They exchanged occasional hellos and even had lunch together twice, sitting on the grass outside. He imagined their intimacy increasing. He elaborated his scheme: thinking of a district they could both sell up and move to. She was oblivious. Like Jamie, he thought he and Rachel were inevitable. Had she known she was considered the target and goal of two ineluctable destinies, she would have bridled, relegated to a prize in arrogant masculine assumptions which considered only their own desires.

Arthur offered to drop Rachel off late one afternoon. She accepted a lift as far as the nursery. Once she had left the car he drove round the district, reconnoitering. It was a reasonable enough place, but he thought he could take her to better. He priced houses. The particulars all but settled in his mind, he now needed only Rachel's approval, a mere bagatelle once she realised the degree of his commitment and the detail of his arrangements.

One afternoon, before she left, he asked her if he could come round and see her at home since he had something to discuss he'd rather not talk about at work. At the time she was coming to the end of a probationary short-term contract, the continuance of which being dependent on the agreement of both parties. Arthur held some unofficial sway in the place. Assuming this was what he wanted to discuss, she agreed.

He arrived with some cans, prepared in this one case to violate his purist standards by drinking canned beer, and a huge bunch of flowers for her. She accepted these with some perplexity, found water for them, and put the beer in the fridge. Arthur was asked to take a seat in the lounge. She returned with one can and a glass.

'You won't join me?' he asked.

'No.'

His ceramic head caught and reflected the light positioned above a picture behind him.

'That man's got no hair,' Suzy said, pointing. She was taken, protesting, by her mother to an early bed. It was half-an-hour before Rachel returned. Arthur had finished his first can and started on a second.

'Did you drive here?' Rachel asked.

'Taxi.' He concentrated on pouring for the correct pro-portion of foam. 'Pouring is an art,' he pontificated, abstractly. She did not listen, too busy thinking of the cost he had incurred on taxi fares and the sinister import of the flowers. She became apprehensive. He finished pouring and looked up.

'Ingenuous things, children. Aren't they.' She did not know whether this was a question and remained silent. 'No guile, no ability to lie.'

'I wouldn't go so far as to say that.'

'No. I defer to your superior knowledge in these things. I haven't had much experience of children since the last school I was at.'

'I didn't know you had taught in schools.'

'I didn't. I attended them, as a pupil.'

'Oh.'

'I think it's good to have children, or I mean, a child. Lends a sense of continuity. Especially if genetically they are yours, such as . . .'

'Suzy,' she said, furnishing him with the name.

'Of course a mother can always be totally sure the child is

hers, but the father never can. Ironical to have your fatherhood usurped by a genetic *droit du seigneur*, don't you think?'

'I can't say it's something I ever considered. Tell me, Arthur, is there any doubt that my contract will be extended? Because if not I'd like to know now.'

'No doubt at all, as far as I'm aware.'

'Obviously that's not what you came here to discuss then.'

'No.' He was still examining the proportion of foam to beer. She waited a moment more. He did not seem in any way put out by the silence.

'Arthur, why are you here?'

'Charming child . . . Suzy. You know some people would consider the prospect of taking on someone else's child daunting. It would inhibit them, no matter how they liked the mother. But,' magnanimously, pointing at his chest with his thumb, 'not me. When you think about it, allying oneself with another person has enough attendant problems as it is. All those unforeseen in-laws for instance. For all one knows they might be insufferable. Add to that a child, half of whose genetic complement one has no way of gauging. They may grow up to rob banks or vote Socialist. It makes one think. At least it makes me think. And, Rachel,' he leaned forward to impress on her the gravity of his ruminations, 'I have been thinking, and you'll be glad to know I've come to a conclusion . . .'

A few moments later a man was seen unceremoniously quitting Rachel's building. His coat, which in his haste to leave he had not had time to don, was bundled under his arm. Nor, evidently, had he had time to phone a taxi and so wandered disconsolately in the direction of the main road to hail any passing cab.

Rachel discussed the matter with Mave, her only real confidante.

'Him, the bald podgy one who dropped you off that day?'

'Yes.'

'He's dried up. You want someone with a bit of a spark,

who'll be a good laugh and good fun in bed. What possessed
the man?'

'I've no idea.'

'I was propositioned once in Ireland by a man like that,
who said I'd deliberately inflamed him the way I hung my
knickers out on the washing line. "Your Grace," I said to him,
"what's it coming to if a young woman can't hang out her
smalls on the line without having her gusset given the glad
eye by every passing cleric?" '

'You're making this up.'

"Course I am. The point is it's none of your doing and
you shouldn't let it upset you.'

'The point is I still have to work with the man.'

The language school was a small enterprise and everyone
in the place could work out what had happened by Arthur's
doleful expression. He at least had the grace to approach
Rachel and suggest they continue as if the incident had never
taken place. 'I don't think we should allow it to affect our
professional relations,' he said. Neither did she because, thankfully, they had very little to do with one another. After a
month, during which he remained subdued with everyone,
she realised the rejection had affected him as much as it was
possible for someone like him to be affected. It was Nick,
with silent pity for the vanquished, who acted as ambassador.

'Perhaps if the three of us have lunch on the grass it would
be easier.'

She reluctantly agreed. The three sat doggedly chewing in
silence. It was a public quietus. She went home that night
with chronic indigestion. So did Arthur. Only Nick felt good
about the whole thing. He felt good enough to ambush
Rachel the following day and launch into a monologue about
the vulnerability of women, especially single women with
children, misperceived as . . . as . . . Nerves overtook him. The
rehearsed piece which he had hoped would continue from
the momentum of repetition petered out to no conclusion
and a limp invitation to a meal or a night at the cinema or,
or whatever . . .

Her first thought was that he knew the position she presently found herself in and was exploiting it. One look at him and she realised how long and how hopefully he had awaited his opportunity. The very way in which the invitation was couched – hesitantly, awaiting the blow he had anticipated but made no provision for – silenced the rejoinder which sprang first to her lips. He accepted a polite refusal gracefully, excused himself on a pretext and, feeling foolish, began to look for employment elsewhere.

She knew things would not be easy between herself and either of them now. She would miss Nick. Why, she wondered, did things go so easily for other people?

51

He began to find himself living between two locations: the spartan rooms where he had moved and lived thoughtlessly, and the space she inhabited, comfortable, sequestered. At his simple remark about her husband's gloomy tastes she had had the place gutted. What she could not sell or give to charity disappeared in a skip. It was a lustral act. The sombre air disappeared with the brooding furniture. She had the floors and the skirtings and the doors taken back to their original colouring. The walls were painted in the muted colours she dressed in, peaches, luminous pearl-greys, warm orchids. There was always food and heat; the place became permanently inviting.

For the first time he experienced a contrast and, when alone in his rooms, for the first time grew disconsolate at the threadbare carpets, the lop-sided furniture, the miscellaneous cutlery and the archaic plumbing that took an hour to draw a tepid and shallow bath. He kept a toothbrush at Sarah's, and then a change of clothes and then some more things. He stopped importing when he realised he was moving in by instalments and had come to depend upon being depended upon.

Mrs Moncrieff missed him. Laura missed him more. They chided him gently for his absence, making daring allusions to the woman in his life, hoping against hope they were wrong. He gave charming disclaimers which left them none the wiser. He always came to hand in his rent in person, even if only by cheque. Previously, this transaction had been used as an excuse for one of their frugal teas: 'We were just pouring a cup, Mr Robertson. Would you care for some pork luncheon meat?' But now he sat with them dissembling his vast depression at their faded gentility. Laura was ageing daily, knitting herself into arid middle age. When he left, he would crane from his lounge window, gulping in air against their suffocating etiquette.

Occasionally, not wishing to appear as if he took his continued presence at her place for granted, he would have Sarah round to his rooms and cook for her as best he could. Although she was only ever complimentary, it was when she was there he viewed the accommodation dispassionately and saw his place for what it was. He made her vinous casseroles or baked fish. They burned cylindrical amaretti papers and watched them ascend. When she came, she brought things for him, small ornaments, cushions of decorative fabrics, and sometimes flowers. When she left he would look at the flowers sadly and think of other times, when a similarly dingy place had seen the incongruity of flowers and a woman's touch.

He began to want to be with her all the more, and could not decide whether it was for her company or the ambience of her home. He was suspicious of himself and did not want to become inured to this convenience. Everything was convenient. They ate together, bathed together, took turns at cooking or cooked together. She laughed at his vulgar remarks, read things she knew he was interested in in order that their conversations and destinies would overlap. She wore exotic underwear to please him, formed herself for his delectation. She would undress and sit astride him in front of the television screen to convince him of her sexual spontaneity, mould her lips to the perfect diameter and take him inside the liquid sheath of her red mouth. She offered her sex to him like a ripe fruit. He had been with enough women to know that all she did, she did for him, that she saw her own wants as ancillary and that the fluidity of her response was only at the pleasure she had given and not taken. Her pleasure came only in giving. He thought it the most unselfish spectacle he had witnessed.

He wondered if she had given as much to the others, whether she had gone to such lengths uniquely for him, or whether or not he was simply the latest incumbent. His speculations were not jealous. If he was right he wondered how much she had left to give. There was so little of him to go round he did not have enough for himself. Why was she still alone?

He was to find out. His initial need to be depended on had been as keen as hers to depend. He recognised this aspect of his character and found it slightly pathetic. It was also an appetite easily satisfied. Three months of being indulged and caressed and having his opinions corroborated by everything she said and did was enough. But with all her money and time, things which people associate with independence, her capacity to depend was limitless.

She derided his clothes. His appearance was of little concern to him; he let the guarded insults go unanswered. When spending a weekend with her he returned to his rooms one Saturday morning to pick up some clean clothes for the next few days. She insisted on driving him and, when they arrived, on coming up. He navigated her up the stairs without arousing the Moncrieffs, not through motives of shame but because he did not want to witness their disappointment at having their suspicions confirmed. While he carelessly threw things into an overnight bag she rummaged through his drawers and wardrobe with unashamed curiosity. Her appraisal was thorough and lasted longer than it took him to pack.

'You don't buy anything with a view to what you already have, do you?'

'I don't even remember what I already have.'

'You choose good things, but you choose haphazardly.'

'I choose what I can afford.'

'No. You could afford good things which match as opposed to good things that don't.'

'I choose not to care.'

'I care enough for us both.'

She gently insisted on exchanging some of the things he had in his bag, despite the fact that they would spend the weekend together without company. When he arrived at her house the following Wednesday night he showered and was handed a deep-pile dressing-gown he had not seen before. It smelled new and expensive. So did all the things arrayed on the bed which she waved to with mock nonchalance saying: 'They're for you.'

He didn't know what to say. 'I'm flattered,' he said, feeling obscurely insulted. She had cooked specially for him. That night she came out of the bathroom having rouged her nipples. When he lay between her legs she manufactured an epidermal climax to come in concert with him. He lay back wanting her to stop trying so hard.

She tried harder. The number of things he had to do for himself merely to exist were diminishing. She had more or less told him he need not work. She wanted to do everything for him besides think, which he could do for the both of them. She was to do whatever was necessary and he was to have all their opinions. Any attempt he made at self-sufficiency impugned her position in this arrangement.

He found the arrangements so cloying he absented himself for a fortnight without explanation. She called incessantly, calls which he let ring out because he knew with certainty who was on the other end of the line. She wrote several times, short notes ending in tones of querulous recrimination. She came to the library, and when he made it clear he could not discuss their arrangement publicly she waited outside, standing martyred in the rain, beside her parked Volvo. She drew stares from the scurrying pedestrians. She drew stares from his parting colleagues. This, he thought, was the next step of perverse logic: if you cannot gain sufficient leverage over another person in private, you do it by the threat of public spectacle. He thought this till he approached her. She was sodden, the fringe of her hair like a streak of oil across her forehead. She was oblivious to anyone else. Her face had a wretched, beseeching look he knew he could not withstand.

'Come home,' she said.

'All right.'

He could not eat. Neither could she, apprehensive at his loss of appetite and what it might inevitably portend. He went to bed early, to read, unable to supply topics for their flagging conversation. She joined him, undressing with feverish haste. She took his fingers in her mouth, one by one. They made love standing, he supporting her by the crook of her knees, she grasping his hair, staring intently into his face. For the first time in his life he realised he was too upset to climax but juddered as he imagined he must at the cataclysm. She did likewise. He put her down and walked to the bathroom to get away, annihilated by this counterfeit fuck.

He visited her regularly, conscientiously staying over, anticipating his departure. He began to see the real world as something which started and finished outside her house. She came three more times to visit him at work, sitting in unnerving quiet in the reference section. None of his colleagues noticed. It was for this reason he asked for, and was given, a transfer to the other library near Islington, requesting his old colleagues to keep his whereabouts private. He never knew whether or not she turned up again at his old workplace, only that she made ambiguous remarks regarding the time it took him to return from work.

He knew, even before he saw Rachel for the first time again in ten years, that this would have to stop. The night of the dinner with Rachel and Mave he took a taxi to her house.

'I can't come here any more.'

'Stay the night and we'll talk about it in the morning.'

'No.'

She looked at him.

'I'm sorry. I really am. Everything I think of sounds trite to me even before I say it. I don't know what to say to you.'

'You had no right to say those things to me. Those things you said in the library.'

'No.'

'You thought I was a plaything.'

'No,' he said. But she was right, and he knew it. And he knew also he had been right when he told her how selfish love is.

'Do you love me?' she asked, with daunting candour.

He thought: I will not insult her with a lie.

'No.'

'Will you ever love me?'

'I will never be in love with you.'

'Are you in love with someone else?'

'I have been in love with someone else for ten years.'

She looked at him in utter resignation and then said, quietly, with great dignity: 'I think you had better go.'

He knew immediately he had not just been an incumbent and felt ashamed at ever having thought so. He left.

He walked most of the way back, pensive. He thought: am I still culpable, froward, a cunt? Do I know anything more? Have I learned anything? He looked at the dark buildings and the lamplight, and when he came to it, the metallic sheen of the Thames, and thought how little he cared for all this. He wondered if he was bad for trying to seek happiness. He thought: what a foolish propensity to expect equity, why do we persist in it? He said aloud to the frowning masonry: 'I'm waiting to care.' And, later, 'I'm in imminent danger of hope.' He knew it was too close, too soon to look back at him and Sarah and evaluate. But even at this distance he knew that the blur of facile days that had become his life had been interrupted, not once by Sarah, but twice by Rachel.

5 2

He has been patient. He has waited over a month since their meal. She has come once in that time to the library while he was there. She was served by someone else. She took a small detour of five minutes to pass the time of day with him. It was not awkward. He suppressed the urge of invitation. He was biding his time. Now it is time. The phone rings for almost a minute. He thinks: if she answers now and knows I've hung on for this long I'll look desperate. He is about to hang up.

'Hello?'

'Hello, Rachel?'

'Yes.'

'It's me. Jamie . . .' The man who has held you in the inviolable recesses of his heart for more than ten years, '. . . the librarian.'

'Yes. Of course. Jamie. How are you?'

'Fine. And you?' It's turning out to be one of those conversations again. I'll be more positive.

'Fine.' What's the purpose of this call?

'I'll get to the point. I wondered, are you free any particular night next week?' He has broached the topic this way to give her the opportunity to decline, invent previous commitments before a specific offer is made. This is both for her convenience and to salvage what will be left of his *amour propre*.

'Nothing immediately springs to mind. Which night in particular were you thinking of?' Another invitation. Arthur, Nick and now Jamie. And I'm not even trying. And I don't think I'm good looking.

'Well I didn't have a particular evening in mind. I'll tell you what I was thinking of, and if it's in any way inconvenient please don't feel embarrassed to decline,' even though a refusal will be mortal. 'I was thinking how enjoyable our meal was and I felt half guilty. I feel to some extent I dragooned you into cooking because the restaurant dinner fell through. I hope you didn't feel that too, did you?'

Yes. 'No. Not at all.'

'Good. I was vaguely apprehensive about that. I wanted to return the favour. I wondered if you would like to have dinner again? My cooking isn't as good as yours. I thought of perhaps a restaurant. Obviously since I invited I'd like to pay . . .'

She says: 'It's difficult . . .'

He produces his last gambit, lest she considers an invitation to a tête-à-tête pushy: 'I thought you might like to invite your friend Mave too, since we both seemed to enjoy her company so much last time.'

He is craning desperately down the phone. She makes an inarticulate sound of indecision he cannot construe.

'I think I might have trouble getting a sitter. Can I call you back?'

'Of course.'

'All right then. Bye for now.'

'Bye.'

In his agitation, the reference to a babysitter has completely escaped him. And he realises he has no idea when she intends to call back, if at all. Presumably before the proposed meal next week. Will she call tonight? or tomorrow? or at the weekend? or is this a means of simply deferring the issue till it quietly evaporates? He treads the room, feeling the pull of a phone that will not ring.

She is treading the lounge biting her lip in vexation. Arthur, Nick, Jamie. Perhaps it is not fair to tar him with the same brush. Beyond these bungling seductions she has had so little male company. She is vaguely worried at her evident ability to do without. Mave is right in some of the things she says. She thinks about Arthur, his arrogant assumptions and pompous stupidity and then about the little of Jamie that she knows, rounded at the corners by contact with the world, intelligent. It is only a meal. She calls Mave to seek corroboration for the decision she has already made.

'Mave. Rachel?'

'Yes, Rachel?'

'Jamie, the one we both had dinner with at my place. He's invited me out.'

'To his place?'

'To a restaurant.'

'He probably wants to get you alone at his place but feels it's too pushy first time.'

'He invited you too.'

'What, up front?'

'Well, no. Not immediately.'

'Window dressing. Besides, I can't come. I've got a prior engagement.'

'You don't even know what night it's on yet. What's your prior engagement?'

'Looking after Suzy while her mother goes out with someone who isn't one of those mealy-mouthed half-arsed academics she works with. I told you he liked you.'

Jamie clamps his hand on the phone with feverish haste on its first ring. He lets it ring three more times before answering with feigned ease.

'Hello?'

'Hello, Jamie.'

'Oh, Rachel. I hope you didn't have difficulty getting through. I've been on the line to a friend.'

'No. This is the first time I called back. Is Thursday week all right?'

'Thursday week. Can you wait for a moment till I check my diary?' and then, feeling as if he is over-playing his hand, 'That would be fine.'

'I've got Mave to sit for me.'

He names a tube station near the restaurant where they arrange to meet. They say a formal farewell. He replaces the phone and puts his arms round his shoulders, clinging to himself. He is ecstatic at having her to himself. He stands on the dilapidated settee and dances frenziedly for half a minute and then stops dead. He is thunderstruck when he realises why Mave cannot come.

5 3

He thinks she has changed in his eyes, even though he has not seen her since the phone call. He literally expects her to look different, as if there were any number of maternal nuances that he failed to notice. The truth is that she has changed in his estimation. Thursday week has given him too long an opportunity to reflect. He has imagined dozens of permutations of their conversation, knowing that none of them will occur. He has spent sixty hours thinking about a rendezvous which will last perhaps one-twentieth of that time. Being alone has given him a disproportionate amount of time for such preparations.

Thursday week has passed for her unconsciously. She has been too occupied with her work and her baby and the effort of cobbling together a home for them to give the meal undue thought. Mave comes home with her directly from the crèche the night she is due to babysit for Rachel. When asked how she feels about the night ahead, Rachel is pleasantly surprised to have to conceal a warm sense of anticipation. She talks to Mave and Suzy as she gets ready. Mave says to her: 'For God's sake, tart yourself up a bit.'

'What's wrong with this?'

'You look as if you're going to hold hands round a bonfire outside a missile base.'

'You don't understand. It's a meal with a friend.'

'Tell that to him.'

'And besides, this isn't the Edwardian era any more. You don't have to deck yourself out just because a man is going to look at you.'

'Call me old fashioned then, but I'll bet he puts himself out for you. He might not be well-dressed, but I'll bet it's as good as he can manage. I call it just common courtesy to return the effort.'

Rachel did not reply, but before she left she made the

surreptitious concession of putting on some cologne behind her ears, on her wrists and, although she could not say why, between her breasts. She thought about him on the tube. Greece was aeons ago. She could not possibly count the number of people she had spent time with in the interim. And yet her memories of him were persistent, and fond. Unbeknown to her, till their recent meeting he had retained a larger place in her memories than the brief time they had spent together would normally have merited. She did not inflate this to anything it was not. But she was glad they were to be together, if only for three hours. She thought: perhaps I miss male company more than I think I do. I won't foist on him the role of panacea.

Mave had been right. He wore a midnight-blue suit in vicuna wool with pale blue shirt and silk paisley tie. His shoes shone with a lustre that immediately made her think of Arthur Puxty's scalp. The ensemble looked like more than a month of a librarian's wage. She was surprised both at the outlay and the taste she had had no suspicions of. He looked as if he had emerged from tissue paper. She felt dowdy and glad at least for the concession of the cologne.

'To quote someone we both know, you beggar description, Jamie.' He blushed. She was moved. She continued: 'If we're going to eat somewhere where you have to dress like that, I'd better go home and get changed.'

'We're not.' He looked ashamed at having made the effort. She found this suddenly child-like aspect of him curiously appealing.

'I'm only kidding. You didn't risk getting crumpled in the tube dressed like that, did you? Did you float here?'

He tried to think of a quick rejoinder that did not come. At her comments he felt both gratified and ashamed: gratified for obvious reasons, ashamed because every outfit he tried on had appeared motley and absurd. Finally he was obliged to go to the section of the wardrobe which, until now, he had fastidiously ignored: that which had been chosen and bought by Sarah. He walked downstairs feeling dignified and hypocritical, to be confronted by the stunned appraisal of Miss and Mrs Moncrieff.

'I'm off for a stag night at Lambeth Palace. The stripper comes in wearing a feather boa and a mitre.'

They watched his pristine back disappear down the stairs.

'That Jamie,' said Mrs Moncrieff.

'That Jamie,' echoed Miss Moncrieff.

That Jamie offered his arm to Rachel in a gesture of archaic chivalry. As soon as he had done so he thought himself absurd. She looped her arm in his with easy informality and if she felt awkward, disguised it well. They began walking. She lengthened her pace to fall in with his. In lieu of conversation he began to point out spurious points of historical significance: 'Carlyle was born there. So was Cervantes, Alfred Hitchcock and Charlie Chaplin. It must have been cramped. Over there is where Mozart is buried, next to the tomb of Karl Marx. Or is it Harpo Marx? The first Graf Zeppelin was launched from that cellar . . .'

'You're not obliged to amuse me. I'll still pay for my half of the meal.'

'Over there is where Alfred burned the cakes to start the Great Fire of London and then hid up this tree afterwards to escape the Roundheads.'

'You don't half talk shite.'

'One of Mave's words?'

'One of Mave's words. Do you think you could slow down?'

He slowed down. They said nothing further till they arrived. He felt the silence somehow had her approval, that she was discomfited at his trying too hard. He tried harder and stayed silent. His nerves felt as if they had been steeped in petrol.

They arrived, a small unostentatious Italian restaurant with a subdued interior. It was busy for mid-week. He had had to book, a good recommendation. A lithe waiter steered them to their table and provided them with iced water while he took their orders for an aperitif. She drank gin. He had some of the dry white wine they would drink with the meal. They spent some time talking about the menu. He could not think of anything else. Finally she handed the embossed booklet across and said: 'You order.'

'Is this a test? All right, I'll order.'

He summoned the waiter across. 'Nothing too heavy,' she said.

He said: 'This is an Italian restaurant.' He ordered Artichoke Salad, Red Mullet Calabrese and, for dessert, Panettone. He was on to his third glass of wine by the time the salad arrived, and ordered a second bottle. She looked at him and realised that Mave had been right. He was nervous. In Greece his tasks had been admittedly simple, but he had carried them out with such self-confidence she did not think him capable of this reaction. It perplexed her that she should be its cause.

They talked in a desultory way about Greece. He seemed to have more vivid memories than she did. In his mind, as he talked, he was comparing her then with now. He had been stunned at the realisation that she had a child. He did not know who she had slept with, did not want to know, but the thought of a child, the undeniable corroboration that she had been penetrated by someone who was not him, hurt. And it made her different. Something about her whole composed manner suggested that she had dispensed with the father rather than been dispensed with. There was nothing wistful about her. Her baby somehow made her more complete. He was jealous of her self-sufficiency. He could do everything required of him to subsist, but unlike her had never been entire.

'And Mave looks after your baby?'

'You know she does. Did you say that to get on to the subject of Mave or my baby?'

'Just passing the time. That's what people do, pass the time. They say things they don't mean or ask questions they don't want the answers to, just to make a noise that means they're trying to be friendly. Like "How are you?" or "Nice week-end?" when really they don't give a fuck. It's the social lubricant.'

She is jarred slightly by the swearing. This is not nerves

and he has not drunk enough to reach the stage of flagrant candour.

'Not you,' she said. 'I don't remember you in Greece ever wasting your time with the social niceties. You either asked direct questions or made cruel remarks at other people's expense.'

'Was it as bad as that?'

'It wasn't bad, it was just you.' And then she said, 'How are you?'

'I don't know really. There isn't really any answer to that besides "fine" is there? I could invent a disease. Something venereal sounding. Something embarrassing.'

'And contagious.'

'Yes.'

'So – how are you?'

'I've got scruporrhea. Hence the galoshes, to catch the discharge. Have some of my wine. Care to share a handkerchief?'

'Is this your usual sally at the social niceties?'

'No.'

'I think people should just be themselves. Falseness shows. I suppose that's what love is, being unaffected in the presence of someone who is the same way towards you.'

He wondered if this was her unaffected. She hadn't had much to drink yet. He was jealous of whoever she had been unaffected in front of.

'Gulag commandants went about unaffectedly standing in other people's faces. I hear the Paris opera never shut up shop during the occupation. Cultivated Gestapo officers wept unaffectedly at performances and then went back unaffectedly to appreciate the aesthetics of torture.'

She was appalled. 'Do you really believe that?'

'Don't you?'

'No. If that was natural for them something had gone very badly wrong.' He thought: now she is wondering what has gone wrong with me. Then she said: 'What makes you say such bitter things?'

'I don't know.'

'I've been bitter before, but I grew out of it.'

'Just a matter of maturity then, is it? I can hardly wait. I'm in training for hilarity. I hope to be ecstatic when I croak. I want to be buried wearing my revolving bow-tie and exploding trousers.'

He had lost his appetite at the sudden burst of earnestness he had tried to keep out of things. He could not stop himself from imagining her being happy and unaffected with someone else. At his last remark, she burst into a peal of girlish laughter that melted him.

'Eat,' he said, pointing at their dinners. She acquiesced and took a mouthful.

'It's getting cold,' she said through the food.

'No it isn't,' he said.

They ate in silence for several minutes. He was surprised at the amount of food she put away, in tidy continuous mouthfuls. He played with his food and poured them both another drink.

'Why aren't you fat?' he asked. She shrugged. 'Most women, when they have children, get to look like a potato on legs.'

'No they don't. You're just bitter and twisted.'

'What's it like, having a baby?'

'What do you mean by having a baby?'

'Having one around the house and things like that. I don't think I could empathise with one coming out between your legs.'

She shrugged again and said: 'It's nice. It changes everything. It's not like anything else.'

'I thought it might be like having a small incontinent house guest who never leaves.'

'No. It's complete.' She thought: Like Arthur and Nick and all the others he's not interested in Suzy so much as how I came by her. He wants to know where and who the father is, and like all the others he's too embarrassed to ask.

'Where's the father?'

'I don't know.'

'What was he like?'

'Feckless and wonderful and sad.'

'Will you tell me about him?'

'I don't know. I think so, but certainly not yet.'

'And when you do, it will be a watershed?'

'Do you always say what you think?'

'No. But with you there's no point in lying. Are you sorry you came?'

'No. But you're more exacting than I remember. Or perhaps you've just become that way because you think you've run out of time and have to dispense with the preliminaries. You haven't and you don't.' She held up her glass. 'Pour me another drink so that I can at least give myself an excuse for talking like this.'

They talked lightly for the rest of the meal. He made her laugh lots of times. He thanked whoever gave him this facility. They wrangled over payment until he realised she did not want him to feel she was in his debt. His concession: 'You pay for the wine.'

She refuses a taxi, deploring the expense. He walks her to the tube. On the platform are several vagrants and some lethargic teenagers. When he can feel the wind of the approaching train he says to her: 'Will you at least call me and let me know you got home safely?'

'You're not in charge of me.'

'Just indulge me.'

'You just want the notoriety of strange women phoning you at your digs.'

'You spoilt little middle-class bitch!'

She looks at him victoriously and presents him with her wrist and a biro. 'I've lost the piece of paper with your number.' Her simplicity stops him. He feels the warmth of her skin as he writes on it. She takes back her hand and her pen and kisses him lightly on the cheek. He pushes his head between the folds of her open coat and smells the fragrance of her breasts.

She touches his face and says: 'Thank you, Jamie.' Again, as in Kyros, he is led to wonder at cause and effect and how a soft word of endearment from her can give rise in him to such disarray.

The train draws away without her looking back. He looks round at the platform. There is nothing remotely frightening here. He realises that for the first time he is more concerned for another person's well-being than his own.

He has to run for his own train. At his lodgings he is waylaid by Mrs Moncrieff, who puts some oblique questions to him and invites him in for supper. At the first ring of his phone he sprints up the stairs, shouting an apology behind him. He wrenches his door open at the third ring and the phone goes dead.

5 4

He is doing what someone once tried to do to him: thinking of her past in an attempt to insinuate himself into the warp and weft of her history as if somehow, by some arcane process, divining the route of their lives, he will plot the similarities which led to their meeting. He thinks his life has been an erratic parabola, as has hers. He wants to think of them as trajectories destined to collide, a love as inevitable as the laws of ballistics.

5 5

In the past, at Mrs Moncrieff's insistence, he has let her occasionally come and tidy his rooms. Not that he ever cared about the clutter. He had done this as much to humour her as for any other reason. He has paid his rent, diligently eaten his sponge cake, and listened to her state, as a kind of *fait accompli*, that she would come up some time in the next few days, some time during working hours so as not to inconvenience him, with a Hoover and a duster, 'Just to lend the place a woman's touch.' He has refrained from saying that the austerity of threadbare carpets and miscellaneous furniture won't be put to rights by a vase of chrysanthemums and the jar of home-made damson jam which she always leaves as her calling card. But he knows that the blowzy decor is the best they can do, given the little money they have, that with his rooms he has the best of a bad lot, and that this little luxury is the nearest manifestation he will get, or she can give, to maternal concern. He knows also that, baffled by the species of solitary male, she tidies for him as much to satisfy her curiosity as for his benefit.

Suspecting one of her forays, he has tried to put out of the way anything she would find offensive. He has smuggled his bed sheets to the launderette rather than let her discover the aftermath of female stains gone crisp, which he has unconcernedly slept on for weeks after the event. He has turned the spines of erotic novels to the wall, knowing her gift for misinterpretation.

But she has noticed now that for a time he has spent more evenings away from his flat and been more reticent in accepting her offers to tidy. The last offer was made when he last paid his rent. 'Wednesday afternoon,' she said. Abstracted at the time he said: 'That would be nice,' without realising the commitment.

Miss Moncrieff has a part-time job in the Victoria and Albert Museum. She works in the shop selling postcards to tourists, pictures of the booty of a faded empire. She took the job to get out of the house. She thought perhaps she would meet someone nice. It was a modest ambition, unlikely to be fulfilled by the crocodiles of schoolchildren, deferential Japanese with their cameras, and fat Americans in plaid trousers to whom she daily sells paperweights, bookmarks and postcards. But it is one of the few things she has.

Unwittingly, Jamie hurt her by his tendency for flippant disparagement. 'What if they came and wanted it back?'

'Who?'

'All the people we stole things from. Cleopatra's Needle, the Elgin Marbles. London's a repository of plunder and it's all up there for public scrutiny. If they took it all away there would be a lot of empty plinths around. Your place would be left with a few Constable paintings, a couple of papier mâché statues and some old rugs nobody else wants.'

She is not foolish enough to pretend to herself it is a vocation, but at least it is something. In her lower moments she has accepted Jamie's flip evaluation. This Wednesday afternoon, her afternoon off, is one of her lower moments. She has walked to the bus-stop in the suburban sunshine dawdling en route, in no hurry to be anywhere. She has looked around at the others who occupy this city with her. Is it her imagination or do they all look purposeful? Have they all destinations? Are there a sufficient number of destinations to go round? Where is hers? A dowdy woman approaching the bus-stop from the opposite direction stares at her vacantly. Closer still and she recognises her reflection which is also nonplussed in guarded disappointment.

She reaches the flat feeling ancient. Her mother is on her way out.

'There's some gammon and a salad between plates for you in the fridge. There might be some of the trifle left.'

'Where are you going?' Yet another destination.

'To the sales. Mrs Parish has seen some reduced napery in Kensington.'

'I've just come from there.'

'I know.'

'If you'd told me I could have met you.'

'I know, but I just found out myself.'

'If it's Kensington it won't be cheap.' She realises she is being fractious. She does not want to look at napery in Kensington with Mrs Parish.

'No harm in looking. Must go dear.' Her mother gives her

an absent kiss on the forehead. 'And by the by, if you've time I told Jamie I would tidy up. If not, just leave it and I'll do it sometime next week.'

She gestures a goodbye as her mother leaves, goes to the fridge and takes out the plates. The gammon she throws directly into the cat's feeding dish and picks half-heartedly at the wan vegetables. The lettuce was crisp two days ago. The cucumber has turned opaque. She makes herself a pot of strong coffee and is roused by its fragrance. It is times like this she almost wishes she smoked. In foreign films beautiful French women imbue such moments of reverie with improbable chic, watching wreaths of smoke curl upwards, following the blue whorls with their beautiful languid eyes.

She realises she has not even taken off her brown coat.

Twenty minutes later, propelled by a sense of curiosity, she climbs the stairs to Jamie's flat, the vacuum cleaner cradled under one arm. Her mother has told her Jamie has a duster and polish provided in his utility cupboard. He has never used them.

She lets herself in with the pass key. The flat is small, a lounge where he usually eats with a table at the oriel window, a kitchen large enough only for one person to stand in, a bathroom with a shower cubicle, and a sizeable bedroom. Each room radiates off a cramped hallway. She enters the lounge. Afternoon sunlight floods the room, pale lemon slanting shafts illuminating the motes of floating dust. The table is cluttered with books, coffee mugs with skinning residue, condiments and two plates with the remains of hardened pasta. Other books are also stacked at random on the coffee table. She glances into the kitchen. Pots with blackened, unidentifiable contents are on the cooker and more dirty plates occupy available surfaces. It looks as if he washes dishes as they are required. She turns on the immerser for hot water, retrieves the dusters and polish from the cupboard and makes a start on the lounge.

As she works she thinks: it is curious, I am almost happy doing this for a man who will be only vaguely grateful. He probably tolerates this to humour us. There is no essence of him here among the things he has accumulated haphazardly. Being around his possessions is the nearest I will get.

She stacks all the dishes in the kitchen, moves the books from each surface before methodically spraying and polishing. Hardened coffee rings require more effort to remove from the veneer. She returns the books in symmetrical piles. Lastly, she vacuums the carpet, moving each piece of furniture in turn to reveal trodden digestives and small change. She does the same in the hall. Twenty minutes and she has warm water. She washes the dishes and wipes down the kitchen surfaces. She takes a look at the bathroom. It looks clean, if untidy. If he wants to clean that, she thinks, he can do it himself. She pours half a pint of bleach round the toilet bowl and goes lastly to the bedroom.

She has been uneasy since she entered his flat and feels increasingly so here. The curtains are still drawn, the room in premature twilight. She pulls the curtains apart, opens the window to clear the smell of exhaled air and turns to look around. The bed is unmade, the duvet peeled back half lying on the carpet. It is a double bed which she remembers he had delivered shortly after his arrival, to the consternation of her mother, who was asked to have the single bed removed. She can see the indentation his body has made on one side only. It is obvious no one has been sleeping on the other. What, she wonders, is the point? Is he waiting for the symmetry of a partner? Beside where he has lain is a small table with a glass of water, an electric alarm silently displaying numerical time, and a novel with a bookmark. The wardrobe doors are open with other clothes strewn where he has left them over a chair. On the wall opposite the bed is a large, felt pin-board covered in photographs, some secured four square, others hanging obliquely. More photographs are scattered over the drawers below. She crosses the room to look.

Her eyes are drawn to a photograph on the pin-board, half concealed by others. She notices it immediately because it is older, folded at the corner and cracked, as if it has been carried often. It shows a group of teenage boys in overalls of some kind. All are standing, with the exception of one who sits on a table lighting a cigarette from a tool of some sort. Even this effort seems too much. He is leaning on a companion. She looks closely. There is an expression of youthful arrogance she has never seen, but the face is unmistakably Jamie's. There are other photographs of recognisable landmarks with Jamie in the foreground. Jamie at Sacré Coeur, at the Statue of Liberty, the Pyramids, Sugar Loaf Mountain, and many others. Sometimes he stands by himself. She has no idea who has taken the photographs. Sometimes he is accompanied by a woman, never the same one twice. Did they take the photographs in which they never appear, or was he capable ever of being alone? She asks herself this question with a sense of chagrin. This catalogue has brought home with brutal suddenness the prosaic uniformity of her past. She thinks: What would I have given to have stood framed with him, or even to have held the camera?

There are some whose location she cannot identify: a fat, jovial-looking man with a beard working over a gridiron and saluting the camera with a raised beer bottle; a slender woman in elegant middle age who sits at a desk on a flat roof-top surrounded by washing. It is hot, the light looks intense. Those given pride of place, pinned above the batch of miscellaneous travel photographs, are obviously more modern. The colour is keener, the canopy of clouds indicative of London, the man who stares out recognisable as the one she orchestrates accidental meetings with on the stairs. But his face is different in these late photographs, subtly suffused in a way she cannot describe. And there is another common denominator: the same woman endures throughout all these later pictures, sometimes accompanied by an infant girl.

And there is Jamie, sitting alone with the infant girl. The woman, presumably the mother, is also, presumably, the photographer. Jamie with the baby at the Science Museum, gesturing towards the skeleton of a Triceratops. Jamie with her in Kensington Gardens, gesturing towards the statue of

Peter Pan. Jamie with her in Trafalgar Square, enduring pigeons perched on his shoulders and head for her amusement. In each case he seems gamely to be trying to amuse a child whose life consists of a series of fleeting distractions. Jamie standing beside a swing, rigid with cold, the girl with a flush of exhilaration on her face caught at the zenith of her short arc. In each of these he has a look which, she imagines, he is unconscious of, a look seeking approbation from the camera, or whoever is behind it.

There are only a few photographs of him alone with this recurring woman. She is not particularly good looking, not the houri Miss Moncrieff has somehow imagined. Indeed, thinks Miss Moncrieff, she is not someone I would feel ashamed to stand next to in a fashionable bar myself, if I ever went to fashionable bars. But there is about her an air of self-reliance Miss Moncrieff can only envy, and she knows this confidence will manifest itself in her deportment, her small movements, her conversations and in a hundred subtle ways. She knows also this is alluring. She knows Jamie finds it so. There is in his face, as he sits beside her, a repressed wistfulness which Miss Moncrieff sees twice and cannot look at again.

She replaces the photographs in as close an order as she can remember. She leaves, quietly, without disturbing or tidying anything else in the bedroom and locks the flat behind her. She knows it was as close as she ever got and she will never willingly go there again. She descends to her trinkets and her knitting, looks at her life of awful rote and goes out for a walk. She walks for hours, till after dark, and returns to find her mother on the landing of their flat shouting goodbye to the ascending back of Jamie. He has, by all appearances, been infallibly amusing yet again. Mrs Moncrieff's face is creased with genteel mirth. She waves a greeting to her daughter.

'That Jamie,' says Mrs Moncrieff.

Miss Moncrieff doesn't say anything.

5 6

'I'm worried about him, Mave.'

'Is he all over you then?'

'No, he isn't.'

'Is that what you're worried about, him not being all over you?'

'No. Of course not.'

'So what is it? Do you want him to make advances or not?'

'It's not as simple as that. If only it were.'

'Nothing's as complicated as people think. They only pretend they see things as complicated so that they can congratulate themselves on being profound. You know what I think, I think you're miffed because the perfume you keep putting on your tits for him since that first night hasn't worked yet. There's no need to be embarrassed.'

'I'm not embarrassed.'

'You could have fooled me.'

'If it was just sex I'd do the asking myself. I've done as much before. Before Suzy came along.'

'I'm sure you did. In my day you let them do the asking, but you let them know beforehand they wouldn't be knocked back. Not now though. When our Angela was at primary school she got sent home with a note. Seems she'd been showing her knickers to all the boys for a Jaffa cake a time. There's the modern approach for you.'

'I don't know what to do. He worries me the way he's not demonstrative.'

'Would you like him to be?'

'I don't know. I get the impression he's holding himself in check all the time. I don't know if I'd like what would happen if he let his composure slip.'

'Do you want to sleep with him?'

'I don't know.'

'God help the man. I always knew, even if I never did it while my man was alive, I always knew. From what I remember of that dinner I thought he was quite nice looking. Don't you find him attractive?'

'Yes, I do.'

'Well then . . .'

'Oh, I don't know.'

'That bald man and the young one and now Jamie. You're spoiled for choice. That Mrs McCruden, two doors down. Ugly woman. Ugly. Husband like a starved whippet. She clings on to him because he's the only thing she's likely to get. Nothing indecisive about her. And I'll bet she's not unhappy. You want to go out and get yourself some ordinary problems. Do you like him?'

'Yes. Very much.'

'Do you love him?'

'I've never thought about it. I suppose if I did I would have.'

'Nice to see a woman who knows her own mind. When Michael was still young and staying at home he used to bring his girls back. He used to wait outside till we had gone to bed before he brought them into the lounge. I used to come down and interrupt. I've even heard him say, "Lie down and try it. You might even like it." I might have shouted the odds but I was never really angry. After all, he was only doing what everyone wanted to. Not much subtlety though. I know these days you have to be more careful, but perhaps you should give it a go. You might even like it.'

57

It has been an Indian summer and it has drawn to its close. It has been, for him, a summer of wildest vacillations. When he has been very happy he has mistrusted the quality of his joy, its precariousness. He has looked so long for something he thought did not exist that he has measured out the pulses for the short spaces of time it is given to him. Mave would not approve. Neither would Rachel, although she suspects it. When he is sad he tells himself he has endured worse. He is not pessimistic but he has come to expect nothing. He is both envious of, and pleased for, the gratuitous happiness he perceives in others around him, flying Sunday kites, holding hands, sipping wine, speaking.

'Where's my fucking cocoa?' he has said, whimsically, thinking aloud.

'It's not what you think,' Rachel has told him.

He is appalled by the prospect that things of such moment can be left to serendipity. Accident has no place in his scheme of things. The contingency of love, for him, detracts from its intrinsic value.

It is Sunday afternoon in Richmond. It is getting late and the early dark is catching them. Rachel has wanted to see Kew. Both he and Suzy are bored by its manicured exactness.

He has much in common with Suzy he is glad for. He talks to her almost the same way he talks to her mother, remembering from his own childhood the offensive superciliousness of adults. She responds in kind, having had enough of the men who attempted to gain credibility with Rachel by assuming surrogate fatherhood. Both mother and daughter have watched several men persevere in the role they sought to fill by forced horseplay or bribery. All failed, decisively. Suzy accepted their sweets and refused their caresses with precocious hauteur. 'You're your mother's daughter all right,' Mave said. 'She's got a line in disdain too that's broke more hearts than she'll credit.' Jamie has had the good sense to treat the child as a friend in the making. She responds in a more tactile way than she ever did with any of his predecessors, even creeping into his arms to sleep.

Denied entry to the pagoda, Suzy has turned fractious. Jamie is secretly glad. Rachel has conceded and they have left the gardens. 'There's no need to look so smug,' she says.

He adopts an appalling cockney accent to annoy her.

'Bloody 'ell. That Kew. Some gaff. An' all those plants and whatnot. 'Ouses too. Architecture an' osmosis. Bloody marvellous what they think of these days. Just goes to show you . . .'

'It's not my fault you're a philistine.'

Suzy walks ahead, tottering into the piles of swept leaves. The trees look bleak. A fragrant pall hangs over the common from the leaves which have been burned, the thin smoke merging with the dropping evening. There is a last yearning twilight, spread wanly across the sky.

'Careful,' Rachel shouts, automatically.

'Did it ever strike you that it's more difficult to be cynical during a sunset.' Again he is thinking aloud. She answers the unasked question.

'No. It doesn't. I don't think it would strike a cynic either. It only strikes people like you who try hard at it.'

'You don't think I'm a cynic?'

'No.'

'I fucking well am.'

'Don't swear within earshot of Suzy.'

'Sorry.'

'If you were, I wouldn't be here with you.'

'Was he a cynic?' Jamie asks, nodding his head towards Suzy. Rachel says nothing. He remains silent, adamant he will not do her talking for her, cover the embarrassment with some appropriately facile remark as he has been doing since they met this time round. She thinks: This is a test. A door is open. Will I walk through?

'I don't know if I would call him cynical.'

' "Feckless and wonderful and sad" is what you called him. I don't know if that's complimentary or not. I don't think I'd like to be categorised like that.'

'What do you want people to say of you?'

'What they will. I just don't want to know what it is.'

Without further prompting she says: 'Yes. Perhaps he was cynical. Or rather, he was becoming cynical, and that was one of the things that made him sad.'

'What were the others?'

'Sometimes he drank too much.' She raises her hands to her lips as if attempting to catch the words she just said. 'No. That's a lie. Even now I lie for him. Everyone always did. He was so charming. He was an alcoholic.'

'If he was a sad drunk, what made him so wonderful?'

'He wasn't defined by three adjectives. That was the nearest I could get off-the-cuff, faced with an awkward question. A kind of hope made him wonderful.' She looked defiant now. He wondered how near the truth he would get. Was she sufficiently in love with his memory to embellish it the way Jamie had his memory of her? 'He had a gift of giving that hope to other people. They wanted his company. They paid for drinks just so some of his optimism would rub off on them. They put him up.'

'Did you?'

'I let him and his two dogs share my one room for months till we were practically evicted.'

In his relentless curiosity he had forgotten for a moment her capacity to hurt him. He thinks of their recent months of politesse, their hesitant farewell kisses, his efforts not to trespass and ruin the edifice he is building, piece by hesitant piece. And here was some drunkard who had walked into her history and her loins. What would he have to do to make her love him sufficiently to tolerate him and the squalor of two dogs in a small room for months?

'He sounds like a lovable parasite.'

'That's what other people have said.'

'What else did he do besides drink and distribute optimism?'

'He was a writer.'

'Had he had anything published?'

'Not as far as I know.'

'Had he ever actually written anything?' She does not answer. He thinks she is becoming angry at him. 'I'm not trying to be insulting.'

'It doesn't sound like it,' she says with an edge. He knows

he cannot tread warily for much longer. It has tired him beyond telling. He throws caution to the wind.

'Was he really a writer or was he one of those people who claim to have a vocation because it's convenient?'

'He was a writer. Is a writer.' She is defiant, prepared not only to stretch the truth, but to project him into the present tense.

'I suppose it depends what you mean.'

'What do you mean?'

'I mean did he scribble things on pieces of paper to give himself a label and keep the world at bay?'

'Everyone does something like that. Look at you and your cordons of books.'

'I don't ask anyone to pay my way. And I don't lie to myself either.'

'Neither did he.'

'Why do you think he was an alcoholic?'

'Are you trying to tell me you don't get successful artists who are alcoholics?'

'No, I'm trying to tell you that successful alcoholics are usually unsuccessful something elses.'

'Like what, librarians?' She realises she has been petulant and that the remark is unfair. She has wanted to tell him of Suzy's father, but not in circumstances like these. She feels she is being goaded into a revelation. 'I'm sorry. There was no need for me to say that.'

'That's all right.' He absorbs both the insult and apology without show of offence. 'Do you believe everyone does something like he did to keep things at a distance?'

'It was something to say but yes, I suppose so.'

'What's yours?'

'I don't know. Perhaps I'm not impartial enough to pass an opinion. I suppose you have an opinion as to what it is.'

'Suzy,' he says, simply. They walk in silence for some minutes. Suzy returns with a stick which she says is a dead snake, proudly displays it to both of them and then scurries off. Rachel is mulling over what he has said. 'The thing about the two of you . . .' he says.

'What?'

'You're complete. You make others feel superfluous. I'll go if you want me to.' It is a botched consecration.

'I don't know what I want.'

He feels he has aged ten years on the spot.

'Is that why Suzy's father left, because he felt he wasn't needed? You don't have to talk about it if you don't want to.'

'No, that's all right. Ask what you want.'

'You conceived Suzy in a squalid room where you lived with him and two dogs?'

Again she surprises him with a sudden girlish peal of laughter.

'God no. I let him stay with me in that room when I was a student – years and years ago, before I ever met you even. He was in love with me. I only realised it later. We both knew I wasn't in love with him. I think it hurt him, very much. I know when we were together he made futile attempts at writing. I used to look at his notebooks when he wasn't there. It sounds tantamount to reading someone's diary, doesn't it? Don't be shocked. I only wanted the best for him. I wanted to be arrested by something brilliant. I wanted to see something there that justified the foibles and the sloth and the drinking and everything else he did, or didn't do. I never read anything that was good. Most of it was scored out. I don't know if I was responsible for its quality or not. He cut his losses and left without even saying goodbye. He wasn't given to histrionics. I think it hurt that much. It's daunting to know you have the capacity to cause another person to feel that way. He limped off with whatever peace of mind I'd left him. That's why I don't want anyone disparaging him. Although it wasn't my fault I feel somehow responsible for him. You can see that, can't you?'

'Yes.'

'And in a way that would never be any use to him, I loved him.'

'Yes,' he says, without being asked.

'I met him again about a year before Suzy was born. Here, in London. I was back. It was a temporary lull. I hadn't intended to return permanently, I just felt rather rudderless. Until I had some other project I intended to stay here. It must have been about seven years since I saw him last. He'd aged terribly. I suppose the drink did that. He'd been a mature student when he matriculated at Edinburgh. I think when he saw me he realised how he'd aged. The difference in me was probably negligible. I don't know. When he saw me he said what he always did, that he wanted to take his liver out and run it under a cold tap.'

'Did you stay with him?'

'No. I never saw where he stayed, but it was probably squalid. He helped me find accommodation though. I got a job, washing dishes, till I found something better. He used to stay sober for a day and then come round and just sit. You could see it gnawing at him. By that time he barely ate. He would look at me and talk, trying to hide his longing for me. It had never left him you see, and there was nothing I could do about it. Does that sound arrogant?'

'No.'

'He could barely remember what had happened to him in the seven-year interim.'

'Did he still write?'

'Yes. I had to ask to find that out.'

'Had he had any success?'

'I don't think so, or he would have mentioned it. I don't think he was consistent enough to have success. He didn't do anything consistently, except drink. He certainly didn't have any money. There was some vital thing about him that had changed. It wasn't hopelessness, or a sense of despair, but you could see he didn't expect anything. I don't just mean with regard to writing or success or whatever, but with regard to everything. I suppose in that way he was a bit like you, although he didn't kid himself that it was cynicism. I think he'd received so many disappointments he considered a low threshold of expectation only prudent. Even though he was always cheerful you could tell he regarded sitting in a room with me as gratuitous. And one time he came round really drunk. It was as if his face peeled off . . .'

'And you took pity on him?'

'Yes . . . It sounds a pathetic consummation, doesn't it.'

'Yes. I've done as much myself. Were you lonely?'

'No. But he was. He had had a bath and had worked himself up to this. And then he was so frightened he got drunk. I honestly don't think his esteem could have stood it if I'd turned him out. He was almost incapable. Perhaps that was why I was careless enough to let it happen. In every other way he was destitute and he gave me a baby.'

'Does he know?'

'God, yes. He was ecstatic. He thought it was the solution, instant family, something you add water to and voilà. I think he imagined us in a two-up two-down, in perpetual bliss. He didn't think of money, or the fact that I wasn't in love with him, or of him being a chronic alcoholic. He couldn't look after himself and yet he somehow imagined looking after me and a baby.'

'What happened? Did he leave?'

'I did. I knew I was going to have to hack it on my own. I would have carried him too, but I think a baby on the scene would just have made it worse for him. I think he would have realised how low his expectations really had sunk. You could endure lots of things for yourself you couldn't for a baby. I went back to Scotland for a while – not to my parents.'

'What happened to him?'

'I don't know.'

'Are you sad the way things turned out?'

'For him – very much. I worry about him incessantly and I think I'll never see him again. For me – no. I have Suzy. And there's something curious: if I had had to choose a father for a baby I was going to have to bring up on my own, I'd still have chosen him from all the men I've known. He was a drunk and a failure as an artist. Drink diluted every one of his virtues, but even watered-down he was still wonderful.'

5 8

He had set himself a task of exorcism and he knows, when he leaves her after Kew, he has failed. He cannot imagine anyone ever talking about him as she did her drunkard. They returned in silence. She sensed something portentous at their parting when he did not arrange a next meeting as he usually did.

She tells herself she understands. She wants to tell him so. She is sorry – for him. She knows he is too proud for sympathy. She wants to tell him he is not alone, but knows for her to participate in his loss would be to abolish its root cause. She tells herself many things, diagnoses her feelings as a natural sympathy. She has an explanation for everything except her dull leaden moods, her irritation at the phone's clamorous silence and Suzy's repeated questions of when will they next go out with Jamie.

She confides in Mave to the extent of missing the social life he provided. The comforting vista of pleasantly filled weekends has now gone.

'It wasn't really fair though, was it?' says Mave, 'going along for the ride, expecting him to fill some role of chaperone cum baby-sitter and keeping him at arm's length because it suited.'

'That makes it sound more mercenary than it was.'

'What was it?'

'I don't know, but it wasn't just that. Perhaps things could have changed.'

'Did you ever give any indication that they would?'

'No.'

'I told you he liked you. If he gave you all that space and time he tried to show that too. You should have known. He wouldn't have known which way to jump, poor bastard, you not cracking a light.'

'No. I suppose not. Poor Jamie. Why do things never quite work out? You love the people who don't love you back and you're loved by those whose feelings you can't return.'

'You make it sound like a conga chain, with everyone facing someone else. I think you like him more than you'll admit to yourself. Make your mind up – for both your sakes. And for God's sake, cheer up!'

His nerves had been taut for months at her continued indecision. He felt nothing till a brief telephone conversation, two months later.

'Hello?'

'Jamie. It's me.'

'Yes.'

'You haven't called, come round . . .'

'No.'

'It was only later I realised I'd always left it up to you.'

She awaits a reply which does not come. 'I don't suppose that was really fair, was it?'

'You have a child, a career. It wasn't unfair.'

'You're being nice.'

There is a pause before he says, 'What do you want me to say?'

The silence is unnerving. Finally she says, 'Are you still there?'

'Rachel, what do you want?' His tone is not unkindly.

'Is it possible to be friends?'

'I will always feel the same way about you.'

'Will we see you?'

'No.'

When he has said this he feels suddenly the irrevocable nature of the way things now are. She is too palpable to reinvent as a myth. He cannot now bear contact, even over a wire. He puts the receiver down.

When he was thirty-five he had decided on a course of action: he would reconcile himself to emptiness or stare it out. When he was thirty-five he realised it was a good plan lacking only one merit: efficacy. He feels now it is a long time since he was thirty-five.

She listens to the line go dead and puts down the phone, realising now that ten years' love resonated in that banal hum.

He does what he does, working and sleeping. Since as long as he can remember he cannot muster the interest or concentration to read. He eats more often with Miss and Mrs Moncrieff and watches fatuous family quiz programmes with them on television. He now understands that there are strata of loneliness. The snow comes, and goes. He is surprised each morning at the whiteness as he walks out inadequately dressed. Returning back indoors for more clothes he realises he has not calibrated anything with anything. Perhaps the spring will also take him by surprise and be a metaphor. He doubts it.

A makeshift meal in front of a television he is not watching. He is absently picking at the remnants of a reheated casserole from a pot. The telephone rings. He picks it up. Before the person on the other end gets the chance to speak he can hear the background gurgling of a child's laughter, recognisable, then sibilant shooshing noises. He thinks: if this is coincidence fate is not blind, but rationally malevolent.

'Jamie?'

He exhales the word with effort: 'Yes?'

'We come as a pair.'

Serpent's Tail

1986 to 1996
TEN YEARS WITH ATTITUDE!

"If you've got hold of a book that doesn't fit the categories
and doesn't miss them either,
the chances are that you've got a serpent by the tail."

ADAM MARS-JONES

"The Serpent's Tail boldly goes
where no reptile has gone before ... More power to it!"

MARGARET ATWOOD

If you would like to receive a catalogue of our current publications please write to:

FREEPOST, Serpent's Tail,
4 Blackstock Mews, LONDON N4 2BR

(No stamp necessary if your letter is posted in the United Kingdom.)

Serpent's Tail

1986 to 1996

TEN YEARS WITH ATTITUDE!

"If you've got hold of a book that doesn't fit the categories
and doesn't miss them either,
the chances are that you've got a serpent by the tail."

ADAM MARS-JONES

"The Serpent's Tail boldly goes
where no reptile has gone before ... More power to it!"

MARGARET ATWOOD

If you would like to receive a catalogue of our current publications please write to:

FREEPOST, Serpent's Tail,
4 Blackstock Mews, LONDON N4 2BR

(No stamp necessary if your letter is posted in the United Kingdom.)